Fusion
By Diana Kane

Fusion

Dedication

To my dear friend Liz who kept me sane at times while writing this, constantly provided feedback and encouraged me to keep going. Without your support Fusion likely wouldn't be available to the public.

Table of Contents

Alexis

The neurosurgery conference is set to feature a new intra-operative imaging technology that the hospital is planning to introduce. Attending the conference is a unique opportunity for me. Typically a surgical technologist would not attend a conference like this, but hospital management and the neurosurgeons agreed that sending representation from the neurosurgical nurses and techs would be a great idea. Our team is small, consisting of eight surgical techs. Being the only one without children to consider for the four-day trip I became the logical choice to attend. I don't mind taking the trip. Not only does the prospective new technology sound intriguing, but things at home have been tumultuous recently, and a break from the tension and stress will be welcome.

We board the plane the morning before the conference is set to start. Sasha is in her own words 'young, single and available'. Six months out of her divorce she has resumed her wild ways and is in search of her fairy tale: a nice doctor to sweep her off her feet and out of the midwest. Sasha is beautiful, bubbly and intelligent. I do not doubt that if she puts her mind to it, she will get what she desires sooner than later. While Sasha takes her work seriously, she has made it clear that the educational aspects of the conference are not going to be her primary focus. I know that once we get off the plane, I won't be seeing much of her. The same for the doctors traveling with us. For them the conference is about more than the technology, it is about networking, which means equal parts conference and golfing. I am on my own for this trip, a fact I am perfectly ok with.

Stepping off the plane in southern California is like a breath of fresh air. The warm breeze feels amazing compared to the chilly air at home. I am delighted to learn that our hotel is right off of the ocean. I have always loved the ocean and have vowed to spend as much time at the beach as I can.

*****

Being at the conference is overwhelming. There are so many people in attendance that the slight unease I always experience in sizable crowds begins to set in. I need space and fresh air to calm down. I am only obligated to attend the portion of the conference focused on the new technology. The presentation has been going on for over an hour, and I've seen what I need to. I start to make my way towards the back of the hall, where the crowd is thinner, the tightening in my chest squeezing my lungs, cold sweat beading on my skin.

"Not sold then?"

I stop, the sense I am being addressed giving me pause. Or perhaps it is the voice itself. I turn to properly address the speaker but am temporarily rendered speechless. She is stunning. She has neatly kept blonde hair, mesmerizing blue eyes and a smirk that I am certain many have fallen prey to before.

"Oh, I find it remarkable and can see how it would be of benefit to the patient, surgeon, and staff. It's just…" I trail off having lost my focus. The overcrowded space I had sought to escape now reduced to just the two of us. As I snap back to reality her smirk transforms into a full grin paired with a small chuckle.

"Dr. Catherine Waters," she says extending her hand.

"Alexis Woods," I whisper meeting her offered hand. The butterflies in my stomach take flight as our hands connect, and I inwardly cringe because I'm certain my palms are sweaty.

7

"Sorry?" she asks releasing my hand. She raises one eyebrow, assessing me. It is one of the sexiest things I have ever seen.

"Alexis Woods," I mutter, trying to regain my senses. Catherine's beauty is disarming, distracting me from adhering to the social etiquette I've always strived to observe.

"So Alexis, what do you do?"

That voice…I could listen to her speak for forever and become lost in the lullaby of her words. "I'm a surgical technologist," I answer, regaining some composure. My voice starting to sound like my own again.

"Ah, very nice," she answers with a smile. Do I sense a small amount of disappointment? Mine is an occupation you do because you love it. Recognition and praise are not common in my field, and I have never required them. The reward has always been in the job itself, in helping to save or improve lives. The thought that she might see it as disappointing bothers me.

"I'm sorry, were you leaving?"

"No, it's just that—," I start to reply before being interrupted by someone calling for Dr. Waters.

"Sorry. It was nice meeting you; I must go prepare for my presentation."

"Nice to meet you as well. Good luck." With that I am free. Free from the din in the hall and the trance I found myself befuddled by in her presence. I look for her before I step out of the lobby, but she is long gone, lost in the crowd.

It is a perfect afternoon to spend on the beach. The crowds are sparse, the weather is warm, and the slight breeze and sounds of the waves crashing wrap around me like a blanket. I haul my book and bottle of wine down to the water, prepared to read and relax until daylight fades. Lost in the story, I read until it is too dark to continue. Still not ready to call it a night, I decide to walk the along the beach for a while. Absorbed in my thoughts, I am aware, yet oblivious to the few people that wander the shore with me. How will Elena and I fix the rift that has grown between us? Can it be fixed? After five years together should we just walk away? The problems from home have followed me to this safe haven, refusing to be ignored.

"So this is where you were in a hurry to get to."

My thoughts are interrupted by the silky voice from this afternoon. I look up to confirm who is addressing me. My eyes meet the deep blues of Dr. Catherine Waters, her smirk firmly in place. "Yes...well no, not really. It is a bit more complicated than just wanting to spend time on the beach."

"Complicated? In what manner?" The smirk is still in place on her full, kissable lips. Lips that I'd love to nibble and suck on. Hold on Alexis, what are you thinking? This has to be a side effect of the issues at home. Catherine's smirk transforms into a full grin, I know she has caught me staring at her lips.

I snap out of my trance, my brain finally processing Catherine's questions. "It's just that I get very uncomfortable in large crowds. I was starting to feel overwhelmed and needed to move closer to the exit in case I needed to leave."

"I see. I thought you looked a little frazzled."

That was it, just her observation, no follow-up question. The silence between us quickly becoming uncomfortable, my social awkwardness making it difficult for me to find anything to fill the space. "So, Dr. Waters—."

"Catherine, please. I'm not operating nor do you work for me."

"Alright, Catherine. What brings you out here?"

"I accidentally fell asleep earlier. It is later at home than it is here, so I fell victim to my normal pattern. A commotion in the hall woke me and now I'm up. I decided a walk might be nice, so here I am. And you, what has you out here at this hour? Not out enjoying the night life with your colleagues?"

"I've been out here for a few hours. Started out reading, now enjoying a walk as I'm not ready to sleep. I'm not big on night life activities." I shrug and run my hands through my short, messy hair. "You mentioned home, where is home?"

"Chicago, for now. You?"

"Lansing. Moved there to go to school and never left. Why for now?"

"A few reasons. Mainly it is just too large and does not feel like home. Would you like to continue walking while we talk?" I am honestly so intrigued by Catherine that I've forgotten that I had been walking.

"That sounds nice." We amble along the water's edge, the silence between us again becoming palpable. A faint hint of vanilla tickles my senses and stirs my desire. I have always loved the smell of vanilla on a woman.

"You never did tell me what has you out here so late."

"Oh, sorry. I don't sleep much. I've never slept much or very well. Not a true insomniac, just sleep issues." Why am I nervous? Why are my sentences so clipped all of a sudden?

"Sorry to hear that." We continue to walk along the shore, the sound of the waves crashing and distant traffic filling the silence between us. "What were you reading?"

"*Fingersmith* by Sarah Waters. It has been a favorite of mine for many years."

"What is it about?"

"Love, deception of both yourself and the person you love. I don't like to spoil a plot though so I hesitate to say more."

"I see. Neither the book or author are familiar to me."

"I'm not surprised; she primarily writes stories centered around lesbian characters and relationships."

"Lesbian centric? Well, that would explain why I am clueless here." Catherine hesitates. I know the question she will ask before she asks it. "At the risk of being rude, does that mean that you are…," she trails off, unable to finish the question.

"You're not being rude. Am I a lesbian? Yes, I'm a lesbian." Surely after catching the way I was examining her lips minutes ago she must have guessed this on her own.

"Ah. Right then." I try searching her face for any reaction but she either doesn't have one or her poker face is strong.

We continue walking in silence while I try to figure out what Catherine is thinking. Had my proclamation made her uncomfortable? I know the lengthening silence and my growing certainty that I have indeed made Catherine uncomfortable, are quickly turning my stomach into a tight coil.

"Well, I think I'll return to my room and retire for the remainder of the night. Thank you for walking with me."

"Goodnight." I watch as Catherine moves away from me, chastising myself for my conversational ineptitude. I continue my walk and deliberate about the issues that I face at home. This time the thoughts are interrupted by thoughts about the doctor, her blue eyes, devilish grin and those lips I would love to lock onto.

Catherine

The conference is like so many others, exhausting. I have
nothing against networking; I am simply not in the mood for
it. I feel drained. The climate at work has been stressful,
and the presentation preparation took much more time
than anticipated. I am looking forward to wrapping up the
presentation and finding some time to relax. I want to
catch the imaging demonstration but will have to leave
early to prepare for my own, so I loiter at the back of the
hall taking in what I can.

As I prepare to exit the presentation, I notice a young
woman moving rather quickly in my direction. She has a
panicked look about her and is weaving through the crowd
as quickly as she can. I've seen plenty of panic attacks in
my time, and I recognize it immediately. In an effort to help
calm her down I blurt out the first thing to come to mind.

She freezes, turning to see who has spoken to her. She
stares at me as if she deciding whether to succumb to the
panic or stay and speak to me. I let her, waiting for her
decision, the war in her mind plainly written on her face.
Finally, she finds her voice and speaks. The
transformation in her features is a dramatic shift. I'm
unsure why but part of me finds it slightly amusing.

I introduce myself and offer my hand. She shakes it but
inaudibly tells me her name. Already becoming distracted
myself by needing to leave I ask for it again. She tells me
her name is Alexis Woods. I ask what aspect of
neurosurgery she is involved in. Not another female
neurosurgeon as I had hoped, but still a valuable member
of any surgery staff. I tell her that it's nice and her features
transform once again, into a state of distraction or panic,
I'm unsure. The silence lasts a brief moment before I offer
her the exit she was so clearly determined to make
moments ago. She comes to again and starts to respond

before being interrupted by my colleague who is co-presenting with me. I've put off leaving too long and have to dismiss Alexis before I know she will be ok. I catch a glimpse of the back of her as she exits the hall, the tension melts out of her shoulders as she takes a deep breath and releases it. I smile to myself and refocus on the task at hand.

*****

A commotion in the corridor wakes me. I curse to myself. I've accidentally fallen asleep, and now it is late. Sleep won't return anytime soon, so I elect to take a walk along the shoreline. I throw on some shorts and a t-shirt and run a brush through my hair, unconcerned with my appearance at this late hour. Most of my colleagues will be out enjoying the city's night life or in bed, not that impressing them is on my list of priorities.

The beach is everything I hoped for. Relatively abandoned except for a few couples here and there. The balmy weather and the salt water scented air are invigorating. I make my way down the shoreline, observing the people I pass and contemplating what I am going to do regarding the issues at work. I'm pulled from my thoughts by a familiar face coming towards me. It is the woman from the conference whose name I cannot recall. Her demeanor calmer, more at ease than earlier in the day. I feel bad about the rushed dismissal at the conference. I decide to say hello, only it comes out as a playful quip. I wince inside and remind myself that this woman doesn't know me, or my sense of humor, often playful and sarcastic. She stares at me momentarily, before finding the words to explain what I already know. She begins to ask me a question, addressing me as Dr. Waters. I must interrupt her; I am not fond of formality outside of the operating room. She accepts calling me Catherine and continues with her question. I tell her a half-truth. A stranger does not want to hear about the drama at work, how my messy divorce is making continuing to operate there unbearable. I turn the conversation back to her, wanting to be lost in someone else's life instead of my own. The conversation moves a bit more smoothly between us; maybe it is the wine she is drinking.

Our conversation moves on, and I learn that she is a lesbian. I think I've overstepped, but she assures me that I haven't. The revelation surprises me; I am unsure why. I have a few lesbian friends and a sister who all fall on different points of the femme to butch spectrum. I don't buy into stereotypes; people are who they are, each one unique. As I wonder to myself why I'm surprised, I also make a mental note of which of my friends would likely adore the short dark hair, green eyes, warm smile and athletic build that she possesses. I realize too late that I've been too short, she looks uncomfortable again. I take my leave; I need to be up early for the conference and hope to get some additional sleep before then.

I search for her the next day at the conference. I want to apologize if I made her uncomfortable and explain that I continually struggle with being too concise, my answers often misrepresenting my intent. I am unable to find her and realize that I will have to live with the unspoken apology, another stranger put off by my inability to fully articulate my thoughts.

Alexis

"The rift has turned into a chasm," I lament to my best friend, Abby.

"What's happening?"

"It always comes back to the same issue. Even when we might be taking a few steps forward, we take one giant leap back. Elena has this sudden desire for children that I've never had."

"Didn't you two discuss this years ago?" Abby's mind is a steel trap; she never forgets the details.

"Yes. Several times. I've discussed it with anyone I've ever thought about being with seriously. I've never wanted kids, have never felt the urge. I'm certain that I do not have the proverbial biological clock that most women have. Apparently, Elena's has started ticking after being off for 34 years." Frustrated, I run my hands through my hair knowing it is nearly impossible to mess it up.

Abby takes a sip of her margarita and eyeballs me. I know she is trying to figure out what I'm holding back. "Is that the only issue?"

"It is the biggest issue, the one that magnifies anything else so that it seems ten times worse than it is. I was hoping this was a temporary thing for her and that it would pass and we could get back to good. I'm not sure that it's going to happen anymore."

We sip our drinks in silence as Abby looks at me. After all these years she knows that I am thinking and waits patiently for me to continue.

"The warning signs are starting to show. I'm starting to notice other women more and more. At that conference a few months ago I met this doctor. She was magnetizing." Although our encounter had been brief, thoughts of Catherine still permeated my mind occasionally.

"Wait, how am I just hearing about this now? Did you..." I can see the shock register on Abby's face, her brown eyes becoming huge.

"No! No. Absolutely not. You know I'm not a cheater. Nothing happened. I had a brief conversation with her at one of the presentations, and later that night I bumped into her while I was walking the shoreline. We walked and talked, but she took off shortly after the conversation revealed that I'm gay. You know me, I struggle to maintain conversations with people I'm not comfortable with." I can't admit to Abby the attraction I felt for Catherine, or the thoughts I had about her lips.

"That's it? You're worried about that?"

"I'm not concerned about the interaction in itself, more about how her presence affected me. That odd I've met you before crossed with a heady dose of lust. I could have spent the entire night walking the beach with her."

"So just the one example then? Nothing to worry about." Abby shrugs and takes another sip of her margarita.

This is one instance where Abby and I will never agree. She doesn't see it as an issue, but I know it indicates a much larger problem. "Perhaps. Let's not talk about this anymore. How are things? What is going on with you and that widower neighbor you told me about?"

Abby, happy to talk about this, quickly kicks into gear. She is a dreamer, longing to find the man who will love her, yet trying to insulate her teenage daughter from any dating life she may have. She sadly has a pattern of trying to force square pegs into round holes when it comes to love. She meets a man who tells her what he is interested in, if it doesn't fit what she is looking for she somehow chooses to ignore it and convinces herself that he will change his mind. This is a conversation we have had before, her trying to force the pegs, me pleading with her to step outside of the situation and examine it, her telling me she knows I am right but maybe this time. I feel for her. If anyone deserves to have that someone who will love them like they need to be, it is Abby.

The waitress brings our meals, and we order another round of drinks. I'm in no hurry to get home, and Abby's daughter is at a friend's house. It is one of the rare occasions where we aren't rushed. I only realize that we have been here for hours when it hits me how empty the place has become.

Catherine

My first day on the new job. I am looking forward to moving on from the toxic work environment my divorce had created and getting a fresh start. Today will be split between clinic and the OR. No patients, just introductions to staff and finalizing the paperwork. The partners at the neurosurgery practice had kept my addition a secret from everyone but hospital administration while the buyout of an old partner was settled. Now it is finally time to put my feet on the ground and do what I do best.

The clinic introductions take up the morning. I meet our nurses and physician assistants as well as get situated in my new office. I like things kept tidy and clutter free, so moving in is simple. I rearrange the furniture to my liking, replace the existing art with my own and am finished. I am ready to move on to the OR where I prefer to be.

The hospital business begins with finalizing my privileges to treat and operate, or as I think of it the paperwork portion. The least appealing aspect of my job is the paperwork, yet it is the most time-consuming. I'm thankful every day for the assistants and nurses who handle the vast majority of this for me. Once done there we break for lunch. The partners take me to a little diner a block away from the hospital. Though not food I typically eat, the fare is amazing and I know I will be back. I realize that I have done what I typically do when eating, I have inhaled my meal, a poor habit picked up from years of operating. In the OR you eat, drink, and use the restroom when you get the chance. You never know when the opportunity might open up again. The habit has sadly carried into all other areas of my life, an issue my new partners don't seem to share. Initially, I tried to learn to control it outside of work, but I never mastered the skill.

It is finally time. Time to get into the OR, to meet my new nurses and techs, to smell the myriad of aromas you can only find in an OR. At first, you find them repugnant, but over time they start to remind you that you are where you belong. I've missed these smells.

We are waiting for the fifth partner to finish his trauma craniotomy. Dr. Hoffman finally finishes, and the room staff sees the patient out of the OR and up to the neuro intensive care unit. One staff member stays behind to clean up and prepare the room in the event another trauma comes down. She zips around the room, cleaning all the surfaces, putting equipment back in the proper location, mopping the floor, putting unused supplies away, making the bed, and replacing the trash and soiled linen liners. The partners finally stop her.

"Alex we'd like you to meet," but Alex cuts them off and beats them to the Catherine portion of the introduction as she removes her mask. I hadn't recognized her. Alex? Her name is Alex? I could have sworn it was something else, but I'm terrible with names, so it comes as no surprise that I am wrong.

"You two know each other?" They look back and forth between Alex and me, waiting for one of us to answer. Alex isn't carrying an expression that gives me any confidence that she can.

"We met at a conference a few months ago. Two brief conversations is all." The partners switch their view from me back to Alex.

"Is that all it was? Just two brief conversations?" I do not understand the need for the interrogation.

Alex nods her agreement; her emerald green eyes fixed on me.

"Well good then. Dr. Waters is going to begin operating here next week. We've spoken to management, and they have agreed that you will be available to help facilitate the creation of her preference cards, instrument sets, and anything else she needs. Additionally, since you will be handling all of that we thought it best that you scrub all of her cases the first few months so that we can make you the resource tech for the other members of the team."

Alex again nods her consent; they haven't left her with any other choice. They take their leave, abandoning me with the woman who looks as if she still doesn't know what just hit her.

Blindsided…totally gobsmacked. What is Catherine doing here? The faint droning of the other doctors brings me back just in time to finish the introduction for them. A mistake, one I realize the I uttered her name. My sexuality is no secret at work. I've never had an issue with anyone about it, before now. It annoys me that the team I have dedicated myself to is questioning me about this. Would they have done so if it was one of my male counterparts? Probably, given what they just went through with their last partner. That doesn't make it acceptable in my book but does lend a sense of understanding to their actions.

They leave, and I find myself staring at Catherine again. So many questions are moving through my mind, and that mesmerizing effect she has on me is in place again. I am tongue tied. Which question should I lead with first? Why is she here? Is my sexuality going to be an issue for her when we work together? Did she know about this at the conference? I am struggling to decide where to begin when Catherine shuts the OR doors.

"I'm going to try to make this come out right this time, given that I believe I failed miserably that night on the beach. Do you remember our last conversation?" Do I remember? There hasn't been a day since that evening on the beach that I haven't thought about her plush lips, sultry voice and gorgeous sapphire eyes. Eyes that seem even bluer against the generic powder blue scrubs.

"I do. Your reaction to my telling you that I'm gay was quite confusing."

"Yes, I'm certain it was. I realized too late what my brevity had likely done. I looked for you at the conference the next day but couldn't find you. I wanted to explain what I really meant and apologize for giving such a vague answer and then essentially running away. In hindsight, I am sure that I gave you the impression that I have an issue with your sexuality when that couldn't be further from the truth. What I'm saying is that I'm more than comfortable working with and being around you."

"Well Catherine —,"

"It is Dr. Waters here I'm afraid."

"Right, Dr. Waters. I can accept that and move on from it." Catherine smiles at my answer making me focus on her kissable lips once again.

"Great. Should we begin?"

*****

It turns out that finding a place to work is going to take some effort. The conference room is closed for a meeting and the afternoon shift is taking up most of the break room for their lunches. I suggest that we could try to work in the dining area upstairs. Catherine indicates that she doesn't mind where we work, so long as it is quiet. The dining area is never quiet. It is impossible to find a quiet space in a hospital, no matter the time of day. I had been lucky and found such a rare spot a few years ago. It is on the overflow floor, utilized only when inpatient counts are high, and the extra bed space is needed. The floor has a little area with small tables set up along the floor to ceiling windows that present an excellent view of the city and take in lots of sunshine. I like to eat my meals there, enjoying the quiet and relative privacy it provides. I've never shared the space with any of my coworkers, could I disclose it to her? I think it over for a moment and decide it will be fine, that Catherine has full use of the doctors' lounge and won't have time to spend on the over flow floor anyway. My secret space will remain safe. Assuring her that I know a place, I grab a laptop and lead the way to the elevator.

The elevator ride allows me to take more of Catherine in. I estimate she is in her early forties. She is taller than me, probably around 5'9". She carries an air of self-assurance, one I've seen many surgeons wear. I know it won't be long before she is the topic of conversation among many of the men in the OR. I am lost in my observations when I realize Catherine is looking at me, a questioning look, her head tilted slightly. Shit, she has been speaking to me, and I have no idea what she has said. I have no idea how I am going to focus while scrubbed in with her.

"Sorry I was lost in my head." Such a lie. It wasn't my head that I was lost in.

Catherine chuckles, the smirk I remember from the conference back in place. "I was just wondering—," The door chimes as we stop to let other passengers on, the crowd forcing Catherine and me closer together.

"Hello darling," chirps a voice that I would recognize anywhere. I look up and smile as Abby pulls me in for a hug.

"What are you doing here?"

"Rounding and a quick consult before I head back to the clinic. What are you doing out of the basement? Finally running away?"

"No, I am working with our new neurosurgeon on her preference cards and stuff. Abby this is Dr. Waters, Dr. Waters this is Abby." They shake hands and exchange pleasantries, Abby quickly returning her focus to me, clearly oblivious to the effects of the veritable goddess I've just introduced her to.

"Time for dinner Friday night?"

"Sure. I'll stop by your room before I leave; if you guys are still working."

"Sounds great." The elevator stops again, and Abby takes her leave along with the other passengers, leaving Catherine and me alone again.

"Your girlfriend?" Catherine's question forces my attention back to her.

"Abby? No. Just my good friend. I've known her for years. My partner is a professor at the university."

"I see. You two seem close."

"We are. As I said, it has been years. You aren't the only one to notice though. When we first started working together, many people thought we were dating. It took a long time to put an end to that rumor. Now, most people just refer to her as my work wife."

Catherine smiles and nods. Nothing more. Mercifully the elevator finally arrives at our destination. "This is nice! The view is gorgeous," Catherine observes as we settle into our chosen table. "Where is everybody?"

"This is an overflow floor, so it typically isn't too busy. I like to eat my lunch up here. I can read or just take in the view. A little relaxation in the middle of the day."

"I can imagine. Not a lot of space here for a group meal though."

"No there isn't. I come alone. I haven't really told anyone where I go; I just make my way here."

"A secret? Well…" Catherine trails off, taking in the view. I allow her to enjoy it a little longer before suggesting we get started.

*****

I realize while changing at the end of my shift that I don't want to go home. The thought depresses me. Home is a place that you are supposed to want to go, not a place you actively try to avoid. I know that avoiding it is exactly what I have been doing, working extra shifts, picking up extra call, volunteering to stay over, all so that I can avoid the issues at home. I sigh as I close my locker.

"Everything ok?"

I turn to see my friend Tara at her locker. Tara and I went to tech school together and have been friends ever since. "Yeah, everything is fine."

"I call bullshit. If everything were fine, you'd say good. Things are always good with you. What is going on? You need to talk?"

"No really, things are fine. All good. You just go home to your husband and make him pamper you. Let him make you dinner, rub your feet, whatever. You're having the baby; he can least spoil you before he gets here."

Tara laughs. "We both know I won't give him a choice on that front; I can't cook."

Now it's my turn to laugh, not only because I know that she can't cook but because I also know her husband worships her. If anyone is treated like a queen by their husband, it is Tara. "True enough. What is he making tonight?"

"I have no idea; I just hope it's ready when I get home. I'm starving!"

"Well, you get home and get off those feet. Have a nice night."

"You too. It's cold out, do you want a ride home?"

"No, I'm good, thank you. Honestly, I don't mind the walk; it helps me to unwind after the day here." I have no idea why I don't tell Tara. Aside from Abby, I haven't spoken to anyone about the issues at home. Tara would keep anything I tell her in confidence.

"Ok, well I'll see you tomorrow."

Ten minutes later I arrive home to find that Elena isn't here. Though I should feel curiosity about where she is, I only feel relief that she is gone. I head to the kitchen for a glass of water and find a note taped to the refrigerator: Spin class and dinner with Rachel—E. A little more relief sets in with the knowledge that Elena will be gone for a long while. I'm certain I will be in bed long before she and her sister call it a night. I head for the shower deciding to enjoy the peace and quiet with a movie and some popcorn.

Twenty minutes into the movie I realize that popcorn and a movie just aren't the same when you're alone. I shut the movie off and head to bed with my book. I should try to get some sleep tonight anyway. I have an aneurysm clipping in the morning, a case that can go to hell in a hand basket in a hurry.

Catherine

I wake in a state of panic, the sweat soaked sheet twisted around my body, the comforter kicked to the floor. The nightmare, always the same nightmare. Every surgeon has that case, the one that will haunt them forever. The nightmare comes at will, never changing, never anything I can do. It has been five years now; I am certain it will never fade. They rush the young girl into the ER. She is four. I know immediately there is little I can do, her pupils are blown, hemorrhaging from both ears, eyes, and nose, face swollen and distorted, no response to any stimuli. Her mother in hysterics, having seen her child struck by the car. I know there is nothing I can do to save her, but I have to try. I order an immediate OR. No time for a CT scan. I know how this will end before it begins. Still, I try. She survives for 26 minutes in the OR before coding, our battle lost.

I know sleep has left me behind. I check the clock, 4:17 am. Good enough. Disentangling myself, I pull the sheets free from the bed and toss them in the washer. On an average day, I would be pressed for time to make it to the hospital to round on my surgical patients before heading either to appointments at the office or down to the OR for the day's cases. With clinic starting tomorrow I elect to enjoy my last truly free morning. I swim, shower, make breakfast and turn on the TV. I will be joining Dr. Hastings for his aneurysm clipping this morning, but have plenty of time before I need to arrive.

By seven I can take it no more, the itch to be back in the OR driving me out the door. I have done all I can to delay any longer; the bed is made, the dishes I dirtied washed. I decide to head in early, maybe that will calm me down.

I arrive at the hospital around 7:15 and make my way to the locker room to change. I still have at least half an hour before Dr. Hastings will make his way down to the OR. With nowhere else to be, I head down to the surgery desk to find out which OR we will be in. Greeted by the stares of people who I have yet to meet and a few good mornings from those I have, I discover we are in OR 4 today. The desk points me in the right direction, and I head down to pull up the scans and meet our staff for the day.

In route to room 4, I bump into Alex's friend from the elevator. She greets me with a smile and a hello. Even this early she is upbeat and full of life. I return her good morning and ask her how she is. We exchange a few more moments of small talk and go our separate ways, each of us having cases to attend to.

A quick glance in the window shows me that the room is already open and the staff is working on setting up. The music is on, and the staff is chatting and joking around with each other. I take it in for a moment. A team that can work together like this is always a great thing.

I grab a mask and head in, greeting everyone as I make it through the door. Their conversation stops briefly as they register who their unexpected guest is and return my greeting. I look around me, recognizing the faces of the nurses, my eyes finally landing on Alex. She is scrubbed in working on the craniotomy set up. I make my way towards her, careful to maintain an appropriate distance, watching her do what she has likely done countless times before. She seems focused and efficient, qualities that make a great assistant.

"Good morning Alex, how are you today?" I inquire, breaking her focus.

"Dr. Waters. Good morning. Will you be joining us today?"

"Yes. Dr. Hastings has invited me to scrub with him."

"Large gown and seven and a half ortho?"

"Yes, thank you." She is all business, an interesting contrast to what I witnessed a few moments ago. I write it off to the staff not knowing what environment I prefer in the OR. I realize then that the music has been turned off. I tell them they are welcome to turn it back on. This seems to lend them all a little ease as they get back to their preparations. I make my way towards the doctor's terminal to call up the films and review them, peeking at the nurse's chart as I pass it to make a mental note of the rest of their names. I notice it has gotten quiet again. I look over my shoulder to see Alex and Erin whispering to each other, their set up forgotten momentarily.

Alexis

"What was that?" Erin has abandoned setting up the aneurysm clips to confront me. Her tone hushed, accusatory. She stops me from finishing my set up.

"Nothing," I answer looking over my shoulder at Catherine, who is watching us. I try to get back to work, but Erin is having none of it.

"Oh no, you are not getting off that easy. What. Was. That?"

Erin and I have worked together for years. We know the other's thoughts and body language like one would know a movie they have seen a dozen times. Catherine caught me off guard by showing up unexpectedly, and I know Erin has picked up on something.

"Nothing, I just wasn't expecting her. Did you know she was joining us?"

"No, I didn't know. I'm not buying that caught you off guard shit either. You hesitated. You actually hesitated. I've never seen you do that. Plus you were cold, to the point of being rude. You didn't even look at her. You always greet the doctor and ask how they are." This is the result of someone knowing you too well, Erin has me cornered.

"I'm just really focused is all. It's early." My set up complete, I break scrub, walking away from Erin. "We have a few minutes before the patient will be back. I'm going to use the bathroom and get a glass of water."

"Fine, but I'm not buying it." Erin turns to finish setting up the clips and microscope as I leave the room.

"Neither am I," I mutter under my breath and head for the locker room. I have got to get it together and fast.

*****

Home. I'm relieved to be home. What a long day. The aneurysm was an anterior communicating artery, which can be difficult. Adding more difficulty was that it was the second one for the patient, which meant scar tissue and a tougher dissection. Taking three hours longer than anticipated pushed us severely behind for the second case. Fifteen hours after leaving this morning I'm happy to be home. I kick off my shoes and head to the kitchen for some water and any sustenance I can eat as I make my way to the shower. All I want is to shower and go to bed. Elena surprises me. It was so quiet I didn't think she was home.

"You're late. Everything ok?" There was a time when I would know if she was upset or concerned. Now I have no idea what she is feeling.

"Yeah, just a difficult case today that took longer than expected. Everything is fine though, thanks."

"I was really hoping we could talk tonight." Upset for the win, I see.

"Sorry, I didn't know. We had two rooms running late, so I volunteered to stay."

"You give too much of yourself to that place. You aren't on call tonight."

"Maybe I do. It's part of the job though. Not everyone is trained to do the cases I do. I can't in good conscience leave my patient and surgeon with someone who isn't efficient. Can we please not get into this right now? I really just want to grab a shower."

"Fine. You're right. I do want to talk soon though. Are you on call the rest of the week?"

"No. I'll try to be home relatively on time."

"Good," Elena answers before turning to head back into her office.

*****

Two days later I manage to get out on time. I had a pretty good idea early in the day that I would so I sent Elena a text letting her know I'd be home. Mixed feelings of apprehension and relief war with one another in my head and stomach. To think that five plus years could boil down to the upcoming conversation is unfathomable, yet the possibility of some resolution is appealing.

"Elena I'm home. You here?"

"In the kitchen." Might as well get this over with. I head towards the kitchen where Elena is busy working on dinner. It looks like blackened chicken caesar salad, one of my favorites. "Hungry?"

"A little maybe." Honestly, I'm not, my stomach feels upset from the anxiety of our impending talk.

"Ok. Want to go grab a shower first?"

"Yeah, that would be nice."

"Go ahead. It will keep."

I head towards the bedroom wondering when we became so formal, so unfamiliar. I really don't feel like eating. I just want to get this talk over with and figure out what has to happen from there. I barely feel like taking my required after work shower to cleanse the germs, body fluids, sweat, and stress from the day away.

Showered and changed I head back towards the kitchen. Elena has dinner set up in the dining room. I take my seat and thank her for making dinner. I realize I have no idea when the last time we shared a meal was. I wait. I have no idea where I am supposed to start. Elena eventually breaks the silence that looms around us.

"I don't think we can carry on like this."

I sigh and put down my fork, my dinner untouched. "Neither do I. I don't like finding reasons to avoid coming home, not connecting with you, and fighting all the time."

"Good. We agree on those points. What are we going to do?"

"What can we do? I honestly thought we were fairly good. I know you want me to cut back at work a bit but the whole wanting a kid thing has really thrown me for a loop."

"I know, and I'm sorry." Elena looks down, studying her hands. "We were doing good. Yes, it would have been great to have you around more, but I understand why you work so much, I know it is part of the job."

"And the kid thing. When did that start? I thought we were on the same page about not wanting them."

"It was about a year ago; when Rachel had Liam. Something just clicked. Until then I didn't think I wanted any."

34

"A year? You sat on this for the better part of a year without mentioning it to me?" Shock, anger, and hurt run through me. How could I not realize that my lover of five years had started to hide something of this magnitude from me? How could my partner of five years hide something like this from me for so long? I struggle to maintain my calm.

"I did. I knew how you felt. I hoped it would pass, that spending time with Liam would be enough. I couldn't send our world into chaos for something that might go away on its own."

I sit in silence. I don't know what to say. I look at the woman I've been with for five years and feel like I'm sitting across from a stranger. At that moment I know for certain that we are over, we have been for months.

"I don't want to fight anymore, this endless argument we've been having, only taking a break when we avoid each other. We've stopped talking, touching, or even looking at each other." Elena speaks these words to me, and all I can wonder is how she cannot see that we are through.

"I know. I don't know what I'm supposed to say. My feelings on the matter haven't changed. I don't really feel like they ever will. I can cut back on the call shifts and volunteering to stay late, but I honestly know that I do not want a child. What do we do?" I feel sad about this. Not in the devastated way, part of me knows that this ship has been sinking since Elena first told me. Sad because something that had been so strong, so stable, so fulfilling for so many years is no longer any of those things. Sad because I know that all the positive things from our relationship are gone, eclipsed by the thing we will never agree on.

"I'm not sure, but I don't think either of us has been happy these last few months."

"No, not really. I'd be happy to get a puppy or a kitten, but it seems a ludicrous suggestion to make as a substitution for a kid."

"Yeah, I don't think that will work. I believe we need to take some time to really figure out what we can and cannot live without. Both of us."

"What are you asking for?"

"Nothing. I just think we should stop fighting and both examine what it is we want in our lives and what we are willing to sacrifice."

"We've been together five years. I don't think you have ever given me an ultimatum. This feels like one."

"It isn't. I have some thinking to do as well. This is a major crossroads, one that could change things in drastic ways. This isn't a decision we should make hastily."

"How long are we talking? What are you proposing? Do I need to find a place to stay?"

"No. I'm not suggesting you move out. I'm suggesting we take some time, a month or two, work on us and allow each of us to examine what we want for our lives and this relationship. Let's try to stop avoiding each other and arguing about this."

"Ok, but Elena, I don't think I will change my mind. I don't want either of us to get our hopes up. I love you and would give you almost anything, but not this. I've never wanted one and am pretty confident I never will."

"I know. Please, just a month and then we can reevaluate."

I acquiesce. I know it is a mistake, but I'm just not ready to give up and let go of the past.

That night I'm awakened by Elena pulling my hair. We are spooning. Everything about this situation has me confused.

"Why'd you stop?" Elena's breathing is heavy, her voice raspy.

"Stop what?" I have no idea what she is talking about or how we even ended up entwined.

"You woke me up. You were grinding your hips against my ass, pinching my nipple and murmuring. You were sleeping?" I hear the sound of her soft chuckle. "That must have been one hell of a dream."

It had been one hell of a dream. I just have no idea who I was having sex with. I realize she isn't joking, her breast is still in my hand, and I'm incredibly horny. The debate in my mind is quickly won. I resume teasing Elena's nipple and grinding my hips against her. We have sex for the first time in months; only it doesn't feel like it used to. It feels like goodbye.

Catherine

It has been just over a month since I started here. The transition has gone smoother than I expected it would. That doesn't diminish the relief that I feel knowing that it is Friday and I just need to make it through the day to have a few days off.

Alex and I are just finishing applying the Kerlix gauze around the craniotomy incision when Dr. Hasting's nurse comes in. "Dr. Waters! Dr. Hastings was just paged for an incoming trauma, but he is still in the middle of his fusion. He wants to know if you can take a look for him."

"Sure. I'll head right up. Are they here?"

"ETA is 5 minutes."

"Ok. Alex, Erin you two alright?" They assure me they are. I've ordered an immediate CT scan, so no need for me to wait for the patient to be extubated. I break scrub and head for the ER.

The trauma team is in place and waiting when I arrive. "What have we got?"

"Eight-year-old boy struck by a car while getting off the bus. Loss of consciousness, pupils unreactive, GCS 2." I feel my blood turn to ice.

It is the nightmare all over again. I can feel it. I text Alex telling her to set up an OR immediately. They arrive with the boy less than a minute later. My gut feeling was right; there isn't anything I will be able to do to save him. Still, I have to try. I order that we immediately go to surgery. The ER staff looks at me like I am crazy, they know what I know. The charge nurse is waiting by the elevators when we get to the basement. She sends us to OR 6.

Alex is setting up when we arrive. Several people float around the room, scurrying to get ready. She looks at the boy and then at me. She sees it too. Bleeding from the eyes, ears, and nose. She knows this war is lost before the battle begins. The look only lasts a second or two before she gets back to work.

He lives for nearly an hour. I still cannot save him. The nightmare is a reality once again. I feel a weight on my forearm.

"Dr. Waters. There is nothing more we can do. Anesthesia is calling it," Alex says as she moves her hand to my wrist, moving to take the suction and bipolar from me. She is right. This fight is over.

We close the incision in silence; the only sound is that of the two nurses trying their best not to cry. With the incision closed we clean him up as best we can. I leave to do the hardest thing I will ever do, tell a mother and father their son is gone. Only this time it isn't just the mother and father. Grandparents, aunts, and uncles wait with them. The family consult room is packed. I close the door and shatter all their worlds with one sentence: "I'm very sorry, but your son did not make it."

*****

Quiet. I just want quiet. I need to be alone for a few minutes. It isn't that I don't want the staff to see me as human, I would just prefer it if they did not see me upset like this. I only know of one quiet place in the hospital. I head there now. The platitudes given by the OR staff won't do any good. I just need a few minutes to get it together before I head back to the OR to speak with the medical examiner.

I take in the evening view, a stark contrast to the sunshine filled daytime. The lights over the city are beautiful. Much smaller in scale than they were in Chicago, but beautiful none the less. I've always loved the night time sky scape of a city. I have no idea how long I've been up here when my phone goes off. A text from Alex asking if I need anything and letting me know that the M.E. will be here in twenty minutes. I have twenty minutes to get it together. I set the alarm on my phone for fifteen minutes so I will be back downstairs when the M.E. arrives.

The floor is closed for the weekend; the only noise is the faint humming of the fluorescent lights. The ding of the elevator arriving pulls my attention away from the calming view. Alex steps off, stops when she spots me, then continues to where I am. Neither of us speaks, we just stare out the window. Minutes go by. Without turning to her I whisper, "Sorry for invading your secret space, I just needed quiet."

"No worries. I can head back if you'd like." I am unsure why, but the thought of Alex leaving me stirs a small bit of panic in me.

"No, stay." I don't want to head back yet, nor do I want to be alone. "Aren't you on call?"

"No. Erin is on call. She had to take over Dr. Hastings room. I was getting ready to leave when I got your text. I told them I would stay to do the case."

What can I say? Alex volunteered to stay to help and will now live with the nightmare. So many emotions swirl through me, anger at my inability to help, grief that a young boy is gone, regret that Alex will be haunted by this forever, gratitude that she would stay to help, relief that she is here with me now. "Want to go for a drink after this?"

"Yeah," she answers as she pulls out her phone. She sends a text to someone named Elena. All it says is 'bad day.'

The alarm on my phone sounds. Without thinking I put my hand on Alex's shoulder. She stiffens briefly then relaxes. "We have to get back."

Alexis

Despite common misconception, death in the OR isn't that ordinary. A majority of cases have a multitude of variables that we examine and control. Patients undergo pre-operative physicals and blood tests; thorough medical histories are reviewed and considered, risks are identified. In most cases, patients are awarded medical clearance to have surgery and given pre-operative instructions to follow for the two weeks before surgery. The factors are known and controlled as much as possible. It is the traumas that get you.

Catherine and I walk into the bar. It isn't any place special or even a place with anything interesting to look at. What it is though is poorly lit, relatively quiet, and generous with the booze. I don't come here weekly, but they know me well enough. Catherine and I are both clad in our scrubs still. I only make it half way to the bar before Lisa sets two glasses on the counter and starts filling them with Patron. I try to give her the cash for them, but she refuses, letting me know that this round is on her. She knows me well enough to know what it means when I come in wearing my scrubs. I give her a slight smile and nod, grab the glasses and make my way over to the small booth Catherine has selected for us.

"Was she pouring those before you made it to the bar?" Catherine's eyes have dulled, and her typical self-assurance is nowhere to be found. In its place is a side of her I haven't seen before, she seems dejected and defeated.

"Yeah, Lisa knows what it means if I come in wearing my scrubs."

"Ah. This wasn't your first then?"

"No. My first was many years ago. An older man, routine procedure. Nothing indicated it would end the way it did. Before intubation, he told me he didn't think he was going to make it through the surgery. It was a scheduled, routine case. I disagreed and assured him I'd see him soon. I found out afterward that he lost his wife of forty some years three months prior. I think he just gave up."

"Huh. Was this your first child?"

"In the trauma setting yes. I've been in a Gift of Life on two children before though."

"That cannot be any easier." Catherine's blue eyes that typically radiate with confidence and energy fixate on her drink, dull and defeated.

"It isn't. I'm very pragmatic about these things though. Death doesn't discriminate. Neither does tragedy. At least with the organ procurements you know that other people will be given a second chance at life. I'm not saying that it doesn't make me sad, I'm aware it's a part of the job. Maybe that makes me an emotional cripple." Catherine gives a half hearted chuckle at the last bit. Her slight smile warms me a little.

"Perhaps. I'm guessing not though. Probably just how you cope."

"Could be. Was this your first kid?" Catherine sighs, taking a few moments to collect her thoughts before answering.

"No. There was one before. Not unlike this one. Four-year-old girl hit by a car crossing the street. It haunts me to this day." The pain Catherine still feels shows plainly in her eyes. When she catches me starting she lowers them, again fixating on her drink.

43

"Hell of a life we've chosen, isn't it?"

"Sometimes it most certainly is," Catherine affirms as she orders us another round. "Are the shots here always this large?"

I point to the sign behind the bar warning that all drinks are automatic doubles.

"This place could get a girl in trouble." She wears a small smirk as she says this. Either the alcohol is working, or she is starting to get back to being herself.

"It has that potential." We sip our drinks in silence, memories of the trouble I had found in this very bar parading through my mind. They feel like they existed in another lifetime, someone else's life.

"Do you have to hurry home tonight? I hope I did not take you away from anything." I want to laugh but restrain myself. I haven't been in a hurry to get home in months, despite the talk Elena and I had a month ago.

"No. I sent Elena a text. She won't be expecting me anytime soon."

"I hope she won't be upset with you."

"I doubt she will care." I try to keep my voice nonchalant but fail miserably.

"Hmm." Catherine pauses a moment as if contemplating her next words carefully. "I don't mean to overstep, but are things alright? I mean I have heard your teammates chatting. They seem to speculate that something is off with you lately."

I shake my head. I generally keep my private life and my work life separate. My coworkers have met Elena and know we are together. It pretty much ends there. What goes on in my private life is independent of what happens at work. "Of course. I shouldn't be surprised. So what exactly did you hear?" I am irritated now, not at Catherine but just about the continual gossip at work.

"Nothing specific. Just speculation on why you have seemed so stressed out lately, are taking so much call, and have been more reserved recently. They have come to the conclusion that things at home are not good."

"Well, they would be correct. I haven't told anyone outside of Abby. Things haven't been good since right before the conference where we first met."

"That was months ago!"

"I know." I look down at the table, my drink, my hands. Anything to avoid showing that I know things are over at home but haven't officially ended yet.

"What happened?"

I sigh. Then give Catherine the abbreviated run down of the past few months.

"You see no hope?"

"Not really. It has been a month since we last talked about it. I haven't changed my mind. I doubt she has either. Aside from an isolated occurrence, we aren't even in a physical relationship at this point. We are simply coding, each waiting for the other to call it."

"That is difficult. Have you been together long?"

"Over five years."

"Five years! How did you meet?"

I look at Catherine for a moment. "You really want to hear that story?"

"If there is a story involved I surely want to hear it."

I take a deep breath. "Alright. Well, I first met her around eight years ago, while camping out overnight for concert tickets. I managed to snag the first spot in line for myself and a few friends. A few minutes later another woman shows up, Elena's friend. Elena ended up joining her friend shortly thereafter. We stayed up all night, chatting, playing games, sharing food. It was fun. Elena and I had instant chemistry. She asked me out after we bought tickets that morning but I was already seeing someone. A month later another show was going on sale. It all happened again. Again Elena asked me out, but I was still dating someone, so again I had to decline. We were stuck in each other's orbit though, just waiting for a collision. I ran into her one day while waiting at an appointment. We were talking when my phone rang. I had messed up and gone to the wrong appointment on the wrong day. You have to understand something; I keep a very organized calendar. I'd never made a mistake like that, nor have I done so again to this day. Somehow though things fell into place, the universe conspired, whatever. Again I was still in my relationship, although it was nearing the end, so nothing happened. A pattern developed after that meeting. Anytime I arrived anywhere late I would run into her. It happened every time. The time after the appointment error I finally ran into her and was single, only she was not. We did this dance for a long time. On a few of the later occasions, we both nearly crossed a line. Our chemistry was palpable. I wouldn't allow anything to happen though it probably could have. My father cheated on my mother as often as he could. I didn't want to be like him. Elena's ex cheated on her several times. I didn't want Elena to sink to her level. Finally after years of trying to connect we met and were both single. We've been together since."

"Wow." Catherine appears contemplative as she sips her drink. "It would be hard to compete with that."

"Yeah, star-crossed. Imagine the story Shakespeare could tell. What about you?"

Catherine seems to close down a little. "What about me?"

"I mean what about you? All we have done is talk about me. Are you married, dating?"

"Fair is fair I suppose. I was married. Divorce was finalized a month before the conference."

"And?" The wall Catherine has erected around this topic is driving me crazy.

"And what?"

"I've spilled the details of my life to you."

"Fine. He was the chief of surgery in Chicago. We dated briefly and foolishly got married too soon. We were only married a little over a year before I found out he was cheating on me. I was done right away. He begged me for another chance, but I could not allow myself to be fooled like that again. The divorce was messy. He tried to challenge me at every corner. Work became miserable. I needed to leave. The partners here saw my presentation at the conference. We had our first meeting there."

"So you knew you were coming here then?"

"I did not know for certain. Only that we had a preliminary talk. Nothing was set in stone."

"I see. Sorry about the situation in Chicago."

"Don't be. You didn't do anything wrong." She shrugs nonchalantly, indicating it isn't a big deal to her anymore. "Another round?"

"Sure. I'll get them."

"Oh no. Drinks are on me tonight." Catherine signals to Lisa before I can argue.

"So then are you dating anyone here yet?" Catherine laughs, leaving me confused. "What? An attractive, intelligent woman such as yourself has to have plenty of options."

"Options yes, interest no. I have a hard time opening up to people as it is. I can count the number of serious relationships I've been in on one hand. Dating is not a high priority for me, so I really don't go out looking for someone. Factor in my career with my overall lack of interest and well it doesn't happen often. I'm good with that. It isn't something I excel at anyway."

"I understand. I have the worst social anxiety when it comes to people that I've never met. Add to that the hours we work. Makes dating difficult. One of Elena's sore spots for a while has been how much I work. I think it is hard for people who don't do what we do to understand the demands of our jobs."

"You have social anxiety?" Catherine is wearing her grin again and has her eyebrow arched. "Never would have guessed." She is playing with me for sure.

"Poke fun if you must. I'm quite used to it."

"You seem to be doing alright tonight."

"Yeah well, liquid enhancement I guess." I stare back down at my hands and drink. Catherine reaches across the table and places her hand over mine. The current that passes through me when our flesh connects surprises me. I look up at Catherine's gaze wondering if she feels it too.

"Hey, you're doing fine. Don't shut down." She pulls her hand back and gives me a moment.

"Lighter subject then?" I'm ready to move on from the doom and gloom of our failed relationships and my inability to function socially.

"Yes, please. Before that, I was wondering if you could illuminate me on a matter I've been quite curious about?"

"Maybe. Depends on what it is."

"I know that I replaced a partner at the practice. The partners never disclosed why the opening was available though."

Now I am in a spot. I know nothing for certain but have heard pretty consistent talk in the OR and amongst the surgeons as to why. Surely Catherine could get this information from someone other than me.

"I promise you I do not plan to divulge anything. I really am just curious." I assess Catherine's face and decide she is being sincere.

"Ok. I don't have any actual proof, but from what I've heard he was carrying on an affair with one of the residents. She got pregnant. He promised to leave his wife. When he didn't, she tried to kill herself. It was a fairly big scandal for quite some time. Apparently it wasn't his only indiscretion with a resident. That is all I've heard though."

"Interesting. What is it with married men and cheating?"

"To be fair, I wouldn't apply the cheater label only to married men. I've known plenty of women who have cheated. Seems fairly equal opportunity to me."

"True enough. Have you ever cheated?"

"Me? No, never. I've been cheated on though. I know what it does to a person. Leaving someone can hurt them badly enough, no need to add insult to injury." I sit there wondering if my attraction to Catherine isn't cheating on Elena in some form, making me a giant hypocrite.

"Well said. I'm with you; I'd rather just have a clean break."

We continue talking over the next few rounds of drinks. I find it is easy to fall into conversation with her. Maybe it is the help from the tequila. We finish our current round, I have lost count now, and Catherine offers another.

I stand up from our booth with the intention of agreeing to another round. I feel the effects of the first few rounds on me and change my mind. "I'm gonna be honest. It is starting to go straight to my head. I don't typically drink more than one or two a week. I haven't eaten since lunch today." I glance at my phone. "That was eleven hours ago! Did you know it is after ten?" Catherine grins at me, I know I must be starting to slur my words a little.

"Is it? I haven't eaten anything either. I have to round in the morning." Catherine takes a moment, seeming to assess her current physical state. "I have to eat something, or else I'm going to be hurting in the morning. I should call it a night."

"Me too. How are you getting home?" I have no desire to go home, but that is my available option.

"I am certainly not driving. I need a taxi."

"I can see if Elena is free. She can always pick us up and give you a ride home."

"No, no. Do not put anyone out on my behalf. I can easily take a cab home. How are you planning to get home? I will not allow you to drive."

"Oh, I can walk home from here in fifteen minutes or so. No biggie."

"It is freezing out there. I will tell the taxi two stops."

"You really don't have to do that. I walk all the time."

"No need to argue. I insist."

The cab arrives twenty minutes later. Catherine settles our tab, and we are on our way. When we arrive at my stop, Catherine exits the car with me. I am looking at her, fully confused, when she pulls me in for a hug. The warmth of her body against mine coupled with her vanilla scent stirring my hormones, not something that I need to happen where Catherine is involved.

"Thank you for drinking with me tonight, for keeping me company." She still has me locked in her embrace. I really have no desire to escape it.

"You're welcome. Thank you for the excellent company, drinks, and the ride home." The porch light flips on, and the front door opens. Elena is watching us. I break off the hug and tell Catherine that I'll see her soon. Elena holds the door open for me, and I enter the warmth of the house.

"Who was that?" I can feel her eyes boring into me; she suspects me of cheating on her. Despite the lust I feel for Catherine, I haven't betrayed Elena. Have I?

"That was Dr. Waters. We lost a kid tonight." Elena's look transforms to sadness.

"I saw something about that on the news." She moves to me and wraps her arms around me. "I'm sorry."

Catherine

It's been another long day in the OR. Closure on the last patient finished, I am waiting for the patient to be extubated and taken to recovery. I'll then be able to talk to the family and hopefully get a bite to eat and a shower before going to bed. Eventually the nurse, CRNA and patient head to recovery, leaving Alex and me alone.

"Alex, how have you been? We haven't had a chance to talk." Alex's body language has been off lately. She just seems so dejected.

"I'm hanging in there."

"You ok?" I don't want to pry, but I know she has been having personal issues. There is something about seeing this typically confident woman like this. I feel the urge to hug her but refrain.

"Yeah, I'm alright." Her body language betrays her; I know this is a lie.

I need to check in with the family, but am concerned about Alex. Something isn't right. "Listen, it has been a long day. I need to get a quick bite to eat somewhere. You hungry?"

"Sure, I could eat. I need about 15 minutes to wrap things up here though."

"Great! That will give me time to dictate and speak with the family. Meet you outside the locker room?"

"Sure, if you don't mind driving. Otherwise, I need to head home to get my car."

"I can drive. Meet you in 15 minutes or so."

*****

We settle into a little Mediterranean place Alex recommended. She orders the falafel meal; I opt for the chicken shawarma.

"Alex, what is going on?" I have been very concerned about her body language recently.

"Oh, well Elena and I have officially called it quits."

"I am so sorry to hear that. Are you ok?"

"Yeah. Just sad. It's been over for the last six months or so. Now it's official. We both agreed that it is probably for the best. Neither of us is going to change our minds about kids, and neither is willing to sacrifice our position on the matter for the other."

"That is tough. Right before the holidays as well. So what are you doing for Thanksgiving next week? Do you have any family to visit?"

"No, no family. I'm just going to relax. Probably watch some football, definitely going to the movies, looking for a place to live, maybe some shopping. I'm on call so nothing too crazy. What about you? Visiting family?"

"No. My sister is in California. I'm on call as well, so I will be around. What movie are you planning on seeing?"

"*Carol* with Cate Blanchett and Rooney Mara." Alex's features shift from sadness to excitement. I can tell she is anxious to see this movie.

"What is it about?" I enjoy movies, but somehow I never seem to know what is coming out.

"It is based on another of my favorite books, *The Price of Salt*. Blanchett plays the title character. Set in the 1950's she is a married but separated woman who meets Mara's character. It is about them falling in love and everything that comes with it."

"Wow, I did not peg you as someone who would be into the chick flick."

Alex laughs. It's a nice sound to hear, one that has been missing in the OR recently. "Don't tell anyone my darkest secret."

"Well now, I am gathering quite the stock pile of those. Promise your secrets are safe with me."

"Thanks," she says half sarcastically, flashing me a lopsided grin.

"Any interest in some company?" A look of genuine shock registers on Alex's face.

"Ok. I'll check the showtimes and text them to you."

"Great. What are you doing for food before the movie? Want to find some place to eat?" I feel like I'm inserting myself into her plans, but she seems fine with it.

"Sure, we could do that."

"Alexis is that you?"

Alex and I turn towards the voice. "Hey Nina, how are you?" Alex stands to greet the stranger as she approaches us. They hug, and Alex slides back into our booth.

"Great, just picking up dinner for Tasha and I before I head home."

"Nina this is my friend Catherine, Catherine this is Nina." Nina's eyes shift back and forth between Alex and me.

We shake hands and exchange pleasantries. Alex and Nina chat for another minute or two before Nina's take out order is ready. She takes her leave, allowing Alex to resume eating.

"Sorry about that."

"No need to apologize. How do you know her?"

"Met her through friends many years ago. We played softball together a few summers. I haven't seen her in a while though." Alex is very nonchalant about the whole thing. It is clear they have never been an item.

"Ah. Does she think we are here together?" I don't know why I am nervous about this, but I am. Perhaps it is because of Nina's obvious analysis of what she interrupted.

"Uh, we are here together. Do I think she believes this is a date? No, not likely. I doubt she knows that Elena and I have separated." Alex eyes me for a moment, forgetting her meal. "Are you ok?"

I realize that I have said something wrong. Alex's tone betrays her irritation. She has stopped eating while she waits for my answer. "Yes, I am fine. I didn't mean anything by it. Just curious what people you know will think if they see us together." Alex is not pacified.

"Does it really matter what people you have never met think? If you are uncomfortable, we don't have to do anything outside of work."

Oh my, I have kicked a hornet's nest. "Alex, I am truly sorry. I did not realize that I was asking the wrong question."

"I can't spend time with you outside of work if I have to be worried that you are uncomfortable. I introduced you to Nina as my friend, not my girlfriend, partner or date. I don't understand why you would automatically assume that people would think we are together unless that idea bothers you." Alex is fuming.

"You are right, again I apologize. I am fine being seen with you outside of work. There really is not an issue on my end."

Alex sits quietly for a minute. "Ok, if you're sure. For the record, I automatically assume that the majority of women I meet are straight. I assume most people do the same."

I feel terrible. I really did not mean any harm but have clearly upset Alex. A third apology seems too much though. "You are right. I'm guessing most people assume that a person is straight when they first meet. Can we move on?"

"Sure."

The silence between us becomes too much to bear, making me nervous. I ask the question I have wondered about before but never bothered with. "Why do some people call you Alex and others Alexis?"

"Not sure. Personal preference on their part probably. Maybe it was how they were introduced to me. I never really paid attention."

"Which do you prefer? When we first met, you introduced yourself as Alexis."

"Either is fine." Her tone is still clipped, I know she is still irritated.

We finish our meals in relative silence. I have upset Alex on a level she isn't ready to easily move past. I drop her off at her house hoping that I have not alienated the first potential friend I have here.

Alexis

It has been two days since the dinner with Catherine. I arrive at work hoping I won't be scrubbing her room. I am not ready to see her yet. Despite Catherine telling me she is more than comfortable being around me, her actions and questions have given me a different impression. Now I will be avoiding drama at work. I despise drama anywhere, much less at work.

I check in at the desk and learn that I will indeed be scrubbing in Catherine's room. Determined to just get through the day I head to our OR and start preparing for our first case. Erin arrives a few minutes later. I am pleasantly surprised as she was not originally scheduled to scrub with me. "Hey. What's up?"

"Nothing. I just felt like scrubbing with you today since we haven't had the chance to lately. So I traded assignments."

"Really? That is great! We're gonna have a great day!" I get along with all of my teammates but scrubbing with Erin always makes the day better.

Erin and I proceeded to chat while I scrub in and start setting up the case. I am just finishing up draping the microscope when I hear the door swing open. I turn to see Catherine walking in, talking on her phone. I speed up a little bit hoping I can finish and break before she ends her call. I am not that lucky.

"Good morning Alex, Erin. How are you this morning?"

"Morning," I quip, breaking scrub and exiting the room as quickly as possible. Erin emerges a few seconds later.

"Well, it certainly got cold in there all of a sudden." One of the things I love about Erin is our ability to be completely sarcastic with one another about everything. We are both so laid back that we enjoy the banter and trying to one up the other.

"Did it?" Playing dumb with Erin never works. She knows me too well.

"Yeah, what the hell was that?"

"Nothing. All good."

"Oh no, I let that go before. What is it? I thought you two were getting along well from what I've heard."

"Yeah, things are fine. She just has given me the impression that she might not be that ok with the whole gay thing."

"How did that even come up?"

I feel my phone vibrating as I prepare to answer. I pull it from my pocket to check what it is and tell Erin not to worry about it. I walk away as I open the text message from Catherine: *I just want to tell you again that I am sorry. I keep giving you the wrong impression. I hope we are still on for next week; I'm looking forward to it.* I audibly exhale, jamming my phone back into my pocket. I will respond later. I've learned that I can be quite a bitch when I answer messages from people I'm a bit pissed at.

"Everything alright?" It isn't even 8 am and I am already tired of being asked that question. I turn to greet Abby, trying to get my surging anger under control.

"Morning love. How are you?"

"Doing great. You?" Always so bubbly. I love her, but sometimes the positivity is too much.

"Fine, I'm fine. I haven't seen you in a minute. Anything new?"

"Oh, you know, still working on the neighbor. Other than that nothing I can think of."

"Well keep me posted. Usual Friday?"

"Of course. Wouldn't miss it." She smiles at me, but I know she has picked up on my sour mood.

"Great. Well, I'm going to grab a bite before our case starts. Talk to you later." I don't want to bring Abby down, and I know that I'm in a bad mood. Best to move on.

"Have a good day," Abby answers as she heads toward her room for the day.

*****

Our first case is a struggle. Fusion revisions come with their own host of issues, and this was no exception. A great deal of scar tissue coupled with difficulty removing the old hardware delays us well into the lunch hour. We are finally closing when Tara arrives to give us break. I am all too happy to drop out and head to lunch. I need to be alone for a few minutes, to regain control of my emotions.

I am sitting at the table in my quiet spot when I hear the elevator chime its arrival. I instinctively know who it is. I didn't bother looking back to confirm, the scent of vanilla does the work for me.

"I sent you a text this morning." Catherine's voice is barely an audible whisper.

61

"Yeah, I got it." So much for correcting my mood.

"Look. I'm sorry to intrude on your lunch. I just feel awful. You're the closest thing to a friend I've made here. I hate that I have messed that up because I am incapable of communicating clearly." I can see the remorse on Catherine's face.

"This isn't something I can do. I'm happy to be friends with you, but I can't do that if I have to worry in the back of my head that you are uncomfortable around me, or worried that someone will think you are a lesbian because they see you with me. I am too old to deal with that shit anymore."

"All I can do at this point is tell you this: my sister is a lesbian, I have several friends who are lesbians. I am fine with it. It does not bother me." Then why all the ridiculous, predictable questions?

I audibly exhale, the fight going out of me. I cannot stand arguments. Maybe it has to do with the daily barrage I witnessed between my parents. Maybe I'm just not wired to enjoy them the way that some people do. It takes too much energy. I would rather just move on. "Ok. However, I am going to call you on anything like this in the future. Just want you to know that."

Catherine smiles. "Good, I hope you do. Now, will you tell me how you are doing? I have been worried about you."

"I'm doing alright; I think it is more nostalgia than anything else at this point. Still looking for a place. Elena isn't kicking me out, but I know we will both be better off the sooner I find a place."

"If you need someplace to stay you are welcome to stay at mine." Catherine's offer comes out of left field. I have no idea how to respond.

"Uh thanks, but I'm pretty sure that is not a very good idea. We work together. We hardly know each other. We don't need to be stepping on each other under your roof as well." I don't bother to mention my attraction to her, only one of us is likely to be bothered by that.

Catherine grins. "That last bit would not be a problem. The basement of my house is essentially a small apartment. It has a large bedroom, a decent sized bathroom and an area that serves as a combo living room and den. We would only have to share the kitchen. I know we do not know each other that well and that we work together, but if it would help alleviate some stress on your end you are welcome to utilize the space. Besides I know that you like football, chick flicks, and peace and quiet."

"You are never going to let me live that chick flick thing down are you?"

"Not if I can help it." Catherine grins. "Just stop by and look at the space. No pressure, just a friendly offer. Stop out tonight if you'd like."

I know this is a bad idea. "I have Friday night dinner with Abby tonight. I could come out tomorrow if you will be around."

"I can be around. I will text you my address. Just text me when you are on your way."

*****

"Well, this certainly is a role reversal." Abby is practically gloating. "Let me tell you I do not think moving into the

63

doctor's basement is a good idea." Abby has always been able to read my mind.

"I know. I had that very thought. It would get me out of Elena's house until I find my own place though."

"So you are considering it?"

"I haven't seen the place. I'm supposed to look at it tomorrow. I feel like I would be under less stress if I got out of Elena's sooner. From the sounds of it, I would have plenty of privacy."

"Why don't you just stay at mine? We can figure out space for you and you stuff."

"Thank you, but no. You have one bathroom for yourself and your teenage daughter. You need more room for the two of you. You certainly don't have room for a third. Things will work out. No need to worry."

"I will worry." Abby pauses. I know she is debating between continuing to speak or giving up. "Alex you like a firm boundary between work and your private life. You've admitted before that you are attracted to her. Just be careful."

"I will. I'm sure I will eventually learn something about her that will eliminate those feelings anyway." I know myself well. I have frequently found myself attracted to women in the past only to find what I think of as the deal breaker, the quirk or personality trait that would make them undatable in my book. "Now tell me about the neighbor. How is that?"

"Well he told me that he is seeing a woman, but it isn't serious. However, her car is at his place every weekend."

"Sounds like it is somewhat serious. Abby if he lost his wife last year he probably isn't ready for a commitment. If you just want to sleep with him and he agrees then, by all means, go for it. If you are looking for something more permanent, then be careful. At least wait until her car hasn't been in his driveway for three months."

"You're right, I know. I'm going to try to be careful."

"Well, take care of you. You need to remember that."

"You too. I still think you should consider staying at my house." Abby would pack every homeless person in the county into her house if she could sort the logistics of it. She has enough on her plate though, and I need some space. In a way moving into her place is likely just as bad of an idea as moving into Catherine's.

*****

I arrive at Catherine's around 9 am. The house is located behind a dense tree line. If it were not early winter, I would have missed it behind the now missing foliage. I am not prepared for how large the house is. It is a sprawling Cape Cod style home. The gray-blue siding feels inviting to me, as if it oozes warmth. I am fairly certain that the three stall garage might be larger than Elena's house.

Catherine is waiting for me at the door as I step onto the large front deck. "Any trouble finding me?" She greets me with an amiable smile, one that is impossible to not respond in kind to.

"No, although if the trees still had their leaves, I'd likely have missed it. I cannot believe how large this place is." I struggle to take everything around me in. I notice that the walls are largely empty except for the few art pieces here and there. No real personal effects such as family photos anywhere. Some people would likely consider it bare or cold; I find it to be perfect, no clutter, no distractions. I realize that Catherine and I might have more in common than I initially thought.

"I will admit that it is a bit much. Shall I give you a tour? Would you like something to drink first?"

"Just some water would be great." I take off my shoes and leave them on the mat near the door. Catherine takes my coat and hangs it in the closet.

"You sure? I have all sorts of juice. I might even have some coffee if I look hard enough."

"Yeah, just water. I don't drink coffee."

"Me either. The kitchen is this way." My head is on a swivel as she leads me to the kitchen. I see that she enjoys things neatly kept, the house hardly appears to be lived in.

"Wow…this is amazing!" Kitchen is probably an understatement for what Catherine has led me to. It isn't just a kitchen; it is a dream. Everything I have ever wanted in a kitchen is here. Dark marble counter tops, all new stainless steel appliances, the large island in the center of the space, a griddle, stove top, and two ovens. I am fairly certain that the kitchen and dining room combined are larger than my first apartment.

"Do you cook?" My awed reaction must be obvious. Catherine is looking at me with that smirk on her face again.

"I do. I cook and bake. I take it you cook as well?"

"When I can. I enjoy it. I have never been very adept at baking though. Ice?" she asks as she grabs a glass.

"Please." Catherine has an ease about her that I've never seen at work. The confidence she wears like a shield at work takes a back seat to the comfort she clearly feels in this house. I feel a familiar twinge as I take Catherine in, my attraction to her stirring my hormones. She is wearing a pair of jeans and a light blue v-neck t-shirt that hugs her curves perfectly and makes her eyes pop.

"Well, what would you like to see next? The apartment or the rest of the house?" If Catherine senses me checking her out, she doesn't let on.

"Whichever is fine by me." I'm still awestruck by the kitchen.

"Very well, let's head downstairs first."

Catherine leads me to the basement. She had not been joking. The first thing I see is a large open space with a fireplace, fully furnished with a couch, TV, coffee table, and two chairs. She hadn't mentioned the bar area, which I discover also houses a small refrigerator. The bedroom isn't just large, it is massive and has two dressers and a king size bed, all stained in a dark cherry color. The walk in closet is larger than I remember my dorm room being. Shelves line one wall of the closet; they would work great for my vast shoe collection. The bathroom is also extensive. It contains a whirlpool tub and boasts two sinks at the counter. It would be easy to temporarily crash here.

"Well, what do you think?"

"I think you understated the size of this place. I thought you said small apartment. This might be larger than any apartment I ever lived in."

Catherine laughs. "I suppose it is all relative. In comparison to the rest of the house, it is small."

"True. This can't span the entire house though; the house seemed larger when I pulled up."

"You would be right; it does not. We will get to that. Shall we continue the tour?"

"Sure."

Catherine guides me from room to room. After four bedrooms (one being her master suite), three bathrooms, a sitting room, a living room, a laundry room, and two storage rooms we finally arrive at the end of the tour. "I promised you that we would come back to your basement observation. This should answer that for you."

I am not prepared for the indoor swimming pool. I didn't even know that people actually owned indoor pools. However, here it sits, and it is beautiful. Natural light drifts in from the countless windows, and the familiar scent of chlorine tickles my nose. The water looks cool and inviting. "So this is hidden on the back side of the house?"

"Yes, privacy on all sides. I own several acres of land surrounding the place. I wanted peace and quiet when I relocated here."

"I don't mean to be rude, but isn't this a lot of house for just you? Were you planning on living here with someone?"

Catherine laughs. She is much more relaxed than I have ever seen her. Somehow I find her even sexier like this than I do any other time. "It is. It is so much more space than I require. However, the price was perfect. The previous owners relocated and were desperate to sell. I likely would have passed on it had it not been for the isolation and the pool. The pool sealed the sale for me. I swam until I finished undergrad. I missed swimming. Now I don't have to. I justified the rest by telling myself that it would be easier to sell a larger house if I ever decide to relocate again."

"Makes sense I suppose." The thought of Catherine relocating bothers me, when I know that it shouldn't. I should take it as the final sign that this is a bad idea, but I ignore my subconscious screaming this fact at me.

"So what do you think?" She asks me this as the sunlight trickles through the windows, highlighting her hair and lightening her eyes. I want to tell her I think she is beautiful, instead; I just enjoy elegant visage before me.

"How much are you thinking?"

Catherine looks at me confused. "How much what?"

"Rent. How much per month?"

"Nothing. I offered the place to you. You do not need to rent it from me." I look at Catherine, my expression relaying my confusion to her. "Why is that upsetting to you?"

"I wouldn't feel right not paying something. I'm not a freeloader."

"I did not mean to make you feel like one. I don't need your money. I have the means to help you out; you need a place to stay. There isn't an ulterior motive. It would be nice to have someone else living here."

"I have to pay you something; otherwise I would feel like I'm taking advantage."

Catherine doesn't look thrilled by my insistence. "Alright. What about $100?" I can hear a measure of irritation in her voice.

"A week?"

"No a month. I can already see you are going to argue. What if you add those cooking skills into the mix? So $100 a month and you cook dinner on the nights that you are not working late?"

I think about it. Part of me knows it isn't a good idea. Moving into Catherine's house would eliminate a barrier between my work life and private life. The other part of me argues that it would be nice not to live alone right away once I move out of Elena's, and that I'll likely never stay any place this nice again. "Yeah, I can do that. When would I be able to move in?"

"Whenever you'd like. I can help you Thanksgiving day if you'd like."

Catherine

Thursday morning arrives and with it move in day for Alex. I stop by her place after rounding so I can take a load of stuff back to the house with me. I am excited to have her moving in. Finally, there will be some life in the house other than myself.

I arrive just as Alex emerges from the house with a few boxes. I quickly kill the engine and jump out to open the door of her Impreza for her. "Good morning Alex."

Alex barely musters a smile. Her sadness is coming across clearly. In my excitement to have her at the house, I have forgotten about how difficult this would be for her. "Hello, Catherine. Thanks for offering to take a load back to yours for me. Anything brewing at the hospital we need to be ready for?" Her tone is flat, and I feel my heart ache on her behalf.

"Not yet. Good start to the day thus far. Hopefully, it will stay quiet for us."

"Yeah." Alex turns to head back into the house. "I don't think this will take too long. I'm a pretty big minimalist, so if we pack up both cars just right, we might get everything in one trip. I already have everything boxed up in the laundry room and entryway."

My first impulse is that I want to give her a hug. I debate this as we make our way to the first stack of boxes. I decide to go for it. I stop Alex from retrieving the top box by gently grabbing her arm. This forces her to turn back in my direction. I take advantage of this and immediately pull her in. Alex initially goes rigid and tries to fight it, but quickly acquiesces, sighing deeply as the resistance goes out of her. "I'm sorry this is so difficult for you. I promise you will get through it."

"I know I will. I've known this was coming; I just didn't realize how bittersweet it was going to be. I've lived here for nearly five years. Five pretty good years. I have a lot of great memories involving this place." Alex breaks off the hug and grabs a box. She moves past me and heads back towards the cars, but not before I catch the tears welling in her eyes.

"Can I ask why you are the one moving out?"

"It is Elena's house. Her parents purchased it after Elena and her sister left the nest for college. It was meant to be their downsized retirement home. They lived here for eight or nine years when they decided they had enough of winter and relocated to Arizona. By then there was only a year or so left on the mortgage, so they let Elena take it over."

"I see."

"I'm sorry, can we talk about anything else? Distract me."

"Absolutely. What do you want to talk about?" I'm more than happy to help distract Alex; I'm just not certain what topics will lead back to her failed relationship.

"I don't know, anything. You said you had a sister. Tell me about her."

"Taylor lives in San Francisco. I think I told you she is a lesbian. She is 37 but typically acts like she is 22."

"It doesn't sound like you two are particularly close."

"We are not. We're polar opposites in so many ways. She is wild, makes rash decisions, flits from one woman to the next, and lives impulsively, unconcerned about the future.

I think you know enough about me at this point to guess that I do not understand her behavior. I am sure she feels the same way about me."

"Maybe she is just living the life that feels right to her, being her truest self." Alex makes a point that I have never considered.

"Perhaps. I think she is planning on visiting for Christmas. Not sure what your plans are, but last we spoke she mentioned coming here." Knowing Taylor, she will change her plans at least a dozen times in the next month.

"Oh, that could be nice for you. Maybe the two of you can find some common ground. Not visiting your parents then?"

"No, they went abroad for a few months. I haven't planned on taking much time off around the holidays. I on call Christmas day for Dr. Hastings so he could spend it with his family. What are your plans?"

"Nothing really. I'm sure we will end up having a gathering of some form either at Dahlia and Derrick's or Shannon and Kevin's house. Aside from that, I haven't planned too far out."

"Do you not have any family to spend the holiday with?"

"Sometimes your real family is the family you chose, not the ones you share blood with." Alex's words and tone more than tell me there is a lot about her past I know nothing about.

"No siblings? Parents?"

"I'm an only child, and I haven't spoken to either my parents in over 15 years. My mother disagrees with my sexuality and the decisions I've made. My father never really took an interest in me. Drinking and philandering were always his top priorities. I'm not missing anything there."

"I don't understand. You are their child. Do you miss them?"

"I certainly do not miss my mother's judgement or constantly pressuring me. My father isn't a good person, nor did he ever make an effort to be a part of my life. I got over all of it a long time ago. There are some people that you are better off not having in your life and those people aren't worth the emotional expenditure they cost you."

I think about everything that Alex has just told me for a minute. While I'm not particularly close to my parents or Taylor, I do not doubt that they would be here in a second if I needed them. I hope they know I would be there for them as well. "Wow, I am failing miserably when it comes to distracting you with something better to talk about."

"No worries. We only have a few boxes left to load anyway. 35 years on the planet and I can pack everything I own into a pair of Lezbarus." Alex eyes our vehicles and the sadness deepens in her features.

"Lezbarus?" I have no idea what she is talking about.

"Surely you have heard the stereotype about lesbians driving Subarus? Well just combine the two and you have Lezbaru."

I can't help it; I laugh uncontrollably. It is absurd yet after the dismal conversation topics this morning a much-needed relief. "I've never heard that before." We are grabbing the last of the boxes when I notice Alex picking up a storage chest. "That is beautiful. May I ask where you got it?"

"I made it." She says it so matter of factly that I almost feel like she is kidding me.

"You made that? Do you make things and sell them?"

"Not really. I enjoy woodworking as a hobby. If I need something and can make it, then I make exactly what I want. I've crafted a few things here and there for friends when they've needed shelves, display cases and what not though." She shrugs and turns towards the door with the chest in her hands.

"Impressive. I could think of a few things I could commission you to make. What do you use yours for?"

"I wouldn't charge you. You pay for the materials, and I can make you whatever you need. I just store some personal effects in mine."

"Well feel free to set up a workspace in the garage if you would like to. That is all the boxes right?"

"Yeah, that is everything."

"Ok. I will see you at the house. Here are your keys and one of the garage door openers."

"Thanks. See you in a few." I want to hug Alex again. I can see the pain in her features. Instead, I get in my car and leave Alex to say farewell to her home of the last five years in private.

Alexis

I don't realize how hungry I am until I start the car to head to Catherine's. Unsure if Catherine has eaten anything yet, I stop to grab some bagels. By the time I get to the house, Catherine is already hard at work unloading her Outback. "Hey, I grabbed some bagels. Not sure if you are hungry."

"Lovely, I could eat for sure. Thanks." I follow Catherine into the house as she hauls one of my boxes in. "Hope you don't mind that I started unloading stuff and taking it downstairs."

"Not at all. You didn't have to, but I appreciate it." We situate ourselves for our late morning breakfast. "Were you still interested in grabbing dinner and seeing the movie tonight?"

"Absolutely. Have you looked into showtimes yet?"

"The movie shows at 9:15, so I was thinking of heading to dinner around 6:30 or 7. There is a sports bar open that has a few different fares if that works."

"Yeah, that would be fine."

"Great. Well, I'm going to get back to unloading and unpacking. I won't be able to stop until things are where they belong."

"Understandable. I can help you get everything downstairs."

"Are you sure? You've been a huge help already, I don't want to take up your entire morning."

"No big deal. I am used to being busy all day anyway. Happy to help out."

"Thanks. So out of curiosity are there any ground rules or anything I need to know about? Any areas of the house you want me to stay out of or something?"

"The house is yours now too. Feel free to use the pool when you want, the kitchen when you want, really no restrictions."

"Ok. Well just as a heads up, before we land in an awkward situation, I sleep naked. So just beware if you are downstairs at night, there is that."

"No big deal. I do the same. I think we will be fine though." I'm immediately distracted by images of Catherine sleeping naked. I lose track of time, my bagel, everything. "Anything else?" Catherine is wearing her smirk again and eyeing me.

"Well if I am doing anything that is irritating you just let me know."

"Like I said, we will be fine."

*****

We are in the middle of dinner when I realize that Catherine is not her normal, inquisitive self. She sits quietly, picking at her food, avoiding eye contact with me. "Everything alright?"

"Yes, everything is fine. Why do you ask?" The fact that she can barely look at me when she says that things are fine tells me she isn't being honest.

"You're being abnormally quiet over there." I don't want to pry so I leave her the open door.

"Well…I am just a little bit nervous."

"Nervous? About what? Big case next week?"

"Oh no, nothing like that. It's just that, well I am nervous about there being sex in this movie." I nearly laugh out loud. Between Catherine's hesitancy to tell me and then her unloading what seems like a ridiculous reason, I struggle to not unleash the laughter I feel bubbling inside.

"I'm confused. Why are you nervous?" I'm not one to minimize a person's feelings, but this just seems absurd to me.

"Well, I am not sure. I just feel nervous." Again she tries to avoid eye contact. Now I'm certain this has to do with it being a love story between two women, meaning we are right back to the gay thing again. I try to stay calm.

"Ok. I'm assuming you've seen movies with heterosexuals having sex before right?"

"Yes of course."

"Did that make you nervous?"

"No."

"Then why would this make you nervous? It isn't like you will be the only straight person at the show. I'm very confused why you are nervous about this, but if it calms you down, I've seen the one sex scene in its entirety already. It is brief and not much more than a make-out scene with breasts."

"Oh. Ok then. You are right, nothing to be nervous about." She says it is ok, but I can tell that she is still ill at east about it.

"I can go see this on my own. I was going to anyway remember?" I offer Catherine an out. I've been looking forward to this movie since it was announced. I want to be able to enjoy it and not worry about Catherine's emotional state.

"No, I want to go."

"Are you sure? I will be fine if you don't feel comfortable going."

"I am sure. All good." I'm not sure if she has convinced either of us, but she isn't budging. "Did you get settled in alright? Do you need anything?"

I am not convinced that Catherine going to the movie is the best idea, but I have given her an out multiple times. She seems determined to change the subject, so I let it go. "Yeah, all settled. You saw that I didn't have too much anyway. I'm a pretty simple creature. I think I have everything that I need. Thanks again for all of your help."

"You're welcome. If there is anything you need, please let me know."

The pause in conversation allows me to realize we have forgotten to discuss something we should have figured out already. "Catherine, what exactly are we letting people at work know?"

"What do you mean?"

"Well, that place is like a soap opera. If they know that I've moved into your house, then that little piece of actual knowledge will spiral into some torrid affair between us. If we don't disclose that information and someone finds out, we will have been having a secret affair. It is a no-win really."

"Oh. Well, I already told the partners that you were moving into the basement apartment in my house. After everything they went through with the old partner, I figured it was best if I was upfront with them about it. As for your coworkers, let them talk. Idle chatter does not phase me one bit."

"Except that I think it would bother you if they all thought you were a lesbian."

"Well, I am not trying to date anyone at work. I made that mistake before, and it turned out horribly. People can think what they want, I won't lose sleep over it."

I'm not buying it. Her words contradict her past behavior when she met Nina. I decide it isn't worth it and let it go. "Fair enough. Well, think about it. I'm not suggesting we put up a flyer or announce it at a meeting, I just don't want to have to lie to anyone when they ask me where I am staying."

"Just tell them that you are renting a friend's basement."

"I suppose I could. Everything eventually comes out though."

"We can worry about that if it happens."

"Fair enough." I don't like it. I've always preferred a preventative maintenance approach to things. This is more of a patch up the holes as they appear stance. I feel confident that it will bite us on our asses sooner or later.

Catherine

"Two for *Carol*, a large popcorn, and two large drinks, please. You ok with sharing a popcorn?"

"I can get my own ticket and snacks."

"Don't be silly; I've got it."

"Catherine you just insisted on paying for dinner. I should be paying for this."

"Let me; I can afford it." I know as soon as the words slip past my lips they were the wrong thing to say. Alex's pupils flare, and her jaw clenches.

"Catherine I am not a charity case. I can more than afford to buy myself dinner, popcorn, and a movie ticket." I can tell she is struggling to keep her voice down.

"I'm sorry. I did not mean any offense by it. I don't see you as a charity case. I just meant that I have a lot more disposable income, it isn't a big deal." I really need to just shut up.

"That doesn't make it sound any better. Don't throw your wealth in my face. If I couldn't afford to do this, I wouldn't be doing it. I make more than enough to take care of myself."

"Alright. How about you pay next time then? Would that be ok?" At this point, I am looking for any way I can to calm Alex down. People are starting to look at us. All I wanted was to do something nice for Alex on a day I know has been difficult for her.

"Sure. I can live with that."

"I don't understand. Why won't you just let me take care of you?"

"I'm not your child. I've been taking care of myself since I was 14. I don't need anyone to take care of me. Nor is this a date. You paying for everything makes it feel like a date."

I admire her fierceness, the way she is never afraid to speak her mind if something bothers her. It is a refreshing change from what I am used to. "Alex, I know you are not my child. I did not mean to imply that. I simply meant that I get enjoyment out of treating people. You are right; this is not a date. I am sorry if I made this uncomfortable, to be honest, it didn't cross my mind that it would make it seem like it was. I just wanted to do something nice for you."

"Fine. As long as we're clear. Next time I am paying though. Trust me I won't forget."

There is no doubt in my mind that she will not forget.

*****

"That was really beautiful."

"So you enjoyed it?"

"Yes. I know I was nervous before, but that was a great movie. Blanchett and Mara have great chemistry; the story was beautiful and tragic. I would have preferred a different ending, but it was a great story."

"Not feeling lickalotapuss fever coming on then?"

It takes me a second before I realize what Alex said and another to calm my laughter enough to respond. "I see what you did there. No, I think I am still me."

"Well that is a relief," Alex says with a grin. The light has returned to her eyes as well.

"Wait a second, what is that supposed to mean? Don't want me playing for your team?" Alex's smile falters, and her face flushes.

"I'm sure we would be lucky to have you. You were the one who was nervous though."

"You aren't likely to let me live that down are you?"

"Nope." Alex smiles, a genuine, having fun smile. It might be the first one today.

"Good. I would be disappointed if you did." I have a question I want to ask. It feels like playing with fire though. "Have you never been with a man?" I'm relieved when Alex stays relaxed.

"No. Never. I had my first crush in the second grade, on our teacher's assistant, a woman. Never been interested in men."

"How do you know though if you've never been with one?" The humor that had returned to Alex's eyes is gone in an instant. Will I ever be able to have a conversation with her without putting my foot in my mouth?

"How do you know you aren't into women if you have never been with one?" Alex asks it with an irritated tone. I know I'm tottering on the edge of angering her.

"Touché." She has a point, at least one that I don't have a counter argument for. "Want to do some Black Friday shopping since we are here?" I know that the stores will be crowded. I am not sure if Alex will be up for it, but I could use a few things.

"Sure we can go see what we can find."

"You'll be alright in the crowds?"

"Yeah, I should be fine. If not I can just step outside of the store and wait for you. No big deal."

"Great. Can we head into Victoria's Secret first?"

*****

I am contemplating buying a lacy black matching bra and panties set. It is cute and cheap and even though I have no idea who I will wear it for, or when, I still want it. "Alex, what do you think about this?" The store is packed. Alex is starting to get a little squirmy. I am trying to distract her, help calm her down. Plus I could use some advice. I've never been able to picture myself in anything.

"Uh…"

"No good?" I feel slightly disappointed; I was certain it was a good choice.

"I'm sure it would be fine." I see her swallow hard. She is trying to look at anything but me, her eyes darting around the store.

"Well, that was not enthusiastic. Is this one better?" Alex is wearing the strangest look on her face. "What is it?"

"I cannot do this with you!"

"Do what?" I have no clue what is happening.

"This." Alex makes a hand gesture that encompasses the entire store. I have no idea what she is referring to. "I can't have you showing me your new lingerie options. I have a very vivid imagination. Every time you show me something new I get a clear picture of you wearing it in my head."

"No big deal," I say with a shrug. "Which one then?" I still do not understand what the issue is.

"Both. Neither. I'm just going to wait for you outside."

She is headed for the door before she even finishes speaking. I couldn't have stopped her if I tried. I have no choice but to follow her out. "Alex are you alright?"

"Yeah. Go ahead and finish shopping in there. I can wait for you here."

"What just happened though?"

"Nothing really, just finish your shopping." Alex is oozing frustration and agitation, and I have no idea why.

"Come on. I know something just happened." I don't understand what the issue is; I just know that Alex is extremely uncomfortable.

"I told you. I see you wearing every little thing you asked me about in my mind's eye."

"It isn't a big deal Alex." Nudity had never been a big taboo for me. Working in the OR, you see people fully naked every day. One becomes a bit desensitized to it.

"Catherine, I know you know you are an attractive woman. I have basically been single and have gone without sex for months. I really don't need the image of you wearing any of those items in my head right now."

Alex's revelation does not bother me. She is right. I have been told more than few times about my appearance. It hasn't ever been a big deal to me. I never really put much effort into it, I just have what I have. It never crossed my mind for a second what I could be doing to Alex. "Ah I see. Well still no big deal for me but if it made you uncomfortable, I am sorry."

"It's alright. You couldn't have known. It was just becoming awkward for me." I realize then what I've done.

"No problem. You have anywhere you want to go?"

"I can go to the bookstore if you want to continue shopping here. You can just meet me there when you are finished."

"Sure, that sounds good." I really do need to pick up a few new pairs of panties and giving Alex a few minutes to herself might be a good idea.

Alexis

I won't be getting those images out of my head anytime soon. Catherine in those lacy black panties. No. I can't continue seeing it. Yet I can't stop seeing it either. To not care that her lesbian, tenant, coworker is picturing it, and it is clearly appealing to her…what is she thinking? I shake my head trying to erase the images and get ahold of myself; the cold November air not having the effect I hoped it would.

Books. I need to find a book. Books can be unsexy. I decide the best place to start is the history section. Surely I can find something about the Tudors, Medici family, or some other dynasty that will get the job done. Try as I might, nothing is working. I look around for another section and see the graphic novels and manga area. I head there next. I am thumbing through a new Wonder Woman omnibus when Catherine finds me, her perfumed scent announcing her arrival before she speaks.

"I never took you for a nerd." She is wearing that grin, the same one she wore when we first met, full of self-assurance, oozing cockiness.

"Well, I have never been in the closet about being a total nerd. I grew up reading Batman, Wonder Woman and their DC counter parts. Never stopped enjoying them. Good escapism."

"I see. I have not read anything related in years."

"You read comics?" Catherine is always so serious that I find this revelation surprising.

"Years ago when I was a child, into my early teens. I used to love Wonder Woman. Also enjoyed Batman. I am sure things are quite different now though."

"Probably not. There are a lot of alternate universe stories or stories that have been rebooted by different authors. Of course, they have added characters and diversified over the years as well."

"And you have kept up with all of it?"

"No. I would have never had the time to. I do enjoy looking at them when I'm at the store though. Do you need to get anything here or do you want to move on?"

"I do need a new book or two to read. I think I will keep looking around if you are good."

"Me? I'm always good in the bookstore. I could stay here all night and be content." Catherine gives me that look. The look I haven't learned to interpret yet, maybe I never will. "What?"

"Hmm? I'm going to head over to the fiction section. If you decide you are ready just let me know."

"Ok." Damn that woman. Why does she always evade answering when you question her? I decide to head over to the sci-fi and fantasy section. I have always had a penchant for the fantasy genre. Maybe something new will catch my eye.

Twenty minutes have passed. I still haven't found anything that looks appealing. I give up, deciding I will check my Kindle for something. I find Catherine in the mystery and suspense section. "Any luck?"

"A few. I doubt they will take me long to read though. You find anything?"

"Nope, but I have stuff at the house and on my Kindle. I have plenty to read. Ready to move on or do you need more time?"

"We can move on if you are ready." We head to the front of the store so Catherine can purchase her books. "Isn't that the book you were reading that night on the beach?"

How does she remember these things? I can't remember what I had for lunch yesterday, but she can remember the name of the book I mentioned reading more than six months ago? "I think it is. I'm not sure how you remember that because I don't."

"Maybe I should get that too." Catherine picks up the copy of *Fingersmith* and starts to read the description.

"You can borrow my copy if you'd like, but if you were nervous about making it through *Carol,* you won't make it through *Fingersmith*."

"Why is it that graphic?" Catherine eyes me; she looks almost as if she thinks I'm challenging her to read it.

"Probably not. It is a bit more in-depth than the scene in *Carol.* Just borrow my copy if you think you want to give it a go."

"Ok, I will borrow yours then." Catherine yawns and stretches her lissome body. "It is getting late. You ready to call it a night?"

I hadn't realized that it is approaching midnight. The stores being open have thrown my sense of time off. "Sounds good."

*****

I'm in bed reading when there is a soft knock on my door. "Alex are you awake?"

Shit, my clothes are in the hamper inside the closet. I quickly dismiss the idea of getting up to retrieve them and simply pull the sheet up as I tell Catherine to come in. Catherine enters my room wearing a blue bathrobe. It matches her eyes, something I'm sure is deliberate.

"You can't sleep either?" Catherine makes her way over and settles herself on the end of the bed.

"I might eventually. I read every night before I try to sleep. It helps me relax. Why are you still awake?" I'm trying not to be distracted by the fact that Catherine is on my bed, in the middle of the night, wearing a short bathrobe. I get my first glimpse of her long, bare legs and feel my insides stir.

"I was just thinking about a few things. You know how easy it is to second guess a decision you've made when it is the dead of night." I understand what she is saying, just not what she is actually talking about.

"Well, I am sleep challenged. I don't need any help being kept up all night most of the time. Anything you want to run by me? Maybe I can help."

"Perhaps you can. I'm not sure that I've made the right choice." Catherine rises from the bed and in one smooth motion unceremoniously opens her robe and lets it fall to the floor. She is wearing the black lingerie she showed me earlier tonight. I am transfixed. The sight of her is better than I had imagined, I can feel the effects between my legs. Catherine moves up the side of the bed, maneuvering like a predator stalking its prey. Her fingers trail over the sheet along the length of my leg as she approaches and I feel the sensation of her touch reverberate through my body. In one smooth motion, she is on the bed straddling me. "Maybe you need a better view." She tosses my Kindle aside and places both of my hands on her ass. I know the sheet I have been using for cover has fallen, but I don't care. "Well my view has certainly improved," Catherine purrs, arching her right eyebrow as she stares at my bared chest. She slowly moves my hands up her sides to her breasts. They fit in my hands like they were tailor made for me. I gently massage them and slowly tease each of her nipples through the lacy fabric. Her breath rasps as I apply firmer pressure to the hardening nubs. My mouth waters as I contemplate which nipple to put in it first. She takes my face in her hands and redirects my attention from her body to her deep blues. "You still haven't told me, did I make the right decision?" I am unable to find the words to answer her. My hands are on Catherine's hips again. As I slide her body closer to mine, she pulls me in for a kiss, teasing at first then fully engaged. I run my tongue along her lower lip before invading her mouth. I can feel her hips grinding against my lap. This is bliss. I'm slowly trailing my way down her neck, alternating teasing her with gentle biting and my tongue. I've nearly made it to her breasts when Catherine takes a handful of my hair and pulls my head away. "Not until you answer me. I want to hear you say it." Her mouth is on mine again. She greedily invades my mouth and continues to grind against me. I bite her lower lip and am rewarded by a long low moan, her sounds turning me on even more. I'm convinced she is hell bent on punishing me and I like it. She breaks off our kiss, biting and tugging on my lower lip as she pulls away.

A sharp pain wakes me. I turn on the bedside lamp and discover that my lip is bleeding. I must have bitten it in my sleep. I'm also aware that I am soaking wet. The dream of Catherine still fresh in my mind. Catherine in that black lingerie, grinding against me. I know I shouldn't be thinking about Catherine like this, no good can come from it. However, my clit is throbbing, and I need some relief. I open the bedside drawer and grab my favorite vibrator. With the dream of Catherine still fresh in my mind, it doesn't take long for me to climax, twice. I hope that sleep will find me again, but after half an hour I know I am out of luck. Resigned to my fate of being awake I decide to take advantage of the pool. It is just after 4 am, but the pool is far enough away from Catherine's bedroom that I shouldn't disturb her.

I love the water, even if I am just swimming laps. I push myself hard, swimming lap after lap without rest, punishing myself for the thoughts I keep having about Catherine. I have no idea how long I have been at it when a movement catches my eye. Catherine is awake. She is wearing a dark blue swimsuit. While it conceals much more than the lingerie in my dream, it still showcases her amazing body. I feel a familiar stirring again and am thankful that I'm likely already flushed from my swim.

"Good morning. Couldn't sleep?" She smiles at me as she pulls on her swim cap. She clearly has no idea about the forbidden thoughts I've been having about her.

"I got a nap in, around three hours I think. What time is it?"

"Just after 5."

"What has you up so early?" I try not to molest her with my eyes, but I'm certain I'm failing miserably.

"I have rounds this morning. I'm used to getting up early anyway, so I take advantage of it and get a workout in."

"I see. I'll leave you to it then." I make my way back towards the shallow end so I can exit the water."

"No need to leave on my account. The pool is plenty large enough for both of us to use. You have pretty good form and are actually reasonably fast. Did you ever swim competitively?" How long has Catherine been watching me?

"No. Never had an opportunity to. We had a pool when I was a kid. I've always had access to one, and I love the water. Guess I just naturally developed whatever skill I have." I exit the water and wrap myself in my towel.

"Alex you do not need to leave on my behalf." My body is begging me to stay; my mind is telling me to leave.

"I've been at it for nearly an hour. I'm going to grab a shower and decide if I want to try to take a nap or make some breakfast." I really can't be near Catherine right now. The memory of the dream along with the view of her in her suit is too distracting.

"Suit yourself."

"Let me know if anything comes up on rounds. I'll be ready."

Catherine

I arrive home exhausted from a long day in clinic. Some days the factors all align so that no matter what effort you make you just fall further and further behind. This was one of those days. Patients were extra chatty, a few wanted to discuss issues they were not scheduled to be seen for, two showed up late, and there was a system issue as well, meaning patient charts were unavailable for a good 20 minutes. I skipped lunch in an effort to catch up, but that effort was in vain. I arrive home wanting food, a drink and something to read before bed. I am pleasantly surprised to find a note from Alex letting me know she heard the office had issues today, so she made dinner. I check the refrigerator to discover some homemade chicken noodle soup. Perfect comfort food for this stressful winter day. I love having Alex at the house for a number of reasons, her amazing abilities in the kitchen being one of them. I put a bowl of soup in the microwave and pour myself a glass of white wine. The peace and quiet of the house is a welcome respite from the chaos at the office today.

After dinner I head towards the basement to thank Alex. I stop at the top and announce myself, "Alex?"

"Hey, Catherine. You can come down."

I head down the steps, thinking I should have a door installed so Alex has some form of privacy. I find her curled up on the couch with the TV on. "Hey, I just wanted to thank you for making dinner tonight. You didn't have to do it, but it was the perfect surprise to come home to. I appreciate it."

"No worries. It is so cold out, and Dr. Hasting mentioned this afternoon that everything was chaos at the office today. Figured you might be hungry when you got home. Good comfort food for this time of the year."

"It was delicious." I am starting to feel the food coma effect. I will be out cold soon enough.

"Thanks." Alex smiles at me. Her eyes never leave me as I make my way around the couch and join her.

"So I was thinking about having a door installed at the top of the stairs."

"Am I being too loud?"

"No, not at all. I didn't even know you were here actually. I just thought it would give you a bit more privacy."

"Oh. Well, that is up to you. I feel like I have a great deal of privacy already. Have it installed if you'd like but please don't do it on my account."

"Ok. I will think about it then." I turn my focus from Alex to the TV, unable to identify the movie that is playing. "What are you watching?"

"*Love Actually.* It is my favorite holiday movie."

"Haven't seen it. I will have to watch it sometime." I sit and watch the movie for a few minutes. "Wow, this has a great cast."

"Want me to restart it? I don't mind."

"Thank you, but not tonight. I am exhausted. I just want to go curl up with a book and fall asleep. Rain check though?"

"Absolutely." Alex's smile tells me she will be more than happy to watch it with me sometime.

"Speaking of books, I was wondering if you have something I can borrow? I intended to visit the bookstore after clinic but was too drained."

"Sure. They are on one of the shelves in the bedroom closet. Help yourself."

Alex continues watching her movie as I make my way into the bedroom. I discover that she was not joking before when she told me she reads a little bit of everything. She has several nonfiction works about the Tudors and Catherine the Great, several Anne Rice novels, a few by Stephen King, and some other works I'm unfamiliar with. I find my eyes drawn to *Fingersmith*. I hesitate initially and then decide to give it a go. As I turn to exit the closet, I again notice the gorgeous storage chest Alex made. I am curious what she keeps in it but my respect for her privacy wins, and I leave without peeking at the contents.

Alex turns when I rejoin her on the couch and eyes my selection. "You sure you're ready for that?"

"What do you mean?"

"I mean are you ready for that? If *Carol* made you uncomfortable, then *Fingersmith* won't be any better."

"For the record, *Carol* did not make me uncomfortable. I was nervous for unfounded reasons. It isn't as if this book is porn is it?"

"No, not at all. There are just a few scenes that are more intense than anything in *Carol*."

"I will be fine. Thanks for your concern." I have very little concern about reading it.

Alex eyes me and then shrugs. "Well don't say I didn't warn you."

"Oh, speaking of warning. Taylor messaged me today to confirm she will be flying in on the 24th."

"That will be nice. I'm happy you'll get to see her. Any big plans?"

"I'm not sure what she has planned, but she will be here until just after the first of the year." I hesitate for a moment. I feel like I have to warn Alex, to protect her from Taylor, or at the very least try to. "Alex, please be careful with Taylor." Her brow furrows as she looks at me.

"Careful?" She utters one word, but I know from her expression she doesn't understand.

"I mean I want you to be careful. I do not know what to expect from Taylor. I do expect she will make advances towards you. I just don't want to see you get hurt."

"I will be fine Catherine. I'm not worried. Thank you for your concern though." Alex seems fairly confident that she will be ok. I hope that she will, but she doesn't know Taylor like I do.

"Ok. Well if she gets too out of control please let me know."

"If that is what you want."

"It is." I smile at Alex, but I can feel that it doesn't replace the concern I feel about Taylor taking advantage of her. Alex and I continue talking while I finish my second glass of wine. Half an hour later I have finished it and am nearly asleep on the couch. I yawn, despite my efforts not to, and stretch as far as I am able. I know if I don't head up to my bed soon I will be sleeping on this sofa tonight. I look over at Alex who is watching me, her expression either unreadable or I am too exhausted to discern it.

"Sorry I interrupted your movie. Thanks again for the delicious soup, great company, and the book. I really need to go to bed, or I'm going to pass out on your couch."

"No worries, I've seen the movie countless times. Always happy to keep you company." She smiles at me as I rise from the sofa. "Feel free to borrow a book anytime. Goodnight Catherine, sleep well." Alex's glowing smile is the last thing I notice before heading towards the stairs.

"Goodnight Alex." I drag my leadened body up the stairs and melt into my cozy bed.

Alexis

Thursday finds Abby and me both available for dinner and a drink. With her daughter's ball schedule and my chaotic call schedule, we have been missing each other on Friday nights. We resolve to rectify the issue tonight since neither of us has to work for a few days. We find ourselves seated at the bar, sipping our first drink and waiting for our lettuce wraps before 5 pm. A win in both our books.

"So tell me how things are shacking up with the doctor." I knew before we arrived that Abby would ask about this. She has asked a few times over text messages, but it is easy to deflect when you aren't face to face.

"Shacking up? Is that even a saying anymore?" I need to steer away from this topic. I haven't told Abby about the dream or my ever-growing attraction to Catherine. I'm still looking for that one thing, the thing that will make Catherine undatable to me. It has been a month, and I still haven't found it.

"Don't deflect. I want to know how it is working out."

"All good. I have my own space. Neither of us seems to be getting on the other one's nerves. We eat dinner together, watch movies together, chat over drinks. It has been a month, and things are good."

Abby is not convinced. "So that little bit of lust you had for her when you first met, all gone now?"

"Gone? Probably not. Held in check? Absolutely." I know I'm lying, Abby does too.

Abby gives me that look, the one where she simply raises one eyebrow to call bullshit. When Catherine does this, it gives me chills. However, I feel nothing seeing Abby do it.

"Let me know when you start having sex dreams about her." I must have a tell that I am unaware of. Abby immediately calls me out. "I knew it! You already have, haven't you? How long did it take?"

"It was one dream." Not exactly a lie, simply one dream that I have repeatedly had over the last month. "It happened Thanksgiving night. I don't even think it was all my subconscious. We went shopping after seeing the movie. She wanted to go to Victoria's Secret, so we did. She kept showing me all this stuff and asking which one was better. Well, you know how my mind works. I told her she needed to stop, but she said it wasn't a big deal. I ended up leaving the store."

"What a tease. So what exactly did you dream about then?"

"She was wearing one of the outfits. That is all I'm telling you."

"She is straight. Be careful." I know Abby is right, but try as I might I cannot cleanse my system of its desire for Catherine.

"Not a big deal. I'm sure she isn't the first straight woman I've had a sex dream about. Things have been fine. Besides I'm only staying there temporarily."

"Temporarily? So how has your search been going for a permanent place?" Abby has always been great at calling me out. Things have been good at Catherine's, and I haven't been looking for anything else yet.

"It hasn't. It has only been a month. I will start looking after the holidays." Abby is skeptical, I can see it all over her face. She sits quietly for a moment before deciding to change the subject. "So what are we doing for our little holiday celebration with our clan this year? Have you talked about it with Dahlia or Shannon yet?"

"I'm pretty sure we are doing it on Saturday at Shannon and Kevin's place. Bring your own drinks and the usual dish to pass. Not sure outside of that."

"Well outside of that I don't think we've ever needed a plan. We always seem to find trouble to get into every year." Abby smiles as memories flash through both our minds.

"Agreed. I think I'm going to invite Catherine and her sister. Not sure if they will come, but since her sister is visiting for the holidays, it could be fun for them."

"That is up to you. What is her sister like?"

"I don't know. Catherine makes her out to be unpredictable, unreliable and a bit wild. Guess I will find out soon enough. She did give me an odd warning the other night though. Told me to be careful around her sister because she didn't want me to get hurt."

"Interesting. It doesn't sound like they are very close."

"Catherine says they aren't. I haven't inquired too much about it."

"You know, a nice little fling with her sister might be just what you need."

"I'm not going to sleep with Catherine's sister." I give Abby a look to let her know that the subject is closed. "What about you? Ready to invite the neighbor to the party?"

"Oh, that? Well, he and I aren't seeing eye to eye at the moment." The disappointment is clear on Abby's face.

"So you slept with him, now you want some commitment, and he doesn't. Am I warm?"

"Basically, yes." Our appetizer arrives just in time. I know we will be going over this a few times. I am going to need food and another drink if I am going to survive it. Poor Abby.

*****

I arrive home just after 10 pm and can hear murmuring voices as soon as I enter from the garage. *This is why I need a private entrance;* I think to myself as I take off my shoes in hopes of sneaking down to the basement without disturbing Catherine and her guest. She never mentioned having someone over tonight, or I would have stayed elsewhere. I don't make it halfway to the basement steps before Catherine rounds the corner.

"There you are. I was starting to worry about you."

"About me? I'm fine. I was, however, trying not to disturb you and your guest. Sorry. Go back to him; I'm going to grab some water and head downstairs." Catherine wears a heated look, I know she is pissed, I just have no idea why.

"Well, you are certainly drunk. I hope you didn't drive home like this."

"Don't worry I didn't. Abby and I went to dinner after work tonight. We ran into Dahlia and Derrick while we were there. They both have to work tomorrow, so Dahlia drove me home, and Derrick followed us in my car. You really should go back to your guest."

"Actually, I thought—."

"Hey Cat, everything ok?" Not a man's voice. It dawns on me as soon as Taylor turns the corner that today is the 24th. Catherine may have alleged that she and her sister are nothing alike, but she may as well have been lying to me. Taylor possesses the same blond hair, blue eyes, and cheekbones that Catherine does. Her hair is kept much shorter and in a messy style. She stands a few inches shorter than Catherine and has a more athletic build compared to Catherine's sleek swimmer's body.

"Right. Anyway, Alex, this is my sister, Taylor. Taylor this is Alex." Taylor flashes me a grin as she shakes my hand. Unlike Catherine's grin, Taylor's is full of mischief and bad intentions. Maybe it is the drink, and the bias Catherine has instilled.

"Nice to meet you, Taylor. Sorry I missed your arrival, I honestly forgot that today was the day."

"Not a problem. Gave me some alone time with Cat." Cat? Calling Catherine Cat is just not working in my book. One glance at Catherine is enough to know that she is not as accepting of my apology as Taylor.

"Taylor, can you give Alex and I a minute, please? I'll join you in a few."

Taylor looks at Catherine, then at me, then back at Catherine. As she makes her exit, she gives me a look that seems to be equal parts cat ate the canary and you're fucked.

"Alex, I really wanted you to be here tonight. You weren't here and now that you are you're drunk." I still don't understand why Catherine is so upset.

"I'm sorry Cat, I really am. I honestly forgot that today is the 24th. Abby and I both have the next few days off, and we've been missing each other lately, so we took advantage of it. Had I remembered the date I would have been here."

"Do NOT call me Cat!" I have never seen anger flare across Catherine's features like this. I only tried it to see if it sounded as wrong coming from me as it did from Taylor. I already have two strikes against me, and I have barely made it through the door. I've hit the intersection of I can't win and I just want to go down to my apartment and try again in the morning. Catherine is not willing to let me off that easy though. "Nothing else to say?"

"I apologize. Yes, I forgot the date, but I honestly didn't even know that it was that important that I be here when Taylor arrived."

Catherine isn't appeased. She simply shakes her head and turns to rejoin Taylor in the sitting room.

*****

About two hours after Catherine's dismissal I hear someone coming down the steps. "Mind if I join you?" There is no familiar vanilla scent to accompany this voice.

"Be my guest. Sorry again for missing your arrival." Taylor seats herself on the couch with me.

"Don't sweat it. Why was Cat so worked up about it anyway?"

"Don't know. I thought she had company, you know, male company. I truly did forget today's date." Taylor sarcastically laughs.

"My sister? Male company?"

"Well yeah, she is into men. I'm sure men are very much into her. Eventually, it is bound to happen."

Taylor scoffs. "I thought you had met my sister before tonight. I doubt she could remove that prudish stick from her ass long enough to think about bringing someone home."

"Come on. She isn't a prude. Maybe she just has different ideas about how relationships work than you do."

I can feel Taylor's cocky facade slip back into place. "So Cat has told you all about me then." Not a question, simply a statement of knowledge. Apparently Catherine isn't the only one who believes that she and her sister are as different as night and day.

"Not at all. Just a logical deduction from your assessment of Catherine's hypothetical behavior." The white lie in this instance feels justified. I have no desire to stir up any animosity between the sisters.

"Uh-huh." Taylor shifts her focus from me to the television. "You stay up late watching Harry Potter all the time?"

"Honestly I have barely perceived any of it. It has mainly served as background noise and a momentary distraction while I have been lost in thought."

"I see. What's on your mind?"

I turn and look at Taylor, Catherine's warning and Abby's suggestion playing in my head again. It'd be easy to have a meaningless fling with her. She is attractive, to be sure. I also have a feeling that she wouldn't be opposed to it. I just can't do it. Something tells me that if it did happen Catherine would end up being the one hurt. Or maybe I just hope that if it happened that Catherine would care enough to be hurt. Either way, I'd only be using Taylor as a substitute to fulfill some fantasy involving Catherine.

"You thinking about Cat?"

"Partly. I've never seen her as pissed off as she was tonight." I have no intention of letting Taylor know any real thoughts I'm having about Catherine. I know my feelings for Catherine are evolving, I just can't find a way to shut them down.

"She'll get over it. She always does. I don't even know why she got so upset in the first place. I wouldn't worry about it."

"Yeah but I will. I hate fighting with anyone." I don't just hate fighting; I actively avoid it. Too many screaming matches between my parents when I was young have given me a natural aversion to them.

"So does she. She will be over it by the time you get out of bed tomorrow."

"Maybe. Speaking of, I really should head to bed soon."

"Kicking me out huh?"

"Afraid so."

"You sure?" Taylor slides closer to me on the couch.

"I'm sure. I doubt that would help me out with the Catherine situation anyway."

"She can't give you everything you need you know." Taylor moves her hand to my thigh to emphasize her point. If I had any doubts about my ability to reject Taylor earlier, I have none now. The soft press of her hand fails to stir any feelings of lust or desire; I simply want it gone. My inner self is applauding Taylor for her effort though. She certainly knows how to bob and weave her way through a situation, and I'm sure into many women's beds.

"I know, and I'm still sure." I gently take her hand and place it on her leg.

"Alright. I had to try though." Taylor rises and heads towards to stairs.

"No worries. Hey, I don't know what you and Catherine have planned, but on Saturday we are having a mini bar crawl followed by our holiday get together we hold every year. It really isn't much about the holidays, just an excuse for a bunch of us to get together, drink, play cards, and whatever else we get into."

"Yeah, that sounds fun to me. You'll have to run it by Cat though."

Catherine

I can't sleep. I have been unnecessarily harsh with Alex. Knowing I won't sleep until I speak with her I leave the comfort of my bed and grab my bathrobe. Time to swallow my pig-headed pride and admit that I was wrong.

As I reach the stairs and am about to head down, I realize that Alex isn't alone. Taylor is with her. I know it is wrong, but I can't help but eavesdrop on their conversation. As predicted, Taylor has wasted no time in trying to bed Alex. She is an expert at this. A surge of emotions hits me, anger that Taylor has little regard for boundaries, sadness that Alex is going to be another notch on Taylor's belt despite my warning, confusion as to whether I should reveal myself and try to derail this train or just step back and let the wreck happen. Alex is rebuffing Taylor on her own before I can make my decision. Firm in her resolve even when Taylor tries to change her mind. I realize Taylor is making her way towards the stairs so I quietly slink back to my room as quickly as I can. As I sit on my bed waiting for Taylor to retreat to her room, a new emotion has taken over, one I can't identify.

I wait 15 minutes before making my way towards the basement again. I need to talk to Alex, to clear the air. I reach the stairs to find that the lights are off and it is quiet. I debate for a moment whether or not I should disturb her. Ultimately I decide she probably is not asleep yet and make my way towards her bedroom door. I can detect a faint light at the base of the door, Alex is still awake. I knock softly just in case. It takes a second before Alex tells me to come in. She is sitting up, the sheet pulled to the top of her breasts, Kindle in her lap.

"Sorry to disturb you. Do you want me to step out so you can put some clothes on?"

"I think we will be fine. I'm pretty certain I lost any modesty about partial nudity many years ago." Despite saying this Alex looks nervous.

"Look, I just want to apologize. I was far too harsh with you earlier. You were not obligated to be here. We never made an official plan." Despite the remorse I feel for treating Alex like I did, I can't take my eyes off of her.

"It is alright. I would have been here had I remembered the date. Are you alright though? I've never seen you go off like that before."

"I am fine. Just stressed out having Taylor here."

"Because of me? If so you can relax, I already took care of that."

"You did?" I opt for the lie of omission. I know it is wrong but so was eavesdropping on her conversation with Taylor earlier. I feel a sense of shame settle over me.

"Yeah, at least I think I did." Alex pauses for a moment debating whether she should finish her thought. "I did it for you."

I am at a loss for words. Did Alex only reject Taylor because I asked her to? I am unsure how long I stand there attempting to figure it out before Alex breaks my concentration.

"Was there something else?"

"Hmm? Oh...no...sorry. I couldn't sleep because of how I was with you earlier. I just wanted to smooth things over. Again sorry to have disturbed you."

"It's alright. Goodnight Catherine."

"Goodnight Alex."

*****

Sleep continues to elude me. 'I did it for you.' What did she mean? I can accept Alex turning Taylor down because I asked her to. What if there is more to it than that? Is there a storm forming, threatening to strain our friendship? What would I do if Alex was developing feelings for me? Better yet, what should I do?

Giving up on sleep again, I switch on the bedside lamp and open the borrowed copy of *Fingersmith*. The writing pulls me in, carrying me along the current. I can feel the highs and lows of the characters involved, can feel a bond of sympathy and understanding toward each one. I am about halfway through when I reach one of the scenes Alex had warned me about. I devour it, not a bit uncomfortable. Instead, I realize I am becoming increasingly aroused. It momentarily gives me pause before I recall Alex telling me that she had found herself aroused by straight sex scenes in cinema and literature before. I tell myself that if it works one way then surely it must work the other and fall back into reading. I'm not sure how long I last before finally succumbing to sleep.

Alexis

We are at the second stop on our holiday bar hopping tour. Catherine and Taylor seem to be fitting in with our gang of misfits perfectly. Derrick and Dahlia are telling Catherine, Abby, Sara and me about their upcoming wedding. Taylor is off playing darts with Shannon, Kevin, and Nikki. From my vantage point, it is easy to see that Taylor is trying her game on Nikki. Catherine either hasn't noticed or doesn't care.

"So how does your open relationship work once you're married?" I hadn't realized that Derrick and Dahlia have shared every detail with Catherine. The rest of us all know how their arrangement works; if they are happy, we are happy for them. They really are perfect for each other.

"It isn't going to change. We will still go to parties and do what we do. Our big thing is to be open and honest about it. Neither of us is going to have a second relationship on the side. At the end of the day, we love each other and want to come home to one another."

"I see. Good for the two of you. Sounds like you are on the same page at least, which I hear is the best place to start."

The four of them continue talking. I realize Abby has stepped away and has been gone for a few minutes. I look around for her, finally finding her near the bar. She is talking with someone I don't know. Good for Abby I think to myself. Then I notice she is quite fidgety. Not like Abby. So I pay closer attention. "Alex, everything alright?" Derrick and Dahlia turn to see what it is that I am looking at.

"Maybe. I'll know in a few." Catherine gives me a concerned look. Sara, Derrick, and Dahlia have seen this before. They always find it amusing, waiting to see how things will play out each time.

"Oh yes, and so early! This should be fun. We taking bets?" Leave it to Derrick to turn it into a game.

There it is. Abby finally realizes that she has my attention. "I'll be right back."

I approach Abby and her unwanted suitor. "Hey baby, there you are!" I put my arms around Abby and kiss her. Not a real passionate kiss, just a soft press of the lips that lingers too long to only be friendly. "I was wondering where you disappeared to."

"Hello, darling." Abby looks back to the young man. The look of sheer confusion on his face nearly causes me to lose it. "Nice talking to you. Shall we?" Abby takes my hand and leads me back to our group. The look of confusion and shock on Catherine's face is one of the greatest spectacles I've seen in a long while. Finally, something dislodges her permanent poker face.

"When did you two?" Catherine barely manages to stutter out the question.

"We aren't. Abby and I have a rescue signal system worked out. If we feel trapped by someone we don't want to be trapped by we wait for the other to be paying attention, scratch our eyebrow with two fingers, play with our hair for a second and then scratch at the base of our ear. Three movements that wouldn't happen together by chance, but can easily be drawn out slowly enough to look natural. If one of us signals the other, we go and rescue them from their unwanted attention. These guys have all seen it and enjoy watching how things play out."

"I've gotta say that one was underwhelming. Hope you two do better later." Derrick clearly had either not been entertained or had lost a bet. I see a small look of triumph on Sara's face and know that she was the winner.

Catherine looks at me. Her grin is back in place, at least she is having fun. She leans in and whispers "For a second I thought you had forgotten to tell me something." The scent of vanilla and her warm breath tickling my ear give me goose bumps. She looks around for a minute then adds, "Does your friend Nikki have the same signal worked out? Taylor appears to be working pretty hard on her."

I laugh. "I wouldn't worry about Nikki. Clearly, Taylor hasn't figured out that Nikki is straight." I notice that Catherine doesn't seem half as concerned about Nikki as she did when she warned me.

*****

By our sixth and final stop of the bar tour, none of us are feeling any pain. After a few drinks and a lot of dancing at Velvet, we decide to head back to Shannon and Kevin's house before anyone gets too out of control. We need three taxis to get to the house, so Catherine and I volunteer to take the last one. We are waiting at the bar for the cab to call when I feel a presence on my left. I turn to see an attractive woman has taken the seat next to me.

"Hello." She has long dark hair, brown eyes, and a warm smile.

"Hi. How are you?" I'm not typically a big flirt or even talkative with strangers when I'm sober, but liquid courage has lifted those inhibitions.

"Very good." She grins at me, revealing the slightest of gaps between her front teeth. "You?"

"I'm well, thanks." I turn to look for Catherine and find she has moved down the bar a few seats and is chatting with a middle-aged man. Sandra brings the woman a drink and shoots me a quick smile.

"Your girlfriend?" The stranger's question pulls my attention away from Catherine.

"Oh, no. Just friends. I'm Alexis." I offer her my hand, she firmly shakes it. Good start, I am not a fan of weak handshakes.

"Laura. So what are you up to tonight?"

"We're having our holiday bar crawl. Most of us have already headed back to the house to continue the party. We are waiting for the taxi to come pick us up."

"You sure that isn't your girlfriend? She keeps looking over here."

I look over at Catherine. She seems alright. I try to suffocate the pang of jealousy I feel seeing Catherine talking to the strange man. I refocus my attention on the attractive Laura who might actually be interested in me. "No, not my girlfriend. What about you, what are you doing tonight?"

"Meeting some friends here for drinks. Nothing exciting." I realize my phone is vibrating. I check it and discover that our cab has arrived.

"Well Laura, my cab just arrived. Nice meeting you."

"You as well. Have a nice night."

I make my way towards Catherine. "There you are darling!" Catherine wraps her arms around me. What is she doing? She must be drunk.

"Hey, the cab is here. You ready?"

"Finally. Let's go." We settle into the cab and Catherine turns on me. "I thought you had a system in place. I was waiting for you to come save me from that self-absorbed man. I hope at least you got her number since you abandoned me." I have no idea what she is talking about, but she is fuming.

"System? What are you talking about? You needed saving? Things seemed fine from where I was sitting."

"Well they weren't, but you were too busy flirting with that woman to notice."

"I wasn't flirting, we were just chatting. I turned, and you were gone. What was I supposed to do, just come over and kiss you?" I feel myself flush as my attention is pulled to Catherine's lips, lips made for kissing, lips that I long to kiss. Somehow I manage to fight the ever growing urge bubbling inside me.

"You did it for Abby."

"Abby is like my sister. It is easy to rescue her."

"What, it would be difficult to do the same for me?" Not difficult at all I think to myself and unconsciously lick my lips.

"Not difficult, just different. Abby and I are in a different place than we are. I didn't even see you signaling for me."

"What does that even mean "a different place"?" Catherine animatedly throws air quotes trying to emphasize her point. I see the driver look at me in the rearview mirror, it seems like even he has it figured out.

I have no filter syndrome most of the time, when I'm drunk, it is all of the time. The words fly out before I know that I'm going to say them. "It means that I haven't had a sex dream about Abby so kissing her isn't a big deal!" My hand flies up over my mouth too late, the words are out, loud and clear. Oh fuck, what have I confessed?

Catherine just stares at me. I have no idea what she is thinking. I'm not even sure I want to know what she is thinking. The fire is still lit in her eyes, the little vein in her forehead that pulses when she is angry starts to slow. "Well did you get her number at least?" Catherine isn't pacified but at least seems willing to move on. I take the subject change and run with it. Maybe she doesn't realize what I said.

"No, I told you were were just chatting."

"Just chatting? She was clearly flirting with you!"

Now it is my turn to be confused. "No she wasn't! I barely got her name."

"Well, name or no name she was flirting."

"Was she? I never know when someone is flirting with me unless they are blatantly obvious. She would pretty much have to come up and just lay one on me for me to pick up on it."

"Trust me, she was flirting." Catherine is still irritated. My drunkenness paired with my ever-increasing desire for

Catherine make me want to slide across the seat and kiss her just so she will stop arguing.

"What are we even arguing about? It doesn't matter if she was or wasn't flirting. Why is it so important to you anyway?"

Catherine stammers then sits silently for a moment, I watch as her poker face easily slips back into place. "It isn't. You're right. I don't know why we are arguing at this point." Is this one of those times Taylor referred to the other night? Has Catherine just given up on the argument? I hope to myself that it is because I am too drunk to deal with it.

Mercifully the cab arrives at Shannon and Kevin's. Catherine pays the fare while I head inside for a drink.

*****

"Hey, you guys are just in time for shots!"

I'm not even sure who said it. My mood has been soured, never a good time for me to be drinking. "Great, make mine a double." Catherine doesn't look pleased. At the moment I don't care what does or does not please her. Then I realize that isn't true. At this moment if she doesn't like it, I'm only going to want to do it more.

"Want to tell me what happened after I left?" Abby knows me so well. At least she keeps her voice hushed so only I can hear her.

"I would if I even knew. We were having a drink at the bar, a woman came up and said hi, Catherine was talking to some guy further down the bar. The cab rang to say they were there. In the cab, she jumped my ass about not rescuing her the way I rescued you and something about the woman I was talking to flirting with me."

"Well, I certainly didn't expect all that. So what you're just going to drink doubles because she won't like it?" I was wrong about everyone being drunk; clearly, Abby is not. Too damn observant is what she is.

"Maybe. Where is Taylor?"

"Oh no. I am not going to let you do that. That is a line you don't want to cross." Abby grabs my upper arm and steers me towards the bar.

Abby is right. She usually is. I take a deep breath and slowly release it. "I know. I don't even know what I did wrong though. I wasn't flirting. I barely got that woman's name, much less her number."

"It sounds like you've just had a miscommunication. Don't let it ruin your night." Of course, Abby is taking the diplomatic approach. Leave it to my best friend to be Switzerland. I see Catherine making her way towards us. I am not ready to talk to her yet.

"It is too hot in here. I'm going outside for a few."

"Yeah stick your head in some snow and calm down while you're out there." Abby smiles at me as I walk away.

I make my way out into the frigid night air, pulling a deep breath in. I hope the cold air and the silence around me will help calm me down. My peace and quiet are short-lived though.

"Avoiding me now?" I stiffen, still not in the mood.

"Nope, just looking for your sister." I know it is a low blow, but I still don't care.

"Really Alex?" Catherine gives up and turns to head back inside.

"Wait! That was wrong. I'm sorry. Why did you follow me out here?" I watch as Catherine wobbles her way to me. She is clearly drunk.

"I want to talk to you."

"Like you spoke to me in the cab? If that is what is happening, no thanks." Catherine has finally stumbled her way to my side.

"I'm sorry ok? Can we just forget it?"

"Catherine I don't even know what I'm supposed to forget. I have no idea what I did wrong."

"You didn't do anything wrong. I'm sorry. Forgive me?"

"Do you ever feel like one of us is always having to apologize to the other one?"

"Yeah, I've noticed that. Probably what you get when you put two strong personalities together. Forgive me?" There is a new look on Catherine's face, a look of defeat mixed with shame. She looks like she might cry, or it could just be the alcohol. I'm not sure.

"I suppose so." Before I can stop her, Catherine has me wrapped up in a tight embrace and won't let me go. Her warmth a stark contrast to the frigid late December air, the vanilla scent she wears making my head spin. She isn't letting me go, and I know I don't want her to. More than anything I want to draw her face to mine and kiss her. Her scent is more inebriating that the alcohol I've consumed as I slowly turn my head to her, softly running the tip of my nose over her clavicle and against the side of her neck.

"Don't let us interrupt." Taylor and Nikki have emerged from the house, Nikki lighting a cigarette. Catherine jumps away from me like I've electrocuted her. I know this problem is mine, but her reaction to being seen by Taylor seems unwarranted. I simply shake my head slightly and head back inside, leaving the three of them on their own.

Catherine

I wake up with the worst case of dry mouth in the history of the world. My head is pounding more than an entire drum line. My memory of last night is a haze. I look across the bed, I'm alone. One checkpoint cleared. I look down. I'm half naked. My bedroom door is open, and I can see my pants in the hallway. I look at the nightstand for my phone. It isn't there. In its place is a glass of water and a bottle of Gatorade. I down the water and grab my robe. I go down the hall to the room Taylor is using, she isn't here. I make my way to the basement, hoping she isn't with Alex. I can't hear any sounds drifting up the stairs. I head down the steps. No sign of Taylor. Alex's bedroom door is open, so she isn't home either. Only I catch from the corner of my eye that she is home, and she is very naked. I catch myself staring at her lying there. Her toned body is beautiful. No wonder Taylor took a shot at her. I make my way back upstairs to find my phone and guzzle more water.

I'm stirred out of my half conscious coma by the front door opening and shutting. Clearly, drunk Alex and Catherine don't bother to close or lock doors. I look up to see Taylor coming in. Of course she looks perfectly fine. "Good night?"

"Great night, unexpected but great." Taylor is wearing the shit-eating grin I've seen too many times. I have a feeling what or more like who she has been doing.

"Managed to sleep with Nikki I take it? Crossing straight girl off your list now?"

"Oh Cat. How many times have I told you, there is no such thing as straight. Speaking of, what is going on between you and Alex? Had I known there was something there I wouldn't have tried to get her into bed the other night. You should have told me."

I have no idea what she is talking about, but feel my heartbeat start to pick up anyway. "Well, you clearly know something I don't. There isn't anything going on between Alex and me."

"Then what did Nikki and I interrupt last night? Looked like more than nothing to me. You only jumped a mile when you realized someone else had joined you. You've never been a jumpy person."

"Taylor I have no idea what you are talking about. I don't remember any of that." My head is still pounding so hard that I can't think.

"Sure you don't. You look like hell, you should go back to bed."

"Good idea." I slump off back to my bed, relishing the darkness provided by the blackout curtains. I lay there, unable to fall asleep. What was Taylor talking about? How can I not remember anything?

Alexis

New Year's Eve brings about another party at Shannon and Kevin's. Kevin's birthday is December 31, so we always combine parties and have it at theirs. I promise myself that I won't be drinking nearly as much as I did at the holiday bar crawl.

Catherine and I arrive at the party to find everyone else already there. Taylor has paired off with Nikki again. If it bothers Catherine, she hasn't mentioned it. I look around for Abby and find her with a man I haven't met yet, but assume he is the neighbor. Apparently that ship hasn't sailed after all. A realization hits me like a bolt of lightning, if no one else shows up Catherine and I will be the only single people here. Sara is on call, so the chances anyone else will be here are slim.

"There you are! I've been waiting for you to get here! Come on I want to introduce you to someone." Abby is overly excited and will drag me across the room if I don't come willingly. "Alex this is Dave, Dave my best friend, Alex."

Dave and I shake hands and exchanged pleasantries. "Who is this?" Dave asks while eye-fucking Catherine. It instantly pisses me off. I know that he has told Abby that he isn't ready for anything serious, but he came here with Abby, at least focus on her tonight. I know deep down that probably isn't that only reason it angers me. At least Catherine ignores it entirely or doesn't realize it is happening.

"Sorry, this is Catherine, Catherine meet Dave."

"Nice to meet you. So you two are together then?" This guy is a creep. Abby deserves and can do so much better.

Catherine gives Dave a grin and shakes her head. "No, Alex and I are just friends." I need to step away from Dave before I say something. Abby apparently has something to get off her chest though.

"Yeah friends who live together, work together and go pretty much everywhere together." I turn toward Abby giving her my best what the fuck look. It is only a little after 9, can she really be that drunk already? Abby, completely oblivious to my irritation, is already refocused on Dave.

"It is true that we do spend a lot of time together." At least Catherine has caught my extreme level of annoyance toward Abby. If she is bothered by Abby's comment, she doesn't let it show. The patented Catherine poker face is firmly in place.

"If you'll excuse me I'm going to get something to drink. Catherine do you want anything?" If I don't move away from Abby and Dave, I will end up saying something I might regret later. I can only bite my tongue for so long.

"Actually I think I will come with you. It was nice meeting you Dave. Abby." There it is, Catherine's voice becomes pointed as she says their names. The slightest hint that Catherine was at least bothered by Abby's comment and Dave's behavior. Catherine grabs my arm and whispers in my ear, "What was that? First, her date is ogling me and then Abby makes that statement!" The smell of her perfume permeating my nostrils combined with the caress of her breath on my ear and neck gives me chills. I want to slam this woman up against the wall and make her moan louder than she ever has. I shake the visual away as quickly as possible and try to free myself, but Catherine won't let go.

"I have no idea. This is my first-time meeting him, and I already dislike him. What a creep. As for Abby, she hasn't even said so much as a word to me about the time you and I spend together. I don't know if she is drunk, jealous, or what is happening."

"Really? Not a word?" Catherine has that eyebrow cocked, I know she doesn't believe me. The fantasy of taking her against the wall darts back into my mind.

"The only thing she has ever said about any of it is that she thought it was a bad idea that I was moving into your basement."

"Why did she think that?" Catherine looks hurt. I didn't say it to hurt her, nor did I think it would.

I realize then that I am still toting around Kevin's birthday gift. I look around for him and see him by the bar. Great, a multi-purpose trip. If I can get there fast enough, maybe Catherine will forget about the Abby question. Of course, that is too much to hope for.

"Alex, why did she think it was a bad idea?" She tightens her grip on my bicep and forces me to stop. There is no getting out of answering her question. I will be forced to admit things to her that I would rather keep to myself.

"In a nutshell: When Elena and I were having problems I told Abby about meeting you…how sexy I thought you were. Then you came to work here, and I still found you attractive. Abby didn't think it was a good idea because of that and because we work together." Catherine relaxes her grip on my arm but doesn't release it. She has a look on her face that I've never seen before. I wish I could read her. We stand there in silence for a brief moment, the din of the party going on around us. Finally, Catherine speaks, but I can't hear her. "It is loud in here. What was that?"

"You never said." I'm pretty sure that I did say the other night in the cab. Clearly she doesn't remember that or falling down in the hallway while she stripped off her jeans, forcing me to help her remove them. Clearly she has no idea that she essentially forced me to put her to bed or the conflicting emotions the entire event stirred in me.

"Never said what? That I find you attractive? Catherine, Ray Charles would find you irresistible. Besides what difference would it have made? Would you not have let me move in had you known?"

Catherine regains her composure, her expression once again betraying nothing. "Don't be silly, of course I would have offered you the apartment. I like having you at the house. Come on, we need drinks."

Forgotten, just like that. Catherine hauls me towards the bar, where we greet Kevin. I give Kevin a hug and his gift while Catherine prepares drinks for us. I'm still chatting with Kevin when Catherine returns to my side and offers me one of the cocktails. I take the first drink and almost cough it back up. Catherine isn't holding back on the booze tonight. In fact, I find myself wondering if she put anything but whiskey in my cup.

Catherine maintains my drink throughout the night. Each time I am certain there is nothing but alcohol in it. Even if she is speaking with someone in a different part of the house, she still has some radar that goes off if my drink starts to get low. Sometime around 11, I start to feel the effects of having not had much to eat, and the alcohol Catherine has been filling me with. I drop out of the game of *Cards Against Humanity* and grab a plate of food. Catherine must be keeping pace with me as she is already sitting on the couch eating. Nikki, Taylor, Abby, and Dave are with her.

"Alex come sit with me." She slides over, so there is just enough space between herself and the arm of the couch. I have no choice, so I join her.

We find ourselves sitting there for some time, chatting with everyone. I'm content because one of the bowl games is on TV and my drink is full. Catherine and I are chatting away when Catherine makes a joke. I'm not sure if it would have been as funny under normal circumstances or if anyone other than Catherine had made it, but because it was Catherine making the joke, I lose it. I'm laughing uncontrollably. When I catch my breath, I make another joke, starting the snowball. Before long we are both laughing uncontrollably. I realize that Catherine and I are leaning on each other, our foreheads keeping us upright. I can feel her soft breaths tickle my lips. I open my eyes to see Catherine is no longer laughing. Instead, she is very aware and very still, staring at me, like a deer caught in headlights. The realization hits me then, I've nearly kissed Catherine. I can also feel the eyes of Abby, Dave, Nikki, and Taylor boring into us. I panic. Without a word I break the contact between Catherine and I and leave the room as quickly as possible. I need to be alone, but in a house full of people there is nowhere to go. I opt to break the rules and lock myself in the master suite off of Kevin and Shannon's bedroom. I call for a cab from the bathroom and wait there for it to arrive. I escape the party by claiming I'm going outside for some air. As I close the door to the cab, I see Abby exit the house. My phone goes off after the cab pulls away, a text from Abby asking if I'm ok. I know that things are well and truly messed up now, but simply reply that I needed to get out of there and tell her to go back and enjoy the party.

Catherine

What just happened? Alex and I were just sitting here joking around, having a good time. The next thing I know our foreheads are together and I'm starting at her. I realize I want to kiss her. It terrifies me. It has to be the alcohol. I can't want to kiss Alex, can I? Shit, Alex has opened her eyes, a beautiful shade of green one seldom sees. She isn't laughing anymore. I have no idea what I'm supposed to do, I'm frozen in a state of panic, fear, and confusion. Alex runs. She doesn't run, she flees. I've crossed a boundary, I'm not even sure how it happened. I want to find Alex, but I'm glued to my seat. Confusion and conflicting emotions have taken over my body, rendering me inert. Taylor sits in Alex's now vacated spot and tries to talk to me, but I can't speak. I'm absorbed by the thoughts swirling in my head. I'm aware that Alex hasn't returned and Abby has left to find her. It should be me searching for Alex but I can't. Abby comes back alone, Alex has left without a word.

Panic sets in. I need to talk to Alex. I excuse myself and search for a quiet spot to call her. She doesn't answer. I call for a taxi, planning to go home and talk to her there. I grab my coat and head outside to wait for the cab. I try calling Alex again but am sent to her voice mail. I realize I feel a need to talk to her but have no idea what I plan to say. What can I say with so much confusion still swirling in my own head?

I arrive home at half past midnight. All the lights are off, just as we left them. I head to the basement. No lights or sound. Alex's bedroom door is open. She isn't here. I check the rest of the house but cannot find her. I try calling her again, still no answer. I text her asking her to come home, that I want to talk to her. I wait, but she doesn't respond. I have no idea where she would go.

I decide to wait for Alex downstairs. I exchange *Fingersmith* for a new book from her collection, *Tipping the Velvet*. It is written by Sarah Waters as well, and since I enjoyed *Fingersmith* so much I figure I'll like this one too. I sit on the couch and try to read, but my focus isn't there. I have no explanation for what happened or how I felt. Does it matter that I wanted to kiss Alex when she ran away so easily? Why did I want to kiss Alex? What has changed? I have never felt that way about a woman before. Was it just a combination of alcohol and loneliness? Have I even been feeling lonely?

I distract myself for a short while by reading, but the questions continue to plague me, eventually tearing my attention from the book again and again. It is after two, where is Alex? Resolved to wait for her I continue the pattern.

I wake up after four. I am initially confused about where I am, then remember I was waiting for Alex. The light is off, and I've been covered with a pair of blankets. I go to Alex's door. It is closed, no light showing beneath it. I can't recall if I shut it or left it open. I need to know if she is here, if she is safe. I slowly open the door and reveal her silhouette. I stare for a moment waiting to see if I feel anything. All I feel is confused. I quietly shut the door and head upstairs to my own room.

Alexis

I come home to find Catherine asleep on the downstairs couch, the light on, and *Tipping the Velvet* open on her lap. Why is she down here? I don't want to wake her, so I grab a few blankets from my closet and cover her up. I shut off the lights and prepare for bed as quietly as possible. I can't sleep. Shortly after 4 am, I hear the door quietly scraping across the carpet. I know it is Catherine. I still haven't worked out what to say, how to explain how I nearly kissed her, so I hold perfectly still, my will to avoid talking to her taking priority over any modesty I feel about being exposed from the waist up. She lingers in the doorway, and I feel my heartbeat increase. After what feels like an hour, she closes the door, and I hear her retreating up the stairs. I finally drift off sometime after five, no closer to any resolution or explanation about what has happened.

I'm awake before eight. I pull on a pair of sweat pants and a t-shirt and head out to the couch. Catherine has folded the blankets I left with her, so I take care of them. I put on an episode of *Game of Thrones*, I've seen them all several times at this point. It is more for background noise and intermittent distraction than anything. If Catherine isn't awake already, I know she will be soon. I need to figure out what I'm going to say, or if anything I can offer as an explanation will change anything. I have only reached one conclusion by the time I hear Catherine in the kitchen, it is time I find a place of my own.

It isn't long before Catherine is descending the stairs. She makes her way over to the sofa and sits on the end opposite mine. We sit there in silence. She seems to be waiting for me to talk, to explain what happened last night. I have no explanation, no idea how it happened. All I know is that it surely is my fault. The silence stretches on, time has to have stopped at this point. Finally, Catherine breaks the silence.

"You disappeared last night." She still hasn't looked at me. She seems so despondent.

"Yeah, I needed some space and quiet, time to think." She still won't look at me. I keep waiting for it, for her to tell me I should find a new place to live.

"You didn't even say anything, you just left. Where did you go?" I still can't read her, my own emotions are clouding my perception.

"To my quiet spot. I just went and sat there for a few hours." It takes Catherine a minute, but she finally speaks again.

"At work?"

"Yeah. I couldn't think of any other place to go. I knew it would be deserted. I needed to think."

"You could have come back here." She is so calm, even seems a little sad.

"No, I couldn't. I needed to be alone, you were waiting for me when I got here."

"I know. I shouldn't have been down here, but I wanted to talk to you."

"It is your house, go where you please. It didn't upset me."

"It may be my house, but this is your space, I should have respected that." We are clearly tiptoeing around the issue. It was my fault, I should just tear off the band-aid and get it out there.

"Look, things are awkward. I don't even know what happened or almost happened last night. One minute we were laughing and joking around, the next...well, you know. I do want you to know that I didn't plan it, but that I accept it as being entirely my fault. I'm sorry I made you uncomfortable. It won't happen again." Catherine sits there in silence, but she finally looks at me. The impenetrable wall is back on her face. I have no idea what she is thinking. I decide I should just go for broke. "I'm going to start looking for a place of my own this afternoon."

Catherine finally looks at me with real emotion. "What? Why?"

"I think it is for the best. This was only supposed to be temporary anyway. I've been living here for weeks."

"The best for who? I like having you here. There is no need for you to move out. Temporary has no definitive end date. Stay."

"I don't know Catherine. I tried to kiss you, or at least almost kissed you. I don't know how it got that far. All I remember is laughing with you then realizing our foreheads were together. I opened my eyes to see you staring at me horrified. I know it is all my fault. Why aren't you tossing me out?"

"I would never do that. In the end, you didn't kiss me. It was probably just the talk from earlier in the night, combined with the alcohol and the growing level of comfort we feel around one another. I want you to stay. Having you here is wonderful. Don't leave." Catherine's words are nice, but I wish that she meant them in the way that I want her to, a way I know she never will.

I have no idea how to answer that except with humor.
"Why Catherine I do believe that is the closest I have ever
seen you come to begging."

Catherine chuckles before regaining control and retorting,
"That is the last bit of begging you will ever see me do." I
really wish this wasn't true, but know that it is.

"So—."

"I'd say we are good." Catherine is headed for the stairs
before I can protest.

Catherine

Alex may be good now, but I am not. I am a coward. First, I can't confess that it was also my fault or that I wanted to kiss her. Wanted to feel her warm lips on my own, to bite and suck on her pouty lower lip. I couldn't tell Alex any of it. I still felt the urge to do those things as I looked at her hurting across from me. Instead, I sat there pretending to be all unfeeling. It worked right up until she mentioned moving out. The mere thought of Alex moving out tears at something inside me. I don't want her to go. Pro move on my part, piling all the excuses for my feelings onto her. I hate myself for allowing her to feel alone in this and thinking that everything is down to her behavior. I do it out of self-preservation. Self-preservation in that it allows me time to figure out my emotions and deal with them or to continue ignoring them now that Alex has taken the blame for herself. I am a coward, so I flee the basement, similar to Alex running out of the party last night.

"Breakfast?" Alex has followed me upstairs pulling my attention from the pit of self-loathing I find myself in.

"Sure what do you have in mind?" I try to keep up the facade that everything is fine.

"Whatever you feel like, something with carbs though." She smiles at me, and the guilt hits me like a shot to the stomach. I try to turn my face to stone, to not let my emotions slip through.

"Surprise me. I need a shower first though." A shower to wash away the filth I feel for lying about my role in what happened, for allowing Alex to hurt and to feel like shit thinking it is all her fault.

"Ok go get in. Food should be ready by the time you are finished."

*****

My shower offers none of the relief it usually does. No amount of scrubbing can wash away the shame and self-loathing I feel for not being honest with Alex. What kind of person have I become? I know what I need to do, but I'm not sure I can do it. I need to tell Alex the truth. What truth? I have no idea. I'm not even certain what is happening. If I confess what will happen? Will she feel like I'm playing a game, leading her on? How am I even supposed to sort all of this out? I decide that I am going to tell Alex, explain everything that I can. I can't let her go on thinking she is entirely to blame.

I finish my shower, get dressed and head to the kitchen. I don't quite make it there when I realize I hear voices. Taylor is back. I realize she and Alex are talking about what happened last night. I hide in the hallway and once again find myself being a snoop.

"That's the thing, I don't know how it happened. I know I can't lie to myself and deny my desire for her. I have wanted her since the first moment I saw her. Who wouldn't? Only I thought it would lessen once I got to know her or that at least I could keep it under control. The problem is that my desire has only strengthened and I clearly can't control it can I? Now I have crossed a boundary I never meant to."

So much information I didn't know. Had Alex really hidden her attraction to me so well or did I just chose to ignore it? I feel torn up inside. Half of me is thankful that I am not the only one struggling with this, the other half is hurting because of how much Alex is struggling with this.

"If I'm being honest that didn't look all that one sided to me. Not after what I saw at the first party."

135

"Want to fill me in?" I continue listening thinking me too.

"Don't you remember out in the driveway? Nikki and I found you and Cat with your arms locked around each other. It went on way too long to just be a hug. When I spoke up Cat couldn't jump away fast enough."

"I remember that. What about it?" Alex remembers, but I don't. I really did drink too much.

"I'm just saying that none of this is typical Cat behavior. She isn't a hugger, much less an embracer. Abby said last night that you and Cat had some argument in the cab on your way back to the first party. Sounds like Cat was jealous. Then last night, I just don't think that ended up the way it did simply because of your feelings. I'm not a Cat expert, you know we aren't that close, but something just seems different here." Thanks, Taylor. I don't know what is going on in my own head yet she has everything neatly broken down.

"I don't know. I can't trust my own judgment here. I would love it if you were right but I doubt that you are. Catherine has told me she has never been with a woman before. Anyway, I offered to move out, but she insisted I stay."

"Well you know, Cat and I look enough alike. We can go downstairs—."

"No, we can't. That wouldn't be fair to anyone. I don't want a Catherine replacement, you are not a Catherine substitute, and no matter what she is or is not feeling she would be the one to get hurt in the end. I don't want to hurt her. If I'm being honest, I'm surprised that you would even suggest it."

There it is, that feeling again. I still don't know if I simply feel a sense of pride for Alex or if it is something more. It is a warmth that spreads throughout my body, hitting my chest the hardest. I'm so lost, maybe more than I have ever been.

"Surprised? Why? Do you even realize how sexy you are? Come to Cali, I can set you up with a different woman every night."

"Thanks, I think. I'm gonna pass on that offer though. That may be something that works for you, but it has never really been my thing. I need more than just physical attraction."

"You have my number if you change your mind." When did they exchange numbers?

My window to talk to Alex is gone, I can't have this conversation with her in front of Taylor. I also realize that I need to make my presence known. Surely this has been the longest shower in the history of showers. I complete the trip back to the kitchen. "Is that bacon I smell?"

"Yes, and pancakes, blueberry and regular." If Alex suspects that I've heard anything she isn't letting it show.

"Smells amazing. Anything I can do?" Good thing I couldn't rid myself of that stain in the shower. I clearly won't be confessing anytime soon.

"Nope all finished. Taylor is getting plates and utensils around. I guess you could grab the juice."

"Got it." Try as I might I can't make eye contact with Alex.

"What time do you have to leave for the airport?"

"Her flight leaves at six. We have to leave by three. Want to join us?" As soon as I ask, I realize that it would mean an hour and a half drive with Alex alone. I don't know what I want to say to her, I just know that I don't want to be driving when I finally say it.

"No, I think I'm going to stay home and relax. Abby has been blowing up my phone all morning, so I'll have to touch base with her as well." My shoulders sag a bit with relief. I know that I am a terrible person.

"I'm jealous. I need a day where I just stay in. Enjoy it. If you change your mind, you are welcome to join us."

*****

"So you wanna talk about it?" Taylor and I are headed to the airport. I am distracted and not being good company. All the questions that have plagued me since last night are still parading through my head. I am no closer to having any answers. I still feel like a terrible person for lying to Alex as well. I'm certain I'm a real joy to be around.

"About?" I try to evade this, to play dumb. Taylor and I have never seen eye to eye, would she even understand anything if I did talk to her?

"Oh come on Cat, cut the crap. I saw that last night. You don't get to pretend that nothing happened. I talked to Alex. She feels like shit because she thinks she did something wrong. She blames herself for all of it, only I was there. That wasn't just her. You've never been one to lie, one to not take accountability for your own behavior. You don't get to start now, not when someone else's emotions are involved. Someone you consider a friend."

Taylor is right, completely right. I still don't have any answers, am not even sure if I should be talking to her about any of this. I take a deep breath and whisper the only response I have. "I know."

"Look, I know you and I have never been close. We've approached life differently for as long as I can remember. You don't agree with how I live my life, I know that. But sis, something is happening and it is time you stop lying to yourself about it or denying that it is taking place."

"I don't even know what is happening though, don't you get that?" Hot tears start to burn my eyes. I fight them back, not wanting to cry in front of Taylor.

"Well start somewhere. What happened last night?"

"I have no idea. Alex and I were joking around and the next thing I knew we were almost kissing. Honestly, I wanted to kiss her. I don't know if I've ever wanted to kiss anyone so badly. At the same time, I was terrified. I don't know what that means. I've never wanted to kiss a woman before."

"Yeah, that didn't look one sided when it happened. So why did you let Alex blame herself for it this morning?" I'm shocked, I thought Taylor would at least do some gloating at my confession of wanting to kiss a woman, but she doesn't.

"I don't know. Last night she ran away. I tried to call her but she wouldn't answer. I went home hoping to find her, but she wasn't there. I waited up for her but fell asleep before she came home. When I tried to talk to her this morning she just took all the blame. I was a shameful coward and let her. She told me she thought she should move out and I felt like someone had cut a part of me off. I basically begged her not to." I can't contain it anymore. The stress, the shame, the self-loathing, and the desperation to find answers that seemingly aren't there all start to cascade down my cheeks.

"Cat, take a deep breath. Try to calm down."

"What am I supposed to do though?" I'm so emotional right now that I'm grateful that traffic is light.

"I can't tell you that. This is something you have to work out on your own. Do you care about Alex?"

"Of course I do. What kind of question is that?"

"Yeah, but do you CARE about Alex. How do you feel when you see her, hear her voice, hear her name? Does it all just feel platonic or is there something deeper there?"

"I don't know Taylor. Before last night I hadn't thought about it. Now I can't stop thinking about it, what it means. I've never been with a woman, nor have I ever wanted to be with a woman. Then last night I nearly kissed one, I wanted to kiss one. How is that even possible?"

"Well, there must be something about her that you find attractive or at least something that attracts you to her. She is pretty damn hot and seems like a genuine down to earth person as well. Either way Cat, no matter what you decide you have to be careful. Alex is a person with real feelings. She clearly has feelings for you. I don't know how strong they are but it doesn't matter. Even if she is just lusting after you, you need to be certain before you start something. The two of you could get through this and wind up the best of friends, or you could fuck it all up and lose her forever."

Alexis

I need to respond to Abby. I hate talking on the phone so I simply text her telling her to get take out and come over. It is a long shot if she is even available. She responds in less than five minutes letting me know she is on her way.

True to her word Abby shows up in half an hour with pizza and ice cream. "You didn't say what you wanted me to get. I figured this might be a carb and sugar kind of night so we have pizza and moose tracks."

"That actually sounds great. Thanks for doing that." Abby always instinctively knows what I need, even if I don't. Probably her maternal instincts spilling over into the rest of her life.

"Where's Catherine?" I put the ice cream in the freezer and grab some plates and napkins.

"Taking Taylor to Metro. She won't be back before six for sure. It doesn't matter though, she won't mind that you are here."

"You sure about that? I think I irritated both of you last night with that comment." As we settle in at the dining room table, I realize I've forgotten drinks.

"You did. I didn't think Catherine cared one way or another until she gave you that look as she was walking away. What was that about anyway? What do you want to drink? We've got water, juice, beer, wine, various liquors." I know I'm having water. I had enough to drink last night and am too stressed out to be drinking.

"Just water. I can't even think about drinking for at least a month!"

"So dinner and drinks Friday after work?" I give her my best devil made me do it smile.

"Probably. I have to check though. Anyway sorry about that comment."

"Abby you don't need to be sorry, I would like to know where it came from." Really that knowledge is my sole concern on this subject. Dave didn't make the best impression and I couldn't care less what he thinks about how things are between Catherine and me.

"I'm just worried about you. You were with Elena for forever and that break up busted you up inside for a while, long before it was actually official. I know you harbor some feelings for Catherine, I get it. I'm just worried that you are going to get hurt again. Hurt if she doesn't feel the same or hurt if she gives it a go and then realizes she can't. I love you and I can't just stand by and watch you get hurt." I'm touched by Abby's sentiment. If the situation were reversed, and really it is, I would feel the same.

"Love you too." Abby is one of the only people I say these words to. "So speaking on this topic, we need to talk about Dave. I know you two have talked and whatever. I don't exactly know where you left off with that, but he was quite clearly into Catherine last night. I'm not just saying he found her attractive, he was eye-fucking her before he even knew her name. It pissed me off, not because of my attraction to Catherine, but because it was disrespectful of you. I just want you to be careful is all."

Abby looks sad. "I know." She grabs my hand and squeezes it. "Good thing we have each other. Someone has to look out for us."

"Absolutely, always." I finish my slice of pizza. "You know you probably could have just brought the ice cream. We should be honest and just admit that is what we really want anyway."

Abby laughs. "I know, but you know I like to fool myself. So you ready to talk about it?"

"Yes. No. I feel like I've been talking about it all day." Abby gives me her oh really look. "No, not just with myself. First Catherine this morning, then Taylor."

"You already talked to Catherine? How did that go?"

"I don't know. I took the blame. I know it was my fault. I don't know how I ended up almost kissing her, but I know it is on me. I offered to move out, but she wouldn't hear of it."

"I bet she wouldn't." Abby's tone harbors sarcasm and a hint of irritation. It is my turn to give the confused look. "Come on Alex. Do you really believe that was all your fault? We all saw it. No way that was all on you. She had plenty of opportunity to pull out of that situation, well before you realized what was happening. She didn't. Even if it were your fault, it really isn't. She has been leading you on since the night you moved in. That whole thing with the lingerie, whatever Taylor said she interrupted in the driveway at the party, the cab ride argument on the way to that same party. Do I need to go on?" Abby gives me time to process this. "If I told you that all of these things had happened between me and some guy what would you think?"

She has me. "I honestly don't know, but probably that he was jealous and had feelings for you."

"Then what makes this any different? This is exactly why I'm worried."

"Well for one Catherine isn't into women, has never been with a woman. Second, it is me. Why would a—" Abby doesn't let me finish.

"Oh no. Don't you dare downgrade your worth! Do you not comprehend that one of the most attractive things about you is that you do not seem to know you are physically attractive? That is just the surface. Adding to it you have a huge heart. Sure you barely let anyone in there or let anyone really get to know you, but when you do who wouldn't love you? So no, don't you dare try to say that there is no way someone could ever have those feelings for you."

Wow. I'm shocked. Abby knows me as well as, if not better than, anyone else. She is one of the only people who knows everything about my past. I so rarely see her so spirited about something that I don't have a response. Abby eventually continues, negating my need for one.

"Look, I'm not saying that she does have feelings for you. I am saying that it looks suspicious. She might not even realize it. I'm just saying there are warning signs all over the place."

"Well Taylor wasn't as passionate about it as you, but she seemed to think something is different with Catherine. I can't sit judge on this one. There are three sides to this situation, my side clouded with my past experiences and emotions, Catherine's side clouded by hers and the truth. I just wish I knew what the truth is."

"I know love, I know." Abby allows me a few minutes to think about the cyclone of thoughts in my head. "What do you say we get that ice cream and watch a movie?"

"I say sounds like a nice Friday night. Anything in mind?"

"Well, I never did get to see *Love Actually* this holiday season? Is it too late? Or do you want to watch something less romantic?"

"It is never too late. Less romantic? I think we could both stand a little hope in our lives right now, even if it isn't practical."

Catherine

I get home from the airport with my head still a jumbled mess, the strange car in my driveway barely diverting my attention. My talk with Taylor only cleared up one point: I need to know how I feel before I confess anything to Alex. I don't want to lead her on if I really am not ready or able to commit to something. I have no desire to hurt Alex, yet I feel like no matter what I say or do, hurting Alex is exactly what will happen. I realize that despite the anxiety I'm feeling I am starving. Breakfast feels like forever ago. I head to the basement to see if Alex is hungry when I notice the pizza box on the table. Odd, Alex has told me before she isn't a big fan of pizza delivery. I head down the steps not trying to conceal my presence. I can hear the TV, I know Alex is here. I am not prepared for what I walk in on though. Alex is curled up on the couch with some woman, their shoulders resting against each other, a blanket draped over them both. I forgot about the car in the driveway. Jealously instantly rears its head inside me. It is foreign to me. I can't recall if I have ever been jealous since childhood. I know I wasn't when I found out Brian was cheating on me.

"Hey, Catherine." How does Alex hear everything? The woman with Alex turns around, I'm shocked to see Abby.

"Hi, Catherine. Want to join us?" I am so confused. What is happening here?

"No thank you. I was just seeing if Alex is hungry. I'll leave you to it." I try to head upstairs, but Alex stops me.

"If you're hungry there is some pizza on the table upstairs and ice cream in the freezer. Help yourself." She never turns to look at me, not once. She and Abby have snuggled together again, my presence forgotten.

I give up on sleeping around 4 am. Emotions I can't reconcile still war in my head. I head for the pool hoping the best therapist I could ever ask for can help. I push myself hard, probably too hard. While my body feels great, I'm just as confused as ever. I need a shower and breakfast. It is nearly five on Saturday morning. I have no idea what I'm going to do with my day.

Showered and dressed I make it to the kitchen around 5:30. Alex is there making our breakfast smoothies, even though she has the day off as well. "Hope you want a smoothie, I sorta assumed you would."

"Yeah, that would be great. Abby gone?" Alex gives me a look.

"Catherine, how many times do you have to hear that nothing is going on between Abby and me? Of course, she is gone. She left around ten last night." Alex shakes her head, it is subtle, but I still catch it.

"It looked like more than nothing last night. You two looked awfully comfortable." Wow, jealousy turns me into an ugly bitch.

"Yeah well, I've heard that some of the things you've done lately looked like they were more complicated than you have suggested they were. Guess things aren't always what they seem." Alex pours half the smoothie into her glass and slams the blender back down onto the counter. "Enough, I can't deal with this right now." With that, she disappears back into the basement.

Alex and I spend the rest of the weekend avoiding each other. I leave the house a little early on Monday morning to avoid another confrontation with her. I know we have to figure something out or our living arrangement will become untenable, but not this morning. I get my rounding done quickly and check on the new consults we have. With nothing left to take care of I head to the OR to review and update charts. I need to keep moving today if I hope to stay awake. My internal struggle kept me awake most of the weekend and sleep deprivation is knocking at my door.

I get to the room to discover Alex is one of my scrubs today. Another reminder of why they say don't shit where you eat. Emotions war within me, distracting me. Is this how it has been for her? If so, she hid it well, her focus has always been laser sharp. She breaks scrub and leaves the room without acknowledging me. I have a feeling it is going to be a very long day.

My hunch was correct, it has been a long day. Alex is ignoring me unless it is related to the case. I don't want to force her to interact with me, but I can't stand it. I try to get her attention all day, nothing works. I think by the end of her shift she has said fewer than 15 words to me, most of them single syllable. At home that night she avoids me, a recluse in the basement when she can be and tiptoeing around me when she can't.

We go on like this for the better part of a month. I am at my wit's end. I am not sleeping. When I do, my dreams are haunted by instant replay of our near kiss. Only in dreams sometimes I run, sometimes we kiss. Even my subconscious has no answers. I need to talk to Alex, to at least try to let her know what is happening on my end, to make the confession I should have made weeks ago.

*****

It is another long day and is just after seven when I arrive home. I have been working myself up to this and need to do it tonight, no matter how tired I am. I can hear the music coming from the basement. I know she is here. If I announce myself she will ignore me, so I head down, hoping she will hear me out. It is already too late when I realize that music isn't the only thing I'm hearing. I'm greeted by the site of Alex fucking some woman I've never seen before. Alex has her pinned against the bar, their backs to me. I need to get out of here but can't look away. Alex is stroking her from behind, pulling her head back by her hair, forcing a brief kiss before releasing her hair and moving her hand down to a breast. Their moans are loud and their breathing quick. I can see sweat coating Alex's body. My senses finally override my arousal, and I quietly retreat back up the stairs. Arousal isn't the only thing I am feeling though. I realize a part of me feels hurt. I have no right to feel this way, but I do.

Alexis

"Wow, you weren't kidding?" I look at Brooke, my eyes half-lidded as I'm nearly asleep. We just put in one hell of a workout, and I finally feel relaxed for the first time in weeks.

"About what?"

"She is hot." I am too tired to follow.

"Who?" I just want to drift off to sleep, but Brooke is intent on talking.

"Catherine. Wait you didn't see her walk in on us?" Alarm surges through me and my eyes snap open, sleep the farthest thing from my mind now. I haven't done anything wrong, yet I want to run upstairs and explain. I stay planted in my bed though. I can't keep playing this game with myself. I need to get over Catherine.

"Are you making that up to mess with me? When?"

"When you had me against the bar. I figured you knew she was there and didn't care. You know I wouldn't care."

"Great." We spend the next few minutes laying there in silence, thoughts of Catherine streaming through my mind. "You staying tonight or do you have to go?" Brooke and I have discussed the Catherine situation, I just don't want to discuss it more after I have just finished sleeping with her.

"What do you want me to do?"

"Either is fine. I'd like you to stay, but that would mean getting up and out early."

"To avoid Catherine? She already knows I'm here."

"No, because I have to work in the morning. I haven't done anything wrong." Brooke knows me well, even after nearly fifteen years and thousands of miles between us.

"Are you trying to convince yourself of that? The you I dated would be trying to convince herself of that." Brooke tilts my chin, forcing me to look at her. "Alex you haven't done anything wrong." I say nothing because every fiber in my body contradicts the notion that I am innocent. I really do want Brooke to stay so I'm not alone. "I can stay," she says as she wraps herself around me. "Happy birthday."

Catherine

Sleep is eluding me again. I am going to go insane, I am sure of it. I can't get the image of Alex and the woman out of my head. I am very turned on. I try giving myself some release, but it isn't working. I'm frustrated. The image of Alex stroking the stranger flashes through my mind, and I finally feel it. I go with it. I imagine how it would have played out had I seen it all, only the stranger is me. I imagine what it would feel like to have Alex go down on me, to fondle my breasts, to pull me in for a kiss by my hair. I imagine that my hand is Alex's, her fingers stroking and fucking me. It isn't long before my much sought after release hits me. I come hard and loud, certain that my closest neighbor has to have heard me. As my body calms itself, sleep finally takes me in her arms.

*****

I reach the kitchen in the morning just in time to see Alex ushering her guest out. I feel hurt and sad. I don't want to argue about it though. Alex hasn't done anything wrong.

"Brooke," Alex says her name; as if by saying it I'll understand. The only reply I can make is a slight nod as I try not to relay the melancholy that I feel. "We dated a lifetime ago." If they dated a lifetime ago, it certainly looked like they never broke up. Alex is headed for the stairs.

"Can we talk tonight? I really want to talk to you." She stops.

"Yeah, I can make sure I'm available." She answers without looking back and heads down the steps as soon as she agrees. There isn't a point in talking to her tonight, I know.

*****

An air exchange malfunction at the hospital results in the last two cases of my day being canceled. I know I will regret making up for those missed surgeries, but today I am grateful. Evening staff members are required to stay in case there is a trauma and with the hope that maintenance will be able to repair the air exchange quickly enough that some of the later scheduled cases can still go. I have plenty of time before Alex will be home, so I stop at the market for supplies to make dinner. I head home and immediately get to work. I am nervous and need to stay busy so I won't talk myself out of this.

Alex arrives home just before six. I am just finishing our dinner of roasted chicken with red skinned potatoes and green beans. "Smells good. You didn't have to make dinner though."

"I did. I haven't had a lot of chances to since you moved in."

"Do you want to talk or eat?" I really need to talk first. Now that it looms in front of me I am becoming a nervous wreck. Plus I am unsure dinner will be comfortable if we don't talk first. Then again I am unsure it will be if we do talk first.

"You want to try both?" Alex is clearly ready to move this along.

"I suppose we could." We sit down to the meal and Alex starts eating. I watch her, too nervous to do anything else. She eventually looks up at me, her eyebrows raised.

"What did you want to talk about?" This is it. If I don't speak now I know I never will. My stomach clenches and my saliva turns to sand. Why didn't I make myself a drink?

153

Instead, I reach for my glass of water and guzzle half of it before I begin.

"Alex I don't even know where to begin. I need you to let me get this out though." I look at her and she nods, letting me know she understands and to continue. "I don't have answers I guess is a good starting place. I am lost and confused. I feel like I'm going to have a nervous breakdown. I miss you." I pause and look down. I can't look at her when I say this, any of it. My shame is too much to bear. "I haven't been totally honest with you." Alex sits down her fork. She stares at me waiting.

"I don't know when it happened; when it started. I do know when I realized it was there." I know I'm not making sense, Alex's expression making that clear. She waits patiently though, kind enough to honor my request to let me talk. "I guess I should lead by confessing that the night that we almost kissed, that wasn't all you. I wanted to kiss you, so badly. I don't know when that feeling developed, but it was there. It terrified me. I know you are comfortable being out, but that isn't a skin that I've ever worn. I'm being honest when I tell you that I've never felt that way about a woman before. You ran before I could process or talk to you. You were the only person I wanted to talk to. I wanted to tell you the next morning, but you just blamed it all on yourself. It was easy for me to let you. I immediately regretted that decision and have felt very ashamed about it since. I planned to tell you that morning after I showered, I couldn't stand the self-loathing, but Taylor was here." I stop to gather my thoughts and try to rein in my emotions. The tears win though and I am trying not to sob as I continue.

"I am so lost right now. I don't understand what this means. These feelings have never been a part of my identity. I tried talking to Taylor about it on the way to the airport, hoping she could provide some clarity. The only thing she gave me was a warning. I needed to know and be sure about what I wanted before I talked to you or I'd risk losing you forever. I never planned to lead you on, please believe me. I have no desire to hurt you any more than I have. I care about you. I am certain of that. I know I have feelings for you that are past the point of being platonic. I just don't know about the rest. I don't want to lead you down a path and realize in a week or a month that I've made a mistake." I finally look up at her. "I don't want to lose you."

Alex stares at me, unreadable. The silence is more than I can take, but I let her process. "What do you want me to say?" Her voice is barely a whisper. It is clear that my confession has shaken her.

"Anything, please. What are you thinking right now?" My heart is pounding, fear cascades through me and the room feels like it is 20 degrees warmer than it was a minute ago.

"Honestly? So many things. I'm pissed because you lied to me, that you let me believe that everything was entirely my fault. That you let me feel like I am a terrible person, that I had violated some boundary. I am sad and hurting because you are hurting and have been going through this alone. I've never wanted that for you. I'm glad that you feel something but I am confused as to what I'm supposed to do with that knowledge." It is my turn to stare at Alex. "Now I'm scared, scared that since I know this, I will start to hope. Hope leads to heartache."

We sit in silence. I'm not sure for how long. Dinner has been forgotten. My tears continue to pour out of me. Eventually, I hear the sound of Alex sliding her chair back. She makes her way to me. I rise to meet her. She embraces me, the contact with her an intoxicant I've never known.

"I'm sorry," she whispers. I start to pull away, cupping her face in my hands. A tear falls down her cheek. I brush it away with my thumb and draw her face towards mine, I have to know. Alex stops me, searching my eyes. "Catherine...I can't." She breaks free from my arms and retreats to her apartment. The void her rejection tears through me bringing a new wave of tears. This time I don't fight it and the sobs take over.

Alexis

Catherine said she wanted to talk not stagger me with a truth bomb. My mind is in overdrive. My emotions battling each other. One minute I want to run upstairs and pin her to the wall, claim her mouth with my own. Then I remember the agony she suffered in front of me and tell myself I need to give her space. I try to put myself in her shoes but cannot, I've always known I was gay. I don't feel anger toward her anymore. I may not understand exactly what she is going through but I know I never thought I'd see Catherine reduced to the wreck she was when I pulled away from her. Rejecting her like that is one of the hardest things I have ever done. The hope in her face erased by my rebuff, her collapse and agonized wail as I walked away. I physically ache each time I replay the scene in my head. After an hour of the same thoughts ruminating in my mind, only one thing seems clear, I need to move out. Living here is no longer the right thing for either of us. Catherine's suffering is more than I can stand.

I grab my laptop and start searching for an immediate occupancy rental near work. The sooner I am out of here the sooner Catherine can start to heal. I find several options, so I start making a list. It is too late to call any of the numbers tonight.

*****

I arrive at work the next morning to discover that we are over staffed. Still rattled by Catherine's words last night and needing to find a new home, I volunteer to leave. By 9 am I am released for the day. I immediately get to work calling the numbers on my list.

The search is tedious. I don't require extravagance, just a reasonable amount of space in a place that is clean, a nice neighborhood, and something away from the students. By noon I am convinced that I will never find something. My phone rings while I am eating lunch. It isn't a number I recognize immediately. After three rings I realize it might be a return call from one of the classifieds I've contacted. I answer to hear the soft voice of a woman who identifies herself as Lydia. We talk about the rental for a few minutes, I get the address and agree to meet her there in half an hour.

I arrive at the property twenty minutes later. I want a chance to check out the surrounding area before I meet with Lydia. I am excited when I realize that the house is located in what is locally known as Dyke Heights. The neighborhood is nice, seems to be well kept and looks like it will be fairly quiet.

A few minutes after my arrival the front door opens, and Lydia greets me. She is probably in her mid 70's, shorter than me, and a little thick. She has short silver hair, glasses, and a warm smile. We shake hands, and she welcomes me into the house. It is warm and smells of fresh baked cookies. She offers me something to drink, and as she leaves to get me a glass of water, I take in my surroundings. The living room offers a lot to take in. My attention is drawn to a wall covered in photos. Some hold Lydia with two young women who resemble her enough that I assume they are her daughters. Others show Lydia with a woman closer to her own age, perhaps a sister. Others show Lydia with four teenagers, who I guess are her grandchildren. My observation is interrupted by Lydia returning with the water and offering me a seat.

We talk for a while, too long if I am honest. I am anxious to see the apartment, find out if it will meet my needs and move on if it won't. The day is passing quickly, and I still need to sort this out. Unfortunately, Lydia seems to want to know all about where I work, what I do for a living, and what interests I have. I learn that she is a retired professor, she has four grandchildren and that her partner died a little over a year ago from breast cancer. I glance at the photo of Lydia with the woman of similar age.

"Yes, that was my Clara," Lydia informs me, my glance having been spotted. My heart breaks a little for the loss this kind woman has endured.

"I'm sorry for your loss." I am unsure what else to say. I feel for Lydia but am not close enough to her to offer any real condolence.

"Oh don't be, it wasn't your fault." I realize I like Lydia. She is feisty. If I could chose a grandmother, I think I'd choose Lydia. We sit in silence for a few moments before Lydia suggests looking at the apartment.

The apartment itself sits over the top of the garage. Lydia informs me that it was originally built to offer one of her daughters a private living space while she went to school. After that, she and her partner had been renting it to graduate students. The most recent tenant graduated in December and had moved out. It is available immediately and is furnished with a couch, full-size bed and a dresser. Rent would include all utilities. So far everything sounds good.

We enter the garage and make our way up a set of stairs on the right. The door opens into a small entryway that is a large enough space for coat hooks on the wall, a small storage cabinet, and a washer and dryer. The short hall ends at a large open space that is comprised of the living room and kitchenette. The two rooms are separated by a small island bar with a set of barstools. The walls and carpet are neutral in color. The sofa is gray. Not a lot of personality, but it would work. The bedroom is tiny compared to the one at Catherine's, but given how little I typically sleep it would suffice. The bathroom is tiny as well but would meet my needs. I doubt that I will find anything that will check off as many of my requirements as this place does. I also like the idea of having a lesbian landlord and not sharing my walls with strangers.

"So what would the lease length be?" I am hoping to avoid a year long lease just in case I end up not liking the place.

"Well, I don't know. Typically the students are here, and they just let me know when they would be leaving. Some stayed for years, others for a few months. I've never really drawn up any formal paperwork with them before."

I am shocked. This is unheard of anymore. "I really don't know how long I will be here. I haven't rented in a long time. I was hoping to avoid a year long commitment, maybe get something month to month."

"I see. So you want to move in right away but don't want a lengthy commitment." It was a statement, not a question. "What are you running from? Bad breakup?" Lydia isn't just feisty, she is smart. It makes me like her even more.

I look at the floor, a slight sting of shame filling me; like I have been busted by my grandmother doing something I know I shouldn't. "Something like that I suppose."

Lydia looks at me a moment. I can't tell if she is assessing me or if she is thinking. "I've been there before and didn't have a place to go. Tell you what, we can make month to month work. All I ask is that you give me at least a months notice if you are going to move out."

I smile at Lydia. "Would I be able to move in tomorrow?"

"Dear, you can move in today as long as you have the rent and deposit."

We go back into the house where I write Lydia a check, and she gives me a set of keys. I thank her and head back to Catherine's to start packing.

Catherine

I lay in bed staring into the dark. All I can think about is Alex. All day during clinic today I was distracted by thoughts of her, our conversation from the previous night replaying in my head. I had bared myself to her, and she rejected me. Still what I want more than anything is to go to her, to make my way downstairs, take her in my arms and capture the kiss that had eluded me. I didn't see her at all today, and I missed her. Still, I lay tethered to my bed, unable to force the movement, unable to confront the woman who does not want me. I know she has Brooke now, and the self-pity I feel for letting my own opportunity pass is nearly too much to bear. It is just after 4 am. I get up and make my way through my morning routine, never seeing Alex.

*****

I have four cases today. Normally this wouldn't bother me, but I'm so distracted that I don't feel up to doing any of them. Despite this, I know that once I scrub in all thoughts will be on the surgery at hand, a welcome respite from the torrent of thoughts in my head.

I get to the room at 7:30 and start reviewing the patient films. Erin is there already preparing for the case. She is alone, which strikes me as odd. A few minutes later someone I've never met arrives. Erin seems to know him though.

"Hey Mike, what are you doing here?"

"Alex called in sick, so I'm filling in for her." He has my attention. Alex is sick? I want to rush home and take care of her, but know that isn't an option.

Erin laughs. "Yeah right, she hasn't called off sick in years. Where is she?"

"I told you, she called in."

Erin realizes that Mike isn't joking. "Wow. Never thought I'd see the day. Well, have you met Dr. Waters yet?"

Mike and I introduce ourselves to one another. I want to text Alex, to see if she is ok but she is likely sleeping and I don't want to wake her. I'm anxious to get started on my cases. I just want to wrap things up so I can go home and take care of Alex.

*****

We finally finish up our day just after 5. I'm exhausted but ready to spend this Friday night at home. Despite my exhaustion, I stop and grab some soup and Gatorade for Alex on my way home. I am not ready for what greets me when I arrive. Alex's car is gone. I enter through the garage and find a note on the counter along with the keys and her garage door opener. My stomach drops, my hands are shaking, I am crying again. She is gone. My trembling hands pick up the letter.

> Catherine,
>
> Sorry to move out like this, but had you known I think you would have tried to stop me. This is for the best. Please know that I never wanted to hurt you, to be the cause of the anguish and suffering I saw when we last spoke. To know that I caused it is more painful to me that you can imagine. I hope my absence allows you the space you need to find clarity and to heal.

Alexis

I read the letter three more times. Denial coursing through my system, I head to the basement. I call to her as I make my way down the stairs, but I'm calling to no one. Every trace of Alex is gone, all but the flashes of my memories of her in this space. Movie nights with her, sitting by the fire and chatting with her, coming down and finding her curled up with a book, seeing her naked silhouette the night of our fight. The last memory stirring up a desire deep within me. What if I had just gone to her then? Had kissed her at the party? So many what ifs, yet I know that even then I had no idea how I felt about her. Do I even really know now?

I want to call Alex, to hear her voice, speak with her. Somehow I know it isn't a good idea, that she will simply ignore any call or text from me. My need to know that she is ok is too strong though. I do the one thing I can, I text Abby asking if Alex is ok. It takes ten agonizing minutes before she responds. *She will be, are you?* It does little to make me feel better. I have no idea if I will be ok, so I don't respond.

I drink myself into an oblivion that night. It doesn't take much given that I never ate lunch or dinner. All I want is anything that will dull the pain. I come to on the couch in the basement, the television on a movie I've never seen. I shut it off and head to the bedroom, where Alex used to sleep. I take in its emptiness for a minute before heading up to my own. I don't bother getting out of bed on Saturday other than to use the bathroom. I just want to hide from the world, to be alone in my solitude.

Sunday morning I wake up starving. It has been two days since I've eaten. I go to the kitchen and fix myself some toast. I feel disgusting, in need of a shower. The realization that tomorrow is an OR day hits me. I'll get to see Alex. I feel hope and comfort at this thought, even though I know I shouldn't, that she has moved on and does not wish to see me.

*****

Rounding and consults take longer than I anticipated they would. I don't make it downstairs until nearly 8 am. I enter the core leading to my OR for the day, running into Abby half way to my room. "Hey, Abby." I know there is no enthusiasm in my voice.

"Hi, Catherine. How are you doing?" Abby surprises me by pulling me in for a hug. I know that she has spoken with Alex, that she knows everything. A few people glance at us as they pass us in the hallway.

"I'm trying." It is the only response I can give her, anything else would be a lie. "How is she?" I have to know.

"Just checked in with her. I think she is alright, although she wouldn't let on if she wasn't. Not here." She is right, Alex won't show it here, not if she can help it. We stand in silence for a brief moment before I dismiss myself, I need to get my case started.

I am scrubbing at the shared sink between rooms four and five; when Alex emerges from room five. She pauses when she sees me, her mask hiding any emotion I might have been able to read. She glances at the floor then takes up position next to me. I am unsure what to say, my heart is pounding, I am so happy to see her, yet saddened by the current state of our friendship. I long to reach out and touch her, yet cannot, despite my skin aching to make contact with hers. I can't tolerate the silence, it makes Alex feel like a stranger, makes me miss her even more. "Hey." One syllable, the one hushed syllable I can manage.

"Hi." Then nothing, the silence between us is torture. My scrub is complete, I needed to get in and start my case yet all I can do is stand there, watching her, my hands above my elbows, the water dripping onto the floor. Alex finishes her scrub and turns to back into her room.

"Alex." I stop her. The compulsion too great for me to resist. "I miss you," comes out of me in a barely audible whisper.

She looks at me, and I see her eyes crystallize as she fights back the tears. "Catherine...please don't." With that, she backs through the door into room five. This is the new normal between us. Taylor was right, I told Alex how I feel, and I have lost her.

Alexis

A knock at the door pulls me from the reverie I have found in my newest book. I know it has to be Lydia, she is the only one with keys to the garage. "I'm sorry to bother you, I just wanted to see how you are settling in. I haven't seen or heard much from you." It has been just over a week since I moved in and I hadn't thought to check-in with her.

"No problem Lydia, please come in. Would you like something to drink?" I get Lydia her requested glass of water and join her in the living room. Lydia is eyeing the book I left sitting on the couch.

"Haven't read that one. What's it about?"

"Vampires mostly. I'm not sure where it will head, but it is distracting me at least."

"Never had time for those. I like a good drama with a happy ending."

I smile at Lydia, and the words slip out before I can stop them. "I don't think I can handle a happy ending right now."

Lydia gives me a look, one that I'm sure is of mild disapproval. "You want to talk about it? Maybe I can share some life wisdom with you, I've been around for forever now."

I can't help but smile and hope I have half the spirit I think Lydia has when I'm older. "I shouldn't bother you with it really. Thank you though."

"Nonsense, what else do you think I have going on?"

I recount the story to Lydia, pausing here and there to maintain my composure. "This isn't how I wanted things. I never wanted to see her hurting like that. I had to leave so she can heal and move on, and maybe I can do the same." Lydia stares at me, or maybe through me. She seems lost in thought. Perhaps she just thinks I'm crazy. I have no idea.

"When I first met my Clara I was married to John. He was a good man, took care of his family, was a great father, would have moved the sky if he thought it would make a loved one happy. We had been married for nearly 10 years when I met Clara that day at the library. We became fast friends, spending as much time together as we could. I knew early on that Clara was a lesbian for she had confided it to me one day. It didn't bother me. The war came, and John rejoined the service, he was loyal to his country and wanted to serve her in her time of need. The girls were still babies. I pleaded with him not to go, but he had made up his mind. It may be the only time he ever denied me anything. Clara was there for me, she kept me company, let me cry on her shoulder, helped me with the girls. I'm not sure I would have made it through those first few months if it weren't for her. John was gone just over two years. He came home, and Clara gradually disappeared from my life. I fell into a depression. John tried everything he could to make me happy, nothing worked. As my despondency grew greater so did John's desperation. One day I saw Clara at the library. It was there she told me her true feelings, that she had fallen in love with me. She had been avoiding me in an effort to get past her feelings. It took me two months to realize that I was actually in love with Clara. I tried to deny it, I was unsure how I could be. I knew that I loved John, it was just that I loved Clara more, needed her more, longed to be with her. Although I struggled to accept my feelings I couldn't hurt John. He had always been an ideal husband, and I could not put him through my leaving. So I stayed.

John and I went on for nearly a year like this, but John was wise. One day he came home and informed me that he thought we should divorce. I was shocked. John told me that he loved me, that he would always love me, but he couldn't stand to see me suffer any longer. He told me he was freeing me to follow my heart. I don't possess the words to tell you how I felt, but imagine your heart breaking and taking flight all in one breath. The man who I tried to honor, who had never done wrong by me once, was sacrificing our marriage so I could be happy. It didn't take me long to track down Clara and confess my feelings to her. We were together for forty years when she passed."

I am stunned, grasping for the appropriate words to respond to Lydia. How does one respond to a story like that, especially when the person it happened to is in front of you recounting it? I finally find my voice "Lydia I—."

"Now I'm not done." I immediately give Lydia my cooperation and stop trying to talk. "My point is this, you have no idea the emotional hell that Catherine is going through. You've taken her world, turned it on its head and spun it for good measure. I'm not sure how she is functioning day to day, I know I couldn't. I'm not blaming you. We love who we love, there is no controlling that. However, I am telling you that it doesn't matter if you ran away trying to spare her the hurt she is going through, if she cares about you, it won't matter if you are there or not. Those feelings don't go away on their own, not if they are real. Hiding here isn't going to make you forget about her either. It seems pretty clear she has feelings for you, she told you as much. You just need to give her time to decide whether she is going to live honestly by those feelings or if she is going to lie to herself about them for the rest of her life."

I sit in contemplative silence, tears streaming down my face. The combination of Lydia's story and the emotional roller coaster I've been on lately are too much to contain. Lydia goes back to the bathroom and brings me a tissue. She takes her glass and deposits it in the kitchen sink. She heads towards the short hallway that leads to the exit and stops before she is out of my line of sight. "Come down to the house for dinner tonight around six. We can talk some more about this, or not. Your choice. It won't be fancy, but I can promise you won't leave hungry." I nod my head, affirming that I will be there. Lydia sees herself out, leaving me to the new round of thoughts weighing on my mind.

*****

Three weeks have passed since Lydia confided her story to me. Things between Catherine and I are unchanged. I am still trying to avoid her at work and will not answer her calls or texts. On the days I have to scrub her cases I keep our interactions to a minimum and strictly case related. Being the ice queen towards her isn't getting easier though. Each day my resolve erodes a little bit more, my feelings for her impossible to deny.

As usual, I don't sleep much past 4 am on that Friday morning. I get up and assume my new routine. I turn on the weather to discover they are calling for a winter storm starting this morning and stretching into the late night. Looking out the window, I observe that nothing has accumulated yet. I get ready for work and head down a few minutes early to spread some salt on the driveway and Lydia's porch before I leave. I've made an effort these last few weeks to keep her driveway, porch, and sidewalks clear and salted after I discovered her outside shoveling one morning. I am just finishing laying down salt when Lydia pops her head out the door.

"I wish you would let me take care of that."

"I don't mind. It is too cold out here anyway. Stay in the house where it is warm and dry. I'll take care of the shoveling when I get home. You need me to pick anything up for you on my way?"

"I went shopping yesterday, so I'll be fine. If you are around Sunday, I am hosting the monthly dykes dinner. You should come. We will eat around five, but people will start showing up around two."

"Thanks. I'll come down if I'm here. Have a good day." 10 hours separate me from my weekend. My plans free, no obligations weekend. Abby is out of town at a conference, so no Friday night dinner. I plan to take advantage of the opportunity to have a 'mental me' weekend. 10 hours and I'll be free to put on my sweats, shut off my phone and be a recluse for two whole days.

Catherine

Today is the day I reaffirm to my reflection as I reach for my toothbrush. Today I will speak with Alex. I need to tell her how I feel. I know she has moved on with Brooke, but I need her to know. I don't think I can last another day without having her in my life in some capacity. I long for her in a way I don't ever recall feeling before.

I get up and ready for work early. I am on-call this weekend, so I pack a bag to last a few days. With the impending snow storm staying at the hospital is my safest bet. I give myself a few extra minutes to get to work this morning just in case, minutes that I end up not needing. I have three cases today and four patients upstairs I hope to discharge before the storm starts. Discharge orders complete, I head down to the OR, anxious to find Alex.

My search for Alex is pointless. I am unable to find her. Determined as I may be, I am forced to give up when my phone rings. It is the Jessica, the PA who is currently on call for us. My second patient has rescheduled their surgery due to the impending weather. Understandable. I ask her to contact my last patient to see if they are available earlier. I intend to resume my search when a colleague stops me to ask if I'd be willing to work his mother into clinic next week. I gladly accept, give him the office number and make a quick call to leave our scheduling secretary a message informing her that the request would be coming. I'm free to seek out Alex again. I finally find her, but she is scrubbed in setting up in another doctor's room. I give up for the time being and head to pre-op to initial my first patient and sign the consent forms. It is time to get this day truly underway.

*****

I finish my last case just after noon. I still need to see Alex, to talk to her. I stop by the OR she is in to find her scrubbed in yet again. I make my way to the consult room and speak with the family. There aren't any new consults yet, so I decide to grab some lunch and head to Alex's preferred lunch spot. It is a long shot, I know she has likely already had her break, but it is an effort I have to make. I eat my lunch without interruption, the compulsion unfulfilled. I am starting to feel like a stalker. I need to stop. I tell myself I will see Alex when I see her. I stare out the window taking in the heavy snowfall, trying to forget the litany of thoughts I can't seem to shake. It is just before three when I pull myself back to reality. I take out my laptop to finish the charting I have left to do. That done I decide I should find an available on call room. Sleep will likely not come, but I need to try before the inevitable trauma consults begin this evening.

I settle into the on call room and run through the mental checklist of things I need to take care of. Aside from responding to a few emails, I am caught up. I try calling Taylor but get her voicemail. The realization of how exhausted I am starts to sink in. I start a movie on my laptop and settle in on the cot.

I come to four hours later. I am in disbelief, still no consults. I also realize that I've missed Alex, she will be long gone by now. Not wanting to sit around idly ruminating about Alex I head to the ER. Perhaps they are busy and can use a hand with something. I check in with Dr. Andrews, the trauma surgeon for the night. He seems relaxed and is chatting with the resident physicians. I am out of luck, even the ER is relatively quiet.

I settle back into the on call room. I should grab something to eat, but I'm not hungry. Instead, I opt for my current novel, a book about a female detective who excels at her job but is falling apart in her personal life. I can relate.

The sound of the trauma pager on my phone brings me back to consciousness. It is nearly 9. I've slept more today than I have all week. I fumble for my phone to see what it is. A motor vehicle accident victim, level one, estimated arrival time of five minutes.

I arrive at the ER trauma bay and meet Dr. Andrews. He begins to fill me in. Unconscious female, driver of the vehicle struck on the driver's side door by a city bus. He is cut-off when the paramedics arrive with the patient.

I stand back and let the trauma team start their initial assessment. Dr. Andrews will alert me when it is time. I pick up what I need to know. Unidentified female, head trauma with a GCS of 6T, facial lacerations. I wait. Dr. Andrews and his trauma residents make their initial assessments. No immediately noticeable abdominal injuries or open fractures. In less than a minute he calls me over. I make my way toward the patient, finally able to get a suitable look. My blood turns to ice, and my heart stops beating, the woman is Alex. The room swims around me. Dr. Andrews picks up on my hesitation immediately "Do you know who this is?"

I'm frozen, the doctor brain pushing me to save her, the personal brain wanting to collapse at the sight of Alex lying there unresponsive. Andrews asks me again. "She is Alexis Woods. She is one of our scrub techs." It is enough. The doctor brain is taking over. I confirm the GCS score. Not good. "I need her in CT immediately."

Andrews doesn't argue. Alex is quickly wheeled down the hall for a head and abdominal CT. I call downstairs for the team to set up an OR immediately, telling them they have 10 minutes. I hang up and realize I need to warn them, they need to be informed and ready. I call back and inform the charge nurse who our patient really is. She is shaken but assures me that they are already preparing the OR. I pace the hall outside of CT, waiting for the results, assuring myself that a GCS of 6T can be recovered from. I need the information, these minutes are taking forever.

The CT is finally finished, the longest two minutes of my life I can remember complete. I scan them quickly. Subdural hematoma, 3 mm midline shift, no noticeable lesion, no cervical injury and abdominal organs do not appear to be bleeding. The best case scenario I can hope for given the circumstances. I still need to intervene, to relieve the pressure from her brain before further damage is done. We are on our way down to the OR less than two minutes after the scan is complete.

The elevator ride to the basement seems to take an eternity, even though it is only one level. During this unending ride, my brain somehow manages to make me realize I have another call I need to make. I take out my phone and call Abby, the closest thing to family Alex has. We are off the elevator and halfway to the OR before she finally picks up. "Catherine?"

"Abby. There's been an accident. I'm taking her to the OR now. You should probably get here soon." It takes all I have to force the miniature sentences.

"Catherine, who?"

"Alex. It's Alex." In my panic I have forgotten that Abby has a daughter.

"I'm in San Antonio, I'll be on the next flight out."

Shit. I need someone here for Alex. "I'll leave my phone with the nurse and will call you when we are out of the OR." I make to hang up the phone when I hear Abby shout my name. "Abby?"

175

"No extreme measures, she doesn't want extreme measures."

*****

The house and my soul are empty shells. Everywhere I look I see Alex, only Alex is gone. Images of her cold, lifeless body flood my mind when I close my eyes. I couldn't save her. I failed her when I couldn't admit my feelings for her, and I failed her when her life was on the line. Despite Taylor, Abby and her daughter staying here the past few days, the house feels more empty than ever. I haven't left my bedroom since the night Alex died. They bring me food that I leave untouched and water that I drink when they force me to.

The day of Alex's memorial service arrives, and I can't bring myself to get out of bed. It takes the combined efforts of Abby and Taylor to push me out the door. How can I go? How can I stand there with Alex's chosen family when my failure is the reason we will all be there? I couldn't save her. A part of me has died with her.

We arrive at the memorial, not a service or funeral. Abby had been entrusted with a copy of Alex's will a few years ago. Alex was adamant that she wanted to be cremated and there was to be no funeral. Her instructions were that she wanted us to move on with our lives, take care of one another, love each other. Abby takes my hand and squeezes it, looking over at me when she discovers how sweaty my hands are. "She loved you you know?"

I nod my head hoping that I could have been so lucky. "I'll never get to tell her how I feel though, that I am ready."

"She knew." But she didn't know really. The thought of my failure compounded by my inability to love Alex the way she deserved sparks a rage in me like I've never felt before. I take in the scene around me. The picture of Alex they have chosen is wrong, it doesn't do her eyes or warm smile justice. The urn is wrong, it is too plain. It fails to reflect any of the beauty or complexity of the person whose remains it now holds. I look at the foods people are eating, none of them Alex's favorites. Even the music is wrong, I've never heard Alex listen to any of these songs. Did these people even know Alex, the beautiful woman that she was? I realize that I have failed her again, that my inability to function these past few days has resulted in a memorial that disappoints her memory.

"I need to get out of here," I inform Taylor as everyone listens to Abby's speech. My skin itches being here, the anger is growing at a fever pitch, I feel an urge to scream.

"Catherine we can't." I am flanked by Taylor and Sara, each of them holding one of my hands.

My agitation is growing by the second, threatening to spill over beyond my control. "No Taylor, I need to get out of here now!" I am shouting by the time I finish the sentence. Abby stops in the middle of her eulogy and looks in my direction. Everyone is looking in my direction, but I do not care. My blood boils, and I am ready to rage.

"Catherine." Someone is calling me. I turn looking for the source. "Catherine!"

I sit up, covered in a cold sweat. My hand is holding Alex's. "Catherine. You were having a nightmare. I thought you were going to toss yourself out of that chair."

Abby has arrived. I look at the clock on the wall, it is after 4 am. The cold sweat and lingering images from the dream give me the chills, despite the room being plenty warm.

"Well?"

I sigh. "I did all I could do. I relieved the pressure, GCS is still at 6T, small midline shift, no lesions on the scan, her ICP is looking good. I gave her a few burr holes and drains. All we can do is wait and continue to evaluate." Abby looks at Alex, then back at me. I know that her weariness and heartbreak match my own. Her chosen sister, lying in this bed, both of us helpless to do anything to help.

"Prognosis?"

I don't want to think about this, to put the same weight on Abby. I know she won't let it go though. "Fair. Any GCS below 8 has a much lower rate of full recovery than scores above 8. That is scoring without intubation. The paramedics tubed her when they arrived on the scene. They indicated that witnesses said she was initially conscious but wasn't speaking coherently. She lost consciousness before they arrived. They tubed her to protect her airway. Positives are that she is young, healthy, and was treated very quickly following the accident. If there had been any sort of delay, the outcome would likely have been much worse than where we are now."

"What are you telling me?"

"There is hope. The next 24 hours are pivotal though. I have another CT scan ordered in the morning. I don't see anything that gives me extreme concern on the original CT other than the bleed. Pray if that is your thing. I'm not leaving her side unless I have to."

We sit in silence for what feels like days. My sole focus is Alex. I barely register that Abby is here. I am not sure why it occurs to me but I realize that someone else should be notified. "Alex's phone wasn't on her. I have no way to call Brooke. You should call her." It tears at my heart to tell her this, but I know it is the right thing to do.

Abby looks at me, her brow furrowed in confusion. "Brooke? Why would I call Brooke?"

Why is she confused? I know it isn't a sensitivity issue. "Because they are together, at least they were before Alex moved out."

Abby's look shifts from confusion to amusement. She accidentally lets out a small snigger. "Sorry, that was inappropriate." She sits for a minute, composing herself and staring at me. I feel like I'm under a microscope. "You think Alex and Brooke are together?" I nod my head. "Look, it isn't my place to tell you, but they aren't together. Sure they were a couple many years ago, and they may have been together for a night recently, but Brooke is usually a reaction for Alex. She lives in Seattle. Occasionally she comes home to see her family. When she does, if they are both single, they get together. They have…good chemistry I guess you could say. Anyway, Alex typically turns to Brooke when something is wrong. What you saw was Alex's way of torturing herself over your situation. Alex tends to get a little down that time of year and all the stress between the two of you didn't help. She and Alex communicated, and Brooke arranged a trip home. Simple as that." Abby's eyes stay fixed on me, but the more information she shares with me, the less I actually see her.

I feel it then, a small blossom struggling for the sunlight. Hope. Abby's words have given me hope. Alex isn't with Brooke, maybe there can still be a chance. All I'm longing for is a chance. A chance to tell her how I feel, that I want to be with her, that I'm sorry for not figuring it out sooner. I just need the chance to say the things that I've left unsaid.

"You love her, don't you?" Abby's question interrupts the endless string of promises I find myself making Alex in my mind.

"Yeah." I refuse to deny it anymore. Abby finally shifts her gaze back to Alex, and smiles.

*****

Transport personnel arrives to take Alex down for her CT scan. As much as I want to go with her, I need to round on my other patients. Abby wakes at the commotion.

"They are here to take Alex down to her CT scan. I've given them the ok to bathe her when she comes back. I need to do my rounds and should grab something to eat. She will be back from CT in a twenty minutes or so."

"Ok. Will you be here? I could take this chance to go home, shower, change, check in with my daughter. Update her on Aunt Alex."

"The only way I'm leaving is if a trauma comes in. Otherwise, I'm not going anywhere. Take your time. I'll update you when you get back."

"Can I bring you anything? Food, something else?"

"Thanks. I'll survive off of the cafeteria though." We walk out together, the two of us behind the head of Alex's bed. This is the longest I've gone without her hand in mine since she got to the ICU. My hand feels cold and empty, I can hardly stand it. As if we possess a psychic link Abby takes my hand and squeezes it.

"Our girl is going to be ok. I know she is." Even at a time like this Abby's optimism never ceases.

*****

I check the time and realize I've finished rounds too quickly. Alex's latest CT will not be in the system yet. I head downstairs to the cafeteria for some food. I settle for an omelet and a fruit smoothie. I head up to the overflow floor, hoping to find it empty. Breakfast finished I find myself staring out the window, recounting everything Alex and I have been through. Could it all have been for nothing? Somehow I start thinking about Taylor. We haven't really spoken since her visit aside from a few text messages here and there, the time difference and our conflicting schedules make it difficult. I check my phone and see that it is just before 10 am, still quite early in San Francisco. I know I'll be waking her up, but I go with the urge and dial her number anyway.

"Cat?" I'm greeted by a raspy, groggy voice on the fourth ring.

"Hey, Taylor."

"What time is it? Everything ok?" I'm not sure why, but her words set something off in me, the avalanche of emotions that I have been suppressing along with those as yet unreleased from last night become too much. I completely lose it and am sobbing in seconds.

"Whoa, hey I'm up." Taylor is certainly awake now. "Cat? Cat take a deep breath, try to calm down." It takes me a few minutes to finally regain some composure. Taylor quietly waits for my breathing to settle and the sobs to stop. That or she has fallen asleep. "Cat what the hell is going on?"

"Everything Taylor. Everything is wrong." I proceed to fill Taylor in on all the events I can recall since her visit, starting with Alex's accident. She listens with only a few interruptions to ask questions or for clarification. I finish and take a deep breath. I know I shouldn't, but somehow I feel slightly better having just said everything out loud.

"Let me get on a plane, I can be there tonight." Taylor's offer surprises me, it is a level of support we've rarely shown one another.

"I truly appreciate the offer Taylor, but there isn't anything you can do. Time is the factor right now. I did all I could last night, of that I am certain."

"Are you sure you don't want me to come out? It isn't an issue. There may not be much I could do for Alex, but at least I could be there for you." Again I find myself shocked, who is this woman that I am speaking with?

"No, stay out there. I can keep you updated on any changes."

"Ok. If you change your mind, let me know." Silence fills the line for a few moments. "So you never told her?"

"Never told her what?"

"You never told her how you feel about her? That you love her. You do love her right?"

I sigh. "Yeah, I do. I wanted to tell her, intended to try to talk to her yesterday, never had the chance."

"So go tell her now! Get off this phone and go tell her!" I've never heard Taylor so passionate about expressing one's emotions.

"Taylor maybe I wasn't clear before, but Alex is comatose right now." The thought drives another dagger into my aching heart. The tears threaten to return to the forefront.

"So what. I've heard about people in comas waking up and reporting that they remember hearing all sorts of things. Cat go do it! At least then you will have told her. You need to do it for yourself."

"You mean in case she doesn't wake up, or doesn't recover?" Tears are burning trails down my cheeks again. Either a possible reality, neither one I can accept or wrap my mind around.

"Yeah, unfortunately. Just think about it."

"Ok. I will."

"Go now Cat! If you change your mind about me coming out, I'll be there."

"Thanks, Taylor."

*****

I go down to the OR locker room for a quick shower before I head back to the ICU. After my talk with Taylor, I'm sure Alex is back from CT and bathed. It adds 10 anxiety filled minutes to my absence. I need to get back up there.

I return to Alex's room and discover she is back and indeed bathed. I don't need to inquire with the nurses, the smell that greets me is wrong. It doesn't smell like Alex. I check her drains and see that the drainage has slowed to very minimal output. I will recheck them later today and if the output is still minimal remove them, reducing the risk of infection. I looked over the facial lacerations caused by the glass from the window. They all look clean and dry. I

183

had essentially forced Sara, the on call plastics attending, to come look at them after I finished the burr holes last night. She was initially pissed off and fought it but quickly changed her tune when I told her who the patient was. We spent half an hour examining each cut, ensuring that the small wounds were clear of glass and adequately washed out. After closing the deeper gash, she assured me that she thought the facial lacerations would heal nicely and leave minimal to no scarring. As if I cared about a few scars when the risks were so much greater.

I want to run another GCS diagnosis to check for improvement but decide that I should look at the new CT results first. I pull out my laptop and log into the server. Alex's films are available. I don't bother reading the written report. I want to see them and form my own conclusions first. The scans show what I have hoped for and expected. The bleed is under control, the midline shift is shrinking, her pressure is still good. I pour over the films searching for the smallest of defects indicating permanent damage. I still cannot find any. I open the written report to confirm. My findings concur with those of the radiologist.

I take up my post next to her bed taking her right hand in mine. I rest my chin on the safety, oblivious to the discomfort the cold plastic causes. I can't get any closer to her without crawling into her bed. Taylor's advice keeps crossing my mind. At one point I realize that I have started caressing her face, alternating between slowly running the tip of my thumb over her cheek and the backs of my index and middle fingers down her jaw line. I don't bother to stop. I need to feel close to her. Without warning, words start spilling out of me. "Alex, I'm sorry. I'm sorry for the hell I've put you through. Sorry that I haven't been honest with you or myself. Sorry that you felt like you had to sacrifice your feelings to save me from my own. Most of all I want you to know that I love you. I need you to wake up.

A part of me will die if you don't, I am sure of it. I love you Alex, and I am ready. Please come back."

A knock at the door interrupts me. I assume it is either a nurse or Abby. I give a cursory swipe at the tears on my cheeks as I tell them to come in. My back is to the door, and I don't bother turning to see who it is.

"Dr. Waters?" Erin is the unexpected visitor. I barely recognize her without her scrubs and a bonnet on. She has seen everything, the image crystal clear in front of her. Me sitting vigil at Alex's bedside, holding her hand, crying. I don't bother moving away or relinquishing her hand. There is no point. I had forgotten that Erin was the tech last night during Alex's surgery.

"Hello, Erin. Thanks for stopping by." She takes a seat on the other side of the bed.

"How is she?" I can see Erin's eyes taking in Alex's condition. She was there last night, she knows the baseline. She also knows that I cannot legally tell her anything related to Alex's case or care. "Not much change then. Drainage looks good though." No questions, just verbal observations, and assessment.

Our silence is broken by my phone going off. I have a consult, a patient has fallen and has a cervical spine fracture. I curse inwardly and start to panic. Depending on the location of the fracture this could require emergency intervention. I release Alex's hand so I can grab my laptop and pull up the patient's CT. The fracture is a small chip of bone off of the C4 spinous process. Thankfully it has dislodged itself posteriorly and should cause no threat to the spinal cord. I could go down and remove the fragment, but it isn't worth putting someone through surgery for that reason alone. I look through the scan one more time, double checking for missed fractures or any compression on the spinal cord. Everything else looks great.

"We have something coming down?" I jump, having forgotten that Erin is here.

"Nope, just a consult. Small chip off of C4 posteriorly."

"Brace it is then." Erin knows her stuff. It makes me appreciate her that much more. I return the call to the trauma resident informing him of my findings, instructing him to admit the patient and put him in a Miami J cervical collar. We will keep him for observation and pain management until he feels like he is ok to go home.

"Erin, why was she out so late last night?" I've resumed my post, Alex's hand back in mine.

"What do you mean?"

"I mean why was she out in that weather so late last night? Her shift ended hours before her accident. What was she thinking?"

"Her shift should have ended. She volunteered to stay late when most of the evening staff had called in, and we didn't have enough techs to handle the cases we had going. We both did."

I shake my head in disbelief. She could have avoided this. If she had just been selfish for once and gone home, we wouldn't be here. Hadn't she told me Elena had said the same thing to her over and over again? Oh crap, Elena! I have no idea what to do about Elena, no idea if they have even spoken since Alex moved out of her house. I will have to leave it with Abby.

"So the two of you huh?" I am so focused on the Elena thing that Erin's question fails to register.

"Sorry?"

Erin looks pointedly at my hand, the one locked around Alex's. "The two of you. Are you the reason she has been miserable these past few months?" Erin isn't known for mincing words, something that I admire. This, however, is dangerous territory. My observations have given me the impression that she isn't one for gossip, but even this might be too much for her to keep quiet.

"Erin, I—."

"Look I don't care about some scandal or stirring up some new rumor for everyone to sink their teeth into. I just want to know if you're the reason why Alex hasn't been herself lately. If you're why she has shut herself off, why she is running on autopilot, why she just wants to work and go home to be alone."

I had no idea that it had gotten that bad, no idea that Alex was suffering so much. Consumed by my own emotions I had failed to see how much she has been hurting. "It's complicated."

"Not really. Pretty basic. You either care about her, or you don't."

"Still way more complicated than that. Look I will give you a brief summary, but I need you to hold it in confidence. Can you do that?" Erin nods that she can. I give her a basic outline of events, keeping things as simplified as I can. When I finish, Erin has no immediate response.

"You know there isn't a rule forbidding it." I have reestablished my focus on Alex, so it takes a second for me to follow Erin's intent. When I don't answer she continues. "They won't allow her to scrub your cases anymore, just in case there is ever a lawsuit. That is it, the whole policy. People in a relationship can't work in the same room." A sacrifice worth making in my book. Hell, at this moment I'd give up operating altogether if Alex would wake up and be ok.

A few minutes later Erin rises from her seat and heads towards the door. She stops at the foot of the bed and looks at me, waiting for me to shift my focus to her. "When she wakes up, you don't get to hurt her anymore. Time to either call or fold doc." I had no idea Erin is a poker player. She doesn't wait for my response, just makes her way out the door.

*****

I realize I've drifted off again as I wake up with my head resting on Alex's thigh. It takes a second for me to sense that I've let go of her hand as well. I reclaim her hand and give it a gentle squeeze. "At least I didn't drool in your lap." Something stops me, real or imagined I'm unsure. Could my wishful thinking be playing tricks on me or did Alex just respond? It dawns on me that I forgot to reevaluate her GCS score earlier. *Ok calm down Catherine, think with your head, not with your heart.* I take a moment to collect myself, steel myself for what I'm about to discover. I squeeze her hand, trying to replicate the pressure I used last time. Nothing. "Come on Alex, I need you to squeeze my hand," I plead as I give hers another gentle squeeze. There! It takes a second, but this time I'm sure. She is trying to respond. I keep hold of her hand, I can't let it go now. "Alex I need you to open your eyes." I wait patiently. "Alex open your eyes." Movement, finally movement, even if it was just the slightest twitch. She can't open them, but she at least has movement. I let go of her hand only to recheck her other stimuli responses.

Still good. I call respiratory. I want to take the tube out, but need to be sure they agree it is the right call.

Abby returns while I'm consulting with respiratory. The look of concern is immediate as she enters the room and sees all the unfamiliar faces evaluating Alex, making their determination. Eventually, Dr. Shaw turns to me. I can't read him, maybe my personal attachment here is serving as a block. I know my anxiety is making me impatient. I want to grab him by the lab coat and shake the answer out of him.

"I agree the tube can come out. She'll need close monitoring though, just to be safe." I look to Abby, the relief visible on her face.

"Neither of us are going anywhere." Satisfied he and his staff get organized, their suction at the ready, a replacement tube on hand just in case. Neither Abby or I can sit, our anxiety is too high. We've clasped hands again as we stand and wait.

"Ok, all good." I don't realize I've been holding my own breath until Dr. Shaw makes the announcement. The exhalation taking a small bit of the weight off my shoulders with it. I can feel Abby looking at me expectantly as the respiratory team takes their leave.

"Tell me what happened!" We take our seats as I fill her in.

"We still have a lot of hurdles to clear, but she is moving in the right direction. When they brought her in she had a good reaction to painful stimuli, but she was unconscious. Her response to stimuli is still good, now she is starting to respond to verbal commands as well. By taking the tube, out we can obtain a more accurate measure of where she is at."

"So right now?"

"I'm cautiously optimistic."

*****

Abby left her daughter with her mother so she would be free to stay with Alex. I am grateful for the company and that she will be here if I have to operate. We set up my laptop and find a few movies to watch, the rule being they have to be movies that Alex loves. Abby makes a quick trip to the cafeteria and gift shop to procure caffeine and snacks. We settle in for a long movie night, neither of us wanting to miss it if Alex shows any improvement. I choose first and select *Carol*. Abby hasn't seen it yet, and I know Alex has been waiting for the digital release so she can own it. I remember when Alex and I saw it over Thanksgiving, how I identified with Therese and couldn't understand how Carol could lead her along that path, knowing what her situation was. Now I know how big of a fool I was for feeling that way, I've now seen it from a new perspective.

We finish *Carol* and take a break to stretch our legs. I use the time to check Alex's drains. They are still nearly empty, so I elect to take them out and put an order in for another CT tomorrow afternoon, just to be sure the bleed is still under control and her pressure is still good. I'm being overly cautious, I know, and I don't care. Abby isn't back yet, so I talk to Alex. I remind her how I feel about her and plead with her to wake up. Abby eventually returns, and we start up her choice, *Sliding Doors*.

Although I've seen *Sliding Doors* before and enjoyed it, I can't help but start playing out all the what if's that could have altered Alex's outcome in my head. I know it is pointless, but I cannot stop it, they play endlessly on. I finally get to the question that I still don't know the answer to. It doesn't matter that the movie is on, I have to ask the one person who might know. "Abby, why did Alex leave?" Abby looks at me, and it is clear that she is not following what I'm asking. "Why did she move out? I never asked her to, never wanted her to. So why?"

Abby sighs and looks at Alex as if she is waiting for her approval. "I'm not sure I should be telling you this. It really is pretty obvious if you think about it, although I doubt she would ever admit to it if you confronted her with it. She ran because she is scared." I don't follow, the pieces of the puzzle I have aren't lining up the way Abby suggests they should. I look at Alex then back to Abby. "Think about it. Everyone who should have been there for her no matter what has abandoned her at some point. Her father never cared or took a real interest in her, her mother was cordial at best when Alex lived by her rules and standards. As soon as Alex fought against those her mother tossed her aside. The people she is closest to have all proven that they aren't going anywhere in some way. When you told her you weren't sure how you felt it set off the alarms. She couldn't allow herself to continue to develop deeper feelings for you thinking you would abandon her. So she protected herself the one way she knew how to, she left."

I've forgotten about the movie, Abby's information playing on a loop in my head. I squeeze Alex's hand, willing her to understand that I'm here, that I'm not going anywhere. A small twitch is her response, not huge but more movement than earlier in the day.

*****

Sunday morning arrives without any change. Abby agrees to hang around so I can complete my rounds, shower and eat. I complete my rounds and discharge one of Dr. Hasting's patients. Rounds and charting finished, I quickly make my way to the cafeteria where I grab a bacon, egg and cheese sandwich on a biscuit. I practically inhale it as I make my way to the locker room for a quick shower and change of scrubs. I just want to get back upstairs to the ICU, to Alex's side. I realize that my impatient nature is not helping, but I really hoped to see some more improvement by now. I am starting to become paranoid that I elected to remove her drains too soon and the bleed is not under control, increasing the pressure on her brain. Constant reminders to myself that her progress is normal are not helping to alleviate my anxiety.

I get back to the room as quickly as possible. I try to tell myself it is so that Abby can take her leave, go home, shower, eat and check-in with friends to update them, but selfishly I know it is because it is where I want to be. I tell her to take her time; that I will send a text if someone comes in that I need to operate on. I know I have been quite lucky so far this weekend, luck that is guaranteed to run out.

I find myself alone with Alex again. I check her incision sites and facial lacerations. Things still look good. Her lips are dry, so I grab my chapstick from my bag. She has some facial twitches while I'm applying it, the sight reinvigorating the hope that was starting to fade. I take her hand once more and stroke her face as I talk to her. I tell her that I can't wait for her to wake up so we can see what this is between us. I tell her that I'm here and I'm not going anywhere. I tell her I need her to wake up so I can tell her all of these things when she will remember them. I take out a book and read aloud to her for a while. Probably not a book she would read under normal circumstances, but it is what I have with me. When I tire of the sound of my own voice, I set up the laptop and start an *Game of Thrones*. Many people have told me over the years that I need to watch it and I know Alex loves it. I am halfway through the second episode when I realize that tomorrow is Monday and I have cases scheduled. I pull out my phone and look at my calendar to see what it is I am supposed to be doing. Three elective back cases, none of them urgent. I contact the on call PA and ask her to contact the patients to reschedule. It doesn't matter to me that I will end up working late several nights to make up for it, I just need to be with Alex.

I am a few episodes into the show when transport arrives to take Alex for her CT. I need to stretch my legs, so I make the trip down to CT with them. I know it will be a little while, so I head down the hall to the ER just to see if anything is happening.

"Dr. Waters, I was just about to page you." I turn to see one of the trauma residents, I am not sure what his name is.

"Have something?"

"23-year-old male with a cervical fracture. I actually have the CT called up here if you'd like to take a look at it."

Shit! This might require surgery. I look over the scans a few times. The patient is young, too young for me to really want to do a fusion if it can be avoided. I look at the scans a final time before deciding to go with a halo application to see how his healing progresses. The fusion can happen later if he doesn't show signs of healing properly, but with his age, a conservative approach is better long term. I'll have to take him downstairs, but it isn't a lengthy procedure. I get the patient information and head over to see him. I'd like to get him downstairs and into the halo as soon as possible.

Alex is back from CT when I return from the short procedure. "Sorry I was gone so long, had to put a halo on someone." I'm not sure what possesses me to do it, but as I take her hand, I lean over and kiss her on the forehead. I pause in the middle of standing up, certain that I just heard her make a sound. "Alex, can you hear me?" Nothing. "Alex, can you open your eyes?" More movement than last night! I ache to see her beautiful green eyes staring back at me. I take my seat and look up her latest CT. Everything looks good.

Abby returns late in the afternoon, carrying a grocery bag. "My mother made chicken noodle soup and bread. She wanted me to bring you some."

I smile, hopefully hiding how surprised I am. "You told your mother about me?"

"Not in great detail, she knows you are holding a permanent seat up here. She likes to make sure people are fed."

I chuckle as I picture an older version of Abby in a kitchen preparing far too much food. "Be sure to thank her for me. It smells delicious."

"I will. You know I can stay here with her if you want to go home and sleep in your own bed for a while."

"Thanks but I'm fine. I've already canceled my scheduled cases tomorrow. I'm still on call until the morning as well. I've been sleeping on and off here. We've been watching *Game of Thrones*."

"Great show. If you are going to stay would you mind if I went home tonight, see my kid and sleep in my own bed?"

"Not at all Abby. I will call you if something major happens."

"Thanks. I'll check in tomorrow before we start our first case. Want to continue *Thrones*?"

"Sure." I start up the next episode and take my soup from Abby. It is good, but not as good as it Alex's. Abby heads home after two episodes leaving Alex and me to continue the marathon on our own.

I wake up with my head in Alex's lap once again, only this time I have drooled. I wipe the side of my face as I stand up to stretch, glad that Alex won't remember this when she wakes up. I use the bathroom and walk around the limited space in the room a few times. I grab the chapstick to keep her lips moist. I know I hear her try to make a sound as I am applying it, this time I have zero doubt. It is brief and incomprehensible, but it was there. "Alex, it's Catherine, can you hear me?" Another grunt. "Alex, can you open your eyes?" It takes a second, but she manages to open them just slightly! I kiss her on the forehead and run my fingers down her right cheek. She twitches and grunts. I kiss her forehead one more time and whisper, "Keep fighting baby." I resume my seat and squeeze her hand. This time there is a soft attempt to squeeze mine back. Knowing I won't be sleeping anytime soon I restart the last episode of the show and continue on.

*****

I don't bother to fight it this time when I start to feel tired. I simply lay my head on Alex's thigh and give into sleep. I'm pulled from my stupor by the sense that something is off, something has changed. In a matter of seconds, I realize that Alex's hand is gone. My eyes fly open as I bolt to an upright position. I must be dreaming, I am not seeing what I'm seeing. Alex is awake, eyes half open, a look of extreme confusion on her face. "Alex?" She looks at me, her confusion still thick like a fog. I fight to hold back the tears that start to form. I need to stay calm for her. "Alex you were in an accident. You are currently in the ICU." Her confusion seems to lessen a little as she takes in what little the room has to offer. Her hazy eyes slowly make their way around the room before landing back on me. She tries to speak to me, but there is nothing. My heart drops, panic at the idea that she might have lost some speaking ability setting in. *Stay calm Catherine!*

"Do you know who you are?" I'll stick to yes or no questions, see if she can answer. A barely audible yes followed by a nod. Relief sets in. "Do you know who I am?" She doesn't answer immediately, and I feel the icy cold grip of what surely must be death around my heart. Finally, she nods that she does, leaving me to wonder if she needed the time or had been trying to speak. "Do you remember the accident?" Again she delays before answering. She finally manages to croak out a no. "What about Abby? Do you remember Abby?" Without hesitation, she nods and whispers that she does. "I need to text Abby, tell her that you are awake. Ok?" She nods her agreement, and I send Abby the text. She immediately responds that she will be here as soon as she can. I need to slip back into doctor mode, to complete a new assessment.

Abby arrives and practically pulls Alex out of the bed to hug her. Alex's facial expression shifts, something resembling happiness taking hold. Happiness that I didn't see there for me. I should go, I will go, but first I need to get Abby up to speed. Abby isn't done though. She bolts around the bed and wraps her arms around me. I'm not sure who is more surprised, Alex or myself.

"Thank you, Catherine, thank you!"

"Alex, I'm going to step out and give Abby an update. She will be right back." Alex scowls and shakes her head. Abby laughs, almost uncontrollably.

"Think you're giving me the update here doc."

"Guess so. Well as you can see she is awake and aware of what is happening around her. She is having difficulty speaking which could just be from being intubated. I haven't done a memory assessment yet, but she did say she knows who she is, and she remembers you. She doesn't remember the accident though, and she hesitated when I asked her if she knew who I am. We'll assess her motor skills more thoroughly once we can get her up on her feet, but so far they look to be ok. I'll come by in a little bit to see how she is doing." I look at Alex one last time before I head for the door, intending to leave.

"Alex I'll be right back. I need to speak with Catherine." Abby follows me into the hall and pulls me into the nearby stairwell. "What the hell was that? You said you were going to be here if she woke up! She is awake, and you're running!" I'm not sure I've ever seen Abby so pissed off.

The tears I fought off when Alex woke up are back. I can't stop them this time. "Abby I was so happy when she woke up, but she either wasn't happy to see me or doesn't know who I am. What am I supposed to do with either of those? I'm keeping her case, but I can't spend every minute with her right now. It is breaking my heart."

Abby gives me a hug. Once finished she puts a hand on each of my shoulders and forces me to look her in the eyes. "Just don't give up yet. We will get this sorted out." She briefly hugs me again before leaving to rejoin Alex. I loiter in the stairwell until I regain control of my emotions. I make my way back to the on-call room, hoping my puffy eyes don't attract any unwanted attention. Thankfully it is the predawn hours of Monday morning, and foot traffic is scarce.

Alexis

I wake up and find myself in a state of total bewilderment. My head is pounding. Where the hell am I? Did I drink way too much last night? Why is Catherine sleeping with her head in my lap? I scan the room and realize I must be in the hospital, the generic furnishings and color seem familiar. I have no idea why. Instinctively I check my head, the right side feels fine. I check the left side to discover that my hair has been shaved and there are some bandages in place. Catherine wakes up while I'm trying to work out what has happened. I focus on wiggling my toes. They seem to work giving me some measure of relief. Catherine is talking to me. I try to answer, even know what it is I want to say but my voice isn't cooperating, my throat is raw. Where is Abby? Abby would be here if it were serious. Catherine continues to question me. The questions, why the questions? What has happened? Was it serious? She asks if I know who she is. Does she think I could forget her so easily? She finally asks if I remember the accident. I try to recall it but I can't. I don't even remember leaving work that night. More questions and a physical exam. Was Catherine my doctor? Did she save me? She doesn't bother revealing her findings to me as she completes her exam.

Abby arrives and nearly throws herself on top of me to give me a hug. Catherine tries to speak to Abby about my condition in private. No fucking way. I need answers. My facial expressions must be working at least because Abby laughs and they speak in front of me. Catherine leaves, and Abby follows her out. When Abby returns she seems happy, yet a bit perplexed. What has Catherine told her?

I look to Abby expectantly. I try to speak. I want to know what happened. I managed a croaked noise, incomprehensible, even to me. I point to the bottle of water, maybe water will help. Abby isn't sure if I'm allowed anything by mouth yet. She sends a text to someone, I assume Catherine (when did they exchange numbers?) and leaves the room. She comes back with some ice chips. It is a start.

I eat some of the ice chips and try to speak again. This time I manage to audibly whisper, asking Abby what happened. Abby looks at me, I'm not sure why she won't tell me. Finally, she relents and starts to fill me in.

"I don't know everything. I was at the conference in San Antonio when I got a call from Catherine. She told me that there had been an accident, that you were hurt and that I needed to get here, that she was taking you down to surgery. I have never heard her sound the way she did on the phone that night. She sounded so shaken and scared. Normally she strikes me as ultra confident, has a lot of bravado to her. Not that night. I knew it must be bad, so I got on the next flight and headed home. You were out of surgery and here in the ICU when I arrived. Catherine was camped out at your side. I told her that I could take over, and she could get some sleep at home, but she refused. In fact, she refused to leave your side at all. She has been on call so she would quickly do her rounds and shower here before I left each day. No one has sat in that chair over there but Catherine. She's basically been holding a vigil of sorts from that chair. She canceled all of her cases for today. She refused to leave your side, said she couldn't." Abby pauses to let this information sink in. I'm hearing her, I know what her point is. I remember clearly how I feel about Catherine, I still ache for her, actually thought for a second that we were together when I saw her sleeping with her head in my lap. Thought that, until it hit me that I couldn't remember being with her. I look at Abby trying to tell her to continue. I finally manage it, another hoarse whisper.

"Right, anyway, I arrived, and Catherine debriefed me on your status. You had been in an accident, hit by one of the city buses in the driver's side door. You were unconscious when the paramedics arrived, bleeding from your face and skull. It seems that you hit your head on the window and the window shattered. The scan showed you had a subdural hematoma with a midline shift. She gave you a few burr holes and drains. This was Friday evening. It is Monday. You have been slowly regaining consciousness since. Your scans look good, she can't see any permanent damage."

Abby gives me time. Time to let everything she has told me to sink in. She knows she doesn't have to elaborate, that I will understand. I've been out for a few days. Not great but could have been worse. I know that means that I was intubated for a decent amount of it. Hopefully that is why I'm having trouble talking. It has to be that, or my cords were strained or damaged when I was intubated. I want to see the damage though. I need a mirror. I managed to croak the word phone to Abby.

"You want your phone?" I nod yes. I can reverse the camera and use that as a mirror. "You didn't have your phone on you when you were brought in. I went to the lot on Saturday and collected anything I could from your car. I found your phone but left it at my place with the few other things you had in the car. I'll pick it up after our cases today and bring it to you."

Damn. I point to Abby's phone. She finally figures out that I want it and hands it over. I reverse the camera and assess the damage I can. I have several gashes and a small slash on the left side of my face. It looks like it was closed expertly. Abby sees me assessing it and informs me that Catherine forced Sara to do it. I'm not sure if I am surprised or not, but I am grateful. My head is half shaved, half not. I feel like Two-Face from the Batman comics.

Better to just shave it all and have an even grow back. I grab a hunk with my left hand and mimic scissors with my right.

"You want a haircut? Now?" The tone in Abby's voice makes it clear that she finds my request unbelievable.

"Yes." A bit above a whisper. Improving, I think and grab another ice chip. Abby takes her phone back and sends another text. A few seconds later her phone chimes.

"Catherine says she will bring the clippers with her when she checks in later. You can wait until then." Irritating, but it isn't like I will be going anywhere. "I've got to get downstairs for our cases soon. You need me to bring you anything?"

I think about it and realize that I have nothing to do. My sole source of entertainment will be the small television with the limited channel selection. It isn't going to be long before I am bored and when I get bored, I get restless and crabby. I look at Abby and manage the word book. "Of course you want a book. I'll see what I can do." With that, Abby is gone. Twenty minutes later she returns from the pharmacy on the corner with a pair of paperbacks and a puzzle book. I smile and hold out my arms to give her a hug. Abby leaves me to head downstairs. I realize I'm exhausted and lower the head of my bed so I can sleep.

*****

I wake up to find Catherine asleep in the chair on my right. She looks so peaceful, her guard fully down. So she really did cancel her day for me? Where was she in a hurry to get to this morning then? I had been actively avoiding her before the accident. I needed to move on, to get over my feelings for her. A part of me felt guilty for moving out of her house without telling her first. As much as I'd like to

201

say I did it for her, I also know that I did it to protect myself. I had let her in and in doing so had fallen for her. She will never be able to be to me what I want her to be. Seeing her there I quickly realize I have not made any progress on this front. I still long to touch her, wish she would crawl into this bed with me and sleep. I don't want to wake her, so I leave the television off, instead opting for the puzzle book that Abby brought me. I open it to the first crossword but instead focus on Catherine, enjoying the serenity she seems to have found in her slumber.

Catherine starts to wake up about twenty minutes later. I look down at the puzzle and realize I have not completed a single clue. I've been too absorbed in the sight of her, lost in a trance of sorts; as if the sight of Catherine has the ability to hypnotize me. I quickly focus on the puzzle trying to fill in as many clues as I can before Catherine comes to. I manage three before I realize Catherine is awake and now she is the one watching me. When I look up she smiles, but it isn't her usual confidence filled smile, this one houses a certain sadness, the smile never reaching her eyes. It is like a dagger to my heart.

"Hey, have you been awake very long?" Catherine tries to stifle a yawn and fails. I shake my head. "Still not able to talk?"

"A little." Still hoarse but improving bit by bit. We sit, staring at one another. I wish I knew what she is thinking.

"Alex, I—," a nurse comes in to record my vitals, something that takes place every hour. She is young, pretty, has a nice smile. She makes some small talk at me and tries to crack a joke. I don't find it that funny, but I still put on my best faking it smile and give a fake chuckle, or at least the impersonation of one since the sound doesn't really come out. Before she leaves my side, she puts her hand on my shoulder and reminds me to use the call light if I need anything. She trails her fingertips down my arm as she leaves.

"I think she likes you." I shrug, it isn't important to me. "Maybe before you leave the floor you should ask her out. She was cute." I shake my head no. "Why not?" I stare back at her instead of answering.

"You were saying?" Three words, they feel like little razors in my throat as I focus on trying to ensure they are audible. Catherine hesitates. I know that whatever she was going to say is gone, she has decided against it.

"Abby said that you wanted these." She pulls the clippers from the pocket of her lab coat. I nod that I do want them. "You sure?"

"Yes"

Catherine stands, grabbing a pair of bath towels as well. She is about to hand me the clippers, but stops just short. "Want me to do it?" I think about it a second and realize I do. I can't see what I would be doing and making sure I do it right and don't end up with strips or patches of long hair would be difficult.

Catherine approaches the head of my bed, leans in and wraps one of the bath towels around my shoulders and neck. I instantly know that this is going to be a torture of its own kind. I can smell her customary scent of vanilla, and her proximity sends chills down my spine. The height of my bed has her breasts at the same level as my face. She is wearing a scrub top under her lab coat, and as she leans in, I am given a clear view of what the top contains. The lacy navy bra and her scent combine to form a lust elixir that I know I cannot drink. I close my eyes, only opening them when I can feel Catherine has backed away.

"Ready?" I nod that I am. The haircut takes an eternity. Catherine's proximity a slow torture that I don't want to end, yet can't stand to have it continue. I want to pull her onto the bed with me but resist the undying urge. When she finishes, she rubs the newly cut hair, brushing away my shorn locks. "Well, at least you don't have an oddly shaped head." She doesn't stop rubbing. I lean into her hand, and by default her. She continues briefly then trails her fingers down the side of my cheek. I want to take that hand, kiss the palm and hold it in my own, but I can't.

Catherine situates herself back into the chair I've been told she has lived in the last few days. She looks at me, and I'm sure she can see it, the desire I feel for her oozing out of my pores. "They will be moving you to a regular inpatient room later today. Do you need anything?"

You, just you, I think to myself. "Laptop, Kindle."

"Ok. I'll grab them…I mean I'll text Abby, ask her if she can get them from your place." Catherine looks sad. What have I done to her? "You didn't have to leave Alex. I never wanted you to leave." I offer her no response. What can I say to her that will make her understand? What can I say to her that won't let her in any deeper than she already is? We sit in silence, Catherine staring at me, me looking down at my own lap. "I'll check back with you later today." She rises from her chair and turns her back to me, to leave. I don't want her to go. Desperate, I slap the table that holds my books and now melted ice chips. She jumps at the sound, but it works, she turns to look at me, eyebrows raised.

"Stay if you want." Another whisper that I am certain she cannot hear. Catherine hesitates momentarily. I am certain she will leave and am shocked when she turns around and takes her seat.

"Have you been out of that bed yet?" I haven't. I've thought about it but haven't. I shake my head. "Do you want to try?" I do. Catherine lowers the rail on the side of the bed. "You need to go slow and be careful." I can feel the stiffness in my lower back as I move to swing my legs over the side of the bed, the muscles there are screaming too. Catherine lowers the bed until my feet touch the floor and positions herself in front of me. I start the upward movement slowly, feeling my legs protest the further off the bed I get. Just as I gain the confidence that I am going to make it my arms weaken and give, sending me stumbling forward, right into Catherine's waiting arms. The scent of her vanilla once again luring me to come closer, the heat from her body igniting my skin. I am now certain that I did not survive my accident, that I am now stuck in my own private hell, where Catherine will torture me for all eternity. We remain locked in this faux embrace until my legs start to shake, threatening to fail me much like my arms did moments ago. Catherine returns me to the bed. "Not too bad."

I eye Catherine, my face relaying my skepticism and sarcastic retort. She laughs. "Ok well, do you want a shower?" I am frozen, unable to answer, the thought of Catherine's hands on my body too much. Catherine detects my panic. "We can get an aide and a shower chair for you." I realize that I do want a shower, badly. I nod my head to let Catherine know. "What else do you want? Food?" Again, yes. "Ok. I'll put in the order for you to get the shower. When they come to help you, I'll call down and see about getting you some food. Want to watch some *Game of Thrones* with me? I finally started watching it." I do. Anything that will keep her here with me.

Catherine

I'm the one who needs a shower, an ice cold one, I think when the aide arrives to help Alex. My physical contact with her has every cell in my body on fire. I want to tell her how I feel, to crawl into her bed and hold her. I nearly kissed her after I cut her hair but the memory of her rejection dampened my ambition, inhibiting my desire. "I'll be back shortly. Do you need anything?"

"No, thanks." She manages it in a strained whisper. Better than it has been. As I leave I feel a small tinge of jealousy towards the aide. I shake my head at my own thoughts and emotions. *Get yourself together Catherine.*

I call in the meal order for Alex. She isn't going to enjoy her broth, jello, applesauce, and juice but she can only have clear liquids to start. I stop by the locker room for a quick shower and my laptop. I grab a pair of scrub pants for Alex. If we can get her up and moving, then she will be able to have her catheter out. I'm hoping the shower helps alleviate the stiffness in her muscles.

I call Taylor to give her an update. This time it sounds like she was already out of bed at least. "That's great news Cat! So did you tell her then?"

"Tell her what?"

"How you feel?"

"No. I'm quite sure that this is killing me though. I want to tell her but now is not the time. She wouldn't be able to leave if she wanted to and I'm still her treating physician. Too much of a conflict."

"Well don't let this second chance slip through your fingers. Never know if you'll be given a third." Taylor is right, I know she is. I can wait a little longer. Besides, I don't really know why Alex hasn't figured all this out on her own at this point. I end the call with Taylor. I've been gone for around an hour, I want to get back to Alex.

When I get back, Alex has finished her shower and is working on her food. "Gourmet broth, jello, and applesauce, exactly what you were hoping for I'm sure." Alex's look tells me it isn't all that she had been hoping for. "You're going to have to start slow, work your way back to solids. How was your shower?"

Alex answers in a raspy whisper, improving for certain, but it still sounds painful. "As great as it could be. I feel cleaner at least. I don't like the smell of this soap though." I chuckle, remembering how I thought she smelled wrong after they first bathed her. "What I miss?"

"Nothing. You just reminded me of something, you had to be there. I'll pick you up some of your usual soap and bring it tomorrow."

"Don't you have clinic tomorrow?"

"Normally, but I'm planning on canceling the day." Alex gives me a look, one that makes it clear she doesn't approve.

"No cases today?"

"I canceled them."

"Why?"

I try to come up with a stalling technique, hoping that someone will interrupt. I'm not that fortunate, and the impatience on Alex's face is becoming clearer by the second. "Because you...because I needed to be here." I wait for Alex's response, but she doesn't seem to have one. After the silence stretches on for at least a minute, she finally speaks.

"I think you should go to clinic tomorrow." Her words hurt me more than they should. She doesn't want me here. I should go, should sign her care over to one of my partners. I try to keep a poker face, to hide the hurt and disappointment, but I must be failing. "It isn't that I don't want you here. Abby said you haven't left this place since the accident, that you have barely left my side. You can't keep postponing your other patients for me. I'm here, and I will be fine." I have no answer, at least not one that I can tell her now, so I say nothing.

Abby enters the room; as if she had heard her Alex say her name seconds ago. I look at my watch, it is just after 2 pm. "Hey, Abby. Late lunch today?"

"Yeah. The first case involved a lot more work than we anticipated. We are hours behind now. How is she?" I wonder if Abby even realizes she is talking about Alex as if she is still in the coma. If she doesn't, Alex does.

"She is doing fine." Her voice is still a bit raspy, but she doesn't seem to be struggling as much to be heard.

Abby turns and faces Alex, her eyes wide, the surprise at hearing some semblance of a voice from her clear. "Hey, I can hear you! How are you feeling?"

"Alright." Alex turns to me. I feel like I should leave them alone yet can't find a reason that I need to leave.

"So we are hours behind. I know I said I'd be able to pick some stuff up for you from your place but we won't be done until late, and I need to get home and see the kid tonight. Maybe Catherine could go?"

I'm pulled from my efforts to find an excuse to leave. Abby has just provided me with one, just not one I was expecting. I look to Alex, then Abby, then back to Alex. This isn't my decision to make, it is up to Alex. She doesn't take long in her deliberation. "Yeah, that would be fine, if she is willing to."

"Sure. I can go now while you two visit. What do you want me to get?" Abby hands me a list and gives me directions. It shouldn't take me long to get there and back.

*****

I ring the bell and wait for an answer. It is still freezing outside. Spring doesn't seem to be anywhere in sight. I am about to leave when the door finally opens. "You must be Catherine. Come in, it is freezing out there."

"How do you—," Lydia cuts me off before I can finish.

"What, know who you are? You look just like Alex said. Have a seat. You want something to drink? I've just got to take care of something in the kitchen. Won't be a minute." Lydia heads back to the kitchen. Instead of sitting I make my way over to a wall filled with pictures. Their varying quality shows that they have been taken throughout Lydia's life.

"First thing Alex noticed too. That's John, my ex-husband. Those are our children. That's Clara, my partner." Lydia glances at the photos with me. "I've been pretty blessed." She hands me a glass of water that I never asked for. "Take a seat. I'd like to know how Alex is doing." I hesitate. Legally I'm not allowed to tell her. I don't think Alex would mind, but I didn't ask her either. "I know you can't tell me much. Abby said she is awake now, so I assume that is a good sign."

"It is. You are right though, as her treating physician I am legally prohibited from telling you more. Abby is with her now. I'll ask her to call and update you."

"Thank you. I don't know how you did it or how you are still doing it though. When my Clara was sick, there were times I could hardly take care of her. We knew she was never going to make it. Sometimes I just lost it."

"I was as scared as I have ever been when I saw that it was Alex. I don't know how I made it through the craniotomy either. I think once the drape went on and I couldn't see her face I just ran on an autopilot of sorts. I lost it after though, and I've had my moments since."

"I can imagine. Well, Abby said you were stopping by to pick up a few things for Alex. I suppose I should get you the key."

"There is actually one thing I was hoping to discuss with you first."

"Oh?" Lydia sits back down in her chair and waits for me to continue.

"Alex is going to be off work for a while. I'd like to take care of her rent for the next two months if I may."

"I know Abby said you haven't left her side, but you really do care about her, don't you?" I look at the floor. It isn't shame that I care about Alex that causes me to do it. It's shame that everyone else seems to have figured it out before I did. "It's alright, nothing to be ashamed of. I told Abby not to worry about rent for now. I doubt I'll have the same luck brushing you off though, will I?"

"Nope. I can take care of it now, and if she is off beyond two months, I'll continue to take care of it."

"Very well. Here is the key. Just go through the door on the side of the garage and up the stairs on the right. If you don't mind, I'll stay in, out of the cold."

"That is fine. I'll only be a few minutes anyway. I'll drop the key off when I'm finished."

I'm not sure what I expected when I entered the apartment. Alex once told me she is a simple creature, this apartment with its small space and sparse furnishings certainly suits a simple lifestyle. I grab her laptop from the coffee table and put it in the messenger bag from the closet. One item off the list. I make my way to the bedroom. It feels so small, the full-size bed taking up a lot of the room. I grab her Kindle from the floor beside the bed and the phone charger from the outlet. I open the closet to grab her a pair of sweatpants, found next to the chest that Alex made. One of them at least. There are now two chests, the newer one finished in a different stain than the original. I continue on my quest. It takes me a second to find the gym bag I am to use. It is out in the coat closet, not in the bedroom closet. Bag in hand I place the sweatpants inside and grab her slippers as well. All that remains is some clean underwear, deodorant, her toothbrush, and toothpaste. I grab her preferred soap as well. Everything in hand I realize I've seen the entire apartment in under 5 minutes. I'm certain I had bigger places in residency.

I put the bags in the car and write a check for the next two months rent. Check and key in hand I head back to the front door and ring the bell. Lydia answers much more quickly this time.

"That was fast. Find everything she wants?"

"I did, thank you." I hand Lydia the key and the check.

"I'm heading down to Texas to see my sister tomorrow. Will they let me visit Alex before I leave?"

"Sure. They will be moving her out of the ICU sometime today. I haven't been given the room number yet. It should be available at the information desk, but I'll have Abby text you with it as well. I'm sure Alex would like to see you."

"Ok then. Tell her hello for me please."

"Will do." I turn and head down the walk towards my car. I hear the door open again and stop.

"It's none of my business, but if you care about her half as much as I think you do, then you need to tell her. These chances don't come around often, and they are rarely given twice. You two can't keep running from each other."

I smile at Lydia. I respect her boldness, her willingness to overstep and speak her mind. "I know."

Alexis

"You shaved it all?" Abby seems surprised. I don't understand why; it was already half gone anyway.

"It looked funny. Gonna be a late night huh?"

"Yep. The case now is a quick one but another long one after that. I don't need to be there for the first one. The residents will help. She knows where I am and the nurse has my number if she does need me. So how you feeling?"

"Alright, I guess. Voice is improving. I showered and drank some sustenance. Tried to stand up, Catherine had to catch me. Eventful day."

"Well, at least you still have your sense of humor. How are things with Catherine?"

"Like torture. I want her here, to be near her but it is so painful. I feel like a masochist."

"Oh, Alex stop it. Can't you see it?"

"See what?"

"That it is the same for her. Come on. I know you can be thick when it comes to another woman being interested in you but it doesn't get more obvious than this. She has barely left your side since you were admitted, she was a wreck when she called me, was a wreck while you were unconscious, she canceled a full day of surgery to be by your side. She was going to cancel her clinic tomorrow as well. I'm not sure if she has, but that was her plan. She cares about you, and she clearly isn't going anywhere." Abby might see a nice sugar coating on her own romantic relationships, but she is never one to have such delusions about anyone else's. I ponder her words for a minute.

"Then why was she trying to set me up with some nurse earlier? It doesn't matter. You can speculate all you want to. It has to come from her."

"Or you could say something. You don't have anything better to do while you're here anyway."

"Can't. It has to come from her. It isn't the same for the two of us. This would be easy for me. For her it means a shift in her identity, how she has always seen herself. I don't want to pressure her into figuring that out."

"I think she already has it figured out. Your call though. Everyone says hello and sends their love. They plan to come see you once you're out of the ICU."

"Catherine said that will happen today. I haven't heard anything else, so I'm not sure. Tell them all hello for me." Abby's phone rings, making both of us jump.

"Well quick case is over. Gonna have to go back in a few. Depending on how late we finish I'll stop up after, but I'm not hopeful. We have office tomorrow, so I won't be by until dinner time."

"No worries. I get it. I'll have something to do at least when Catherine gets back."

"Talk to her Alex. One of you has to take the first step here. This is like watching a standoff where both gunmen refuse to shoot."

"I has to be her. It has to come from her." Abby shakes her head as she walks out the door.

I'm awakened by the sound of people in my room. I open my eyes to see that Catherine is back and asleep, her head lying on my leg. "Hi. We're here to move you to your new room."

"Ok, just a second please." The pair step out into the hallway. I don't want to wake Catherine. I can't imagine she has had much quality sleep if she has been here with me for days. I don't have a choice though. "Catherine. Catherine wake up." Nothing. She is out. I sit up and brush the hair from her face, then find myself lightly running my thumb over her cheekbone. I cup her cheek in my palm and slowly trace the length of her jawline with my finger tips. I stop with my thumb hovering just over her lips. She looks so peaceful. I shake myself out of it and move my hand to her shoulder. "Catherine. Catherine, time to wake up." This time I give her shoulder the slightest of shakes. Just enough to jar her from sleep. She opens her eyes, sees me and smiles, her smile quickly fading into a look of panic when she realizes where she is.

"So sorry. I—." The two unknown individuals come back into the room, this time with my nurse.

"Hey, Alex. Looks like you're leaving us. They are here to take you to your new room. Good luck with the rest of your recovery." Catherine rises from her chair and begins to grab the few things we have to take with us.

"Just put the bags on the bed Catherine. Plenty of room." Plenty of room for you too, I think to myself. I still feel the warmth from her face on my thigh. I need to stop. It is difficult enough being around her, no need to make it worse.

A trek down one hallway, a short ride in the elevator and a few turns later we are in my new room. Seems bigger than the ICU room did. Probably due to less equipment and maybe because the window allows a view of something other than the side of the building. Catherine immediately starts to settle in. The chairs are further from the bed in this room. I immediately like it less. My new nurse comes in to introduce herself and take my vitals. Once she is gone, Catherine and I are alone again.

"Well, at least this room has a recliner you can sleep in." I cringe as I hear myself say it out loud. The look on Catherine's face makes it even worse. "I didn't mean it that way. You using my leg as a pillow is fine. I just meant the recliner will probably be a bit more comfortable." Catherine gives me a small smile but says nothing. "Before I forget could you text Abby the room number please?"

"Sure." Catherine sends the text. "Lydia says hello. She is planning to come see you tomorrow I think."

"Yeah, I need to talk to her. Try to figure out the rent situation."

"Do you want to try to get up again? The sooner we get you up the faster that catheter can come out. Faster that comes out the sooner you can have your sweatpants."

"Excellent motivation Dr. Waters! We can give it a go when you're ready." Catherine moves to my bedside, waiting for me to move. I swing my legs over the side and plant my feet on the floor.

"Oh hold on a second. Don't stand up just yet." Catherine leaves the bedside and opens the gym bag she got from my place. She comes back to me with my slippers in her hand. "These will keep your feet warm and give you a little

216

more traction." She squats and places a hand on the back of my right calve, slowly moving her hand down to draw my foot to her. The sensation of her touch on my bare skin sends chills down my spine and elicits gooseflesh. If Catherine notices she doesn't say anything. She repeats the process on my other leg, my body again betraying me. I become embarrassed when I realize it has been a few days and that I probably need to shave. Catherine stands again and looks at me. I want to bolt up off of the bed, pull her body against mine, feel her lips on mine but sit, frozen and waiting. "There. When you're ready." I shake my head to clear the fog my imaginings have left me in.

"Ok. Ready?" Catherine holds out her arms, indicating that she is. I plant both feet and stand. The motion creates a Charley horse in my right calve and sends me back to sitting on the bed.

"What happened? Are you ok?" Catherine's concern fills her voice and face.

"Yeah. Just a Charley horse. Shouldn't be surprised I guess." I lean over to grab my toes just as Catherine squats down. Her chin connects with my head, sending her backwards and causing me to fall from the bed. Catherine springs back to my side.

"Alex are you ok?" She is already helping me up to my knees.

"Yeah, just my pride I think." Catherine has my face in her hands, tilting my head at all angles, first to examine the burr holes then everywhere else. She finally stops tilting my head around but keeps my face contained in her hands.

"Where did we connect?" She is so close it would be easy to shrink the distance, to use the press of my body to pin her against the floor. I finally look at her knowing that she has to see how badly I want her. The thoughts quickly go away, ice water putting the fire out.

"You're bleeding." I instinctively reach up and gently wipe the blood from Catherine's lower lip. I'm vaguely aware that my thumb lingers longer than necessary. Catherine doesn't move away immediately but steps back after a prolonged moment.

"I'm not worried about me. Are you ok?"

"Physically fine." Catherine releases my face and stands. "Ok, we need to get you off of this floor and back onto the bed. Let me call the nurse."

"No. I can do it. Just give me a hand." Catherine stops, clearly planning to argue with me. I don't give her a chance though, and begin the process of trying to stand. My muscles fight against me, taunting me that Catherine was right. I make it back onto the bed and this time swing my legs back up onto it before attempting to grab both sets of toes.

"Here let me help." Catherine moves to the foot of the bed. "Straighten out your legs." I do as she commands. "I'm going to push back on your feet, see if we can't get those cramps to ease up." She does as promised. It aches in the way that breaking up a Charley horse does, painfully good. She repeats this a few times and moves to the side of the bed, taking a seat on the edge. She proceeds to start to massage my right foot. I pull away and slide back up the bed. "Relax. Those muscles need to stretch. Just relax." I obey, and she resumes massaging my foot. It feels amazing. She does the same with the other foot. I think she is finished, but she isn't. She slips her hands behind my heel and starts to massage my calve, stopping just below the back of my knee. My muscles tighten in response, and I try to pull away. Catherine is quick though and has a lock on my leg. "Honestly Alex, relax." I have no choice. I will my muscles to relax. Her touch is driving me insane. She moves her attention to my other leg. I nearly moan but suppress it in time. "Want to try again?"

"Sure," I whisper, catching the breathless rasp of my own voice.

Catherine resumes her position at the side of the bed as I pivot, placing my feet on the floor. She extends her arms, and I take my cue and stand. My legs shake causing Catherine to place a hand on each of my hips, not knowing that of all things that probably won't help. I will my legs to get control of themselves. It takes a second, but they finally do.

"You alright? Do you want to try to take a step or do you need to sit back down?" I am acutely aware that Catherine's hands are still on my hips. I look up to find Catherine staring at me intensely. She isn't looking away, and I am unable to. The pull of her proximity, her hands on my hips, the intensity of her stare is all too much. I can't stop myself this time. I take a step forward, moving in to kiss her. She doesn't stop me. A knock on the door brings me back to my senses, stopping me before I force Catherine's decision.

"Hey, you're out of bed!" The nurse has come to check my vitals again. I can't decide if she is a blessing or a curse. Either way, she is oblivious to the fact that she has interrupted something.

"Yes. Just managed my first step I think." Did I or did I imagine it?

"Great! You'll be up and down the hall in no time. Do you need anything?" I shake my head no, but Catherine has other ideas.

"Can we get her one of those heating pads from therapy, please? I think the heat will help her muscles." Catherine has no idea that my body is on fire right now, her hands still on my hips. I must have taken a step as her arms are slightly bent now.

"I'll work on that. I'll bring you some more water as well." We thank her as she leaves the room.

I turn and find Catherine staring at me again. My legs are starting to shake a new and the moment has been lost. "I think I should get back to the bed."

Catherine

Not now Catherine. Not yet. I keep repeating this, my inner monologue running on a loop. All this physical contact with Alex is driving me mad. Now is not the time for me to tell her, this is not the place. Alex needs to focus on her recovery, not on me. My head and my heart are at war, my heart urging me to shout if from the rooftops and my head reminding me that now is not the time. She is so close though, my hands locked on her hips, hers on my biceps, our eyes locked on each other. My heart is pounding so hard that it drowns out my brain. Fuck waiting. Just as I start to close the gap, the nurse comes in to check on Alex, spoiling the opportunity. My brain resumes control, the loop continues to play.

I help Alex back onto her bed. It takes every ounce of control I have to not push her down and straddle her, to claim what my body is screaming for. I know that she can't for many reasons, so for now just sharing a space with her will have to do. I settle back into my chair and find my eyes fixed on Alex. The gorgeous green eyes that were so wrong in my nightmare are perfect here, filled with life and an indescribable spark that draws me into them. A knock at the door interrupts the connection. I figure it is the aide with the heating pad and am surprised to see Erin.

"Hey, Alex! Great to see you awake and out of the ICU!" Erin gives her a big hug before turning to me. "I sorta rushed up here to warn you that we just wrapped up our cases for the day. A group of nurses and techs from the team are heading to the gift shop and then up here to see Alex." I don't need Erin to elaborate. It is one thing for Erin to know, but if the others find out the whole OR will know within five minutes.

"Right then. Well, I do need a shower and could stand a bite to eat. I'll leave you to it." Alex's brow furrows.

221

"I thought you showered this morning." Her voice is becoming stronger, I no longer struggle to hear her.

"It's hot in here, I feel sweaty." I look at the thermostat, it reads a cool 68 degrees. Erin and Alex look at each other, Alex seems more confused than ever. I don't give her time to argue as I rush to get out the door. I can't risk the elevators. Instead, I burst into the stairwell and run as quickly down the steps as possible. I need a cold shower and clean panties. I already know before I get to my locker that I've depleted the bag I packed Friday morning. After thinking for a moment, I decide I have time to head home. There I can shower and grab clothes for clinic tomorrow. It should take around an hour, which I estimate will be enough time for Alex's visitors to be long gone. I grab my keys and coat from my locker and head towards the parking ramp.

The stuffed mailbox serves to remind me that I have been gone for a few days. I realize that I need to take care of a few things while I'm here. I toss the mail on the bar knowing there is nothing there that won't wait. I immediately head to the pool and add the needed chemicals. The water looks so inviting, but I don't want to be gone long enough to get a good workout in. I water the few plants I have and head back to the kitchen. I open the barren refrigerator and realize with a pang how much I miss having Alex here. The pang is quickly eviscerated by the desire I have been struggling to contain. I need a shower.

The cold water assaulting me from the four shower heads does nothing to extinguish the fire my hormones have blazed throughout my body. Giving up I switch them to hot, steam quickly billowing out of the stall. My forearm brushes over my nipple as I reach for the loofah. Little jolts surge through me. My body craves relief. I lean back against the warm tile and imagine what it would be like to be here with Alex. I imagine her behind me, running her hands down the back of my shoulders, snaking them around to cup my breasts, slowly working them down my abdomen, then my hips, trailing her fingers along my inner thighs. I imagine that the warm trails of water running down my body are Alex's lips and tongue working all over me. I start to massage myself with one hand and work a breast and nipple with the other, imagining that it is Alex sending the surges of heat through me again and again. I want to feel her inside of me so I slowly insert two fingers, angling so I can keep pressure on my clit as well. I imagine Alex working me, forcing my hips to move faster and faster. I come quick and hard and realize that the fire has only been dampened. Feeling somewhat better I finish my shower and pack up my bag with fresh clothes to last a few more days. I get in the car and head to the cafe near the hospital to pick up some soup for us. I figure she will be alright as long as it is soft food, so I go with chicken noodle and cream of chicken with rice. I see the dessert offerings and add a pair of red velvet cupcakes, deciding that Alex needs a treat of some kind.

I return to her room and stop just short to listen for any conversation to indicate that I've returned too early. All I hear is the sound of a movie or show. I enter and immediately see the flowers and balloons her coworkers have brought her. They add a little warmth to the coldness of the hospital room. I mentally kick myself. Now that Alex is out of the ICU she can have these things. I've never been big on flowers or balloons, they seem impractical as they wither away so quickly. I make a mental note to brainstorm something better, something permanent. Alex is sitting on the bed stretching her calves as they lay on the heating pad. I warm at the sight of her, my desire for her immediately amping back up, like a fire that has had gasoline tossed on it. The green eyes I can't get my fill of, and her warm smile greet me.

"You're finally back." She eyes the bag of food in my hand, I realize she is probably starving. "Any chance I can at least have a bite of yours? I want something other than broth and jello." A small pout replaces her smile making me laugh.

"I suppose it is a good thing I brought enough for the both of us then." Alex's eyes light up, and her smile returns. I love knowing that I can do something so small to make her so happy. "What are you watching?" I reach into the bag and remove the two bowls of soup keeping the cupcakes hidden, a surprise for later.

"Some movie Erin told me to watch. I can't get into it at all though. I was waiting for you to see if you want to watch some more *Thrones* or something."

"*Thrones* is fine, unless you aren't in the mood." I set the bowls on the table in front of Alex and remove the lids. She eyes them greedily. I'm afraid I'll have to wipe drool off her chin soon.

"But what are you going to eat?" We both laugh. I love seeing her so relaxed.

"Which ever one you don't want." I put a spoon in each bowl as she makes her choice. Alex takes the bowl of cream of chicken and immediately digs in. She moans with pleasure as the first spoonful hits her tongue. I immediately flush, the sound of her moaning causing me to recall the memory of Alex and Brooke, morphing my desire into arousal.

Alex eyes me carefully. "You alright?" I've been busted.

"Yeah, the soup is just a little hotter than I expected." A terrible lie, but she either accepts it as truth or is too hungry to press.

Sara and Abby knock at the door bringing more balloons and flowers for Alex. Their visit is a brief one. I check the clock and discover that it is well after seven. "Want me to put those with the others?" Alex nods her head and watches me. She smiles and shakes her head slightly. "What? Did I do something?"

"No. It'll sound terrible if I tell you."

"Now you have to tell me."

"I don't want to sound ungrateful, but I do not understand the whole flowers and balloons thing. The sentiment is nice, and it is nice to be thought of, but they just fade so quickly. Seems like a waste of money is all." I laugh, clearly shocking Alex. "What is so funny?"

"Nothing. When I came back earlier I saw them and kicked myself for not getting you any. It honestly never occurred to me though because I feel the same way you do about them. They wither so quickly, what makes them so great?"

Alex surprises me by taking my hand. "You don't have to get me anything. You've basically lived here since the accident. I don't know why, but you have. You've run errands for me, brought me food and kept me company. All those things are better than flowers and balloons." I don't let go of her hand and am surprised when she doesn't release mine. We lock eyes with one another, and I will her to see everything I am feeling, everything I am unable to say.

"Feel like watching something lighter? A cheesy comedy maybe?"

"Sure. Sounds like you have something in mind." We can watch anything Alex wants to. I just want to be here with her.

"I do, but it has a lesbian love story in it." She eyes me, trying to assess if I'll be ok with it. I smile at her.

"A love story and a corny plot? Sounds good." I watch as Alex starts up *D.E.B.S.*, never releasing my hand. Her thumb absentmindedly strokes the back of my hand, sending ripples of sensation through the rest of my body, as if her thumb were stroking me everywhere. We watch about half of the movie before she looks over and stares at the bag.

"Anything good in there?"

"What makes you think—," I stop myself. Alex has always been perceptive of the things around her. I grab the bag and am forced to release her hand. The cold and empty feeling returns as I open the bag and extract the cupcakes, watching Alex's eyes grow at the sight of them. "I thought we could use a treat, if you think you'll be ok to eat it."

"I will be. First I want to try walking again. I want to get this catheter out so I can go home." The words hit me like a hard slap. Home?

"Home? We haven't discussed discharging you yet."

"I know we haven't, but I'm fine, and I'm ready to get out of here. I'm slowly going crazy being confined to this room."

"Slow down Alex. For starters getting the catheter out is only a small step. You need to be ambulating with a walker at least before I will consider discharging you. You also need to consider the fact that your place is up a narrow flight of stairs and that you live alone. I'm not sure how you plan to get up those steps, but you cannot go home and be alone." Alex sits in sullen silence. "Look I'm not trying to bring you down. I just want you to realize that you will probably be here the rest of the week, at least. Alex, you suffered a head trauma. You are going to need someone to help you out for a while. You need a plan."

"I know." She sighs heavily. "That just isn't me. I don't like to be a burden on anyone. I can take care of myself. I need to get out of here and get back to work, get back to some semblance of the life I had before the accident."

"I'm sorry Alex. I need you to realize that you will need to accept help this time. Even when I do discharge you, it will be on a very limited activity basis. You have to take it easy and continue to rest. You understand that means you won't be going back to work for at least a month, probably longer."

Alex sighs again, sounding defeated. She won't even look at me. "I know, only I can't—." I cut her off.

"Come back to the house with me." My heart is pounding as the words come out. I'd like to say that I offered for entirely altruistic reasons but I'd be lying. I want her back at the house, need to be near her. "You wouldn't be a burden. I'll arrange to have someone there with you when I'm working. Think about it."

"Catherine...I don't know. Is it really a good idea?"

"Just think about it. I'm offering because I want to do this for you." I'm such a liar. I do want to help Alex anyway that I can, but I'll selfishly be fulfilling a need of my own as well.

Alexis

Catherine acquiesced and went back to work on Tuesday. I am lost in a new book when there is a knock at the door. I am surprised to see Lydia.

"Well, you look like you're doing alright. Nice to see you awake. Abby has been keeping me updated."

"Lydia it is nice to see you! How are you?" I am truly happy to see Lydia, she quickly became like a grandmother to me before the accident. It doesn't hurt that her presence also distracts me from thinking about Catherine.

"Oh you know, I'm good. Getting ready to visit my sister. Tired of this gloom and doom weather we keep having. What about you, feeling ok?" I laugh a little. I understand being sick of this weather for sure but would give anything to be able to walk outside and take in a lung full of that crisp, fresh air.

"I am. I can walk a little, but they won't let me get out of bed without paging for help and using a walker. As soon as Catherine left, they turned the fall risk alarm on. If I even try to get up, the damn thing goes off."

"Good. You need to be careful. So you finally got the doctor to leave your side. How is that going?" I sigh. How is it going? Great with a side of torment? Lydia chuckles. "Never easy is it?"

"Guess not. Honestly, it has been great having her here. Things are relaxed, and we are getting along just fine. It is also like being water boarded. I can't fight my feelings for her. I've agreed to go back to her place after I'm discharged until I am able to take care of myself again. I know it isn't a good idea. I need to distance myself from her, but I can't." Lydia doesn't respond. She does this often. Whenever you speak to her about a problem, she will let you sit and think about it, letting you reach your own conclusion. I know I won't find one.

"Anyway, I need to talk to you. I'm going to be off work for a little while I guess. I'm not sure I'll be able to keep paying rent beyond another month or so. I will make arrangements for someone to come pack up my stuff as soon as I can. I'm really sorry about the short notice."

Lydia looks at me. I can tell she has something on her mind but is debating whether she should tell me. She is always easy to read. I wonder if she knows she would make a terrible poker player. "You don't need to worry about it. It has already been taken care of."

"I don't understand. What do you mean taken care of? Lydia you can't just let me stay there rent free."

"I'm not, although I would have been fine giving you a month or two if that is what you needed. You're a good kid. You help out around the house even though you were never expected or asked to. You've kept this lonely old woman company. It has been nice having you around."

"Then how? Who?" She doesn't answer me, typical Lydia. It only takes a minute for me to figure it out. "Catherine?"

"She loves you you know. You might not want to admit it to yourself because it is easier to keep running, but she loves you. She insisted on paying for two months now, and any other time you might need covered."

I'm speechless. I want to be angry at Catherine's brazen intrusion into my private affairs but I can't. I vow to pay her back, every penny of it. As soon as I can return to work, I'll pick up all the extra shifts and call I can until the debt is repaid.

"Oh, I almost forgot. I made you some cookies. Peanut butter with peanut butter chips and white chocolate chips. Your favorite if I recall correctly." Lydia pulls the massive freezer bag stuffed with cookies out of her oversized purse, my mouth watering at the sight of them. "Is there anything else you need?"

"Thank you so much. You know how much I love your cookies. I think I'm good. Abby and Catherine have been keeping me stocked with what I need. How long are you going to be gone?"

"I'll be down there for a week. If I feel like staying longer, I'll change my return flight. I thought about just booking the flight there and booking the return flight when I felt like coming home, but usually, I'm ready to come back after a week. I don't have anything to rush back to anyway. That is the beauty of retirement, no commitments." I laugh, Lydia is as feisty as ever.

"I'd love to have some commitment to rush off to right now." I stare out the window for a second, as if I'll find some obligation there.

"Your commitment is here. Rest and get better. Address the situation between you and Catherine too." I smile at Lydia, the only response I can give to her orders. "Alright kid, I need to get on the road. Flight leaves in a couple of hours. Please have Abby keep me updated."

"I will. Have a great trip." Lydia and I hug before she leaves me on my own again.

An early afternoon visit from Kevin, Shannon, Derrick, Dahlia, and Nikki adds some joy to my day. They bring with them more flowers and balloons along with a stuffed penguin. I don't know how they remember that I love penguins, but they do. Their visit lasts for just over an hour before they all must leave for their respective obligations. I find myself counting down the hours until I know Catherine will return.

By Wednesday I am going stir crazy, and I realize I am falling deeper and deeper for Catherine. Not good considering she hasn't given me an indication of where she is regarding her feelings. I can't lie though, it is nice spending so much time with her. Things are relaxed and easy. Catherine enters and pulls me out of my own head. I forgot that she operates on Wednesdays, so she has been right downstairs this whole time. She smiles as our eyes meet.

"Hey, just thought I would come up for lunch, see how you are doing." *Better now*, I think to myself.

"Going stir crazy. You don't look like you're planning to eat." Catherine has a bottle of water with her but no food. I hate that she doesn't eat during the day.

"I know. Hang in there." Catherine grins and makes her way over to the shelf where my cookies from Lydia are. "I didn't stop for any food, figured I'd just eat your cookies." She flashes her grin in my direction as she opens the bag and pulls out a cookie and takes a bite. "Damn these are good. You need to make these."

"Have all the cookies you want, but I wish you would eat some real food as well."

"I know. I'll grab some fruit in the doctor's lounge and eat dinner tonight. Has inpatient rehab been here yet?" This is news to me.

"Nope. Should I be expecting them."

"I put the order in this morning. You want to get out of here, this will hopefully help that happen a little sooner." Catherine checks the clock and frowns. "I've got to get back downstairs for my last case. Should be an early evening."

*****

Catherine finishes her day later than she expected. I don't see her again until nearly seven. "Want me to get us some takeout for dinner?" She smiles at me, but it isn't as vibrant as it typically is and it doesn't reach her eyes. I know something is wrong.

"No. You don't need to make a trip anywhere." I continue to search Catherine's features, with the hope that I will find the answer written on them.

"You sure? I don't mind if there is something you want."

"I'm sure. Maybe we can go down to the cafeteria. Get out of this little room."

"Sure if you're up for it." Catherine is clearly distracted. The happiness she exuded earlier today is gone.

"You ok? Do you need to be somewhere?"

"Yeah, I'm fine. Nowhere to be other than here." I want to press her but know better, at least for now. She doesn't seem to want to talk, so I turn our next episode of *Thrones* on. We are nearing the end of season three. I know what is coming and wonder if Catherine even suspects. We sit in silence as we watch the episode with the Red Wedding.

I had read the books before I saw the show, so I knew it was coming. I know Catherine has not read them and the shock is clear.

"I can't believe…they just…" I laugh, uncontrollably. Admittedly the first time I read the books I didn't catch it either. I thought the show however made it obvious if you paid attention. "I mean I knew something was off when Bolton let Jaime go, but that…" I laugh again.

"At least you picked up that something was off. Most people don't even blink when Bolton sets Jaime free. Really though you shouldn't be surprised after the way season one ended. That alone should have warned you all bets are off."

"You're right. It does seem obvious now that you say it. Wow."

"Yep. I doubt it will be the last time the show shocks you."

"Great. Anyone going to be left by the end?"

"Maybe. It hasn't finished yet so who knows. You do know I have the books, you can borrow them if you'd like."

"That would be nice. Thanks." Catherine is still bothered by something, something that she doesn't want to share with me.

"Dinner?" My stomach is making itself heard, grumbling loudly.

"Sure. You want me to bring something up or do you want to go down there with me?"

"I'll go down there with you. I'm pretty sure I can make it and really want to get out of this room." Catherine slides the walker over to the side of my bed and shuts the alarm off. I have been making it a little further every day, but this would be the longest trip yet.

"Don't push it too hard. If you start to tire we can rest or get you a wheelchair. There is no shame in either so don't try to be all tough like I know you will."

We make our way to the elevator and start the trip down to the main floor. I hear Catherine let a small sniffle slip. I look at her and can see that her beautiful blue eyes have turned glassy. I place my hand on her shoulder, offering her support. She jumps at my touch, the contact startling her, she is clearly preoccupied. Catherine looks at me, giving me a half hearted smile. We arrive at the main floor before I can ask her what is wrong.

Catherine grabs a tray and loads up our dinner. We look around and find that it is busier than we anticipated. "Upstairs?"

"Yeah, I suppose so." We get on the elevator, and I am surprised to see Catherine press the button for the overflow floor. I had assumed she meant back to my room. She looks at me, and a small smile touches her lips, but not her eyes. Something is very wrong. I start to wonder if it is about me; if my latest CT scan has revealed an area of permanent damage.

We eat in relative silence. The silence continues afterward as we both stare out the window. I want Catherine to tell me what was wrong, but know I can't push. I have my own question weighing on my mind though.

"Why did you do it, Catherine?" She finally looks at me, her raised eyebrows indicating she needs clarification. "Why did you pay my rent and not tell me?" Catherine turns away from me.

"Because you needed it. Because I could do it and you needed it. I didn't tell you because I knew you would argue and be upset."

"I'm not upset. Thank you for doing it. I will pay you back though."

"You don't have to. You had a need that was easy for me to fulfill, so I did. You never had to know it was me."

"I guessed." More silence. I can't take it anymore. "Catherine." She still won't look at me. I grab her arm. She still avoids making eye contact. "Catherine please tell me what is wrong."

"Nothing is wrong. I'm fine." She continues to stare out the window. I am fed up. I stand up to make my way around the table using the walker. The sound of my chair sliding across the floor finally causes Catherine to look over at me, too late. She leaps up out of her chair and meets me half way.

"You will tell me what is going on. Something is clearly weighing on your mind."

Catherine stands there staring at me. I wish I can read her blue eyes, but unlike Lydia, hers seldom betray anything. "Alex...I...," she stops. Just stops and stares at me, or through me. I want to shake her, but I wait, my impatience has to be rolling off of me. Is there permanent damage on my latest CT? Is she finally going to tell me her decision? Has she finally make up her mind? Tears started streaming down her face. It can't be good news if she is crying. She exhales, trying to regain her composure.

"I had a trauma patient before I came upstairs this evening. MVA, similar to your own situation, only she will never recover. There was too much damage to her tissues. I had to tell her husband and her parents. She has two children, one three and the other five. They will never know their mother. I had to break this news to them, and the entire time I was feeling completely selfish because it could have been you and I was so grateful that it wasn't. I was actually happy on some level that it was her and not you. She is upstairs on life support while organ donation is arranged and all I can think about is how grateful I am that it isn't you. What is wrong with me? What kind of person feels like that?" She breaks down sobbing. I reach for her and embrace her, cursing the walker for getting between us. I hold her as best I can and reassure her that she isn't a bad person. Her sobbing eventually ceases, and she breaks off the embrace. "We should get you back downstairs. You've been up longer than you have at any point."

"I'm doing fine. Really." I actually am doing alright. My legs feel tired and a little achy but I'm still doing well.

"All the same, back downstairs."

Catherine

Back in Alex's room I sit and ruminate, the book I hold a poor attempt to cover up the fact that I'm clearly distracted. Alex is also reading, but I know she isn't as fully immersed as she usually is. I can see her stealing sidelong glances at me. Mercifully she doesn't press anymore or ask if I am ok. I know that if she were to, I would tell her how I feel. I nearly confessed upstairs but stopped myself. She still needs to focus on her recovery, and this isn't the right place for me to admit my feelings. How she has not figured it out on her own yet is a mystery to me. I know I will tell her soon. Everything that has happened has shown me that I'm lucky to have this chance and I need to take it. Alex reaches out and lays a hand on my forearm, a silent comfort. I set the book down and place my hand on top of hers. I long to crawl into her bed and just be held by her. I find myself staring at Alex. She picks up on it after a few of her glances. She puts her Kindle down and looks at me as a tear I've been fighting to hold back escapes, trailing its way down my cheek. She takes her hand from my forearm and gently wipes it away with her thumb. I move to cover her hand with my own but am too slow. Alex has already removed it and is in the process of lowering the safety rails on her bed. "What are you doing?" I reach over and silence the obnoxious alarm. She swings her legs over the side of the bed and extends her arms.

"Come here." I balk, glued to my chair. Alex isn't having it though. "Either you come here, or I come to you. Your choice." I don't want her out of bed again so soon, so I give in and close the short distance between us. In two meager steps, I am in her arms. This isn't sexual, it isn't supposed to be sexual, yet my heart is pounding as she holds me. I can feel the pounding of her heart as well. Neither of us speaks. Alex slowly trails her hands up and down my back as I methodically rub the back of her head and neck. We are lost in this state for a while, Alex comforting me. There is a knock at the door as the nurse announces herself, tearing me from drowning in the comfort. I try to pull away, but Alex won't let me. I quickly give up the fight and resume the track my hand has been running. My heart is still pounding, Alex's embrace threatening to be just the supplement my hormones need to overtake my emotions.

"I know I shouldn't say anything but seeing you two together warms my heart. It is nice to see two people who love each other so much." I stiffen a little at her words, my hands frozen in place. I didn't think it was possible, but my heart starts beating even faster. I realize Alex has frozen as well. It wasn't the nurse's responsibility to tell her. These feelings are my secret to confess. "I'm sorry I have to separate you, but I need to check her vitals." I break the embrace with Alex, this time meeting no resistance. "Heart rate is higher than your normal. So is your blood pressure. Take it easy you two." She is right. The elevated stats are not what Alex needs right now. The nurse leaves us, but I can't look at Alex. Instead I stare at the floor and unsuccessfully try to steal glances to assess what she is thinking.

*****

Friday morning arrives, and Alex is sound asleep still when my alarm goes off. I try to quietly retract the recliner, but it is loud and wakes her. Her sleepy eyes look over at me, and she smiles. I imagine what it would be like to wake up to that beautiful sight every day. "Morning."

"Sorry, I tried not to wake you. This chair is so damn loud." Her smile grows larger, and her eyes finally adjust to being awake, the brilliant green coming back to life.

"Don't be. I don't mind. How many do you have today?"

"Four. Two rescheduled from Monday. It could be a late evening if any of them are a struggle." I hope to myself that they aren't, I want to get back to Alex as soon as I can.

"I'll be here." It's like she can read my mind. "I am wondering though if I can leave today. Do I really need to be here any longer?" She doesn't. I know that she can leave today. She has made great progress over the week and can walk short distances on her own now. I know that I'm keeping her here because I'm too emotionally invested and want her to be safe.

"I'll discharge you tonight after I finish my cases, as long as things go well today. I want you to use the walker at the house though. You are still going to need to take it easy and be careful. You have to keep your blood pressure and heart-rate down. What you can do at my place is going to be the same as what you can do here." The smile that lights up Alex's face is infectious. I smile back at her, I can't deny how happy the thought of having Alex at the house again makes me.

*****

"In a hurry today doc?" Erin eyes me as I help them start to clean up after the first case. Normally I don't do this. I could, but I typically dictate and review the films for my next case while I wait for the patient to be extubated. I'm normally not in a hurry, but with Alex waiting I want to do whatever I can to move things along. As the nurse and anesthesia take the patient to recovery, Erin and I are left alone. Before she can page for turnover help, I stop her.

"If today goes well I'm going to discharge Alex this evening." Erin smiles and eyes me for a moment.

"Where is she going?"

"Back to mine. I've arranged for a service to help out when I'm not there." Erin's smile falters a little.

"Is that a good idea? Have you told her yet?"

"Not yet. I don't want to do it here. Plus I want her to focus on her rehab, not worry about anything else."

"Be careful. I don't want to see her hurt again." I'm happy that Alex has so many people looking out for her well-being.

"That isn't what I want either. I'll be careful, promise."

"Alright, I'll make it sure we kick it into high gear then. I know I don't really feel like staying late tonight if we can avoid it."

"Sounds good. Thanks."

True to her word Erin pushes things along, and we finish my last case just after six. Not bad for a three level lumbar spinal fusion, an ACDF, a three level bilateral decompression and a brain tumor biopsy. I'm tired. The week of not sleeping in my own bed coupled with pushing it today is all catching up with me. The thought of getting Alex out of here keeps me going though. Alex lights up when I enter her room.

"Earlier than you thought you'd be. Nice." I smile back at her, exhaustion be damned, I can't help it.

"Erin moved things along really nicely, especially after I told her I was planning to discharge you tonight." I look over Alex's vitals. Everything looks good. Just a physical exam to pass then. "How have things been today?"

"Uneventful. Made it a little further without the walker during rehab."

"Good. Well, as long as the physical exam looks good I don't see why you won't be able to leave. The CT I ordered today looks good. I still can't see any permanent damage, and you seem fine." I check Alex's eyes, reflexes, sensation detection, and her wound sites. Everything looks good. "Ok. Let me see you walk." She rises from the bed defiantly, making it clear how badly she wants to get out of here. I stand in front of her ready to catch her if needed, taking a step back each time she takes one forward. My back hits the wall on the other side of the room. Alex stops, her pulse point in her neck visibly pounding away, her eyes fixed on mine. I long for her to close the space between us, to keep me pinned against the wall and make me hers.

"So?" Her questions shakes me out of my momentary fantasy.

"Yeah, everything looks good." I know the words have come out in a whisper. Neither of us have moved.

"Good. You gonna put the order in then?" She turns and heads back to the bed. I detach myself from the wall and follow her. Once she is back in bed, I head into the hallway to put orders in and calm my surging hormones.

*****

I realize that I don't have any food the moment I park the car. "Shit. I forgot about dinner. You're probably starving. What if I order one of those BBQ chicken pizzas you like?"

"Honestly, that sounds amazing right now."

"Good." One crisis averted. "Let me come around, and I'll help you up the steps into the house." I expect her to put up a fight and am surprised when she doesn't. Once back in the house Alex situates herself on the couch in the den.

"Feel like watching a movie or something? I just want to do something normal, in a normal setting."

"That sounds nice." I glance at the clock, it is just after 7. I call and order the pizza. "I'm going to take care of our bags, I'll be right back. You need anything? You warm enough?"

"I could use a blanket actually. What do you want to watch?"

"You pick," I call back down the hallway. I deposit our bags in the master bedroom and grab a blanket for Alex. I stop in the kitchen and gather two glasses of ice water. I settle myself on the couch in the den, sitting closer to her than necessary. Alex offers me half of the blanket, so I slide underneath it, her body heat bombarding me.

"It's nice to sit on something other than that hospital bed, to not hear those monitors and all that background noise." I understand how she feels. I try to calm my racing heart and raging desire. There are no barriers between us, and we have complete privacy. My emotions beg me to wrap my arms around her, to eliminate the minimal space between us, but my brain prevails, and I refrain. I realize now how difficult being at the house with Alex is going to be.

"So did you find a movie?" I feel like a nervous teenager spending time with her secret crush. Alex turns her head to face me and our eyes lock. Her eyes glow as they dart back and forth from my eyes to my lips. I feel the excitement, knowing she is contemplating kissing me. She bites her lower lip before turning away from me. Alex audibly exhales, abandoning whatever she had been thinking about seconds ago.

"Well, I never did get you to watch *Love Actually* did I?" Crap. Abby and I watched it in the hospital. I know I promised Alex I'd watch it with her, but it was Abby's pick.

"Sounds good." She starts the movie, and we settle in. It isn't long before we have to pause for the pizza delivery. We both over eat, which only serves to compound my exhaustion. I'm pleased that I don't have to work tomorrow, but I know I won't make it past 11 tonight. Alex yawns as this thought crosses my mind. Good, doesn't look like she will either.

"Well, what did you think?"

"I loved it. Easily one of my favorites. I'm glad you shared it with me." I try to stifle a yawn but fail miserably.

"Glad you liked it. You must be exhausted though. Why don't you go to bed?"

"I can make it until you are ready. No biggie." Of course, I'm already yawning again, Alex eyes me with skepticism.

"I'm ready when you are." We head down the hallway to the bedrooms. "Ok, which room do you want me to use?"

"The master." Alex looks at me, confusion wrinkling her forehead as her eyebrows pull inward. Clearly, she hasn't comprehended that she will be watched closely.

"I can't kick you out of your own room. You have plenty of rooms right here."

"You aren't kicking me out. I can sleep in the chair. I want you to sleep in here as the bathroom is connected. If I put you anywhere else, there isn't a guarantee that I'll hear you if you need help. You know I sleep quite soundly."

"But—," Alex opens her mouth to protest, but the look on my face warns her not to argue. She heads into my bedroom. I put the bag of stuff Abby picked up for her on the bed so she can grab something to sleep in. I realize I'll need to find something as well. Normally this would be an issue for me as I don't sleep well unless I'm naked, but I'm so exhausted I could sleep in a polyester sack. Alex makes her way into the master suite. I quickly change and pull a few blankets out of the closet. I toss them on the ottoman in front of the chair. Alex exits the bathroom in a t-shirt and gym shorts. She still looks sexy, even dressed in that. The shirt hugs her curves perfectly, accentuating her breasts. I catch myself staring. Thankfully Alex does not notice.

"All yours," she informs me. I'm shaken out of my trance. It takes me a minute to realize that she is talking about the bathroom. I use the toilet and brush my teeth. Finished I exit the bathroom and head towards the chair.

"You don't have to." Alex's words stop me. I turn and look at her. "It's a California King Catherine. Plenty big enough. You don't have to sleep in the chair; unless you are more comfortable there." I hesitate, not because I'd be uncomfortable, I know I would be too comfortable. The proximity to Alex would be both stimulating and tormenting at the same time. I don't answer her, I just make my way to the far side of the bed. She is right, it is huge.

I shut the lights off, but despite my exhaustion find myself unable to sleep. Alex is in my bed, yet it feels like a canyon separates us. I lay on my side facing her. I can barely make out her silhouette in the dark. Her breathing is even, so I watch her sleep. I long to reach over and touch her, to run my fingers over her face, to hold her as she sleeps, but I don't. I want her to get some decent, undisturbed rest. My feelings can wait.

Alexis

Lying in bed next to Catherine has me on edge. She is so close I can feel her body heat, but I can't reach over and touch her. I long to run my hands over the length of her lithe body. To take my time caressing every one of her curves. Instead, I lay there staring at the ceiling. I'm too on edge to sleep even though I know I need to.
Catherine's breathing has evened out into a rhythmic pace. I'm glad she is asleep. She has to be exhausted from trying to sleep in that damn chair. I lie there wondering if I will ever drift off. Eventually, I do.

I wake up to total darkness. It takes me a second before I realize there is a warm body against mine, that my arms are wrapped around someone. Where am I? I shake the cobwebs away, and that is when the scent hits me, that warm vanilla scent that is Catherine. Fuck! Somehow after drifting off, I ended up rolling over and wrapping my arms around Catherine. I slowly extract my arms from around her, putting physical distance between us. How did this happen? Thankfully she doesn't stir. I'm hopeful she has no idea what has happened. I feel dirty thinking it, but we've found a certain peaceful rhythm, and I don't want to disrupt it. I grab one of the pillows and roll away from Catherine. I hug it to me hoping that it will keep me from repeating my unconscious act again, but the pillow is cold and doesn't feel anywhere near as good against my body as Catherine did. I sigh heavily, eventually drifting off to sleep again.

I wake sometime later to find myself on my back. At least the pillow kept me off of Catherine for the rest of the night. I wonder if she knows what I've done. It is then I realize that she is awake. She has been watching me sleep. I look over at her, dreading the response, scared that she knows. "Hey." It sounds sheepish and guilty to my own ears.

"Morning. Sleep alright?" I can't tell if she is baiting me, if she knows and wants me to confess. Would she say anything if she did know?

"Yeah, not bad. You?"

"I slept very well actually. I'm afraid I'm going to need to run to the store before I can make you breakfast. Any requests?"

She doesn't know then. Good. It is for the best. "Pancakes sound amazing. Oh and bacon too." Catherine laughs.

"So easy to please. I can do that. I'm going to put the order in online and just use curbside pickup. That will minimize how long I have to leave you here alone."

"I'll be fine, I promise."

*****

Catherine returns with several bags of groceries. It looks like she is prepared to feed an army. I try to help her with the bags, but she refuses, telling me to sit down. She deposits the first few bags on the counter and stops, her eyes examining me, her nostrils flaring. I can tell she is pissed. "Did you shower while I was gone?" I look at the floor. I knew when I did it that she wouldn't be happy about it. I had hoped she wouldn't notice. "I know you showered. You smell different. What would you have done if you had fallen?"

"But I didn't fall. I'm ok, really. That shower is amazing, and I just wanted to feel clean, genuinely clean." I look Catherine in the eyes, watching her anger melt away.

247

"I'm sorry I got upset. I just..." Catherine stops speaking but never breaks eye contact. I don't speak. She has something on her mind, but it is something I can't read. "I just worry about you is all. I wish you would have waited until I was back so I could make sure you were safe."

"I'm sorry. What is your plan for next week though? Eventually, I'm going to be alone."

"Yes but not next week."

"What do you mean? Tell me you didn't cancel your appointments and surgeries to stay here with me!" I feel anger starting to bubble up in me. I told her I didn't want to be a burden on anyone.

"Relax, I didn't. I've arranged for a nursing service to be here while I'm at work. I will be here the following week though. The office is going to be closed for the week for some renovations the partners wanted, so I figured it was a good time to take the whole week off. Most of us are actually." I feel relief at this bit of information until it hits me that she was probably going to actually go somewhere.

"So where were you going to go?"

"I was going to go visit Taylor. Not a big deal. She knows what happened. She wants me to stay here with you, just like I want to stay. I can go visit her another time."

"I never wanted you to put your life on hold to take care of me." I can't look at her. I feel shame for needing help, and I feel like a burden, one she never asked for. I hear the soft patter of Catherine's steps as she makes her way to the barstool I'm perched on. She takes my chin in her hand and forces me to look at her.

"You are not making me put anything on hold. You are here because I want you here; because I want to be here for you. You are not a burden." I nod because if I speak I know I will cry. I hope that Catherine doesn't notice, but it seems that she does. She pushes my knees apart and pulls me into her chest. All of my senses are assaulted at once. Her tantalizing vanilla scent that I can't get enough of permeates my nostrils awakening my desire for her. I open my eyes and discover her breasts are against my face. My mouth waters at the thought of teasing her nipples through the fabric of her shirt. I can hear the beating of her heart as she holds my head against her chest. The touch of her body against mine ignites all of my nerve endings. She holds me like this for a few minutes, neither of us speaking. Finally, she pushes away. I want to pull her back to me. Maybe I do reach for her, I'm not sure.

"I've got to get the rest of the groceries and put them away. Then I need to feed you."

Catherine makes me the promised breakfast of pancakes and bacon. She even remembers that I prefer mine with fresh strawberries and a little bit of whipped topping. After, we put together a jigsaw puzzle. It takes us a decent chunk of the day and serves as a nice break from the continual onslaught of movies we've been watching. Being this close to her is maddening though. Occasionally I look up to see her gazing at me, but she looks away and doesn't say anything. We finish the puzzle and Catherine sighs. I don't know what it is, but she is clearly preoccupied. I look at her and raise my eyebrows. She smiles momentarily then finds her voice.

"I hate to do this to you, but I would really like to go for a swim. I can't let you swim though, it would be too much for you at this point."

"It's fine. You should go for that swim. I know you love it and haven't been in the pool in at least a week. Go for it." She smiles at me again, her relief evident.

"Why don't you come to the pool with me. I want to swim some laps but after we could get you in the shallow end, let you walk in there for a bit. Might be good for you."

"Yeah, it might. I don't have my suit though."

"No biggie. Wear one of mine or your gym shorts and a top if you want. You up for it?" I realize that I am. Something different to break up the monotony of movies and books that have consumed my time lately. The thought of the lukewarm water engulfing me too much to deny. I nod to her that I am. "Great! Let's get changed."

*****

Watching Catherine swim is a thing of beauty. She slices through the water like she is a daughter of Poseidon. She is fast and seems tireless. I have no idea how long she has been at it. I turned my iPod on when we came out here and have barely heard the music, I've been so absorbed in watching her. Eventually, she makes her way over to the side of the pool where I sit with my feet dipped in the water.

"Ready?" I am. I peel off my shirt electing to do this in a pair of my gym shorts and a sports bra. I notice Catherine falter a little, but I am unsure if it is out of desire or because I've made her uncomfortable. Ever unreadable, she quickly snaps back and grabs me by the waist to help me into the water. Her strength comes as a surprise to me. She is certainly stronger than she looks.

"Think you can make it all the way across the pool?" Catherine is issuing me a challenge, one that I don't plan to back down from.

"Across and back I'd bet."

"Now you're just being cocky." She is teasing me, I know. She takes her hands off my hips. "Alright, let's see it then." She backs up, her retreat matching my forward progress. I warn her before she hits the far side, not wanting her to hit her head. She quickly darts around me, preparing for the return trip. "Still think you can make it back?"

"I know I can." We head back, and I realize how great a metaphor this little exercise is for our relationship. Me chasing her, yet never catching her, Catherine always just out of reach. I complete the return trip, and Catherine asks if I want to go again. I do. Our second lap complete I'm starting to feel a little tired but know that I have one more in me. "One more," I inform her. She darts back around me, and we continue our pattern.

"I like this song. Who is it?"

I've been so focused on Catherine that I have to stop and listen for a second. "Florence and the Machine."

"Wow her voice is amazing."

"She even sounds this good live."

"You've seen her?"

"Yep, fantastic show." I have half a lap left. We make the turn and head back. It takes me a little longer, but I make it.

"Great job Alex! You'll be running around without that walker in no time." I laugh, and Catherine eyes me questioningly.

"I only use that walker because you make me. I don't need it." Catherine defiantly looks at me for a moment.

"So get rid of it then."

"Maybe I will." I'm close to being rid of it, I know I am. Once in a while though I feel my legs get shaky, like they are uncertain. "Why am I having this issue still? Is there damage you aren't telling me about?" Catherine's smile fades, and I become certain that she has kept something from me. I start to feel a mixture of panic and worry.

"Calm down Alex." She makes her way to closer to me. "Your bleed was located at the anterior portion of your parietal lobe. There was a lot of pressure on your parietal and frontal lobes. I haven't withheld anything from you. There isn't any permanent damage showing on your scans. It is likely just residual trauma from the pressure on the brain. You're improving quickly, and I expect you will fully regain your motor functions. If I had any doubt you'd still be in the hospital. I wouldn't risk it with you."

"Ok." I don't sound convincing, even to myself.

"Come on. I'll remotely log in and show you everything." We make our way out of the pool. Catherine seats me in one of the chairs at the small table that sits pool side. "Stay here. I'll be right back." She returns quickly, her laptop in hand. She pulls up a chair next to mine and logs into the system. We go over each of my scans, starting with the one she ordered on my arrival and ending with the final one taken yesterday. "I don't see anything. The radiologist didn't see anything. I know you can read these. Did you see anything?"

"No. Just improvement from one scan to the next. None of the tell tale white spots."

"Exactly. I would never lie to you about this Alex. It is too important." All I catch is the 'about this' part of her proclamation.

"About this? Aside from the stuff before I moved out what else have you lied to me about?" Catherine looks down, and I feel my blood run cold.

"I had already seen *Love Actually*. Abby and I watched a bunch of your favorite movies when you were in your coma. I had promised you before that I would watch it with you. I felt like I had broken that promise. Abby picked it though so we watched it. I'm sorry. I really do love the movie though."

"And?"

"And nothing. Nothing else. I don't want it to be like that with us." Catherine has taken my hand, her eyes look as if she is going to cry.

"Ok." I don't care for the fact that she just didn't tell me but can appreciate her wanting to honor her promise. This is minor and easy for me to let go. "So what else did you two watch? What do you mean her pick?"

"We alternated picks. We watched a few movies. We were both miserable and worried. Abby had heard that people in comas often find comfort in having their favorite music played or can recall what loved ones say to them. So we had a movie night where we played a bunch of your favorite movies. She chose *Sliding Doors* and *Love Actually*. I chose *Carol* and *Batman Begins*. I can't remember after that honestly."

"Good picks. Gotta represent the nerd side of me."
Catherine laughs. "You talked to me?" Catherine nods
that she did. "I don't remember anything. What did you
say?" Catherine stares out the windows for the longest
time even though it is dark and there is nothing to see. I'm
certain that she isn't going to answer the question.

"I begged you to come back, to wake up and to be ok. I
begged you to open your eyes so I could see them again.
I—," she stops herself, tears streaming down her face. I
take her face in my hands and force her to look at me. I
gently use my thumbs to wipe her tears away. I'm certain
that if I tried to kiss her now that I could. As badly as I
want to, I don't. I need her to tell me she has come to
terms one way or another with her emotions. I can't open
the floodgate only to discover it is too soon. Catherine's
stomach growls loudly, forcing both of us to chuckle.

"Hungry?"

"Yes, actually I am. I was thinking of making a stir fry.
How does that sound?"

"Really good, actually. I need to get back to eating
healthier. I'm gonna get fat if I don't." Catherine looks me
up and down and laughs.

"I think you have a long way to go before you lose that tight
stomach. Come on let's make dinner."

*****

I wake up that night to find Catherine pressed against me,
her arm wrapped protectively around me, our hands and
legs entwined. My heart races while my head questions
what the fuck is happening. I need to remove myself from
this situation. I want it too much. How to do it without

waking her though. I slowly lift her arm and try to snake my way out from under it. After I've created a little distance between us, I slowly lower it back to the bed. She doesn't stir. I swing my legs over the side of the bed and stand.

"Alex? Where are you going?" Shit! I freeze momentarily as Catherine switches on the bedside lamp, the light spurring me to take a step towards the bedroom door. "Alex wait!" I can hear Catherine behind me getting out of the bed. She cuts off my path to the door. "What's wrong?"

"I woke up, and you were spooning me! It's hard enough being around you all the time Catherine. This is too much."

"But last night…" My blood turns cold again. I've been busted. She knows.

"I honestly don't know how that happened. I woke up and found you in my arms. I must have done it in my sleep. I was hoping that you had slept through it."

Catherine looks so confused. "Why?"

"Because we've been here before." I rub at my temples before running my palm over my face. "I need a little space." I try to move around her, but she refuses to let me pass.

"Damn it Alex stop! I'm not running from you, so please stop running from me!" Catherine's words have frozen me in place. What is she saying? "Isn't it obvious by now?" She doesn't wait for my reply. She quickly closes the space between us, takes my face in her hands and kisses me.

Catherine

Alex's movement combined with the cool air chilling her vacated space pull me from my slumber. Something must be wrong. I call her name, and she freezes. I'm wide awake now, but she is trying to leave again. I tell her to stop, and she hesitates but is determined to leave. I know I can't let her. I have to tell her now or never. I race from the bed and block her path. She went to bed before I did tonight and was fast asleep when I got there. After waking up in her arms last night, I thought it would be okay to hold her. She doesn't know that I know. I was wrong. She is going to run again. I can feel my last chance slipping through my fingers, like the last few grains of sand in an hourglass as it empties. My frustration has reached its limit. Her unwillingness or inability to see what is clearly in front of her combined with my longing for her are too much. I kiss her, and she freezes for what feels like forever before she responds. Relief surges through me as I feel her hands find my face and slowly start to snake their way down my body. Her tongue invades my mouth before quickly darting away. She bites my lower lip as she makes to pull away but follows it back to continue our kiss. Our mouths are fused together. I know now that I've never wanted anyone this badly. Alex's hands are on my hips as she slowly pulls us back to the bed. I try to break off the kiss, but she darts one hand up and presses the back of my head forbidding it. She breaks away from me just after I feel her bump against the bed. As soon as she is seated, I tower over here and reclaim her lips. I feel greedy, but our chemistry burns through me. Alex slowly slides back onto the bed, never breaking our rhythm. I can feel her hands snaking under my shirt as I press my body on top of hers. She bites my lower lip again as she starts teasing each of my nipples. I moan into her mouth, certain that I could come now if I allowed myself to. Alex deftly flips me over and this time sucks on my lower lip as she pulls away.

She looks into my eyes, her greens are on fire. It only turns me on more.

"You're sure?" My chest is heaving, my breathing ragged, my nipples are so hard they ache, and my sex is throbbing. I answer her by pulling her back in for another kiss. I'm not sure I will ever get enough of her lips on mine. Alex is tugging on my shirt, trying to pull it off of me. The cool air meeting my feverish body brings me back to my senses. She is trailing her way down my neck and working my nipples as my chest heaves with desire.

"Wait!" She freezes, and I can see confusion, disappointment and hurt in her eyes. She hangs her head, her shoulders slumped in defeat as she starts to untangle herself from me. I pull her back on top of me and kiss her again. "It isn't that. I want you more than I've ever wanted anyone, please believe me. It's just you aren't ready. You aren't physically ready for that level of exertion." Alex eyes me the fire back in her eyes. She kisses me again. I allow it but break it off before it becomes too intense. "I'm serious Alex. This is indescribably difficult for me, but now that I've got you I won't risk your health. We can wait. It won't be much longer." Alex sighs and kisses me again before rolling off of me. She sits on the edge of the bed, her back to me. It takes me a minute, but I slowly see the heave in her shoulders, she is crying. "Alex?"

"I'm fine, I'm fine." I know that she is not fine though. I move behind her and wrap my arms around her. I hold her tightly and slowly guide her back onto the bed. She hasn't said a word. We lay together on the bed, her back against my chest. I can feel it when she gains control of her emotions, her breathing leveling out.

"You asked me what I said to you while you were in your coma." Alex rolls onto her back and then onto her side. Our faces are mere inches apart. She doesn't speak. I wish she would, I am paralyzed by fear, fear that if I admit the rest, it will be too much too soon. I slowly stroke her face as she looks at me expectantly. "I didn't tell you everything Alex. I did beg you to come back to me. I also told you that I am ready and that I love you." Fresh tears spill out of both our eyes. She kisses each of mine away and then kisses me. Not a frenzied kiss like those we shared moments ago. This one slower and filled with emotion. We separate too soon, and Alex rolls onto her back pulling me into her arms. My head rests on her chest, our legs entwined. I can hear her heartbeat, the rhythm is soothing. "I'm not going anywhere Alex. I promise you I'm not going anywhere." She softly kisses me on the top of my head as she lazily trails her fingers up and down the length of my spine. I squeeze her tighter, attempting to close the imaginary space between us. The combined rhythm of her heartbeat along with the caresses along my spine lull me back to sleep.

Alexis

I can't sleep. As I lay here holding Catherine my mind is swirling with emotional overload. Catherine's kiss has somehow validated everything I have been feeling every time our eyes met, every time she touched me, what I had felt the first time I laid eyes on her. We have a natural rhythm, as if we've been with each other for years. We simply fit. But what if she decides that this isn't right for her, that she was wrong and she can't do this? My first instinct is to run, to get out and protect myself as if it isn't already too late. She said she loved me. People who say that always leave though. Catherine lays asleep in my arms, her head on my chest while I slowly trail my fingertips up and down her back. *She is right here. She didn't run. She stopped me from running.* Over and over I try to reassure myself, but doubt and fear keep creeping back in. Confusion coupled with exhaustion and unreleased sexual frustration combine, eliciting a heavy sigh from me.

"Mmm...what's wrong?" Shit, I've woken Catherine. My fingers freeze, my heart rate speeds, my mouth turns into a dessert. I can't pretend I'm asleep and I can't answer. "Alex?" Catherine lifts her head from my chest and looks me in the eye.

"Nothing. Go back to sleep." My fingers resume their trek along her spine. Catherine doesn't budge.

"I think not. Talk to me." She slides a little up the bed and positions herself so that her face hovers over mine. Her eyes bore into me, searching for what it is I refuse to say. Her hand moves up and strokes the side of my face. "I'm here Alex. I'm right here."

"For now. What happens when you decide you can't though?"

259

"Oh, Alex." Catherine kisses me softly, our lips meeting too briefly. "I meant what I said."

"Why now though? Is it because of the accident? Is it some reaction out of pity or something?"

"No Alex. I'm here because I want to be here; because I can't ignore how I feel about you. I wanted to tell you before the accident. I looked for you all day to tell you that I was hoping we could talk. I just kept missing any chance to connect with you. I thought you were with Brooke, but I was still going to tell you, not to separate the two of you but just to…I don't know. I just wanted you back in my life in some capacity. I missed you so badly that a constant ache tore through me. I missed you that day, the day the accident happened. When they wheeled you into the ER, and I finally saw that it was you, I was a wreck. I wasn't sure how I was going to operate on you, I have never been so scared in my life. I was a mess afterward as well. Abby knew, Taylor knew, even Erin quickly figured out how I feel about you. They all told me to tell you, but I insisted that it needed to wait, that you needed to focus on healing first. I thought it was obvious how I feel, surely it must be if everyone else can see it, but you never did, or you chose to ignore it. Last night when I woke up in your arms, I thought finally. Nothing had ever felt so right to me. When you tried to run I could feel it, my chance was slipping through my fingers. I had to tell you, or you would be gone again."

I lay there in silence, contemplating everything she has just said. The added information turning the storm into a tornado. "Erin knows?"
Catherine releases a small chuckle as she shakes her head in disbelief. "Out of everything I just told you that is what you're focused on? She was there during your surgery. She saw me with you after. She figured it out

quite quickly. She told me that I needed to tell you, and warned me that I better not hurt you. She also assured me that she wouldn't tell anyone."

"No, we can trust Erin." I sit and contemplate everything, trying to quiet my fears, trying to be in this moment.

"Alex tell me the one thing I can do to make you believe me. I'm here, I want this. I'm not going to run." I sit and think about it. Catherine keeps stroking the side of my face, her worry becoming evident.

"Nothing…I can't think of anything."

"Then I need you to trust me. Give me time, give us a chance. I don't let people get close to me, and I am not fast and loose with my emotions." Catherine continues to stare at me, her blue eyes pulling at me like a riptide in the ocean. I pull her face to mine and kiss her because, in the end, she is what I want, what I've wanted for months. The kiss intensifies, and we are quickly back at it again, pawing at one another like teenagers left to their own devices. Just like before Catherine breaks it off. I roll off the top of her and flop back onto the bed, letting an audible growl escape me.

"I know baby. It is hard for me too. Soon though. Soon you'll be healthy enough. Just let the anticipation build until then." She rolls on top of me and kisses me again before sliding back down, resuming her position in my arms. This time I sleep.

*****

I wake up in the morning to find Catherine gone. I look at the clock and discover it is almost nine. How in the world did I sleep so late? I get out of bed and quietly pad my way down the hall towards the kitchen. I can hear sounds coming from there. Catherine is busy cutting up fruit, her back to me. She isn't aware that I'm awake. I tiptoe across the space between us, waiting for her to put the knife down. As soon as she does, I strike, coiling my arms around her waist, kissing her on the side of her neck. "Morning beautiful." She tenses momentarily before giggling and turning to face me.

"Good afternoon sleepy head," she teases me as her arms wrap around my neck and she presses her lips against mine. Could every morning be like this? "I thought you were going to sleep all day." I grin at her as I see the playfulness in her eyes.

"I pretty much did. Why didn't you wake me?" Our arms are still locked around one another, our foreheads together, keeping our lips apart.

"You need to rest."

"So do you."

"I slept very well, thank you." Catherine kisses me again. I could stay like this all day. As if reading my mind she slowly backs me up to the bar. "Have a seat. I'm working on our breakfast."

"I know what I want for breakfast." I arch an eyebrow at her and grin.

"That's not on the menu…yet." She is teasing me, making this seem so easy for her. I want to leap off this stool and pin her against the bar. To take her here and now. But I know that she will stop me, and I know that she deserves better. I'm staring at Catherine's ass, which even in sweatpants looks amazing. She turns her head and catches me, raising her eyebrow in that questioning manner.

"Forget something?" I raise my eyes to hers, I've been too focused on what I'd like to do to her ass to even register what she has said. "Where is your walker?"

"I'm good. I don't need it." She raises that eyebrow again but says nothing.

After breakfast, we head to the pool. Catherine swims her laps tirelessly. Initially, I stay perched on the side of the pool, where she commanded me to, but once she is in a rhythm, I slip into the water. She continues her laps, and I'm certain she is in the zone, that my disobedience has gone unnoticed. I'm enjoying the feel of the cool water around me when I notice the pattern of the ripples has changed. Catherine is making her way towards me.

"What do you think you are doing Miss. Woods?" Miss. Woods huh? Well, two can play this game.

"Just soaking in the pool, Dr. Waters." Catherine raises her eyebrow at me. I know I am skating a dangerous line, that she isn't pleased that I've disobeyed her.

"No soaking. In the water means time to work. Come on." This is an order I obey. I start making my way toward the opposite side of the pool. I complete six laps this time. I'm ready to start the seventh, but Catherine stops me. "You're making great progress Miss. Woods. Must have some great motivation." She still wants to play.

"I do. She's a little taller than me, eyes like the ocean, a smile you could melt over, a brilliant mind and a killer body. She has blond hair that rests just above her muscular swimmer's shoulders. Maybe you've seen her around." Catherine darts towards me, pinning me against the side of the pool.

"I haven't, but maybe you could get her number for me."
Her mouth latches onto mine, my hands roving over the
skin tight fabric of her swimsuit. She grabs my ass, then
slides her hands down my thighs tugging at the back of
them until I wrap my legs around her waist. Our kiss
continues as she slides her hands up my sides. I pull her
as close as possible, my pelvis finally making contact with
her. I slowly start to grind my hips against her. A low moan
escapes me, and she breaks off all contact. My feet
reconnect with the bottom of the pool as my throbbing clit
protests. She moves back in and pins me against the wall
with her chest. She trails a few light kisses up my neck
before whispering "Do you have any idea how badly I want
you?" She takes my earlobe in her teeth and gently tugs
at it before letting go and moving away. "Come on. I need
a shower."

Catherine jumps in the shower, and I change into a pair of
sweats. The sound of the water running on the other side
of the door has me envisioning Catherine in the shower,
the streams of water rolling over her body. I want to join
her so badly, but I refrain. Instead, I head to the kitchen,
open the sliding door and stand in the cool air, hoping it will
help. It isn't long before I hear the door open behind me.

"There you are! I was worried when you weren't answering
me." She eyes me for a minute, sees the few stray drops
of pool water along my head and neck. "You're wet.
Come in before you end up sick."

"I know I am. I was hoping the cold would help."
Catherine falters momentarily before grabbing my hand
and pulling me back inside.

"Go take a shower smart ass. Want to go out for lunch?"

"Yeah, that sounds great."

We pull into the small family owned Italian restaurant. I have been meaning to try this place for years but never seem to remember it when I'm hungry. "Reservation for Waters," Catherine informs the hostess. She takes my hand as we follow the hostess to the back of the dining area, away from the other diners. A few heads turn as we pass their tables, I can't tell if it is because of Catherine or if it is because of the hand holding. Either way, I don't waste any emotion on it. The hostess stops at a long rectangular table with place settings for 10. I'm confused. Catherine pulls me down onto a chair next to hers and lightly kisses me as the hostess walks away. We are completely absorbed in each other when the waitress comes over and asks what we'd like to drink. Neither of us have touched the menu and thus have no idea. Catherine quickly flips hers over and finds the drinks listed on the back. "I'll just have water thank you."

"I'd like a lemonade and a water please." I turn my attention back to Catherine and brush my lips lightly against hers.

"OH MY GOD!!! YOU TWO FINALLY!!!" Abby is basically shouting and squealing for all the restaurant to hear. She is practically jumping up and down. She runs around the table as I stand to give her a hug, never letting go of Catherine's hand. The patrons around us have all stopped their conversations and eating to look at the source of the commotion. After a few seconds pass they gradually resume their activities.

"Everyone is coming, aren't they?" I look back and forth between Catherine and Abby.

"Yes. Catherine sent me a message last night telling me you were doing really well and asked if I could get everyone to come here for lunch today. Everyone misses you."

I turn to Catherine and just look at her. "You did this for me?"

"Abby did most of it. I merely made the suggestion." It is one of the sweetest things anyone has ever done for me. I give Catherine a lingering kiss and thank her before turning to Abby and hugging her again. Abby looks at us and fixes her eyes on Catherine.

"So when did this happen? I thought you were going to wait." Catherine laughs and shakes her head. I realize that the two have formed a stronger bond since my accident, the shared experience something only the two of them can understand. The thought makes me happy.

"I was going to wait, but someone forced my hand." Catherine squeezes my hand under the table and kisses me softly on the cheek. Abby is positively beaming.

"You tried to run again didn't you?" I look at my lap. Abby knows me too well. She is one of the few people in my life that stoutly refused to let me push them away. I nod my head slightly, confirming that I did. "Well, I'm glad she didn't let you."

Shannon, Kevin, Derrick, Dahila, Nikki, and Sara show up as the waitress returns with our drinks. They all line up to hug me before sitting down. I never let go of Catherine's hand. I refuse to. As they look over the beverage offerings, I lean into Catherine and slowly whisper, "Thank you, this really means a lot to me." I make sure my breath tickles her ear just enough and know it has worked when she grips my hand harder. The invigorating scent that is Catherine assaults me causing me to intensify my grip in return. As I lean back out of Catherine's space, we both relax our hands again.

"Hey Alex, you want a drink?" Kevin's offer is nice, but I don't want a drink, nor do I think Catherine would approve.

"No thanks, but you guys feel free."

"I don't think she needs a drink. She already looks like she is drunk on love." Derrick's words make everyone laugh. I turn and gaze into Catherine's eyes. If this is what feeling drunk on love is then keep them coming.

Lunch is a great time. It is nice to see my family and have everything be so relaxed. It is nice to laugh so much after everything that has happened. I am finally forced to let go of Catherine's hand when our meals arrive. I've selected a Cajun Alfredo pasta with chicken, sausage, and peppers. Catherine chose the more traditional meat lasagna. We share a sample of our meals with each other, and I hear Derrick jokingly groan. "Look at them. They are one of those couples." I look at Catherine and smile, we both laugh.

I finish my lunch and let my hand fall back under the table, placing it on Catherine's leg, just above the knee. I slowly trail my fingers a little up her thigh. I feel her muscles tense and see her pupils dilate, but nothing else in her posture betrays my behavior. I slowly trail them back down to her knee and feel her quad relax. I continue to do this, inching further up her leg each time. Each time her quad tenses and relaxes with my movement. Each trip up her thigh brings me closer and closer to its apex. I continue slowly moving my fingers, engaging in the conversation taking place all the while. Catherine clears her throat, and I realize there is no more north to travel, I can only move south or west. I have no intention of moving west. I only intend to tease her, so my fingers lazily travel south and

267

then make the journey northward again. Catherine grabs my wrist this time and places my fingers between her thighs. She closes her fingers over mine and slowly starts to massage herself through her jeans. I can feel the heat radiating off of her and the moisture soaking through the thick fabric. I allow her to continue using my hand to stroke herself until I notice her rhythm pick up, then pull my hand away. I fake a cough just so I have a reason to bring my hand to my face. I inhale deeply and close my eyes, stifling the moan Catherine's scent elicits from me. Just like that Catherine has turned the tables on me. I squirm uncomfortably in my seat feeling my own juices soaking my panties. Our friends are oblivious to the game we are playing.

"Feel like taking any dessert home?" Catherine asks me in a normal tone, but I see the look in her eyes. I lean over and kiss her before pulling back slightly to lock eyes with her.

"I doubt they offer what I'm craving," I whisper, just loud enough for Catherine to hear it. Abby begins tapping me on the back as I lean in to kiss Catherine again.

"Umm...Alex." I pull away from Catherine and smile at Abby. I notice she isn't looking at me but off to the side of the table. I follow her gaze and discover Elena and Rachel staring at Catherine and me. By now the entire table has caught on and has gone quiet.

"Elena, Rachel hello." I'm not sure what to say, but I can feel the tension take hold of Catherine. I realize that she has never met Elena, she has no idea who is standing there. Elena's eyes dart between Catherine and me. She eyes the fading wounds on my face and my knit cap. She knows me well enough to know that I would never keep the hat on while eating. "So how are you?" I reach back under the table and find Catherine's hand. I want her to relax, to know that she has nothing to worry about.

"Fine. You?"

I look at Catherine and smile. "I'm great! Catherine this is Elena and her sister Rachel. Elena and Rachel meet Catherine." I hear Catherine say hello, but it lacks her usual confidence. I squeeze her hand under the table trying to reassure her.

"We will let you get back to your meals." Rachel pulls Elena away from our table. I don't watch them leave. Instead, I immediately refocus my attention on Catherine. She seems a little shaken. I lean over and ask her if she is ok. She nods that she is, but I don't believe it.

"Dessert anyone?" The waitress is back. No one at the table has any room for dessert, and it is clear that I'm not the only one that has noticed Catherine's change in mood.

"I think we will take our checks please." I'm thankful that Abby understands I want to get Catherine out of here.

"Ok, how am I breaking up the bill?"

"One check, please. Lunch is on me." Catherine has been pulled from her state. She fights off the protests of our friends and insists that she receive the bill. She pays the check, and we all stand up to make our way back outside. I'm still clutching her hand, so I slow her, pulling her back to me.

"Baby what's wrong? What happened?"

"Not here," she whispers as she pulls away from me. Outside we say our goodbyes to our friends as they each hug me in turn. I notice Abby giving Catherine a hug and whispering something to her. Catherine nods her head, but the sadness remains on her face, and her shoulders continue to sag a little.

We get in the car, and Catherine remains silent. I stare at her, but she doesn't look at me. I sigh out of frustration. "Do you think we could stop by my apartment and pick a few things up while we are out?" She nods and starts the car.

The ride to my apartment is filled with silence. We get there, but Catherine won't let me go upstairs. Instead, I give her a list, and she heads up. I quickly text Abby asking what happened. My phone goes off right away, and her one-word response is Elena. I text back three questions marks. I don't understand what has happened. Abby responds that I just need to talk to her. Catherine is taking a while to come back to the car. I want to go up and find her, hold her and make her tell me what has shaken her so. I know if I do she will only be more upset because I took the stairs without help. So I wait. When Catherine returns to the car her eyes are red and puffy. She has obviously been crying.

We drive back to her place without saying a word. I can hear her occasionally sniffle, trying not to cry. I am going crazy trying to figure out what happened. Catherine parks in the garage, grabs my stuff and heads into the house without looking back. I step through the door in time to see her head down the hall towards the bedroom. I follow her and try to wrap my arms around her, but she pulls away.

"Will you please talk to me? I'm going crazy here. I don't know what happened." Catherine won't even look at me. My desperation amps up and fear starts to choke me. "Please Catherine, please." She finally looks up at me. I take it as a sign and move closer to her, taking her hand. I pull her towards the bed and sit down. When she does the same, I slide back and sit with my knees bent and my feet together. Catherine pulls herself up onto the bed and faces me. She draws her knees up to her chest and wraps her arms around her legs. I slide closer to her so I can grab one of her hands and rub my fingers across her arm with my other. I do this and wait for her to talk.

"She is very beautiful." Catherine's voice is a whisper.

"Elena?" Catherine nods. "I suppose she is. So?"

"I saw how she looked at you." What is she talking about? "She still wants you."

"Don't be absurd. So what if she does?"

"I've seen that look before." My phone chimes from my pocket. I ignore it. I'm so confused about what has rocked Catherine so badly. It takes me a minute, but the answer finally comes to me.

"Is this about Brian?"

"The woman he cheated on me with looked at him the exact same way that Elena looked at you." My phone chimes again. "You should get that."

"Whatever it is isn't as important as this. Catherine, I'm not Brian. No matter how Elena may or may not have looked at me, I wasn't looking at her. I would never do what he did to you."

"You say that, but you were together a long time, you have history together. What happens if she decides she wants to try again?" My phone chimes again, irritating me. "Really Alex, just see who it is."

271

"Sorry," I tell her as I pull out my phone. Elena has sent me three text messages. She hasn't contacted me once since I moved out and now this. I enter my password and read them. *It was great to see you today. What is with the hat? Please talk to me.* I quickly type my response: *had an accident, busy.* I don't want to encourage her. "Catherine you just said it yourself. It is history. I am where I want to be with who I want to be with." My phone chimes again. A realization hits me. I'm an idiot. Catherine has told me she loves me three times and I have never told her how I feel in return. "Don't you know that you're the only woman I see? That you are the only woman that I want? Don't you know that I love you?" Catherine finally looks up at me, she still has tears in her eyes. They are like daggers being driven into my heart. I slide a little closer to her, spreading my legs out to surround her. I wipe her face with my thumbs. "Don't you know that a part of me has belonged to you since you stopped me at the conference? I've been a fool for not telling you sooner. I love you, Catherine." My phone chimes again. I quickly switch it to mute. Catherine seems to relax a little. I slide behind her and wrap my arms around her. I slowly pull her down to the bed and continue to hold her. Eventually, she spins around to face me.

"Say it again."

"I love you, Catherine. I love you." She kisses me and then pulls me to her, burying my face in her neck. We lie there holding each other until I drift off, the warmth of her body combined with her heartbeat lulling me to sleep.

Catherine

I know I'm being irrational, but seeing the way that Elena looked at Alex has reopened an old wound. I can tell how Alex feels about me just by the way she looks at me. I know she doesn't intend to hurt me, yet the fear and insecurity somehow make their way to the forefront. Alex loves me. I have suspected it, but now she has said the words. Words I know she takes seriously, she would never use those words if she didn't mean it. As Alex lays here asleep in my arms, I can feel my heart soaring. Nothing has ever felt this amazing. No one I have ever been with, not getting married, not graduating at the top of my class, not even my first solo surgery. It seems irrational and a bit foolish, but it feels right. I slowly pull the knit cap off of her head, hoping I don't wake her. She doesn't even stir. I lower my head and breathe in the scent that is Alex, musk mixed with citrus and something else that I can't identify. It is inebriating, and I love it. I kiss the top of her head and allow myself to drift off to sleep.

I wake up before Alex. It's dark outside, but I don't need the light to know that neither of us have moved an inch. We still lie facing each other with my lips planted on her forehead. I start trailing my fingers along her back. It is another twenty minutes before she finally stirs. Twenty of the best minutes I have known. She looks up at me, and I can see the concern on her face. "Are you ok?" I'm more ok than I can ever communicate to her.

"Yeah, I'm good." She smiles sleepily and slowly kisses me before sliding back down and burying her face in my neck again.

"Sorry I fell asleep. I'm never going to sleep tonight."

"I did too." I kiss her on the crown of her head. "I'm sure we will find some way to pass the time." Alex groans.

"Do you have any idea what it is you're doing to me?"

"No less than what you are doing to me." We lie there a few more minutes, enjoying the comfort of our embrace. "I hate to break this up, but I really need to pee." Alex laughs, her warm breath caressing the skin on my chest and neck. Gooseflesh covers my arms as chills work their way through my body. "This is what you do to me," I tell her as I flip her onto her back and straddle her. Her hands dart to my hips. I lean over and give her a slow kiss, deepening it as I pull her hands from my hips and pin them over her head. "I told you I have to pee," I remind her when I break off the kiss. I pull myself off of Alex and jump off the bed heading for the bathroom.

When I come out of the bathroom, Alex is sitting on the side of the bed, her phone in her hands. She is clearly bothered by something. I look at her and smile, but I know I have stopped in my tracks.

"Come here please." I do as she asks but a sense of dread starts to creep in. I sit next to her on the bed waiting. "I'm torn between showing you this and not showing it to you. I want to show you so you can stop worrying. At the same time, I don't want to show it to you because it might make you worry more." She types in her passcode and hands me her phone. The display shows a text message conversation from Elena.

> Elena: It was great to see you today.
> Elena: What is with the hat?
> Elena: Please talk to me.
> Me: had an accident, busy.
> Elena: An accident are you ok?
> Elena: Where are you?
> Elena: Talk to me
> Elena: I think I made a mistake

Elena: I miss you

Me: I am fine. I am at Catherine's house. We haven't spoken since I moved out. I need you to know that I love Catherine. I'm not saying this to hurt you, I just want you to know that I love her, that I have moved on. We wanted different things when we separated, and I doubt those desires have changed. You need to find your happiness the way that I have found mine. I am where I belong.

Elena: I'm glad you are happy. You deserve it.

I hand Alex's phone back to her. "Did you say that for me?"

"No. Yes. I said it because it is how I feel and I don't ever want to see you feeling like you did earlier."

I stand up and turn to face Alex. I take her head in my hands and kiss her. "You know you don't have to cut her out of your life for me. I wouldn't ever ask you to."

"You didn't ask me to. I did it because it is the right thing to do for us right now. Maybe one day down the road when you fully understand that I would never cheat on you and that I simply want to be with you, then maybe the three of us can meet again. If that never happens, well Elena and I had some good times, but it wasn't right. This feels right."

I kiss her again, slow and deep before trying to pull away. This time her hands on my hips prevent me from going anywhere. I don't resist and continue the kiss a while longer, until I feel like I'll suffocate if we don't break for air. This time I stop the kiss and take each of her hands in mine. "Come on. We need to find some way to entertain ourselves tonight." Alex resists and gives me the look. I know what she is thinking. As badly as I want the same, I know it is too soon. "Come on, let's go watch a movie or something."

*****

I lay out on the couch while Alex starts the movie. Up first is *Fingersmith*. I'm excited to see the film version since I've read the book. Alex joins me. She lays on her side with her head on my chest. I wrap my legs around hers and can feel the slight pressure of her hip against my sex. I long to start grinding myself against her but hold back. Ten minutes into the movie Alex turns her body, dragging her self over my crotch. Electricity courses through my body. She smiles and quickly kisses me.

"I thought we were going to watch the movie," I ask once I pull back. She stares at me, wearing her up to no good grin.

"You've read the book." She kisses me again, hard. My body responds, and we are back at it like we have been all day. Teenagers aren't this bad, but it feels too good to stop. Alex adjusts herself over me, straddling one of my thighs as she positions one of hers against me. She lowers herself against my leg and starts slowly grinding her hips, staring me in the eyes the entire time. I can't stop myself. I rub myself against her, slowly. Every movement sends jolts of pleasure through my body. We continue our rhythm as she kisses me again. I moan into her mouth. She speeds her grinding a little more, giving me permission to do the same. My hands snake under her shirt and make their way over her abdomen. I start teasing her nipples through the fabric of her bra. They immediately respond to my touch and this time Alex moans into my mouth. We never break off the kiss. The sound of her moan only turns me on further, and I push myself against her thigh even more, speeding my pace. Alex responds and does the same, breaking our kiss, her breath ragged against my ear. I know I need to stop this but I can't, my resolve is nearly gone. I'm still fully dressed, and I'm close to orgasming. No one has ever had this effect on me. I continue rubbing myself against her, I know I am close.

"I'm so close," I pant. "I want you to come with me." I increase my pace even more, ready to finally find some release. Alex practically jumps off of me. Not the reaction I was hoping for.

"This isn't right."

"What?" I am so confused, my raging clit temporarily forgotten.

"This isn't right, this isn't how it should be. I want it to be right." She slowly rubs her hands over her face as she catches her breath.

"Alex what?"

"Our first time. I want it to be right. This isn't right, this fumble on the couch. Don't get me wrong, I'm so turned on right now, and I was right there with you, but it isn't right."

"I'm not a virgin you know. I've had sex before."

"I know that. But not with a woman, not with me. I want to do it right."

I try to pull her back on top of me, wanting to pick up where we left off. Alex won't allow it though. She finally kneels on the couch between my legs, careful to not make contact with my pelvis. She lowers her face to mine and looks me in the eye. "Don't get me wrong. I long to know how you taste, to be inside of you, to watch you lose all control, to hear you scream out in ecstasy." I swallow hard. She lowers her voice, making it sound deeper. "When the good doctor finally declares me healthy enough for sexual activity, you had better be ready." She leans in and whispers "I am going to worship your body like it is a temple and you are my god." It is my turn to growl, her words have traveled straight from my ears to my throbbing core.

"Do you have any idea what you're doing to me?" I whisper as Alex climbs off of me.

"No less than you do to me." She winks and smiles at me.

I extract myself from the couch and head towards the kitchen. I down a glass of ice water hoping to calm the fire coursing its way through me. Naturally, it fails. My sex is throbbing. *I am going to worship your body like it is a temple and you are my god.* Nothing has ever sounded hotter to me. The burning in her eyes when she said it only making it sexier, I know that she means it. I start to imagine what she plans to do to me. She is in the next room, but I can't help it, I slide my hand down my pants and start rubbing myself, imaging that I am back on the couch with Alex. I'm so horny it shouldn't take long. I'm not surprised to find myself dripping wet. I undo the button and zipper of my jeans for a better angle. I insert two fingers into my pussy easily finding my engorged g-spot. I apply pressure to it as I use my palm to massage my clit. I'm already on the edge before I begin rhythmically fucking my own hand. I imagine it is Alex's hand and quickly lose myself. I bite down on my left forearm to stifle my moan and lean against the bar to support myself as the spasms disperse throughout my body, leaving my hand where it is until the tremors stop.

"That wasn't bad, but you shouldn't hold back." Oh my god, Alex was watching me! I right myself from the bar and quickly try to pull my hand out of my pants. I can feel my face flushing with embarrassment. Alex is in front of me in a split second. She looks at me and grabs my hand, the one I've just taken out of my own pussy. I can see my juices running down my fingers. "Don't be embarrassed. I like to watch. It was even sexier knowing that I did this to you." She holds up my hand and inserts my fingers into her mouth. She licks and sucks them clean, moaning the whole time. I can see her erect nipples through her shirt, I know she isn't faking her pleasure. "Do you know how amazing you taste?" I shake my head no, unable to speak. She pulls me in for a forceful kiss, quickly pushing her tongue into my mouth. Her mouth tastes different, good but different than normal. I realize that is me, that I am the difference. It tastes nothing like I thought it would. It only lasts a moment before she breaks it off. "You do now." She walks out of the kitchen leaving me there, speechless.

I take a few minutes to compose myself. Alex is completely undoing me. I am losing all of my inhibitions with her. It is like falling into the abyss and being comfortable, drowning in the ocean and not needing to come up for air. I've never felt so free or so desired. I shake myself from my thoughts. Ice cream, we need ice cream. I walk back to the den with one bowl and two spoons.

"Feel better?" Alex looks at me and grins. I just smile at her. "Too much?"

"Surprisingly no. I was embarrassed, but you even made that seem hot."

"It was hot. I meant it, I like to watch. I just want you to be free. No holding back." I redden again.

"What if I'm too loud or do something you don't like."

"Impossible. Nothing that comes from your pleasure could displease me. It isn't as if I haven't masturbated thinking about you before."

"You have?" I feel my face flush again.

"Don't be embarrassed. The first time was the night we went to Victoria's Secret, and you kept showing me all the stuff you were thinking about buying, asking my opinion. I had a very vivid dream about you coming downstairs and seducing me in one of them that night. I was so turned on I couldn't go back to sleep." She tells me this in a low, slow, seductive voice. She knows what she is doing.

I'm panting again, how does she do this to me? "Which one?"

"The black one. It was very, very sexy."

"I might have bought that one. I might be wearing it now."

"You might have bought it, but you aren't wearing it. The panties you have on aren't black."

"How do you...oh right." I feel myself flush again.

"What's in the bowl?"

"Huh? Oh ice cream, I bought you some the other day. Moose Tracks. I'm not sure what other flavors you like."

"I can think of one, but I doubt it is an available flavor." I'm not sure I have any blood left in my body at this point. Surely it has all migrated to my face. Alex takes one of the spoons from the bowl and takes a bite. "Mmm, delicious. Want to restart the movie?" I nod that I do, afraid that if I try to speak no words will come out.

Catherine and I continue our juvenile sessions, nothing seems to stop them. We try going for a walk, but that ends with Catherine against a tree in the woods. We try sitting on opposite ends of the couch, even in different chairs, but one of us always caves and attacks the other. No place is safe, but physical contact with her is better than no contact at all, even if we have to stop before things go too far. I know she is worried about me, worried about my blood pressure staying level, but contact with her sends my heart racing every time, and I am fine. I won't be able to hold back much longer, and it feels like her resolve is slipping away more each day. This is how we pass the next week. Catherine goes to work, and I spend the day with my aide Judy, waiting for Catherine to come home. Judy is a retired nurse. She works as an aide occasionally, to stay busy and make a little extra money. If Judy has an issue with Catherine and I being together, she doesn't let on, nor do I ask.

Monday I finally start working on stairs. Judy and I use the two steps in a garage. I am surprised when I don't have any trouble with them. On Tuesday I start to swim laps under Judy's supervision. The burning in my arms and shoulders feels amazing. My heart rate is up, and everything is fine. No headaches, vision problems, seizures or other issues. On Wednesday Lydia stops by for lunch. It is nice to see her and find out how her vacation was. She seems genuinely happy that Catherine and I are together. She and Judy chat with one another while I take my midday call from Catherine. It seems as though the two of them have become fast friends by the time Lydia heads home, leaving me to wonder if there isn't possibly a deeper connection there. By Thursday I am convinced that I no longer need the aide, but I know Catherine won't hear of it. Friday sees me pacing the house all day, impatiently counting down the hours until Catherine is home and off of work for a week.

Friday night we are cuddled together on the couch watching more *Game of Thrones*. I've lost count of how many times I've seen every episode, but I never tire of it. Catherine has a hard time switching it off, so for us, it is a relatively safe thing to watch. Our third episode of the night is just starting. Catherine is laying on my chest our legs tangled together. With one hand my fingers caress the trail along her spine over and over. With the other I hold her head against me, slowly rubbing my thumb along the length of her jawline. As the opening credits for the episode roll, Catherine rises up and kisses me, sucking on my lower lip as she pulls away. I open my eyes and find her staring at me, the now familiar fire stirring in her eyes. She kisses me again, this time deeper and with more urgency than the first. When she breaks it off, she lays her head back on my chest. I know she can hear my heart thundering. She lazily trails her fingers up and down my arm. I rest my head back and try to focus on the show.

About halfway through the episode, I feel Catherine's weight shift as she slides off of me. She grabs my hand and looks down at me. "Let's go to bed," she orders as she pulls me off of the couch, baffled. She never shuts *Thrones* off mid-episode.

Catherine releases my hand when we get to the bedroom, I am certain she is heading toward the bathroom. I turn to move to the bed when I feel her grab my arm, stopping me. She pulls me to her and crushes her lips against mine, our tongues colliding. Her hands move down to my hips, and I obey as she directs me to the bed. When I feel the edge of it collide with my ass, I slide up onto it and spread my legs, pulling Catherine against me. She breaks off our kiss and starts trailing kisses across my cheek, biting my earlobe and moving down my neck. She moves back to my mouth, and we greedily clamp onto each other again. I can feel her gently pushing me back onto the bed. I slide back and pull her down on top of me. She straddles me at my waist and kisses me again. I can feel her start to slowly work her hips against me.

"Ok Catherine, time to stop." My breath is ragged. I'm giving the order I have no desire to give. She gazes at me for a moment, her eyes sparking with fire. She leans down and kisses me again forceful and urgent. My need for her responds in kind, and I find my hands sliding up her torso, stopping on her breasts. I cup one in each hand, careful to secure each nipple between my fingers. I massage her breasts, pulling on her nipples with each new motion. Her hips start to grind against me again causing me to groan. She breaks off the kiss and trails her way down the other side of my face. I move to sit up, but she pushes me back down against the bed.

She leans in and licks my earlobe before whispering, "My body is a temple, worship me like I'm your god." Holy shit! How does she remember that? I freeze, my hands locked on her breasts and look at her.

"You're sure? You know what you are saying?" Catherine responds by kissing me. She quickly pulls away to take off her shirt, but I stop her. "Oh no. This will not be over quickly." I kiss her as I sit up and quickly flip her underneath me. "Only I get to unwrap my gift." I grab Catherine's hands and pin them up over her head as I move in to kiss her. I slowly trail my fingers down each of her arms but feel her attempt to move them. I stop to force them back against the bed, breaking off our kiss to give her a warning look. I start my path down her arms again, my fingertips barely making contact. Our eyes are locked, and I can feel her squirm beneath me. She wants to move but doesn't, she accepts that I am in control now. I kiss her again and continue to memorize her body, my fingertips moving over her like her body is written in Braille. I caress my way up her arms and lock hands with her, breaking off our kiss once again. Her breathing is heavy, her lips swollen and dark red, her pupils like black holes that have swallowed the sky.

"Please let me touch you." I barely hear her request but let go of her hands, giving her permission. She quickly seizes my face and pulls me back down for another searing kiss. I feel her hands move down over my shoulders and stop on my hips. She is gently pushing me backward. I oblige, sliding back just enough to allow her to sit up. My fingers slowly work downward until they find the waist of her shirt. I slowly lift it, breaking our kiss to pull it over her head. I lean back for a moment to enjoy my new view. My fingers never stop reading her body, creating a road map, noting her reactions to being touched in each place. I run my hands repeatedly along the length of her torso and kiss her again. I feel Catherine as she slides her hands under my shirt. She slides them up along my back, and I feel them falter when she discovers that I'm not wearing a bra. I've bummed around in shorts and a t-shirt all day, so I never bothered with one. I deepen our kiss as my hands make their way to her breasts, still contained by her bra. I massage them and pull at her nipples, making her moan. Her moaning drives me wild, but I slow down, reminding myself to take my time. I feel Catherine's hands slowly moving up my abdomen until they reach my breasts. Her flesh feels amazing against mine as she rubs her thumbs over my erect buds. I lean my forehead against her and release the moan that her fingers elicit. My body begs me not to, but I pull Catherine's hands off of my breasts as I slide a little further down her legs. I kiss her again, taking my time. My hands resume working her breasts as I kiss my way over her chin and down her neck. I slowly trail my tongue down her chest, deliberately ignoring her nipples. I watch her reaction as I tease her, her breathing picks up, and I feel her once again try to move her hips against me.

I trail my tongue down her stomach rolling it around the edge of her navel. I hear another change in her breathing, so I stop to enjoy this spot a little longer. Her breath hitches and her hips push up against me as I lick, suck and gently bite the area around her belly button. Satisfied that I have mapped the area I kiss and lick my way to her side, slowly making my way back to her breasts. I finally give in and gently nibble the nipple that struggles against her bra. She groans and pushes her pelvis against me forcefully. I love her reaction, so I bite down a little harder and gently pull back.

"Oh fuck," she groans as her fingers struggle to grip the sheets on the side of the bed. I let her calm a little before darting my tongue around it and sucking it into my mouth. She bucks against me again, and I see her look down at me. She puts her hand on the back of my head, forcing me back to her breast to do it again. I oblige and am thrilled by her response. Her head falls back, and her hands move to pull the obstructive fabric off. I grab her wrists and look at her. When she finally looks back, I shake my head. I focus my attention on her other breast, alternating between biting, sucking and licking her nipple. Catherine screams as she pushes forcefully against me.

"That's right baby, don't hold back." I loosen my knees slightly and raise myself up. Catherine sits up to meet me and pulls me to her for a kiss. She tugs at my shirt, and I allow her to finally pull it off. She quickly latches her mouth onto my breast, her tongue circling my nipple. Fire courses through my body and I forget for a moment that I'm supposed to be in control. I shift the angle of my hips slightly and lower myself onto her thigh. I know my shorts are soaked through and the silky mesh fabric offers little resistance. Catherine and I groan together as I start rocking along her thigh. She reaches down to touch herself, and I stop her. Instead, I pull her up onto my thigh and reposition myself on hers. Our lips fuse together again as we rock against each other, my hands tangle in her hair, pulling her to me. We break it off as our breathing and rocking intensifies. I feel Catherine take my nipple back into her mouth and bite down. I nearly fall over the edge, but I want her there with me. I fight it as I move my hand down to her breast and circle my thumb around her nipple. I feel her pace quicken in response and her mouth release me. I kiss her again before whispering, "Let go with me." I make sure my breath tickles her lobe before I take it into my mouth. We both start bucking harder against each other, and I try to fight it but end up screaming out as the orgasm courses through my body. Catherine reaches her climax right after me, and I feel her body tremble against mine. She falls back onto the bed, her breathing ragged. I lean over and kiss her again, slowly, the urgency calmed for now. I continue the slow pace of the kiss until our breathing has relaxed some.

"I hope you know I'm nowhere near done with you yet." I feel her heartbeat pick back up. I kiss her one more time, this one with more force. I gaze down at her, and she smiles back at me. "Roll over." I'm surprised when she obeys, I was certain that I would have to convince her. I trace my fingers along her back, marveling at the incredible musculature she possesses. Sick of the bra that lays between us I unhook the clasps. I slowly massage her back and shoulders while gently rocking my hips over her ass. Her breathing picks up, and she finally moans. I slide back, pushing my arms under her and gently pull her up to her knees. My body craves the feel of her naked flesh against my own. I pull her back into my chest and feel the burning of her flesh. Catherine turns her face to me, and our lips meet, our urgency expressed in the kiss. She holds my head firmly as our tongues clash and our lips meld together. I move both my hands up her stomach until each slide their way under the now unfastened bra. She groans as my hands find her breasts and continue their work from earlier. I break off the kiss and slowly move my way down to the nape of her neck. She drops her head forward exposing it to me. I instantly know this is another sensitive spot for her, so I slowly run my tongue along it, my hands still manipulating her nipples. Catherine reaches back and grabs my hips, pulling me forward as she slams her ass into my pelvis. Heat surges through me, but my hands and mouth remain focused on their tasks. Catherine grinds against me with more and more force until I can't contain my breathing. I quickly move my hand downward and inside the band of her sweatpants. I slide my fingers into her panties and caress her bare lips. She moans and presses herself downward, forcing my fingers between her folds where the warm pool of Catherine's juices engulfs my fingers. I moan when I discover how wet she is and carefully slide two fingers inside of her. She responds by pressing herself into my hand as I slowly circle my fingers inside of her. I position my hand, allowing her to ride it as she continues to grind against me. I pin her to me with my free arm as she continues to rock against my hand. Her head is tipped back, and her breathing is hot and fast in my ear. I focus on the shoulder in front of me licking, kissing and biting my way across it. Her pace and breathing become frenzied, and I know it won't be long now. She finally loses herself as I trail my tongue slowly along her jawline, her head thrown back against me. I hold her tightly against my chest until I feel the spasms stop and her muscles relax. I realize I have become an insatiable beast, and all I crave is Catherine. I slowly remove my hand from her panties and ease her back down onto her stomach, her breathing still ragged. I study the length of her spine, contemplating for a moment before covering her body with mine. I kiss her forehead as she recovers, content to just lay with her for now.

"What are you doing to me?" she whispers, her breathing still uneven.

"I'm worshiping at the temple. Did you forget?" She lets her sated smile answer. "Besides, you should be more concerned about what I have yet to do to you." She looks at me confused. "You are still half dressed," I remind her.

"You're out of control." She smiles at me, and I can see excitement and curiosity in her eyes.

"You made me this way," I grin at her. "Need a break already?" She lazily smiles at me. "Ok. I have an idea, but you need to trust me." She furrows her brow and looks at me. I can see a little fear start to set in. "Relax, it won't hurt. If you don't like it or you want me to stop just say pineapple. Ok?" She eyes me again but warily nods her agreement. I press my lips to hers, keeping the contact chaste. "Close your eyes and stay here. I'll be right back." She opens her mouth to protest. "I won't be gone half a minute. Just relax."

I peel myself off of Catherine and slide off of the bed. I turn to make sure she isn't watching. Her eyes are closed, the only indication that she is awake is the nervous shifting of her feet back and forth. I almost abandon the idea, it wasn't part of my original plan, but I think she will enjoy it, and the thought of her pleasure sends another surge of energy through my body. I move over to my chest, glad that we brought back here on Sunday, and quietly open it, extracting a small packet. I quietly close the lid and make my way back to the bed. I drape myself back over Catherine, my nerve endings lighting up as our flesh reconnects. I lean in and kiss her again. I work my way back to the nape of her neck and delight when her body responds to me yet again. I slowly work my way down the length of her spine, trailing my tongue lazily along it. I work my way back up and down again, kissing my way across her shoulders, my hands roving along her sides and over her back as I work. I pull the back of her sweatpants and her panties down, exposing her tight ass. As good as it looks in the sweats, it is a work of art laid bare in front of me. I slowly work my way around one cheek, kissing, licking and biting. Catherine arches her back up, forcing her hips into the bed. "Want me to stop?" She quickly shakes her head no. I continue my work on the other side then slowly make my way back up her spine. I kiss her as I lazily knead her ass. "I want to know you, Catherine. All of you. Are you ready?"

"What are you up to?" I can see the fear reenter her eyes.

"Relax. Remember if you want me to stop, just say pineapple." She nods again, but the fear remains. I hate seeing her afraid, but the site of her bare ass has me wanting to do this more than I expected. "I'm not going to hurt you. I need you on all fours though." She does as I ask, the apprehension still on her face. I kiss my way back down to her ass and rework both cheeks. Her apprehension starts to melt away as her excitement builds again. I open the packet and spread the dental dam across her hole. The connection of the cool barrier with her warm body causes her breath to catch. She looks back at me as I slowly lick her taint and circle my tongue around and around her hole. She responds immediately, driving me on. I repeat the pattern over and over. When her excitement really starts to build, I stick my tongue in, knowing there isn't enough strength to push too far.

"Fuck, Alex." Hearing Catherine moan my name causes me to quicken my pace. I pull out my tongue and reinsert it, circling while it is inside, pulling it out and circling, licking down and then back up her taint, repeating the pattern over and over again. Her breathing is heavy, and she begins to move more erratically against my face. I grab her hips to help control her, the smell of her sex so near to my face is making my mouth water, only making my task easier. My tongue glides over the dam easily, and I reinsert it and moan as the smell of her sex assaults me again. Catherine loses control and comes again, falling back to the mattress before I can stop her. I cast aside the dental dam and lazily make my way up her back until I am draped over her again. Her hand finds the back of my head, and she pulls me to her for a kiss.

"What was that?" she gasps, her fingers still gripping my head.

"What the dental dam?"

"No what did you just do to me?" I look at her in disbelief.

"A rim job? Please don't tell me no one has ever licked your beautiful ass before."

"Oh my…I never…" Catherine is speechless. I wonder what is wrong with the men in her past that they never took the time to explore her body. Fools.

"Roll back over when you're ready." Catherine eyes me but does as I ask, casting her bra aside. I look down and marvel at the sight of her breasts. I lean over and kiss her then immediately move my mouth to her breasts. I circle her nipple with my tongue and alternate flicking and biting it. Catherine arches her back up, pushing her breast further into my mouth. I tease her left nipple a little longer before switching to the right. Her breathing picks up again, and I start to trail my way down her smooth stomach. I get back to her navel and tease it again, her response encouraging me to continue. I can smell Catherine's sex through the sweats, several inches away. She arches her hips upward, and I take the opportunity to pull off her sweats and panties. She lays sprawled, fully naked and breathing heavy in front of me. I've never seen anything as breathtaking. I'm frozen in my adoration of her body. Catherine sits up, confusion written on her face.

"Hey. What happened?"

"Nothing. You are just so fucking beautiful." She kisses me deeply, and I follow her back down onto the bed.

"I love you," she whispers as our lips part. My eyes meet hers and I smile.

"I love you too." I kiss her again, this time slowly, trying to demonstrate the passion and love I feel for her. Our lips part and I work my way down again, stopping to worship all the spots I've learned give her the most pleasure. I kneel between her legs, bringing one up to my lips. I slowly trail my tongue over her inner thigh, stopping just before her sex. Unencumbered her scent hits me like a blast, requiring all the resolve I have to refrain from just diving in. I work my way back to her knee and keep her leg draped over my shoulder. I pull her other leg up and repeat the tease. Both of Catherine's legs are wrapped around my neck. I grab a pillow and slide it under her ass then slowly lower myself down. I look up at her as I slowly tease her, running my tongue along her outer lips. Her scent is too great a temptation though, I just want to plunge in. I separate her lips and run my tongue up one of her inner folds and then the other. Her hips rise up forcing my mouth to meet her sex. The taste is amazing, and I groan against her, causing her to respond even more. I slowly run the tip of my tongue over her nub and circle it before starting over again. I watch her body respond and realize I want a better view. I pull away from her and unwrap her legs from around my neck. I move over Catherine again and kiss her, letting her taste how amazing she is. I roll over forcing Catherine on top of me. She relishes in her new position and has me pinned to the bed in seconds. I pull at her hips, trying to move her upward. She balks, stopping to look at me. "I want to watch you. I want to see you come. I want you to ride my face." Her eyes glow as she moves up the length of my body. I grab a pillow and

slide it under my head to make the angle better for her.
She lowers herself onto my face, and I can feel my own
juices dripping down between my cheeks. She locks eyes
with me as she starts to grind herself against my mouth.
My tongue circles and flicks her clit. I suck on it and moan
at the sight of Catherine dominating me like this. The
combination causes her to moan, so I do it again. This
time she arches her back and starts fondling her own
breasts. I increase the speed with which I circle her nub
and continue to moan and suck on it. She becomes more
and more aggressive with her own breasts, her hips
pumping harder and harder. She makes eye contact again
before quickly snaking her hand into my shorts. She
continues riding my face as her fingers spread my lips.
She moans when she discovers how wet I am. We find a
new rhythm as she rides my face and I ride her hand. The
more I watch her, the more turned on I become. I'm
tottering on the edge while Catherine gyrates over my
mouth.

"Come for me baby," she orders as she locks eyes with
me. I lose it, screaming my orgasm against Catherine's
pussy, the vibrations from my moaning sending her over
her own edge. I lock my hands on her thighs and hold her
tightly in place, picking my pace back up where I left off. I
suck and I moan, circle and lick until she topples over the
edge again. The view of her body on fire sending surges
through my own. I clamp down again, trying for a third but
she forces separation, sliding back down my torso. She
lays on top of me, and I feel the last of the spasms roll
through her body. She kisses me again, deeper this time.
I try to flip her onto her back, but she has the leverage and
won't allow it. Instead, she latches onto my nipple and
works it with her mouth. I put my hand on the back of her
head, letting her know how great it feels. She switches to
the other one and the current courses its way through my
body again. She works her way down my stomach and
deftly strips me of the last of my clothing. She snakes her

way back up my body making sure her hip grinds against my lips. When I arch myself into her, she repeats the motion. She kisses me as she does it a third time. I wrap my legs around her, trying to pull her against me again. "My turn," she says as she repeats the motion before sliding back down my body. Her mouth connects with me, and I'm certain the world has exploded. If I thought she might be apprehensive about this, I was sorely mistaken. She moans as she plunges her tongue in, lapping at my juices as I move against her face. She hums and sucks at me, making me moan loudly in response. She reaches a hand up and plays with my nipple as she licks and sucks me, causing my hips to quicken. She sticks her tongue in my pussy, and I nearly come unglued. I wrap my legs around her head as she circles her tongue, moving it in and out causing me to aggressively buck against her. She pulls out her tongue and flicks it over my clit, then sucks and hums at the same time. I scream her name as I climax, my legs trying to pull her inside of me. I free her head as the aftershocks leave my body and she moves up and kisses me again, letting me taste myself on her lips. We gaze at each other as my breathing slows. I'm exhausted, but I still haven't had my fill. I take advantage of Catherine being off guard to flip her back onto her back. "More?" Her eyebrow is arched, challenging me.

"I'll never get enough of you," I inform her. I kiss her again as I reach down and part her lips with my fingers. She is still soaking wet. The combination of her juices and my saliva make for an easy entrance. I start with one finger and slowly roll it around her walls. She moves her hips against the intrusion. I slowly insert a second and then a third. I feel her walls tighten as I flick her g-spot the first time. She slowly pushes me off of her and mounts my hand, riding the fingers I've inserted. She pulls me in for a kiss, crushing our lips together, as she quickly skirts her hand along my inner thigh and finds what she is searching for. She runs her fingers along the inside of my folds, lubricating them, before inserting one and then another. I flatten my palm against her as she rides my hand, my fingers flicking over her g-spot again and again. Kneeling with our bodies pressed against each other we find our rhythm. Our lips are melded together, our tongues vying for dominance. Our pace amping ever upward. We lock eyes, and I can feel Catherine start to tighten around my me. Her approaching orgasm is enough to kick off my own. We climax in unison, and it feels like we have been doing this together for years. We fall back onto the bed and I kiss her again.

"Alex I don't think I can take any more right now. I don't even know if I can walk." I laugh and kiss her forehead, wrapping my arms and legs around her. She responds by pulling me tighter to her. "Have we really been at it for nearly four hours?" I laugh again and look at the clock.

"Well I wasn't timing it but probably close, yeah."

"Is it always this intense?" she wonders aloud.

"No, but this is different." She kisses me again and tightens her arms a little more.

"I love you, Alex."

"I love you too."

Catherine

I wake up in a haze. My heart is pounding from the dream I've been pulled from. I've had sex dreams before but never like this. My body aches. I can feel Alex's arms around me, protectively holding me against her, her heart beating a slow, steady rhythm, her soft skin warming the side of my face. It hits me then, my face is pressed against her flesh, I don't feel any fabric. I open my eyes and realize that it wasn't a dream. I press myself closer to her and revel in the events of last night, the memory of our bodies pressed together, her doing things to me and making me feels things I've never imagined, the sounds of her moans and screams whenever I touched her. I can smell her on my lips still, the tantalizing scent of her sex stoking the flames of my desire for her anew. I want to wake her and pick up where we left off, but the peaceful look she wears while she sleeps stops me. I hope that last night wasn't too much for her, I hope that we haven't pushed her too far. I look at the clock to discover it is after 11. I don't remember ever sleeping this late. I lie with her a little longer, listening to the steady drumming of her heart before nature calls, forcing me to carefully untangle myself from her.

I realize that I am starving. Apparently, a night of marathon sex will do this to me. I'm certain Alex will be hungry as well, so I head to the kitchen to figure out breakfast. Carbs are in order. I dig through the refrigerator and see what we have. I'm happy to discover that I have everything needed to make one of my favorite guilty pleasure breakfast meals. I set to work dicing the apples and making the streusel topping.

"Do you know how sexy you are when you cook?" Alex is awake and has joined me in the kitchen. I turn to the sound of her voice and discover her naked body making its way toward mine. I've lost focus on making breakfast, I've forgotten to breathe. Just the sight of her toned body slowly stalking towards me awakens every fiber of my being. I swallow hard and take a deep breath, longing to feel her heat against me. She doesn't take me in her arms though. She stops just short, reaching up with her hand to lightly trail her fingers along the side of my face. Her gaze locks onto me. I can see her searching my eyes looking for something. "You ok?" I know what she is asking me and wonder why she would even worry. I smile at her, a dopey smile that I know probably looks foolish, only it causes a visible shift in Alex. I can see the trepidation in her eyes being replaced with something else, love.

"I'm not sure ok is quite the right word for it. I'm still processing last night. I think my mind has been blown." Alex smiles and closes the distance between us, enveloping me in her arms, and kissing me lightly.

"Mmm. You smell amazing doctor."

"I smell like sex," I answer, laughing.

"I know," she replies and looks at me, hunger burning in her features. Her stomach rumbles, breaking me out of the trance we've fallen into.

"I'm making you breakfast."

"Yeah, that smells pretty good too. What is it?"

"French toast with sautéed apples, a caramel drizzle and a little bit of streusel topping. Whipped cream also, if you'd like." She smiles at me, and I know I am in trouble.

"I can think of something else I'd like to do with your caramel drizzle and whipped cream." She pulls me towards her again, and her lips claim mine, still tender from last night. I let the kiss linger for a moment before breaking it off.

"Breakfast is going to burn. Go get dressed. We have all day, and after last night we need to eat."

"Yes dear," she mocks me as she releases her hold on me and retreats to the bedroom.

*****

"You shower, I'll clean up the dishes."

"You sure baby?"

"Yeah, you did all the hard work making that amazing meal for me. I'm sure." Alex's eyes are on me, undressing me. I slowly uncross my legs and linger just long enough for her to discover that I'm naked under my robe. When I see her eyes widen and her pupils shift, I know I've succeeded. I saunter down the hallway enjoying the effect I have on her. As soon as I enter the bedroom the smell of sex hits me. Knowing that it is a product of our night together only turns me on more. These aren't things that I would have ever admitted to myself before, yet somehow being with Alex has removed my inhibitions.

I drop my robe on the bed and inhale a deep breath of the aroma we made. "Alex forget the dishes, I want you to join me." Her hands are on my body as she forces me against the full-length mirror on the wall. My breath quickens, fogging its surface, excitement tearing through my cells. The cool surface against my nipples causes them to harden even more. I didn't hear her following me down the hall. She slowly drags her fingertips up the back of my thighs and over my ass. Gooseflesh covers my body in response. I try to turn, to pull her body against mine but she holds me in place.

She winds her hand in my hair and gently pulls my face back from the mirror. Her tongue glides up the length of my neck and finds my earlobe. She knows it drives me crazy, so she nibbles and sucks on it. I can feel the juices escaping from me, my breathing picking up even more.

"Want to know a secret?" Her voice is raspy in my ear, and her breath on my skin is maddening. I try to force contact, but she continues to hold me pinned against the mirror. I am inexplicably so turned on that I can barely answer.

"Yes." The voice sounds nothing like my own, I'm practically panting. Who is this woman that has taken over my body?

"You know I like to watch." She presses my face back against the mirror. I nod. "Well, I know you like to watch as well. I know you saw me fucking Brooke that night." My eyes fly open and my body tenses, panic taking over. How does she know? "Relax. I don't mind. Think about what you saw. I think it turned you on. Did you enjoy watching me fuck Brooke?" The panic disappears, and I feel like I'm trapped in an inferno. I long for Alex to touch me but she keeps one hand on my lower back, and the other between my shoulders, pinning me to the mirror. Images of what I saw that night flood my mind, the jealousy I felt and the orgasms I had thinking about it later, turning me on even more. "Are you thinking about it now? Does it still turn you on?"

"Yes," I moan. I am out of control.

"Good. Do you remember our word from last night?" The odd question pulls my mind back into focus a little.

"Pineapple?"

"Mhm. Pineapple. You know you can say no to anything right?" I nod, fear and curiosity taking over. After last night I long for her to show me everything else that I've been unaware of. I pant against the mirror, still longing for Alex's touch.

"Please touch me." I'm begging her. I've never begged anyone to touch me before. I see her reflection grin back at me, our eyes never losing each other. She sweeps her leg between mine and forces me to spread a little wider. I feel her tongue on the nape of my neck as she shifts her hand down over my ass and glides her fingers over my lips.

"Mmm. I thought it turned you on. Did you pleasure yourself that night thinking about it? Did you touch yourself here?" She applies pressure against my clit as she questions me. I find my self grinding my hips against her hand, trying to force more pressure but her hand moves away. I groan in agony. What is she trying to do to me? I see Alex's reflection pull her shirt over her head and she slams her body against mine, driving me into the mirror. Her warm flesh connects with mine, and I'm certain the world is on fire. She grinds her hips against my ass, and that is when I feel it, the firmness pinned between us. I try to turn around again, but she still won't allow it. She grinds her hips against me again. "I want to fuck you with this Catherine. But I'll only do it if you ask me to." My body explodes as she grinds against me. More juices spill from me, and I'm certain I can feel them running down my inner thigh. I feel the cool touch of the strap on as Alex grinds against me again, causing it to swipe over my lips and retreat. She does it again, watching my reaction in the mirror, our eyes still locked. She does it again, and I press my ass against her and moan, waiting for her to fuck me. "Do you want me to fuck you?" I nod, too lost in her teasing to form words. She arches her brow at me and grinds against me harder this time.

"Yes," I pant. But she simply grinds against me again and pulls back. This is torture, and she is enjoying every second of it. "Fuck me, Alex!" I scream it out, my body unable to take any more of her teasing. She pulls away from me momentarily, and I start to panic that this has all been a cruel prank. She pushes me back against the mirror, and I feel the cold lube make contact with my entrance as she slowly penetrates me. My insides clench against the cold and the fullness, electricity surging through me. My head falls back as I moan, "God yes!" She pushes in further and pulls back slowly, the rhythm slower than my body desires. She does this again and again, and I see her enjoying it in the mirror, a cocky grin gracing her lips. Her hands grip my hips controlling my movements as she trails sloppy kisses along my back. I long for her to fill me but she keeps me under control, refusing my efforts to push back.

"Now that you're warmed up, I'm going to fuck you. You're going to watch." She drives the shaft deep within me, and my head explodes. She slowly pulls back and drives back into me again, pulling my hips to her. She makes a small circular pattern with her hips before pulling back and pounding me again. Again and again she does this, picking up her pace with each invasion. The sensation of her hips grinding against my ass combined with feeling Alex moving inside of me is too much.

"I'm going to come Alex. Don't stop." Just like that her hand leaves my hip and I feel her arm curl around my pelvis, her fingers begin massaging my clit. She keeps up the pounding rhythm, and I push my ass back against her in response every time, wanting every inch of her inside of me. My legs start to shake and collapse as the initial tremors of my orgasm set in. Alex removes her last guiding hand from my hip and coils it around my chest, holding me up as she pushes me back against the mirror.

She continues her assault on my sex with her hand and the toy. My vision blurs as I scream out, "Oh fuck, Alex," my excitement crescendoing, no longer willing to be contained. I feel myself return to earth as Alex slowly lowers us to the floor, laying me on top of her, my back against her chest. I wait for the spasms to stop before sliding off the toy and Alex. I roll over and close the space between our bodies and kiss her. When I pull back and look at her, she has a serious look on her face. Something is bothering her.

"Baby what's wrong?" She smiles at me, and I can see her love for me in her eyes.

"Nothing, you are amazing." The peace that fills my body roils into a panic.

"Did I do something wrong?" She laughs and brushes her fingers along my cheek.

"No, you are amazing! I can't get enough of you. I crave you, my body burns when I touch you. When I said that I fucked Brooke, that is all it was. I want you to know that if I say I want to fuck you, it is so much more than that. I like to play, and sometimes I like to play a little rough. Even if I say I want to fuck you, please know it is so much more than that, that even when I want to play rough, I'm still making love to you."

"You are so mushy." I can't help but tease Alex. Her face reddens, and she tries to hide it from me. I lean into her and kiss her. I pull back and find her still studying me. "I know baby. I can see it in your eyes."

"I love you, Catherine."

"And I love you." I lay down on her chest, and she locks her arms around me. I can see my juices running down the purple shaft. I pick my head up and look at Alex. "Where did that come from?" I see her eyes quickly dart to the chest she made. "Your personal items in the chest? That is what you keep in there?" She laughs.

"All the opportunities you had and you never looked? What did you think was in there?"

"I never. I was tempted. I thought you had some keepsakes or something. I never thought…"

"Not sure I have any keepsakes, at least not enough to warrant storage like that."

"I want to see." Alex stills at the request. My curiosity is piqued. "Now I really want to see." She sighs, I can hear her resignation in it. She undoes the harness and slides it off. She takes my hand, and we slide across the floor to the closet where the chest sits waiting. She sits upright on the floor, spreading her legs and positioning me in front of her. She wraps herself around me, pinning my arms to my side.

"Remember you always have the right to say no, to anything I might ask of you. Don't be afraid or ashamed to say no. I won't be disappointed. I revel in your pleasure and only long to give you more. The things in this chest are all options, not requirements for me to be happy with you."

I realize that Alex is nervous to share this with me, to let me in. Her nervousness scares me a little. I kiss her, and she releases my arms, giving me permission to open the chest. She wraps her arms around my chest and clings tightly to me. It occurs to me that she is scared, scared that what I find will make me run. I lift the lid and take in the chest's contents. I see a few more silicone toys, the sizes and variety surprise me. I wasn't aware they varied so much. A few of them have already drawn my interest, and I feel my body respond as I think about using them with Alex. I look to Alex, confused at what she is so afraid of. "That top level lifts out." I feel her body tense against mine. I lift out the tray and discover leather, a lot of leather. I can feel Alex's body tense even more as I process what I am seeing. Confusion and apprehension take control of me. I loosen Alex's grip and turn to face her.

"Whatever you're thinking please hear me. I don't want a master and submissive relationship with you. I don't want to hurt you. You don't ever have to see anything on that level again, and I would be perfectly happy with that. I enjoy giving pleasure, and those items can all be used to enhance that. They can give you sensations you aren't used to feeling. I don't need to use them though."

"I don't understand. You want to beat me with those things?" I see the horror flash in Alex's eyes and know I am way off base.

"Never. I never want to hurt you. I only want to make you feel all the depths of pleasure I can give you. It doesn't have to be a part of us, of who we are."

I sit and think, I still don't understand how one works without the other. I look at Alex, she looks shattered. My confusion and quietness have her convinced I'm going to leave her. Then I think about last night, how she licked my ass, something no one has done to me before, and how great it felt.

"How do you use any of that without hurting me? It doesn't make sense. Show me."

"You want me to show you? Now?"

"Just a demonstration. Show me how you use those without hurting me." I pull out one of the implements, a stick with a folded swath of leather over it. I put it in Alex's hand and look into her eyes. "Show me." I can see her deliberate. She leans her body over mine and kisses me, forcing me to lie down on the floor. Her kiss is long and deep but lacks urgency. Her hands are rubbing their way up and down my body, my body responding to her touch. She breaks off the kiss and looks at me.

"Relax. Close your eyes." I feel the heat of her body shift away from mine, then I feel something else. Something cool trails its way across my torso, teasing my nipples, slowly rubbing around and over them. Then there is a gentle slap, the sensation surging through my body. The residual sting is minimal and momentary, but the surge that it creates is worth it. My breathing hitches as I take in this new sensation. Alex takes the assaulted nipple in her mouth, the moisture of her saliva like a balm where the leather made contact. She releases my nipple and blows air gently over it. My body is raging again. She slides back up and kisses me, and again I feel the cool air touch my body as she moves away from me. I open my eyes to find her sitting back, watching me, nervousness and fear still fill her features. I close the space between us and wrap my arms around her.

"You can't scare me away baby. I'm still here." I kiss her and feel her relax. I take the implement from her and move back to the chest. I watch her as I put it away and replace the top tray. Her eyes and her body language never change, she never shows any disappointment. I know she is telling me the truth. She doesn't have to have it. But I also know that we will be revisiting the lower level soon. "Come here baby." She slides over to me and wraps herself around me again. I look over the assortment of vibrators and other toys. I'm intrigued by the double-headed dildo, but it doesn't feel right for the current situation. Another one catches my eye, but the semantics of it seem off. I pick it up and look at Alex. She knows the question without me asking.

"You use it with a harness. This end goes inside the person wearing the harness, the ridges provide some clitoral stimulation. Works best during face to face sex." This is the one. I want to make love to Alex while she can see me. I want her to know that I'm not going to run away.

I extract myself from Alex's embrace and stand up, taking the selected toy with me. I make my way over to where the strap on lies and take the harness. I can feel Alex's eyes on me, but she doesn't move. I take the harness and dildo to the bed and leave them there. Alex still hasn't moved. I understand now that someone in her past has run before because of what the chest contains. I am not scared, I need her to know it. I make my way back to her and hold out my hand. She takes it, and I help pull her to her feet. I can see the hurt and the fear still lingering in her eyes. I pull her to me and kiss her deeply letting it linger on while I back up to the bed, pulling her with me. I slide back onto the bed, pulling her with me, positioning myself under her.

"I want you to make love to me with that. I want to look into your eyes as the ground falls away from us." Alex's response is what I hoped it would be. She kisses me, slowly at first but it quickly escalates. She pulls away and looks at me again then repeats the kiss. I wrap my legs around her, pulling her as close to me as I can. This is going to be slow, has to be slow. My body argues against this, but the thought of Alex's emotions keeps me in check. I drag my fingers across her back and feel her response as her kiss deepens, and she bites my lip as she pulls away. I pull her back to me for another kiss, the urgency becoming frantic. I rock my hips against her. This needs to be slow for her, but I can't control my body's desire to have her inside of me. She seems to understand as she breaks off the kiss and backs off the bed grabbing the harness and toy. Her eyes never leave my body, so I start pleasuring myself as she watches, rubbing my fingers over my swollen clit and pulling on my nipples, grinding against my own hand. She stands in a trance watching me, and I see her eyes darken with hunger. She throws the strap on back on the bed and is tongue deep in my pussy before I know it. Her moan reverberates through my body. She swirls her tongue around my walls before pulling it out and reinserting it. She repeats this over and over but stops when my hand creeps back down to add some stimulation to my throbbing clit. She moves my hand away and focuses on my bud, licking, sucking, swirling her tongue and humming against me. I buck against her mouth harder and faster. There is no way that I can hold back. Alex pushes her fingers inside of me, and I feel her massaging my walls, her fingers flicking my g-spot. "Jesus Alex!" My excitement only eggs her on, and she locks her free arm over my hips, giving her mouth a choke hold on my sex. She increases the pace of her fingers and tongue, sucking harder and humming more and more. The reverberations melt into one another, and I come fully undone. "Oooh, Alex! There!" Spasms shake my entire body, but Alex doesn't stop. She keeps mouth and finger fucking me until the quake starts anew. "Fuck!" I scream and grab her head. I need her to stop. I pull her up to me and kiss her, fighting to catch my breath. The taste of me on her lips only makes me crave her flavor more. I put my hands on her ass and gently push towards my head. She looks at me but doesn't argue. I greedily lift my head to meet her sex as she lowers herself onto my face. My salivary glands go into over drive as her scent hits my nose and her warm juices run over my tongue. She adjusts herself slightly, and I focus on her. I slowly lick my way around her enjoying her reactions, feeling her move against me. Her pace quickens with my tongue. I lightly run my teeth over her clit and feel her buck harder. I wrap my arms around her thighs and do it again, this time holding her in place. She moans loudly, her pace becoming frantic. She drops her head, and our eyes meet as she starts riding my face harder and harder.

"Mmm Catherine. That's it." The intensity in her eyes and the movement of her on my face sends new juices gushing out of me. I moan as they escape but keep my eyes locked on Alex's. I suck and hum at the same time, pushing her over the edge. She falls forward onto her hands, but I refuse to let her escape. Her gaze is fire as I continue to feast on her and she continues to move against me. "Oh god! Oh, baby!" I feel the spasms take hold of her as she quickly comes again. I try to hold for more, but she looks down at me and shakes her head. She slides her hips back down my body and kisses me, heedless of the puddle of her fluids on my chin.

Alex looks at me, over at the harness, and back at me. "I still want you to make love to me with that." She kisses me quickly and backs off of the bed. I hand her the harness but before she pulls it on all the way she takes my hand and places it under the base of the toy. She slowly starts pulling the harness the rest of the way up, and I understand what she wants. I explore her folds with my free hand, finding the juicy destination. I guide the shorter end into her and slowly push back rolling the ridges over her clit. Her head falls back, and a groan escapes her. I pull one of her nipples into my mouth and bite down as I again shift the ridges over her clit.

"Fuck!" I meet Alex's eyes, and the two emeralds burn into me. She kisses me, forcing me back onto the bed. I take her hand and wrap it around the shaft, guiding it towards my sex. She slowly enters me, her eyes boring into mine as she does. I bite my lip and moan as I lift my hips into her, forgetting that every motion I make shifts the other end that is inside of her. Alex's head tips back as I lift my hips into her again. She kisses me and starts to slowly circle her hips against me. I lift myself into her again, and she groans, increasing her pace. I want Alex to watch me, to see me.

"Roll over. I want you to watch me." Her hands grab my hips, and she pushes herself into me as she rolls us over. I look down at her as I ride her, each of my movements sending a ripple effect of pleasure into her body. Her hands are working my breasts, and mine hers as my movements become harder and faster, our panting synchronized with the motions of my hips. I can feel that I'm close. I lean down and kiss Alex hard, increasing my movements even more. "I'm gonna come, baby. Look at me. Come with me." I drop my forehead against hers, our eyes locked on each other, our hips pounding together in time, hers bucking up as I slam back onto her. The tremors start to ripple through me, I want to throw my head back and scream, but I force myself to stay draped over Alex with my eyes glued to hers. We explode together, our eyes never breaking contact, even as our bodies cool. "I'm here. I'm not going anywhere." She smiles up at me, giving me relief.

"I know."

Alexis

Catherine's screams pull me from the depths of sleep. I try to sit up but her weight pressed against me keeps me pinned to the bed. A nightmare? Her body is covered in sweat. "No! Alex!" She bolts up off of me her breathing heavy. I switch on the bedside lamp and wrap my arms around her. She jumps at my touch.

"Shh, baby it's ok. Just a dream."

"Alex?" She whips her body around to face me and pulls me to her tightly, holding on for dear life. Her tears burn hot trails over my shoulder and down my back. I hold her tightly and keep telling her that everything is ok. When her breathing calms, and her tears stop, I pull her back down to the bed with me, covering her goose flesh covered body with the sheet. I rub my hand over her back with one hand and wipe the tear trail from the side of her face.

"I lost you." I look at Catherine confused. "They brought you into the ER after the accident, but I lost you." Tears start spilling onto my breast as Catherine's emotions take control.

"Baby I'm right here. You didn't lose me. Just a bad dream." I kiss her forehead and pull her tightly against me, doing my best to calm her again.

"Before you were already dead, I was a wreck, and Abby forced me to go to your memorial." I'm lost again, but I let her tell me in her own time. "When you were in the coma, I had a dream that you were dead and that I lost it at your service because nothing was right." I want to laugh at how absurd this sounds but refrain. Abby has told me that Catherine was a disaster for days after my accident, her pain isn't a source of amusement.

"You didn't lose me. Unless you tell me to, I'm not going anywhere." I lightly kiss her lips and run my fingers along her jawline. Even these little intimacies between us awaken the rest of my body. Catherine has an effect on me that I've never known before.

"I used to dream about the first kid I lost during surgery, the one I told you about before. That was bad enough. I've never felt sorrow the way I do in the nightmares where I lose you." I kiss her again. I'm at a loss for what to say. I take her hand and press her fingertips lightly to my lips and then run them along my cheek. Then I move them to my chest and place them over my beating heart.

"I'm right here with you, safe and alive." Catherine moves her hand back to my face. Her fingers trace along my jawline as she kisses my chest and then lays her ear against it, listening to my heartbeat.

"It's 3:30 am. I'm not going to be able to sleep again." She lifts her head from my chest and looks at me.

"What do you normally do when this happens?"

"Swim, read, something productive."

"Ok, well what are you thinking?" I really just want to go back to sleep. Our love making lasted well past the midnight hour, and I am still tired.

"Oh, I'm thinking something else entirely." Catherine has the look in her eyes that I've come to know so well these past few days. She slowly inches her way up my body and kisses me, licking my lower lip as she pulls away. The flick of her tongue over my lip sends an adrenaline rush through my body.

"Now who is the insatiable one?" I ask as I kiss her again. Catherine pries herself from my arms and crosses the room to the closet. We had feasted on one another's bodies earlier, leaving the toys in their chest. I watch her naked body move with feline grace, curious to see what she will chose. As she makes her way back to me, I can see that something has shifted, that her confidence has taken a hit. I reach out to her and pull her back onto the bed with me. "Baby what is it?" Her eyes burn into my soul and then she looks away. I turn her face back to mine, "Talk to me." I can see the movement of her teeth as she rakes them over her lower lip, one of the few tells she has. She is nervous.

"It's just…well…never mind." I look at her and raise my eyebrows. Catherine is nervous, it seems impossible yet here it is on display before me. "Well, I was wondering… do you ever…"

"Do I ever?"

"You know…do you ever bottom?" This time I can't help it, I laugh out loud. Once I regain control of myself, I kiss Catherine and lock eyes with her.

"You were nervous about asking me that?" She chews her lower lip again and looks away. "Ok, first, I don't ever want you to be nervous about asking me something. Just ask. Second, it depends on the dynamic I guess. I have with some women and not with others. Why? Is that something you want?" Her eyes meet mine, I can see the answer there.

"Yes. I would at least like to try it, if you are open to it."

"On one condition." Catherine raises a single eyebrow as she tries to assess my thoughts. "I don't want you to be nervous when it comes to your fantasies or desires. If you

312

want to try something tell me. Think of it like the chest, the worst that will happen is that I will say no." Catherine smiles and kisses me. I look over to the strap on she has chosen, "Is that the one you want to use?"

"Yes." Her breathing is already picking up, her nipples are hard. I can tell she has been thinking about this, wanting this.

I lean in and whisper "How do you want me?"

Catherine presses her body against mine, forcing me onto my back. She draws my legs around her hips and trails her fingers over my torso. "I want to watch you." Her eyes are radiating hunger.

"That's my girl."

*****

"Holy shit! That was...I just feel so...I don't know, powerful I guess." I can't help but laugh a little. Catherine scowls, "Was I bad?"

"I just came four times, and you think you were bad?"

"Oh right." Catherine's grin returns and I can't help but feel the warmth from it spread through my body. "It's just that you are so fucking good at playing my body. I want to be that good for you."

"You have yet to disappoint me."

"So would you ever let me blindfold you?"

"Of course."

"Tie you up?"

"Yes please."

"Spank you."

"I've been a very naughty girl."

"Threesome?" I panic, pulling myself off of Catherine to look in her eyes. She laughs at me and strokes my face. "Relax baby, I just wanted to see if you would actually deny me anything. I don't want anyone else."

*****

"What time are we meeting everyone tonight?"

"We are supposed to be there no later than 6."

"We could just watch the games here…by ourselves." I grin at Catherine. I know that arguing is futile.

"We can't stay holed up here alone forever."

"I'm willing to give it a go if you are. Unless you're bored already." Catherine laughs and kisses me.

"Hardly. I'd love it if we could but you know I have to go back to work eventually."

"Party pooper." I start to sulk. I know it is childish and selfish.

"You're kinda cute when you pout."

"Seriously?"

"No." She laughs and kisses me. I love seeing her this relaxed and happy. Her fingers trail along my abdomen, tracing imaginary patterns. "So what are we going to do about work?"

"How do you want to handle it?"

"I thought I'd just draft an office memo telling them how often you make me come on a daily basis."

"Oh good idea, then you can read it on the overhead paging system in the OR." We think about it, and both dissolve into a fit of laughter.

"I thought about not telling the partners. It isn't any of their business." Catherine sighs and the relaxed mood she was in follows her breath out.

"Won't work. We have to tell my supervisors. They will just keep us from scrubbing together. That is all they can do. Doesn't matter though. Once they know, everyone at work will talk, everyone will know, including your partners. You have to tell them."

"I plan to. We have a partners meeting every Tuesday morning. I'll do it then."

"It's going to be fine. Promise me one thing though."

"Hmm?"

"Sunday is naked Sunday, as in if we have to put clothes on to do it, we aren't doing it." I can feel Catherine smile against my stomach.

"Deal. Come on we need to start getting ready." She grabs my hand and attempts to pull me from the bed.

"Already? I thought you said six. It's only two."

"I know, but we need to take a shower. Could take a while." I instantly abandon all efforts to resist and obediently follow Catherine into the bathroom.

*****

The drone of the alarm Monday morning is perhaps the evilest sound I have ever heard. It signals the end of me having Catherine mostly to myself. While I know it was inevitable, I don't have to like it.

"Morning baby." Catherine sleepily smiles at me, her half lidded blue eyes oozing peace and love. She kisses me softly and lays her head back on my chest. "For the first time in a long time I don't want to go to work," she whispers, running her fingers absentmindedly over my hip and up my side.

"You could call in sick." She looks at me, and I wiggle my eyebrows, giving her my best evil grin.

"No. Even if I did, I would still have to go in tomorrow. You go back to sleep, no need for you to be up too."

"Nope, I'm up. I'm going to watch you swim."

"You could swim with me." Catherine gives me a devilish look, making my body respond instantly. We have enjoyed the pool together several times during the last week.

"If I do that you won't be going to work."

Catherine swims, and I watch. I inexplicably love watching her in the water. Her strong, agile body moving gracefully through the pool, never tiring. The peace she seems to find as she swims. The water as it parts for her and then moves over her body, the body which I have mapped countless times now. As I sit mesmerized by the flow of water around her, Catherine changes course and slices her way over to where I sit poolside. She lifts herself from the pool, her long arms displaying the unexpected strength that lies within. My breath catches at the sight of her body as the water slowly rolls downward and pools at her feet. She pulls off her swim cap and tosses it on the table next to me. Aphrodite stands before me, glistening as the small rivulets trail slowly down her neck and over her breasts. I want to reach out and touch her but know that I can't, she can't be late.

Catherine leans in and kisses me, her nipples hardening, showing through the skin tight suit. "Come on," she orders taking my hand.

"You'll be late," I remind her. Catherine looks at the clock then back at me and smiles.

"I'm changing my routine. I'll take the rest of my cardio in the shower."

Showered and momentarily sated I head to the kitchen to make a quick breakfast. I make our usual fruit smoothie, scramble up some eggs and prepare some toast. Catherine joins me in the kitchen, looks at my handiwork then smiles at me. "I could get used to mornings like this."

"Me too, well it'd be better if I had something productive to do all day, like go to work."

"What are you going to do today?"

"No idea actually. Everyone will be working…except me. Probably read, maybe watch a movie. I'll figure out something I guess." Catherine clears our plates, our habit of inhaling our food one that will never be broken. We return to the master bathroom and brush our teeth at the dual sinks. I watch her reflection in the mirror, she is still sexy even when doing something as routine as brushing her teeth. I walk her back to the kitchen and hug and kiss her goodbye at the door.

Catherine grazes my earlobe with her lips and whispers, "I know what you can do today. I want you to think about touching me, doing whatever you want to with my body. I want you to think about me touching you, what you want me to do to you. Do this all day, but don't touch yourself. I'll know if you have when I get home." She bites my earlobe and I groan in frustration, eliciting another of Catherine's devilish grins. "I'll call you between cases." She kisses me and walks out the door, leaving me soaking wet and unable to do anything about it.

*****

Catherine's parting words reverberate through my mind all morning. I try to distract myself by any means necessary. I go for a swim, and my mind flashes to images of Catherine swimming and of our liaisons in and around the pool. I take another shower, but that proves futile. I attempt to clean the house, but Catherine and I are both neat freaks and the maid service comes on Mondays and Fridays. I find the little bit of laundry that needs to be washed and start the first load. The problem is that laundry only intermittently occupies your time. I try reading but Catherine's orders for the day and the thoughts stemming from those orders prove too distracting. When my phone rings I nearly drop it, I'm dying to hear her voice. I'm surprised to see Taylor's name on the caller ID.

"Taylor, how are you?"

"I'm good Alex. How are you? How is your recovery coming?"

"Good actually. I'm feeling good. Moving around well again, no walker, no fatigue. So far no headaches or seizures so good things there as well. I thought Catherine was keeping you updated. Had I known she wasn't I would have at least texted you." I start to wonder if they have had a falling out that Catherine failed to mention.

"She had been pretty regularly until a little over a week ago. I just figured she got busy at work and then I got super busy at work. When I didn't hear anything this weekend, I started to worry a little. I'm glad to hear everything is alright though. How is being back at the house?" I quickly do the math in my head and realize that Taylor has no idea that Catherine and I are together now. I also don't know if Catherine wants her to know or if it is even my place to tell her.

"Things have been fine. No tension, no fighting, no drama. How is life out there treating you?"

"Great. I've started bartending at one of the dyke bars here. I make great tips. The fringe benefits are quite nice as well." Taylor laughs, and I can't help but smile and shake my head.

"I'm guessing you meet a lot of new friends through this job."

"Oh yes, quite a few. This might be the best job I've ever had." I can picture Taylor's devil may care grin in my head. I laugh hard. "Really Alex, maybe you should think about a career change."

"I'm good, thank you."

"Wait a minute. Did she tell you? Did you two finally Slytherin her Hufflepuff?"

"Slytherin her Hufflepuff?"

"Well, you were watching Harry Potter that night when you turned me down. Just trying to be funny. Stop diverting. Did it finally happen?"

"How did everyone know about this but me? You don't even live here, and you knew."

"I knew it! About damn time. I've been waiting for this to happen since my visit. Took you two long enough. Is that why I haven't heard from her? When did this happen?"

"About two weeks ago. We've been...busy."

"Um hm, I bet. Wait a second. Cat was supposed to visit me last week. You two spent all week in bed didn't you?"

"Not just bed." I can't help but tease Taylor a little bit. I know she was sort of put in the middle of our drama during her visit.

"I knew it. Well, at least that takes a little bit of the sting out of you rejecting me. Maybe someday though." I know Taylor is teasing me right back.

"Sorry Taylor, no rain checks or substitutions. Maybe you could pick up an extra shift at work. Help you forget all about me."

"Not a bad idea. So you have big plans for Cat's birthday then?"

"Uh, when is that exactly?" I can't believe that I have no idea when her birthday is.

"Of course she didn't tell you. She doesn't ever tell anyone. It is Wednesday actually." The wheels start turning when I hear this. What can I do for Catherine on a limited budget and without a vehicle?

"Interesting. This just might work out well then. I could surprise her with something."

"I'd be careful, Cat isn't big on surprises." I run a few ideas by Taylor, getting her input on them. By the time we hang up, I have a rough sketch of a plan I think might work. The problem is that I'm going to need help to pull it off. I send Abby a text asking if she can help me for an hour or two Wednesday morning. She is quick to respond that she absolutely can. For the first time all day I'm able to focus on something other than erotic thoughts about Catherine. I'm so absorbed in finalizing a plan that when my phone rings again, I jump, knocking it off of the table and across the floor. By the time I manage to retrieve it voice mail has intercepted the call. I check the missed call log and discover that it was Catherine. I quickly hit the return call button.

"Were you touching yourself?" Catherine's voice sounds low, like she is whispering. Her breathing is slightly uneven.

"Nope. Doctor's orders. I have to abstain from such behavior."

"Mmm. Good girl." Catherine's purr causes my insides to twitch. That is when it hits me.

"You are so breaking the rules right now aren't you?"

"I'm not pinching my nipple right now, you are."
Catherine's breath hitches and my body instantly reacts.

"Where are you?"

"The on-call physician's room. He is operating right now, so he doesn't need it." Catherine lets out a low moan. "That's it, baby. I like it when you do that." My free hand is tightly clenched around a fistful of my t-shirt.

"What am I doing?" I know she is tormenting me, but I can't help but play along. The thought of Catherine touching herself drives me wild.

"You just raked your fingers along my inner thighs. Now you're teasing me, coaxing me open. My clit is throbbing for you." Catherine moans again, and the line goes dead.

"What the fuck?" I'm so turned on that I've uttered the words out loud. That's when the video chat request comes in. I automatically know that I'm in trouble. I can't help myself though. I accept the request, wanting to see Catherine's show no matter how frustrated I'll be after.

Catherine's image immediately pops up, but all I can see is her face. "Are you on your laptop?" I nod. "Good. Push it away from you a little bit until I can see your hands. Lay them on top of the table. Remember doctor's orders." I do as she says, wanting to see how far she is willing to take this. "Good." She slides what I assume is her iPad back and leans it against something. When she comes back into focus she is revealed to be wearing black lingerie, the black lingerie I dreamed about her wearing. "Now where were we?" Catherine immediately begins to stroke herself as she massages her breast and pulls at her nipple. I want to crawl through the screen to get at her. Her undulating hips pick up their pace as her excitement builds. "Mmm baby. No one has ever fucked me the way that you do." Catherine slides her fingers back and inserts the middle two into herself. "Fuck. Alex!" Her hips pick up their pace even more as she strokes and rides herself. She begins pulling at her nipple harder as her breathing becomes frantic. I know she is close. My hands are locked together, my knuckles are whiter than fresh snow. I suck in my lower lip and bite down hard. If I had any hair, I'd be pulling it out. "Just like that Alex. Fuck me like that. I'm so close." I can see the muscles in her body begin to twitch and then convulse. She bites down on her forearm to muffle her scream. I'm so inflamed that I'm certain there will be a puddle on the barstool when I get up.

"Damn baby. You know just what I needed to get me through this next case." Catherine is putting her scrubs back on. She looks at the camera and smiles at me lasciviously. "I only have two quick cases left. I'll talk to you soon. Don't forget, doctor's orders." I've lost the ability to speak, I sit staring into the camera gape-jawed. "Miss you, baby." Catherine blows me a kiss as she switches off the feed.

"FUCK!!!!" I scream out at the top of my lungs.

Catherine

I have never done anything like that in my life, certainly not at work. Being with Alex has changed me, I feel a confidence and freedom about my sexuality that I have never known before. I no longer feel shame about my darkest desires and fantasies. More than that, Alex has shown me what it is to be loved and how it feels to truly love someone. She is the unexpected gift the universe has given me, and I vow to show how grateful I am for her every day.

I call Alex between my second and third case. It has been just over an hour and a half since I last checked in with her. The image of her face as she watched me remains singed on my brain. Part of me knows that it was a cruel thing to do after the mandate I laid down this morning. The other part enjoyed it and never really believed she would be able to stick to my orders like she did. Alex finally picks up on the third ring.

"Hey, Catherine."

"Hey, baby. What are you doing?"

"Laundry. What are you doing?" I can hear the tension in her voice. She really has followed my orders today. I'm going to have to make it up to her somehow.

"Getting ready to start my last case. Just a washout and drain insertion. I should be home soon. Why are you doing laundry?"

"Because we dirtied every set of sheets in this house last week. I need something to keep me in line." I grin knowing the torment I've put her through today.

"It won't be long now baby. I should be home in an hour. Patient is on the table and being draped as we speak. I've gotta go. Love you."

*****

I arrive home half expecting Alex to attack me as soon as I get through the door. Maybe I am hoping for it honestly. Either way, it doesn't happen. I feel a modicum of disappointment as I set my bag down next to the door and toss my keys on the counter. "Baby where are you?"

"In here," I hear her call from the den. I make my way there and discover her sitting in the armchair reading. She doesn't tear her gaze away from her book, not even as I lean in to kiss her. I try it again and am met with the same reaction. Undeterred I attempt to take her Kindle from her, but she doesn't allow it. "Just give me a few minutes baby, I want to finish this chapter." Now I am dumbfounded. She has never rebuffed me like this before.

I kneel down in front of her and run my hands up her legs and through the opening of her shorts. Nothing, she doesn't even look at me. I kiss her on her knee and slowly trail my tongue up her inner thigh. She doesn't so much as twitch. I start to panic. I think I've pushed her too far today.

"Baby I'm sorry."

"What do you have to be sorry for?" She never takes her eyes off of her book.

"Please look at me, I'm begging you." Alex sighs deeply, not the sighs I've grown to love hearing, this one is filled with annoyance. She sits her Kindle down on the table next to the chair she is sitting in and finally looks at me. "I'm so sorry Alex. I thought it would be sexy and fun."

"You planned the whole thing." I can hear the anger in her voice.

"Yes."

"Without regard for what it would do to me? How torturous today would be? I don't have anything here to distract me like you do while you're at work." Alex is pissed, and I had no idea.

"Baby I'll do anything. Please. I really thought it would be fun and you would like it." I'm desperate for her to not be angry with me.

"Anything?" Alex's whole demeanor shifts, she cocks one eyebrow and dons a sly grin. That is when I know that I've been had. Relief floods through my body, even though I know I'm about to make a deal with the devil.

"Anything." I can feel my cockiness return to me. I grin at Alex and wait for my punishment.

"You looked like you really enjoyed putting on that show earlier. Time for the prequel." Prequel? What am I supposed to do before masturbating on camera while thinking about my girlfriend? I am about to ask when I hear music start to play. "I'm going to need you to dance for me. Seduce me, like your life depends on it." She turns the volume up, and I recognize the song, Massive Attack's *Black Milk*. It has a sound that oozes sex, perfect for a striptease. I smile up at Alex, whether she knows it or not I'm going to enjoy teasing her more.

I shift my weight from my knees to my feet as I force Alex's legs apart. I slowly arch into her as I make my way to a standing position, never taking my eyes off of hers. My top three buttons are undone, so I make sure my trajectory gives Alex a full view down my shirt. I still have the lingerie on. When her pupils dilate I know I've succeeded. I lean in closer as my neck and breasts approach her face, pausing as my breasts linger just out of reach of her mouth, yet close enough that I know she can smell my perfume, the vanilla scent that drives her wild. She slowly licks her lips as her pupils betray her once again. I want to move in and bite the lip that she just licked, but I hold back. It is too soon. As I make my way to full vertical I grab each of Alex's hands and slowly run them up along the outside of my thighs, stopping when her hands linger just over the lacy fringes of the black panties. I let her leave them in place until she tries to grab my ass, at which point I pull them off and force them away from my body. The black pencil skirt that I wore today for rounds doesn't afford me all of the mobility I would like, but I'm determined to make do. I slide Alex's ass forward in the chair a little bit and force her shoulders back, exposing her crotch to me. I put a hand on each shoulder pinning her in place and slowly dip down and grind the length of my body along hers, increasing the pressure against her crotch the higher I rise, until my pelvis makes contact. I grind my pelvis against her crotch in a slow pace that mimics our love making. I dip back down and repeat everything again. I can hear Alex's reaction this time as she clenches her jaw and draws in a breath through her teeth. Her reactions are an aphrodisiac, and I'd be lying if I didn't admit that grinding my pelvis against hers wasn't turning me on as well. So I dip back down and repeat the process again. This time Alex lets loose a low moan as I grind against her. The skirt is not working out as I hoped, so I swivel my hips until my ass is level with Alex's face. I slowly lower myself in time with the music until I again reach Alex's pelvis. I methodically grind my ass against her until she makes a move to grab my breasts. I catch her hands and look back over my shoulder at her, shaking my head in disapproval. I

327

continue to grind against Alex as I slowly move her hands around to my lower back, stopping near the zipper. I allow her to unzip me, knowing she takes great pleasure in undressing me. I let the skirt fall to my feet knowing that the lavender shirt I'm wearing will keep most of me covered. I lower my ass against Alex again and grind with a slightly increasing pace. I can feel her wetness soaking through her shorts and have to stifle my own moan. The song switches over to Massive Attack's *Angel,* and I continue my assault. I swivel my way back around and grind my way up Alex again. I can smell her sex as I make my way up. I need to keep this moving as I know I won't be able to hold out long. I force Alex's knees back together and straddle her. She tries to grab my hips, but I pull her hands away and set them on the arms of the chair. I start rubbing myself against Alex's lap, starting slowly and increasing my pace as my excitement builds. Confident that Alex will leave her hands where I've put them I grab her face and pull it between my breasts as I continue to masturbate against her lap. I know she can hear my heart pounding, my rapid breathing, and feel my moisture against her lap. I feel my excitement building too high, so I slow my rhythm down, pushing Alex's face away from me, quickly licking her lower lip as I do. She looks punch drunk at this point, and I love it. No one has ever worshiped my body the way she does. Still needing a moment to quell my threatening orgasm I take Alex's hands and move them to buttons of my shirt. I allow her to undo the buttons but stop her from pushing the shirt off of my shoulders, liking how the way it drapes down revealing some, but not all of me. Shirt unbuttoned I guide Alex's hands to my hips and slowly move them upwards. I resume masturbating against her lap as I inch her hands up to my breasts where I finally allow her to touch me. My nipples immediately respond to her touch and the sensation combined with my grinding has me close to spiraling out of control again. I pull her hands from my breasts and inch them up a little more, allowing Alex to remove my shirt. Longing to feel

Alex's flesh against mine I lift her hands over her head and pull off her t-shirt. I slide back off of her and force her legs apart again, meeting no resistance. I trap her left leg between my own and lower myself onto her thigh, taking care to sink my right knee into the cushion so that my thigh makes contact with her. I start to grind against her, and she responds by moving against me. I move her hands to my hips while I work myself closer and closer to climax. Our breathing seems synchronized as we pleasure ourselves against one another. Alex trails her right hand down the side of my neck and onto my chest. I arch back pushing my breast into her hand and grind faster and faster. Just as I am about to come she strikes like a viper, wrapping her arms around me and lifting me off of her thigh. Her strong arms coil around my waist, supporting my weight as she carries me to the bedroom. I have no choice but to wrap my legs around her and hold on.

Alex deposits me onto the bed but doesn't release her hold on me. Instead, she secures her balance on her knees, picks me up and positions me in the center of the bed. With my legs still locked around her waist Alex leans over me and kisses me, her tongue greedily invades my mouth as she slowly starts to roll her hips against me. I try to press myself against her, longing for the orgasm I have staved off three times now. By the time I realize Alex is reaching for something it is too late. I feel the silkiness of the blindfold over my eyes before I even know what has happened. Only then does Alex break off the kiss, as she grabs each of my arms by the wrists. She pins them to the bed over my head and holds them there until I stop fighting. "Are you ok?"

"Yes," I pant.

"Good." Alex's nipple brushes over my lips as she reaches for something else. In less than a second, I feel the first restraint being placed around my wrist, and my arm snugly secured. She repeats this on the other side, and I can feel my arms secured at either side of my head, with my palms facing upwards. I have a little mobility, but not much. "Too tight? Comfortable?" I nod that I'm ok. "Good. Do you remember our word?"

"Pineapple."

"Yes. Do you trust me?"

"Yes." I do. I know Alex will stop if I ask her to and that she won't hurt me. I feel Alex's weight shift off of me and off of the bed. The cool air moves over my body as Alex moves around the bed. She grabs each of my ankles and spreads my legs. "Now I could secure your legs much like I have your hands, but that might interfere with what I want to do later. Will you behave or do I have to tie you down like you're about to be drawn and quartered?"

"I'll behave."

"Good answer." I feel the bed shift as Alex climbs back onto it from the foot. She licks her way up my inner thigh as her fingers rake their way up the outsides of each. Currents flow up my legs and into my pulsating clit. I long to be in Alex's mouth. I arch my hips towards the source of heat I feel over my body. Alex puts her mouth against me and runs her tongue over the black lace that separates us. I feel her teeth graze over me before she sucks and then nibbles. I rock my hips against her begging for release. She continues the assault until my breathing is heavy, then stops. "You enjoyed your little game today, didn't you? Tormenting me. Making me stew all day."

"Yes." I can feel Alex's weight shift as she moves up my body and straddles me at my waist.

"Are you enjoying this game?"

"Yes. Please fuck me, Alex. Please make me come." She slowly moves her hands up my sides and over my breasts. She teases my nipples until I'm forced to suck in my next breath from between my gritted teeth.

"Hmm. I could, it would be so easy. I can play your body like Hendrix played his guitar. I can make you moan, sing, scream and groan at will can't I?"

"Yes, baby." I'm starting to get a sense of what Alex has felt like all day.

"I can, but I won't. Not yet at least." Alex's weight shifts again as she moves further up the bed. I can smell the sweetness of her sex hovering over my face and feel the bed dip where her knees support her weight on either side of my head. "I think it only fair that I be freed from this lust filled prison that you locked me in, don't you?" I strain my neck towards the smell of her. I want her in my mouth. I'm so focused on finding her that I can't answer. She must see my struggle and realizes that I agree. She lowers herself onto my mouth, and I moan with pleasure. She is wetter than she has ever been. She wasn't lying, she really did languish all day without relieving herself. I greedily lick and suck at the pool of nectar over my mouth, relishing in the flavor. I moan again as Alex starts to slowly rock her hips. She moans and increases her rhythm slightly, encouraging the pattern my tongue weaves around her clit.

"When I fuck you later it isn't going to be fast. It is going to be slow, so slow. You are going to beg me to let you come. If you get close before I want you to, I'm going to stop and then start all over again." I groan in protest, the vibrations feeding into Alex's stimulation. I lick and swirl and suck at her hoping she'll have mercy on me. Her rhythm becomes frantic, and she comes hard and loud.

She keeps bucking herself against me, so I continue my pace. She comes again, and I think she will stop, but she doesn't. She presses on, and I jerk my hands against the restraints, longing to touch her, to help her to her third orgasm. The third one takes a little longer than the second, but Alex rides my face like her life depends on it. The convulsions rock her body hard this time. I continue lapping up her juices until she removes herself from my mouth and off of the bed. "That was exquisite my love, I wish you could have seen me come." She strokes my face as she taunts me. She takes her hand away and the room falls silent. I lay there, tied up, listening for her but hear nothing.

"Alex?"

"Yes, my love?" Her voice strengthens as she approaches me. She has clearly left the room and returned.

"Did you leave just now?"

"I did. All that riding and screaming made me work up a sweat and a thirst." I can feel the grin on her face. "Are you thirsty?"

"Yes baby, for you." Alex laughs.

"I know you're thirsty for me. I can see your panties are soaked from here. Are you thirsty though?" I am so I nod. I feel Alex's weight return to the bed and the heat of her body as she straddles my waist. I feel the press of her fingers to each of my forearms a few times. I realize she is checking my capillary bounce back. "Still ok?" she whispers against my ear.

"My arms are." Alex is right, I will be begging for it soon. I feel her reach towards the table for something and then the sound of something being sat back down. She leans in to kiss me, and before our tongues touch, I feel the cold. Alex holds in her mouth an ice cube. The tips of our noses rub against each other as she rubs it over my lips with her mouth. I let the cool drops roll over my tongue. She pulls away momentarily, and when her lips crash back against mine, the ice is gone. She kisses me hungrily, sucking on my bottom lip, invading my mouth and biting my lip as she pulls away. She repeats this three more times.

"Are you burning for me yet?"

"Yes! Please!" Alex is taking a leisure stroll when I long to run a sprint.

"Hmm. Where do you burn?" I feel the ice as Alex trails it down the underside of my chin and over my neck. She slowly makes her way down my chest. I hadn't realized it, but it isn't one cube forming the trail, Alex has two. She splits them just before she reaches my breasts and rubs each cube over and around my nipples. "Do you burn here?" The cold combined with my arousal have my nipples so hard I'm certain they will tear through the lace restraints at any moment. "You do." Alex brings the cubes back together and starts trailing down my stomach. I know where she is going before she gets there. "What about here?" The frozen cubes meet with my juices, which I am convinced have to be boiling at this point. The mixing of the two cools my temperature but not my arousal. I gasp as the two meet, emptying my lungs. "So that's where you burn."

"I'm begging you Alex. Please. Please make me come." I hear the soft clink as Alex deposits the remains of the cubes back into the glass. The cool air chills my body as Alex moves back to the foot of the bed. She lifts my hips and slowly pulls off the lace panties. I can feel her kneeling between my legs as she trails her fingers up and down my length, always avoiding my most sensitive spots.

Finally, she moves each of my legs up to her shoulders and lifts my hips up off of the bed. She supports my angle by laying my back on her thighs. I tighten my leg lock around her neck pulling her head towards me. My hips strain for her. Finally, she relents, and I feel her mouth connect with me. White light flashes under the mask as my body finds a small bit of relief in the stimulation. She slowly licks and savors my juices, moaning as she parts my lips. The small vibration from her hits my over stimulated clit full force, and I buck against her. Alex tightens her grip around my hips and speeds her pace. Each lick, swirl and sucking sensation giving me more and more relief.

"Thank you, baby. More please." I'm surprised when Alex obliges. She speeds her tongue and shockwaves hit me like a typhoon. "Mmm, please don't stop." She doesn't. I scream out as she plunges her tongue into me. She swirls it and moves it in and out with incredible speed. "Damn baby!" My hips have a mind of their own, one that seems to be in collusion with Alex. I feel her shift her hand and her thumb starts massaging my clit as she continues to tongue fuck me. I buck wildly against her, convinced she is going to stop at any second. "Oh god. Please let me come, Alex! I'm so close." I ride her face as hard as I can from this angle, and somehow she finds another gear. Her tongue and thumb work me in a rhythm my hips can't match. I scream out as Alex finally gives me the relief I've been burning for. I buck hard and try to pull away but Alex holds me tightly to her mouth, and I'm soon screaming in ecstasy again. This time Alex lets me down and kisses her way up my body as I pant heavily, trying to regain my breath. I feel her release the restraints, and the blindfold slip away. She looks into my eyes and kisses me.

"I thought you were going to make me wait all night."

"I was going to. You made me wait all day. I changed my mind though."

"Why? What happened?"

"Nothing. I changed the plan. I'm not done with you yet. I want to come with you, and I want to see your eyes when we do. You ok?"

"Mmm…amazing. You always amaze me."

"And you me. You ready for something new?" My curiosity is piqued. Is there really much we haven't tried at this point? Alex extracts herself from my arms and ambles over to the chest. I lay and watch her, still trying to catch my breath. When she makes her way back to the bed with the double-headed dildo, I feel my insides jump, and I smile.

"Finally! I've been anxious to try that."

"All you had to do was ask."

*****

After we lay on the bed, our bodies spent, our breathing still heavy. "That was amazing! Can we use that again sometime?" Alex pulls me to her and stares into my eyes, a lazy, sated smile on her lips. She kisses me lightly and then looks at me.

"What else aren't you telling me? What else do you want to try?" I laugh.

"A girl can keep a secret or two up her sleeve can't she?"

"Sure as long as it isn't out of fear or embarrassment," she says before kissing the tip of my nose. "You are incredible, do you know that? That tease you did for me earlier was so sexy. The video from work…wow. I don't know what I did to deserve you, but I'm glad I did it."

"I'm incredible? No, you're incredible. How do you know just how far you can push me each time? It is so thrilling. My body just follows you."

"I don't know how far. You never stop me, so there is that. Your body doesn't follow me, I follow your body. I read how it responds to what I try. That first time we made love I started my roadmap of your body. I add to it each time. You will stop me though won't you?"

"I promise I will stop you if I think something is too much."

"Good. Baby, I'm starving." I laugh, I can't help it because I am too. The clock reads that it is just after 6:30.

"Come on, let's see what we can find for dinner."

*****

The partners meeting goes about as well as I had expected it would. They initially insist that I end it with Alex, immediately. After much wasted time, I am able to convince them that it isn't just a fling, that we genuinely care about one another. We are finally able to reach a tentative agreement, though I am concerned how Alex is going to feel about it. Alex texts me to see how it went. I don't want to tell her via text message and the meeting running late pushed us all behind for the day. I send her a quick reply telling her not to worry that we will talk when I get home. She asks me to call her over lunch, but I skip lunch in an effort to regain some of my lost time. By the time I pull into the garage I feel exhausted, my head is pounding, and my anxiety about telling Alex is through the roof. Alex is in the kitchen working on dinner when I walk in. I must look as crappy as I feel because the smile fades from her face when she sees me. She sits down the knife and wipes her hands on the towel before coming to me.

"Hey, are you ok?" I melt into her arms as she opens them to me.

"Yeah, just a headache."

"Here, sit." Alex leads me to one of the nearby barstools and pulls it out for me. I sit down, and she gets me a glass of ice water. "Did you eat today?" Alex massages my shoulders and neck attempting to help. It feels amazing, her strong hands forcing the tension in them to slowly ease away.

"A little. The meeting this morning ran way over. I skipped lunch to make up for some of the lost time." I take a few big gulps of the ice water, the cold liquid helping my headache some.

"That bad huh?" I turn away from the bar and hold out my arms, drawing Alex to me. She stays at arm's length assessing me. "What is it?"

"It isn't necessarily that bad. I just don't know if you are going to like it."

"Well not telling me isn't helping." I can hear the anxiety and agitation building in her voice.

"Alright. I know you are strong willed and don't like to be told how to live your life. Just keep an open mind for a few minutes. Initially, they wanted me to end things immediately. Understandable, I guess, given what happened with the previous partner and his indiscretions. I refused though and eventually convinced them that this isn't some meaningless, sordid affair. They finally admitted that the relationship isn't an issue, just the possible ramifications."

"Ramifications?"

"They'd like to have their lawyers draft a waiver, similar to a non-disclosure agreement. It won't contain anything life shattering, just a guarantee that you won't sue them for sexual harassment if things between us don't work out. Please just think about it."

"What about our jobs? If things don't work out, do we both have job protection or would it be in there that one of us would have to leave?"

"Nope, no stipulations about that. They really just want a document signed waiving your right to sue them for harassment."

"Would it specify you alone or anyone from the practice?"

"Just me. Why is someone harassing you?" I can feel anger start to surge in me.

"Calm down. I just want to understand this clearly. I just want to be able to openly be with you and not have to worry about our careers. Even if something did go wrong, I still wouldn't be likely to sue you. I'll meet with their lawyer and look over whatever they draw up." I feel relief course through me. I had been dreading this all day, dreading that Alex would resist simply because she doesn't like to be told what to do. "So when do they want to meet with me?"

"Next Tuesday. They want this sorted before I clear you to return to work."

"Fine, no problem."

*****

Surgery is rolling along smoothly today. I get lucky and have Erin as one of my techs again. She pushes turnovers along quickly, and I find myself getting ready to finish up dictating and speaking with the family of my last patient at 4:30. I should be out of the hospital by 5 at the latest. I wait impatiently for my patient to head to recovery. As I wait, I dictate the case, leaving one less thing to take care of. Once the nurse and anesthesia head to recovery I find myself alone with Erin.

"Hey Erin, I just wanted to thank you for moving things along today. I really appreciate your hard work and ensuring we are always ready."

"No problem, but I appreciate the recognition. How's Alex doing?"

"Good, really good. A few more weeks off just to be safe and I might be able to clear her to come back. She is physically back to where she needs to be and doesn't have any after effects like seizures or headaches."

"So did you tell her yet?" I just smile at Erin as a response. "Really? About damn time! I thought you seemed more relaxed, even happier since you came back from vacation. On Monday I just thought it was because you had a nice trip somewhere. Then I remembered that you are taking care of Alex, so I wondered how you did both. Alex is still staying with you, right? She hasn't moved back to her apartment?" Erin has brought up something that I haven't thought of, Alex doesn't actually live with me. Sadness flows through me when I think about it.

"Yes. I canceled my trip when Alex had her accident. We had a nice staycation. I'm very happy, thank you. I think Alex is as well. You should text her and get the address. You are welcome to visit her."

339

"Really? That would be nice. So how do you two plan on keeping this under wraps?"

"We aren't. I told the partners yesterday. Once we take care of a few things there, we will meet with management here. We want everything sorted before she comes back."

"Well good luck. Go home and take care of our girl."

"You got it, thanks again."

*****

I make it home just after 5. As I park the car, I think about seeing if Alex would like to go out for dinner. I open the door and am immediately greeted by a mouth watering aroma. Suddenly dinner in tonight sounds perfect. "Alex?" I can hear soft music playing from the sitting room. I kick off my shoes and deposit my bag and keys at the door. I follow the music, wondering why Alex isn't answering me. I start to feel panic creep in as I worry that something has gone very wrong. I turn the corner to the sitting room and stop in my tracks, taking the scene in. The fire is lit and before it lays a blanket spread over the floor. Next to that is a small table that sits about a foot off of the floor. It is covered with a table cloth I recognize. A small feast surrounds the three lit candles. It looks like roasted lemon pepper chicken, with red skinned potatoes and asparagus, a salad and chocolate covered strawberries. As I stand there in shock, I feel Alex's strong arms wrap around my waist from behind me.

"Happy birthday baby." She softly whispers in my ear that she loves me and kisses the side of my neck. I'm overcome with emotion. No one has ever done anything like this for my birthday, so my birthday has never felt like a big deal to me. Suddenly it does feel like a big deal, I feel like the most important person in the world. Tears burn my eyes. I turn to face Alex without breaking her embrace. Her hands move from my waist up to my face, and her thumbs caress away the tears I couldn't contain. "Hey what is it?"

"Nothing. I'm happy, just really happy. I feel like the most important person in the world. No one has ever done anything like this for me. How did you know?" Great not only am I crying, I've turned into a babbling mess. Alex just stares at me with those green eyes that make me swoon and her radiant smile.

"You are the most important person in the world. I live to see you happy. Taylor called to check in on Monday. Said you hadn't updated her in a little over a week."

I laugh because it dawns on me that I hadn't, and I know the precise reason why. "So she knows now?"

"Yeah. She figured it out. I wasn't sure if you wanted me to say anything, so I didn't, but she guessed. So that prompted her to ask me what my plans were for your birthday. I felt like a terrible girlfriend. I didn't even know when it was."

"You aren't a terrible girlfriend. I don't know when your birthday is."

"That isn't important. You hungry?" Alex takes my hand to lead me over to our indoor picnic, but I refuse to budge. She turns back and looks at me questioningly. I pull her back to me, take her in my arms and kiss her. I know why she doesn't see her birthday or holidays as important and it breaks my heart.

"It is important. I want you to feel the way I feel seeing this. You matter, you're important to me." She eyes me momentarily before resting her head against mine.

"It's in February." Alex looks down as she tells me this.

"I'm so sorry I missed it. I didn't—," I cut myself off. The pieces slowly start to fit together. I know we had been having a lot of tension filled issues around that time. I also remember Abby mentioning that Alex always tends to get down that time of the year, and that whenever Alex is reacting to something emotionally she tends to call one person. "Brooke?" She drops her eyes and loosens her grip on me, allowing me to walk away if I chose to. I tighten my arms around her and kiss her forehead. "You're going to have to try harder than that to get rid of me." Alex finally meets my gaze. "You did nothing wrong when you spent the night with Brooke. I wasn't honest with you much less myself. Everything that has happened has led us here. Nothing to worry about baby."

"Yeah?"

"Yeah." I take her face in my hands and gently kiss her letting her know how much I mean it. "Let's eat. It smells amazing."

I take my time eating dinner for a change. I want to savor every bite and remain in this moment with Alex for as long as possible. By the time we finish the salad and the main course I'm too stuffed to consider any of the tantalizing strawberries. "So you did all of this by yourself today?"

"Sort of. I had Abby pick me up as soon as you left this morning. She ran me to the store for the food and over to my apartment to get something. She dropped me off and went into work a little late. I prepped everything here though, yes. Erin kept me updated all day on your progress and sent me a final message when you left." Alex stands and leads me to the other side of the furniture she pushed out of the way to accommodate our picnic. There on the floor sits a blanket covered object. "So I didn't really have any idea what to get you. You sorta just buy everything when you decide you want or need it and since I'm not exactly working right now, money is an issue. I started to make this for you before we had all of those issues. It was meant to be a just because gift. Then I was going to give it to you as a thanks for taking care of me gift. But now this feels right." I pull back the blanket and expose a chest, like the one Alex has.

"This is the second one from your closet isn't it?"

"Yeah, it was never mine though. It was always meant to be yours." I squat down and examine the chest. It has been finished in a color slightly different than Alex's, one that matches my bedroom furniture perfectly. I lift the lid and discover that instead of the black material Alex had lined hers with, this one has an interior covered in a beautiful blue velvet lining. I turn and look at Alex. "I wanted it to match your eyes, only there isn't a material that captures that vibrant shade of blue properly. I got as close as I could." I stand back up and pull Alex to me, kissing her deeply, letting it linger.

"I love it. Thank you so much."

"Yeah? I wish I could have done more."

"Are you kidding me? That is probably the most meaningful gift anyone has ever given me. And all of this? Nothing short of perfect."

"Really?"

"Really." The sounds of Momma Cass singing *Dream a Little Dream* start oozing out of the speaker. I look at Alex and raise my eyebrow. "Well this never struck me as a song I'd find on your playlist." She smiles back at me.

"It's beautiful. You're beautiful. Dance with me?" She pulls me away from the furniture and the feast into a small open space. We lock our arms around one another and gently sway in time with the music. I have no idea how long we spend dancing like that, but forever wouldn't have been long enough.

"So Dr. Waters, anything else you want for your birthday?" I sigh, knowing there is something that I want, but I'm afraid to ask. Alex pulls back just enough to look me in my eyes. "What is it? Anything, just ask." I continue looking at her eyes and see nothing there but love and caring and hope. This is just like before, I have to tell her how I feel.

"I want you." Alex gazes at me, and her naughty grin emerges.

"You already have me."

"No, not like that." Alex's look shifts from amusement to confusion. "I want you to move back in with me permanently. Not to the basement apartment, I want you up here with me." Alex eyes me, and I can't read her look.

"Is that what you really want?"

"That is what I really want."

"You don't think it is too soon?"

"Alex we already lived together once. We basically live together now. I can't imagine you leaving here and sleeping 10 minutes away from me several nights a week.

I don't want to imagine it. You belong here with me. If you want to stay at Lydia's I'm happy to cover another month of rent, but you asked what I want, I want you here with me, permanently." I feel my insides twist as I wait for her response. I'm too invested in this to read her emotions.

"You're sure?"

"Not a single doubt in my mind. The thought of you leaving here breaks my heart."

"Well, when you put it that way how can I say no?" The grin returns to her face, giving me hope she will say yes.

"What are you talking about, you never tell me no. Are you saying yes?"

"Of course yes. I've been dreading returning to the apartment. I don't want to be away from you if I don't have to be." I pull her in for a long, slow kiss.

"Now you've given me everything that I could want for my birthday" Alex lets out a soft chuckle against my ear.

"Not yet I haven't, but there is still time." Alex leads me back to the fireside. She pulls the cushions from the sofa and other chairs in the room and arranges them into a makeshift bed, draping the blanket back over them. She pulls me down onto them, and we make love for hours, no games, no toys, just the two of us reveling in one another, our bodies finding the synchronization that we've had since day one. "I love you, Catherine" Alex softly whispers against my lips as we slowly rock ourselves against each other.

"I love you, Alex," I whisper back before continuing our bliss.

Epilogue

I roll over and am greeted by a ray of warm sunshine blasting me in the face, further diminishing my desire to open my eyes. The scent of warm vanilla mixed with sex permeates my nostrils and awakens the longing that our time together has yet to extinguish. Catherine lays soundly asleep facing me, her hand draped over my hip, oblivious to the bothersome sunshine that has roused me from my slumber. I look over at the clock and discover it is only 8 am. I'm exhausted, our lovemaking had taken us into the early hours of the morning. I give up on going back to sleep with the persistent ray on my face and leave the bed to fix the dislodged curtain. I make my way around the bed and discover the culprit, Catherine's jeans. A memory of Catherine hurriedly peeling them off last night and tossing them, shifting the curtain slightly, flashes through my mind. I smile to myself. Catherine had been away at a conference since Monday morning. Despite evening phone sex and a few video sessions we were still on each other as soon as she arrived home from the airport, leaving her bags in the car for another time.

I make my way back around the bed and slowly try to lay back down without waking Catherine. I fail miserably. "It's too early baby. Go back to sleep, we both took the day off remember?"

"I know I just had to fix the curtain."

"Ok. Come here." I slide closer to Catherine, and we entangle ourselves in one another, Catherine already half asleep again. "I missed you," she mumbles as she dozes back off.

"I missed you too," I whisper as I kiss her forehead. In no time I rejoin Catherine in dreamland.

*****

I lay next to Alex's slumbering body, watching her sleep. This is one of my favorite things, watching her like this. She typically wakes before me, so I take full advantage of my opportunity to just lay here and admire her, gently caressing the outline of her body, ensuring my fingertips merely graze her skin. "Mmmm." Alex's low purr pulls me out of my meditation. My hand freezes, suspended just over her hip, the heat of her body teasing my finger tips. She lays still and quiet, and I feel my fingers begin moving again, as if they possess a mind of their own. "Mmmmm." Alex moans again, this time deeper and drawn out. Again my hand freezes, this time over her taut thigh. Recognition fires across my synapses. I glance down at Alex's nipples and discover that they are erect. She lets out a quick breath, and I feel her hips slowly start to rock. This happens every now and again. Alex will have a very vivid sex dream and will wake from it as she climaxes in the dream, often having a small orgasm as she does. I watch her as she moans again and slightly increases the pace of her hips. I know I only have a few minutes before this opportunity will be lost.

I slide across the bed and make my way to the closet and Alex's chest. I already know what I'm looking for before I get there. I quickly slide the leather harness up my legs and secure it around my hips. I hear Alex moan again and her respirations increasing. I grab one of our favorite toys and tiptoe back to the bed as quickly as I can. I slide across the silky sheets and lay on my side, facing Alex once more. The heat radiating off of her body coupled with her breathing elicit the response my body always has for her. Alex is nearly impossible to wake when she is like this, yet I take every precaution I can not to do so as I slowly work my left leg between hers and glide it upwards until her sex glides over my thigh. Her pace increases and

347

I wonder if the real stimulation has somehow reshaped the events of her dream. Alex moans my name and the flood gates between my own thighs open. Her respirations increase yet again, and I see her pulse has picked up as her carotid begins to thunder in her neck. Any second now she will wake, but the seconds feel like years as she rubs herself against me and my own lips swell and my clit throbs. I long to touch her, for her to touch me but I wait, biding my time. Her lips part as she groans and her body shudders slightly. She squeezes her thighs around my leg as her hips stop moving and her heavy lids move to half mast over her hazy emerald eyes. I press my thigh gently upward, and she slowly starts to glide herself along it.

"Mmmm. It happened again didn't it?" I can't help but give her my best lascivious grin, as I fight the urge to pounce on her. My desire is amping up with the passing of every second.

"It did," I whisper. "What was I doing to you this time?" Alex eyes me sleepily and grins, still slowly working herself on my thigh.

"Who said it was you?" I know she is messing with me. I take the hand she has just placed on my face and guide it between her own legs, making her touch herself for a few strokes. I pull back on her wrist and raise her hand to her face as she slides down slightly to reconnect with my thigh.

"Because only I can make you this wet." She moans as I take her dripping fingers into my mouth and slowly lick and suck them clean. I feel her shift as she guides herself closer to me, increasing the friction between my thigh and her sex. She opens herself a little further, and I can feel her engorged clit rub over my upper thigh. I groan and release her fingers, lest I bite down on them. She snakes her hand under the sheet that clings to our hips, seeking out the warmth of my sex. Instead, she is greeted by the cool leather of the harness. Her hips stop as she quickly throws back the sheet and eyes my selection. Her fingers snake around the harness and stroke my aching sex. She glances again at the toy before staring into my eyes. She slowly grins as she resumes grinding her hips against me.

"Lucky guess." Our lips quickly collide as our mouths work to consume one another. Alex breaks off the kiss and looks at me. "Do we have time to go to the lower level before you have to pick Taylor up?" Her fingers never stop working me as she slowly inserts one, teasing me with soft swirls around my inner walls.

"I wish," I moan as a second finger enters me. "I don't have to pick her up though, she said she has it covered."

"Too bad. I would love for you to tie me up and tease me today." I groan thinking about it.

"Soon, maybe tonight if you're lucky." Alex's eyes travel between us again and take in the toy, then look back to me. She pitches her voice into a perfect southern debutant accent and asks, "Why Dr. Waters, were you planning to fuck me with that?" I laugh. I love that she never takes life too seriously.

"Only if you want me to." Alex takes the toy and feeds it through the harness, slowly rocking my end of it along my sex, lubricating it. When she is satisfied that it is wet enough, she gently guides it inside me, my breath catching as my body accommodates it. She tightens the straps around my thighs, and I shift to mount her, but she prevents it by quickly flipping me onto my back. She presses her her pelvis against mine and traps the shaft between her legs. She slowly grinds it along her slit, lubing it up for herself, knowing that every movement she makes stirs the end inside me. I moan at the sensations it causes, longing for her to mount the other end. She slowly raises herself up, and I guide the head into her warmest part.

*****

"We really are going to have to get out of bed sooner than later."

"Just one more baby and then we'll get up." I give Catherine the look and push against her and glide my sex against hers. United by our second favorite toy, we fall into our natural rhythm of pushing and grinding against one another.

"Mmmm. Maybe you're right." We work ourselves against each other, steadily building ourselves to one final orgasm. I look down the length of our united bodies at Catherine who has her head tipped back and is pinching and twisting her nipples. She abandons one and reaches her hand out as far as it will stretch, searching for mine. I lock my fingers with hers, and we quicken our pace to a frenzy, both of us teetering on the edge. Catherine freezes when the doorbell rings. "Fuck!"

"Come on baby we're close." I grind myself against her again. "Stay with me now." A little encouragement wins her back to the dark side. Her rhythm melds with mine. We step back and peer into the abyss when the doorbell chimes again. I don't stop, but Catherine does. She lets goes of my fingers and screams out of frustration. Neither of us will find the ending we seek. I slide my end of the toy out of my aching sex and pull the sheet from the bed, wrapping it under my arms.

"Go get in the shower, I'll let her in." Catherine eyes me.

"Like that?" I just shrug and make my way toward the front door. I inspect my reflection as I pass the mirror in the entryway. My face is flushed, my shoulders bear tokens of Catherine's affections, and my hair is standing in at least 10 different directions. The doorbell rings again and I mutter, "fucking doorbell," under my breath as I pull the door open. Taylor stands on the porch, her eyes bulge as she takes in the sight of me.

"Man you reek of sex. You two still can't keep your hands off of each other after all this time?"

"Clearly. No such thing as too much of Catherine."

"I'm sure. How about a hug?" Taylor gives me a look, not that different from one Catherine has given me countless times. Their eyes the same shade of blue, but where Catherine's is tempered with love, Taylor's is filled with nothing but lust. My body is still burning to finish what Catherine and I have started. The only hands I want on me are Catherine's. The fact that I'm wearing nothing but a sheet doesn't phase me for a second.

"Maybe later, when I'm dressed. Catherine just got in the shower, she should be right out."

"Ok. The bar still in the same spot?"

"Of course."

"Alright. I'm going to go make myself a drink. Why don't you go join my sister and finish what you were doing. You are oozing frustration in tidal waves right now." I don't hesitate and start back down the hall to our master bath. I turn back toward the kitchen before I forget and let Taylor know that we set up the basement apartment for her visit if she wants to get settled in.

Forty-five minutes later Catherine and I emerge from the bedroom feeling much better. Catherine takes my hand

and leads me down the hall in search of Taylor. We find her downstairs enjoying a beer as she watches TV.

"Good grief you two are insatiable."

"What can I say, I've created a monster." I wrap my arms around Catherine. She gives me a light kiss.

"Wait, I thought I was the one that created the monster." She winks and smiles at me.

"Are you two always like this?"

"Pretty much." Catherine leaves my arms and makes her way toward Taylor. "It's nice to see you." They hug briefly before Catherine makes her way to the side of the chair I'm sitting in. She takes my hand, and I pull her down onto my lap, locking my arms around her waist, pulling her close to me. "I didn't see a rental out front, did you take a cab?"

Taylor blushes slightly and avoids making eye contact with either of us, her beer bottle becoming the most interesting thing in the room. "No, I actually got here yesterday. Nikki dropped me off."

Catherine and I look at each other, both of us shocked. "What is going on there? Didn't realize you two were still a thing."

"We aren't a thing. We've kept in contact since my first visit. She has flown out to visit me, and we've met in other cities as well."

"So technically this is a record for you, your longest relationship."

"We are not a couple. She has hinted she would like to be, but I want her to go out and explore what the world has to offer. I don't want to be the only woman she has ever been with." Taylor's words invade my mind and start to fester. I hadn't ever thought about this when I started dating Catherine. I wonder if she has ever felt like she was missing out on something. Taylor sees my mood shift. "Shit, sorry Alex." I feel Catherine's head whip around to look at me, but I avoid her gaze.

Catherine and Taylor continue to exchange small talk. I try to participate but can't shake my own nagging thoughts, much less focus on anything else. Taylor's phone blares out a catchy ringtone as she pulls it from her pocket. She excuses herself to the apartment's bedroom to take the call. As soon as the door clicks shut I feel Catherine leave my lap. She turns around and straddles me. I feel my insides twitch with desire as I recall the first strip tease she ever gave me.

"Where are you right now? What happened?" I sigh, needing to ask the question, fearing the answer.

"Do you ever feel like you are missing out on something else? Do you regret not seeing what other women have to offer? Is that something you want?"

"Alex, in all this time you have never denied me anything that I have asked for. If I wanted that I would ask for it, and somehow I know no matter how badly it would hurt you, you'd allow me to have it. But I don't want or need it. What we have is rare. No one, male or female, would ever compliment me in the ways that you do, understand me like you do, worship my body like you do or most importantly make me feel like I am the only person on the planet that matters; like you do every day. I love you, Alex. You are all I want, you are all I need." Catherine grins at me, and I see a familiar glint burning in her eyes. "I am yours and you are mine. Nobody else, not ever." She locks her fingers in my hair, tilts my head back and kisses me.

"Wow, that was nauseatingly sweet. When you two gonna get married?" Taylor stands in the now open doorway to the bedroom. Catherine and I lock eyes and smile. We've talked about this before and already know where we stand.

I lean into Catherine's ear and whisper "You sitting here like this reminds me of that first strip tease you did for me."

"Oh yeah? Wait until you see what I've got planned for you tonight." I return the look she is giving me, she isn't the only one with a surprise to unveil tonight.

"Well, you two tying the knot?"

"Nope. We've talked about it. Neither of us feels it is necessary. We know how we feel about one another and what we mean to each other. If the world can't see that without a ring and a piece of paper, well that isn't our problem."

"Really? I'm surprised you two don't have something in mind."

Catherine's blue eyes meet mine, love radiating from them, filling me with the warm sensation I've only known with her. I hold her gaze, hoping she can feel my love for her flowing out of me. We smile at each other, the intimate smile that only lovers share. The memory of our trip to the Caribbean last Christmas takes hold of my brain. The white sand beaches that looked almost like piles of sugar at times. We learned to snorkel. We swam and sunbathed. The lovely gay couple we met who had been together for 12 years and recently wed. They asked if we planned to marry and set everything in motion. We hadn't discussed it before, it had never really occurred to me as it was not something I had ever pictured or wanted. That night as Catherine and I held each other by the water, Catherine asked me if I had thought about it or if it was something I even wanted. I told her that I would do it if it were something she truly desired. She confessed that she had always found it to be pointless, but had gone along with her ex-husband because he wanted it. We agreed that it would be nice to find some way to symbolize our commitment to one another, but a ceremony and expensive jewelry weren't for us. It was there on the beach that Catherine and I pledged ourselves to one another. With the moon shining down on us, the warm breeze caressing our skin and the relaxing sound of the tide in our ears we promised that we would always put us first to help minimize selfishness. We vowed that no matter what happened we would never go to bed angry, nor would we be a couple that screamed and shouted at one another. We swore that we would hold each other every night when we went to sleep. We agreed that we would always listen to the other's wants and needs without judgment. We assured one another that we would never take life too seriously, we both knew it was too short. We committed ourselves to ensuring we had us time every day and would give each other me time when either of us needed it. We promised one another that we would never hold back, that we would love one another fiercely and honestly, no secrets, no regrets. We finalized our pact by telling one another I am yours and you are mine, the words we have always used to assure and remind one another of our love. Just Catherine and I under the full moon and the stars. We made love on the beach and in the ocean that night. When we returned home, we got matching tattoos on our left ring fingers. A small, nearly complete heart that trails off into one another's EKG reading winding around our fingers where a ring would traditionally sit. A reminder of the pact we made that night on the beach and the heartbeat to remind each of us whose heart we hold and who holds us in their heart.

"Do we tell her?" We haven't told anyone. It isn't as if we want to keep it a secret, we just didn't think it required a big announcement. No one has asked about the tattoos, so either people have not noticed, or they aren't bothered by it.

"Up to you, she is your sister. I'm fine with it." Catherine turns herself around to face Taylor.

"Come, sit back down." Taylor reclaims her seat on the couch. Catherine clasps my left hand in hers and extends them for Taylor to inspect. It takes her a second, but she finally notices the tattoos.

"You guys already got married? When?"

"Not married, as married as we are going to get though. Over vacation in December. Just Alex and I on the beach, no one else. We haven't even told anyone yet." Taylor continues inspecting our fingers.

"December? But it is May, why doesn't anyone know?"

"We felt it was something between the two of us. We never felt the need to make a big deal out of it." Taylor's brow furrows as she releases our hands.

"Your tattoos don't match. Why? What are they?"

"They aren't supposed to. Alex wears my heartbeat, and I wear hers. We gave each other an EKG at work to get them for the artist. Neither of us can wear jewelry in the OR, and neither of us wanted a real ring." Taylor is quiet for a few minutes before looking at us and smiling.

"We have to have a party! Time for you two to make this known." Catherine turns and looks at me, the question hanging between us. I shrug my shoulders and nod my assent, as long as we know how we feel about each other the rest of the world might as well too.

Author's Note

Thank you for taking the time to read Fusion. The idea for this work came from a dream I had one night. After a few months of toiling and tinkering in my free time, it finally had a life of its own. The story of Alexis and Catherine was originally intended to be a stand alone novel, but somewhere along the way, their friends started to tell me their stories as well. The next work in the series will tell Sara's story and will hopefully be out in the next month or two.

If you enjoyed this story and would be kind enough, please leave a review. For independent authors such as myself, reviews are critical in helping to spread the word about our work.

To stay up to date on my future releases please follow me on Facebook and Twitter.

Email: dianakanebooks@gmail.com

Printed in Great Britain
by Amazon